中国汉籍经典英译名著

THE CHINESE CLASSICS

诗经

国风

THE SHE KING
LESSONS FROM THE STATES

［英］理雅各　译释

JAMES LEGGE

上海三联书店

图书在版编目（CIP）数据

《诗经·国风》译释：汉英对照/（英）理雅各（Legge，J.）译释
——上海：上海三联书店，2014.1
　（中国汉籍经典英译名著）

　ISBN 978-7-5426-4455-8

Ⅰ. ①诗⋯Ⅱ. ①理⋯Ⅲ. ①汉语—英语—对照读物
②古体诗—诗集—中国—春秋时代Ⅳ. ①H319.4∶I

中国版本图书馆 CIP 数据核字（2013）第 268276 号

诗经·国风

译　　　释／理雅各
责任编辑／陈启甸　王倩怡
封面设计／清风
策　　划／赵炬
执　　行／取映文化
加工整理／嘎拉　江岩　牵牛　莉娜
监　　制／吴昊
责任校对／笑然
出版发行／上海三联书店
　　　　（201199）中国上海市闵行区都市路 4855 号 2 座 10 楼
网　　址／http：//www. sjpc1932. com
邮购电话／021-24175971
印刷装订／常熟市人民印刷厂

版　　次／2014 年 1 月第 1 版
印　　次／2014 年 1 月第 1 次印刷
开　　本／650×900 1/16
字　　数／500 千字
印　　张／15. 75
书　　号／ISBN 978-7-5426-4455-8/I・789
定　　价／58. 00 元

中国汉籍经典英译名著

出版人的话

出版这样一套书与当今中国文化走出去的需要分不开。

其实，仅仅就中国传统文化走出去而言，近代以来已经有浓重的笔墨，只是那时的走出去大都是由西方的传教士实现的。那时的好多传教士在向中国人传播教义及西方科技的同时，自己更是为中国文化所吸引并且深入其中，竟然成就了不少有名的汉学家。在这些人中，英国传教士理雅各是非常典型的一位。

理雅各(James Legge，1815—1897年)是近代英国著名汉学家，伦敦布道会传教士，曾任香港英华书院校长。他是第一个系统研究、翻译中国古代汉籍经典的人。

理雅各在传教和教学的过程中，认识到了学习中国文化的重要性："只有透彻地掌握中国的经典书籍，亲自考察中国圣贤所建立的道德、社会和政治生活，才能对得起自己的职业和地位。"理雅各系统地研究和翻译中国古代的经典著作。在中国学者王韬等人的辅助下，从1861年到1886年的25年间，陆续翻译了《论语》《大学》《中庸》《孟子》《春秋》《礼记》《书经》《孝经》《易经》《诗经》《道德经》《庄子》《离骚》等中国的经典著作，共计28卷。当他离开中国时，已是著作等身。

理雅各之前的西方来华传教士虽也对中国的经典著作做过翻译，但都是片段性的翻译，而且由于中文不精，译文辞句粗劣，歧义百出。理雅各在翻译的过程中治学严谨，博采众长，他把前人用拉丁、英、法、意等语种译出的有关文字悉数找来，认真参考，反复斟酌。除此之外，他还与中国学者反复讨论，最后才落笔翻译。理雅各翻译的中国经典著作质量绝佳，体系完整，直到今天还是西方世界公认的标准译本，他本人也因此成为蜚声世界的汉学家。理雅各的译作是当之无愧的英译名著。

从英译的水准来看，或许是现今不易超越的。主要是译者当时所处的语言环境是中国文言文作为书面语言的原因。精晓文言文的直接英译，与现实白话理解后的英译相比，前者肯定会与原意更为贴近，况且理雅各又是得到了当时精通中国经典著作的中国学者王韬等人的辅助。当然，今天的人们有理由去挑战一百多年前的译作,但作为历经一个多世纪仍为西方世界普遍认可的英译经典,依然还会继续发挥其曾有的版本作用。

理雅各译作的重要代表《中国经典》(*THE CHINESE CLASSICS*),首版于 1861 至 1872 年的香港。此次以"中国汉籍经典英译名著"名义出版的各书,是依据牛津大学 1893 至 1895 年出版的理雅各《中国经典》的修订版。

"中国汉籍经典英译名著",是从理雅各的《中国经典》中选出对中国典籍原著的译释,舍去了各卷含有的绪论、前言及所附的参考文献,这样也就更为突出了典籍原著。

原《中国经典》实行的是汉英对照加英文注释的方式,汉语部分使用的是当时的书面语言繁体竖排。为了适于现实的阅读,此次出版均将汉语的繁体竖排,改为简体横排,并将英文注释中的汉字繁体改为简体。

在原《中国经典》中,理雅各对中国经典著作汉字的多音字和需要特别注明的字,都在字的四角画圈以示在注释中说明。这次出版将其改为在字的正上方标注着重号(黑点)。

原《中国经典》对汉语原文的断句标点,采用的是当时的方式,与今天现代汉语式的断句标点存有很大差别。为了保持理雅各译释的面貌,仍然用原断句标点。

另外,为了改变原书过于厚重的形态,这次出版还将原书的大开本改为小开本;将原《中国经典》的 1—4 卷拆分为七种书,即《论语·大学·中庸》《孟子》《尚书·唐书-夏书-商书》《尚书·周书》《诗经·国风》《诗经·小雅》《诗经·大雅-颂》。每书 300 页左右,便于选择使用。

理雅各的译作至今还是西方世界公认的标准译本,说明它适应着西方世界的语言和理解。这种影响了西方世界一百多年的情形,从接受心理的角度看,是很难被取代的。

随着中国在世界的影响力不断提升,中国学者的对外学术交流也更加活跃,交流中对中国文化的讲解和诠释,需要有相应的英译本作为参考,理雅各的译作无疑是适当的选择。

同时,理雅各的经典译作,还是翻译学、语言学、比较文学、历史和经典诠释的重要文献,是研究和实践汉译英的重要参考和借鉴。

相信,借用昔日西方学者译释中国文化经典并传播到西方的成果,延续和助推当今中国文化在世界的影响力,一定可以取得事半功倍的收效。

2014 年 1 月 1 日

目　录

THE SHE KING.

PART I.

LESSONS FROM THE STATES.

BOOK I. THE ODES OF CHOW AND THE SOUTH.

I. *Kwan tsʻeu.*

诗经　国风一

周南一之一

关雎

一章
关关雎鸠。在河之洲。窈窕淑女。君子好逑。

二章
参差荇菜。左右流之。窈窕淑女。寤寐求之。求之不

1　*Kwan-kwan* go the ospreys,
　　On the islet in the river.
　　The modest, retiring, virtuous, young lady:—
　　For our prince a good mate she.

2　Here long, there short, is the duckweed,
　　To the left, to the right, borne about by the current.
　　The modest, retiring, virtuous, young lady:—
　　Waking and sleeping, he sought her.

TITLE OF THE WHOLE WORK.— 诗经, 'The Book of Poems,' or simply 诗. 'The Poems.' By poetry, according to the Great Preface and the views generally of Chinese scholars, is denoted the expression, in rhymed words, of thought impregnated with feeling; which, so far as it goes, is a good account of this species of composition. In the collection before us, there were originally 311 pieces; but of six of them there are only the titles remaining. They are generally short; not one of them, indeed, is a long poem. Father Lacharme calls the Book.—'*Liber Carminum*,' and with most English writers the ordinary designation of it has been 'The Book of Odes.' I can think of no better name for the several pieces than *Ode*, understanding by that term a short lyric poem. Confucius himself is said to have 'fitted them to the string.'

VOL. IV.　　　　　　1

TITLE OF THE PART - 国风 一, 'Part I., Lessons from the States.' In the Chinese, —, 'Part I.,' stands last, while our western idiom requires that it should be placed first. The translation of 国风 by 'Lessons from the States' has been vindicated in the notes on the Great Preface. Sir John Davis translates the characters by 'The Manners of the different States' (art. on the Poetry of the Chinese. Transactions of the Royal Asiatic Society; May, 1829). Similarly, the French Sinologues render them by 'Les Mœurs des royaumes.' But in 'Lessons' and 'Manners,' the metaphorical use of 风, 'wind,' is equally unapparent. Choo He says:—'The pieces are called *fung*, because they owe their origin to and are descriptive of the influence produced by superiors, and the exhibition of this is again sufficient to affect men, just as things give forth sound, when moved by the wind, and their sound is again sufficient to move [other] things (谓 之 风 者，以 其 被 上 之 化 以 有 言，而 其 言 又 足 以 感 人，如 物 因 风 之 动 以 有 声 而 其 声 又 足 以 动 物 也)'. He goes on to say that the princes of States collected such compositions among their people, and presented them to the king, who delivered them to the Board of music for classification, so that he might examine from them the good and bad in the manners of the people, and ascertain the excellences and defects of his own government. 'Lessons from the States' seems, therefore, to come nearer to the force of the original terms than 'Manners of the States.' It will be found, however, that the *lesson* has often to be drawn from the ode by a circuitous process.

The States are those of Chow, Shaou, P'ei, Yung, and the others, which give their names to the several Books.

TITLE OF THE BOOK.- 周 南 一 之 一, 'Chow Nan, Book I. of Part I.' The first 一 is that of the last title, - 国 风 一. By Chow is intended the seat of the House of Chow, from the time of the 'old duke, T'an-foo (古 公 亶 父)', in B. C. 1,325, to king Wăn. The cniefs of Chow pretended to trace their lineage back to K'e, better known as How Tseih, Shun's minister of Agriculture. K'e was invested, it is said, before the death of Yaou, with the small territory of T'ae (邰), referred to the pres. dis. of Woo-kung (武 功) in K'ëen-chow (乾 州), Shen-se. Between K'e and duke Lew (公 刘), only two names of the Chow ar cestry are given with certainty, — Puh-chueh (不 窋) and Kuh (鞠, *al.* 鞠 陶). Sz'-ma Ts'een calls the first K'e's son, but we can only suppose him to have been one of his descendants. In the disorders of the Middle-Kingdom, it is related, he withdrew among the wild tribes of the west and north; and there his descendants remained till the time of duke Lëw, who returned to China in B.C. 1,796, and made a settlement in Pin (豳), the site of which is pointed out, 30 *le* to the west of the present dis. city of San-shwuy (三 水) in the small dep. of Pin-chow (邠 州). The family dwelt in Piu for several generations, till T'an-foo, subsequently *kinged* by his posterity as king T'ae (太 王), moved still farther south in B.C. 1,325, and settled in K'e (岐), 50 *le* to the north east of the dis. city of K'e-shan (岐 山), dep. Fung-ts'ëang (凤 翔). The plain southwards received the name of Chow, and here were the head-quarters of the rising House, till king Wăn moved south and east again, across the Wei, to Fung (丰), south-west from the pres. provincial city of Se-gau. When king Wăn took this step, he separated the original Chow—K'e-chow—into Chow and Shaou, which he made the appanages of his son Tan (旦), and of Shih (奭), one of his principal supporters. Tan is known from this appointment as 'the duke of Chow'. The pieces in this Book are supposed to have been collected by him in Chow, and the States lying south from it along the Han and other rivers.— We must supplement in English the bare 'Chow Nan' of the title, and say—'The Odes of Chow and the South.'

[The above historical sketch throws light on Mencius' statement, in Book IV., Pt II. i., that king Wăn was 'a man from the wild tribes of the west (西 夷 之 人).' I have translated his words by 'a man near the wild tribes of the west.' But according to the records of the Chow dynasty themselves, we see its real ancestor, duke Lëw, coming out from among those tribes in the beginning of the 17th century before our era, and settling in Pin. Very slowly, his tribe, growing in civilization, and pushed on by fresh immigrations from its own earlier seats, moves on, southwards and eastwards, till it comes into contact and collision with the princes of Shang, whose dominions constituted the Middle Kingdom, or the China of that early time. The accounts of a connection between the princes of Chow and the statesmen of the era of Yaou and Shun must be thrown out of the sphere of reliable history.]

Ode 1.—CELEBRATING THE VIRTUE OF THE BRIDE OF KING WAN, AND WELCOMING HER TO HIS PALACE.

Stanza 1. 关 关 are defined to be 'the harmonious notes of the male and female answering each other.' 关 was anciently interchanged with 管, and some read in the text 管 管, with a 口 at the side, which would clearly be onomatopoetic; but we do not find such a character in the Shwŏh-wăn. It is difficult to say what bird is intended by 雎 鸠. Confucius says (Ana. XVII. ix.) that from the

得。寤寐思服。悠哉悠哉。辗转反侧。

He sought her and found her not,
And waking and sleeping he thought about her.
Long he thought; oh! long and anxiously;
On his side, on his back, he turned, and back again.

She we become extensively acquainted with the names of birds, beasts, and plants. We do learn *names* enow, but the birds, beasts, and plants, denoted by them, remain in many cases to be yet ascertained. The student, knowing *kew* to mean the wild dove, is apt to suppose that some species of dove is intended; but no Chinese commentator has ever said so. Maou makes it the 王雎, adding 鸟挚 而有别, which means, probably, 'a bird of prey, of which the male and female keep much apart.' He followed the Urh-ya, the annotator of which, Kwoh P'oh (郭璞), of the Tsin dynasty, further describes it as 'a kind of eagle (雕类), now, east of the Këang, called the *ngoh* (鹗).' This was for many centuries the view of all scholars; and it is sustained by a narrative in the Tso Chuen, under the 17th year of duke Ch'aou, that the Master of the Horse or Minister of War, was anciently styled Ts'eu K'ew (雎鸠氏). The introduction of a bird of prey into a nuptial ode was thought, however, to be incongruous. Even Ch'ing K'ang-shing, would appear to have felt this, and explains Maou's 挚 by 至, as if his words= 'a bird most affectionate, and yet most undemonstrative of desire;'—in which interpretation Choo He follows him. But it was desirable to discard the bird of prey altogether; and this was first done by Ch'ing Ts'ëaou (郑樵), an early writer of the Sung dyn., who makes the bird to be 'a kind of mallard.' Choo He, no doubt after him, says it is 'a water bird, in appearance like a mallard,' adding that it is only seen in pairs. the individuals of which keep at a distance from each other! Other identifications of the *ts'eu-k'ew* have been attempted. I must believe that the author of the ode had some kind of fish hawk in his mind.
在河之洲 (the Shwoh-wän has 州, without the 水),—河 is the general denomination of streams and rivers in the north. We need not seek, as many do, to determine any particular stream as that intended. 洲 is an islet, 'habitable ground, surrounded by the water (水中可居之地).'
窈窕淑女—窈 is to be understood of the lady's mind, and 窕 of her deportment.

So, Yang Hëung (杨雄. Died A. D. 18, at the age of 71), and Wang Suh. 淑 (has displaced the more ancient form with 人 at the side) is explained in the Shwoh-wän by 善, 'good,' 'virtuous.' The young lady, according to the traditional interpretation (on which see below), is T'ae-sz' (太姒), a daughter of the House of Yew-sin (有莘), whom king Wän married.
君子好逑,—if we accept T'ae-sz' as the young lady of the Ode, then the *keun-tsz'* of course is king Wän. 逑 and 仇 (in Ode VII.) are interchangeable, = 匹, 'a mate.' K'ang-shing explains the line by 能为君 子和好众妾之怨, 'who could for our prince harmonize the resentments of all the concubines.' He was led astray by the Little Preface. [There is a popular novel called the 好逑传, the name of which is taken from this line. Sir John Davis has translated it under the misnomer of 'The Fortunate Union.']
St.2. 参差 (read *ch'in ts'ze*) 荇菜,—参 差 expresses the irregular appearance of the plants, some long and some short. 荇菜 is probably the *lemna minor*. It is also called 'duck-mallows,' that name being given for it in the Pun-ts'aou and the Pe-ya (埤雅; a work on the plan of the Urh-ya, by Luh Teen (陆佃, of the Sung dyn.),—凫葵. It is described as growing in the water, long or short according to the depth, with a reddish leaf, which floats on the surface, and is rather more than an inch in diameter. Its flower is yellow. It is very like the *shun*, which Medhurst calls the 'marsh-mallows,' but its leaves are not so round, being a little pointed. We are to suppose that the leaves were cooked and presented as a sacrificial offering. 左右 流之,—the analogy of 采之 芼之 in the next stanza, would lead us to expect an active signification in 流, and an action proceeding from the parties who speak in the Ode. This, no doubt, was the reason which made Maou, after the Urh-ya, explain the character

三章

参差荇菜。左右采之。窈窕淑女。琴瑟友之。参差荇

菜。左右芼之。窈窕淑女。钟鼓乐之。

3   Here long, there short, is the duckweed;
     On the left, on the right, we gather it.
     The modest, retiring, virtuous, young lady:—
     With lutes, small and large, let us give her friendly welcome.
     Here long, there short, is the duckweed;
     On the left, on the right, we cook and present it.
     The modest, retiring, virtuous young lady:—
     With bells and drums let us show our delight in her.

by 求, 'to seek;' but this is forcing a meaning on the term. 流之 simply—'the current bears it about.' The idea of looking for the plant is indicated by the connection. 寤寐 至反侧,—we have to supply the subject of 求 and the other verbs; which I have done by 'he', referring to king Wăn. The commentators are chary of saying this directly, thinking that such lively emotion about such an object was inconsistent with Wăn's sagely character; but they are obliged to interpret the passage of him. To make, with K'ang-shing and others, the subject to be the lady herself, and the object of her quest to be virtuous young ladies to fill the harem, surely is absurd. 思服,—服=怀, 'to cherish in the breast.' 悠哉,—悠, here, acc. to Maou,—思, 'to think.' In other places, in these Odes, it=忧, 'to be anxious,' 'sorrowful'; and also=远, 'remote,' 'a long distance.' Choo He prefers this last meaning, and defines it by 长, 'long'. The idea is that of prolonged and anxious thought. 辗转反侧,—the old interpreters did not distinguish between the meaning of these characters. The Shwoh-wăn, indeed, defines 辗 (it gives only 展) by 转 Choo He makes 辗=转之半, 'half a chuen or turning;' 转=辗之周, 'the completion of the 辗;' while 反 and 侧 are the reversing of those processes. This is ingenious and elegant; but the definitions are made for the passage.

St.3. As the subject of 菜 and the other verbs, we are to understand the authors or singers of the Ode,—the ladies of king Wăn's harem.

The Pe-che (备旨), however, would refer all the 之 in the stanza to the young lady, and the verbs to king Wăn, advising him so to welcome and cherish her; and this interpretation is also allowable. Maou, further on, explains 采 by 取, 'to take', and here, 芼 by 择, 'to pick out', to select' But the selection must precede the taking. It was not till the time of Tung Yĕw in the Sung Dyn., that the meaning of 芼, which I have given, and which may be supported from the Le Ke, was applied to this passage. 友之,—'we friend her,' i.e., we give her a friendly welcome. The k'in and shih were two instruments in which the music was drawn from strings of silk. We may call them the small lute and the large lute. The k'in at first had only 5 strings for the 5 full notes of the octave, but two others are said to have been added by kings Wăn and Woo, to give the semi-notes. The invention of a shih with 50 strings is ascribed to Fuh-he, but we are told that Hwang-te found the melancholy sounds of this so overpowering, that he cut the number down to 25.

In Chinese editions of the she, at the end of every ode, there is given a note, stating the number of stanzas in it, and of the lines in each stanza. Here we have 关雎三章,一章四句,二章章八句, 'The Kwan-ts'eu consists of 3 stanzas, the first containing 4 lines, and the other two containing 8 lines each.' This matter need not be touched on again.

The rhymes (according to Twan Yuh-tsae, whose authority in this matter, as I have stated in the prolegomena, I follow) are—in stanza 1, 鸠.洲.逑, category 3, tone 1: in 2. 流, 求, ib.; 得, 服, 侧, cat. 1, t. 3; in 3, 采, 友,

ib.. t. 2; 芼, 乐 *, cat. 2. The, after a character denotes that the ancient pronunciation of it, found in the odes, was different from that now belonging to it. A list of such characters, with their ancient names, has been given in the prolegomena, in the appendix to the chapter referred to.

INTERPRETATION OF THE ODE. I have said that the Ode celebrates the virtue of the bride of king Wăn. If I had written *queen* instead of *bride*, I should have been in entire accord, so far, with the schools both of Maou and Choo He. During the dyn. of Han a different view was widely prevalent,—that the Ode was satirical, and should be referred to the time when the Chow dyn. had begun to fall into decay. We find this opinion in Lëw Heang (列女传 仁智篇), Yang Heung (法言, 孝至 篇), and up and down, in the histories of Sz'-ma Ts'ëen, Pan Koo, and Fan Yeh.—By the E Le, however, IV., ii. 75, we are obliged to refer the *Kwan-ts'eu* to the time of the duke of Chow. That a contrary opinion should have been so prevalent in the Han dyn., only shows how long it was before the interpretation of the odes became so definitely fixed as it now is. Allowing the ode to be as old as the duke of Chow, and to celebrate his father's bride or queen, what is the virtue which it ascribes to her? According to the school of Maou, it is her freedom from jealousy, and her constant anxiety and diligence to fill the harem of the king with virtuous ladies to share his favours with her, and assist her in her various duties; and the ode was made by her. According to the school of Choo He, the virtue is her modest disposition and retiring manners, which so ravished the inmates of the harem, that they sing of her, in the 1st stanza, as she was in her virgin purity, a flower unseen; in the 2d, they set forth the king's trouble and anxiety while he had not met with such a mate; and in the 3d, their joy reaches its height, when she has been got, and is brought home to his palace. In this way, thinks Choo, the ode, in reality, exhibits the virtue of king Wăn in making such a choice; and that is with him a very great point. The imperial editors, adjudicating upon these two interpretations, very strangely, as it seems to me, and will also do, I presume, to most of my western readers, show an evident leaning to that of the old school. 'It was the duty,' they say, 'of the queen to provide for the harem 3 wives (三 夫 人, ranking next to herself), nine ladies of the 3d rank (九 嫔), 27 of the 4th (二 十 七 世 妇), and 81 of the 5th (八 十 一 御 妻).' Only virtuous ladies were fit to be selected for this position. The anxiety of T'ae-sz' to get such, her disappointment at not finding them, and her joy when she succeeded in doing so:—all this showed the highest female virtue, and 'made the ode worthy to stand at the head of all the Lessons from the Manners of the States. Confucius expressed his admiration of the ode (Ana. III. xx.), but his words afford no help towards the interpretation of it. The traditional

interpretation of the odes, which we may suppose is given by Maou, is not to be overlooked; and, where it is supported by historical confirmations, it will often be found helpful. Still it is from the pieces themselves that we must chiefly endeavour to gather their meaning. This was the plan on which Choo He proceeded; and, as he far exceeded his predecessors in the true critical faculty, so China has not since produced another equal to him.

It is sufficient in this Ode to hear the friends of a bridegroom expressing their joy on occasion of his marriage with the virtuous object of his love, brought home in triumph, after long quest and various disappointments. There is no mention in it of king Wăn and the lady Sz'. I am not disposed to call in question the belief that that lady was the mistress of Wăn's harem; but I venture to introduce here the substance of a note from the 'Annals of the Empire', Bk. I., p. 14, to show how uncertain is the date at least of their marriage.—In the Le of the elder Tae, king Woo is said to have been born in Wăn's 14th year, while, in the standard chronology, Wăn's birth is put down in B. C. 1,230, and Woo's in 1,168, when Wan was 62. But both accounts have their difficulties. First, Wăn had one son—Pih Yih-k'aou—older than Woo, so that he must have married T'ae-sz' at the age of 12 or thereabouts, when neither he nor she could have had the emotions described in the *Kwan-ts'eu*. Further, as Wăn lived to be 100 years old, Woo must then have been 85. He died 20 years after, leaving his son, king Ching, only 14 years old. Ching must thus have been born when his father was over 80, and there was a younger son besides. This is incredible. Again, on the other account, it is unlikely that Wăn should only have had Pih Yih-k'aou before Woo, and then subsequently seven other sons, all by the same mother. And this difficulty is increased by what we read in the 5th and 6th Odes, which are understood to celebrate the numerousness of Wăn's children.

These considerations prove that the specification of events, as occurring in certain definite years of that early time, was put down very much at random by the chronologers, and that the traditional interpretation of the Odes must often be fanciful.

CLASS OF THE ODE; AND NAME. It is said to be one of the allusive pieces (兴). At the same time a metaphorical element (比) is found in the characters of the objects alluded to:—the discreet reserve between the male and female of the osprey; and the soft and delicate nature of the duckweed. The name is made by combining two characters in the 1st line. So, in many other pieces. Sometimes one character serves the purpose; at other times, two or more. Occasionally a name is found, which does not occur in the piece at all. The names of the Odes were attached to them before the time of Confucius, of which we have a superfluity of evidence in the Ch'un Ts'ew. From the Shoo, V., vi. 15, some assume that the writers of the pieces gave them their names themselves; and this may have been the case at times.—The subject of the name need rarely be referred to hereafter.

II. *Koh t'an.*

葛覃

一章

葛之覃兮。施于中谷。维叶萋萋。黄鸟于飞。集于灌

木。其鸣喈喈。

二章

葛之覃兮。施于中谷。维叶莫莫。是刈是濩。为絺为

1   How the dolichos spread itself out,
     Extending to the middle of the valley!
     Its leaves were luxuriant;
     The yellow birds flew about,
     And collected on the thickly growing trees,
     Their pleasant notes resounding far.

2   How the dolichos spread itself out,
     Extending to the middle of the valley!
     Its leaves were luxuriant and dense.

Ode 2. CELEBRATING THE INDUSTRY AND DUTIFULNESS OF KING WĂN'S QUEEN. It is supposed to have been made, and, however that was, it is to be read as if it had been made, by the queen herself.

St. 1. 葛之覃兮,—葛 is the general name for the dolichos tribe; here the *D. tuberosus*, of whose fibres a kind of cloth is made. 覃 =延, 'to stretch out.' 兮 is of very frequent occurrence in the *she*; a particle of song (歌辞). According to the Shwoh-wăn and the gloss of Seu in it, it denotes an affection of the mind, over and above what has been expressed in words. 施 (read *e*, =移) 于中谷,—中谷, 'mid-valley,'=谷中, 'the middle of the valley'. Ying-tah says that such inversion of the characters was customary with the ancients, especially in poetry. 维叶萋萋,—维 here, and nearly every else in the *she*, is simply an initial character which it is not possible to translate. 萋萋 expresses 'the appearance of luxuriant growth.' This repetition of the character is constantly found, giving intensity and vividness to the idea. Often, the characters are different, but of cognate meaning. The compound seems to picture the subject of the sentence to the eye in the colours of its own signification. This is one of the characteristics of the style of the *she*, which the student must carefully attend to. 黄鸟于飞,—'the yellow bird' is, probably, an oriole. It has many names,—博黍,黄丽,

黄莺, &c. Twice in this st., 于 occurs as a preposition.=*in, on*; but in this line, we can only take it as a particle which we need not try to translate. So, Wang Yin-che (王引之); the Urh-ya also, defining it by 曰=聿=聊. Ying-tah erroneously explains it by 往, 'to go.'

L.5. 灌木='trees growing together,' shrubs.

L.6. 喈喈 is explained as 'their harmonious notes heard far off.' The characters are probably like 关关 in the last ode, onomatopoetic.—I translate the verbs here in the past tense, because the things referred to all belong to the season of the spring, and the speaker is looking back to them.

St.2. L.3. 莫莫 (read *moo* or *moh*) adds the idea of denseness to *ts'e ts'e* above. L.4. 濩=煮, 'to boil.' The boiling was necessary in order to the separation of the fibres, which could afterwards be woven, the finer to form the 絺, and the coarser to form the 绤.

L.5. K'ang-shing takes 服=整 'to make,' 'to work at', giving not a bad meaning.—'T'ae-sz' worked at this cloth-making without weariness.' 斁 is interchanged with 射, both=厌 'to be satiated with,' and then 'to conceive a distaste for,' 'to dislike.'

St.3. Ll.1,2. Choo He takes 言 here as a particle, untranslateable (言-辞也); Maou and K'ang-shing make it=我 'I,' 'me,' which is a meaning the Urh-ya gives for the term.

绤。服之无斁。

三章
言告师氏。言告言归。薄污我私。薄浣我衣。害浣害
否。归宁父母。

> I cut it and I boiled it,
> And made both fine cloth and coarse,
> Which I will wear without getting tired of it.
>
> 3 I have told the matron,
> Who will announce that I am going to see my parents.
> I will wash my private clothes clean,
> And I will rinse my robes.
> Which need to be rinsed, and which do not?
> I am going back to visit my parents.

Wang Yin-che coincides with Choo He. Wang T'aou would take it in the 1st line as=我, and as a particle in the 2nd. I regard it as a particle in both. The 师 氏 here is difft. from the officer so styled in the Chow Le, Books VIII. and XIII. That was a teacher of morals attached to the emperor and the youths of the State; this was a matron, or duenna, whose business it was to instruct in 'woman's virtue, woman's words, woman's deportment, and woman's work.' Childless widows over 50 were, acc. to Ying-tah, employed for the office. There would be not a few such matrons in the harem, and the one intended in the text would be the mistress of them all. The 1st 告 is to be understood of the lady's announcement to the matron; the 2nd, of the matron's announce-ment to the king. Maou is led by his interpreta-tion of the whole Ode to understand 归 as='to be married.' but we must take it as synony-mous with the same term, in the concluding line.

Ll.3,4. 薄, acc. to Choo He,=少, 'slightly.' It is better to take it, as a particle, with Maou, and Wang Yin-che, who calls it 发 声, 'an initial sound.' 污, 'dirty,' is used for 'to cleanse,' just as we have 乱, 'disorder,' in the sense of 治, 'good order,' 'to govern.' This cleansing was effected by hard rubbing, whereas 浣 denotes a gentler operation, simply rinsing. The 私, as opposed to 衣, is understood of the private or ordinary dress, whereas the other term refers to the robes in which T'ae-sze as-sisted at sacrificial and other services, or in which she went in to the king. All this and what follows, is to be taken as a soliloquy, and not what T'ae-sz' told the matron (乃 后 妃 自 审 之 词, 非 告 师 氏 也) L.5. 害 (read hoh)=何, 'what.' 否 simply =不, the negative. L.6. 宁=安, i. e., 问 安, 'to inquire after their wellbeing.'

The rhymes are—in Stt.1,2, 谷, 木, cat. 3, t. 3: in 1, 姜, 飞, 嗜, cat. 15, t. 1: in 2, 莫, 濩, 绤 *, 斁 *, cat. 5, t. 1: in 3, 归, 私, 衣, cat. 15, t. 1; 否 *, 母, *, cat. 1, t. 2.

INTERPRETATION; AND CLASS. The old in-terpreters held that the ode was of T'ae-sze in her virgin prime, bent on all woman's work; and thus interpreted, it is placed among the al-lusive pieces. The first two stanzas might be so explained, but the third requires too much straining to admit of a proleptical inter-pretation as to what the virgin would do in the future, when a married wife.

Choo He makes it a narrative piece (赋), in which the queen tells first of her diligent la-bours, and then how, when they were concluded, she was going to pay a visit of duty and affec-tion to her parents. If we accept the tradition-al reference to T'ae-sze, this, no doubt, is the only admissible interpretation. The imperial editors prefer Choo He's view in this instance, and add:—' The Le of Tae only speaks of the personal tendance of the silkworms by the queen and other ladies of the harem; but here we see that there was no department of woman's work, in which they did not exert themselves. Well might they transform all below them. Anciently, the rules to be observed between husband and wife required the greatest circum-spection. They did not speak directly to each other, but employed internuncios, thus showing how strictly reserved should be intercourse between men and women, and preventing all disrespectful familiarity. When the wife was

III. *Keuen-urh.*

卷耳

一章

采采卷耳。不盈顷筐。嗟我怀人。置彼周行。

二章

陟彼崔嵬。我马虺隤。我姑酌彼金罍。维以不永怀。

三章

陟彼高冈。我马玄黄。我姑酌彼兕觥。维以不永伤。

1   I was gathering and gathering the mouse-ear,
    But could not fill my shallow basket.
    With a sigh for the man of my heart,
    I placed it there on the highway.

2   I was ascending that rock-covered height,
    But my horses were too tired to breast it.
    I will now pour a cup from that gilded vase,
    Hoping I may not have to think of him long.

3   I was ascending that lofty ridge,
    But my horses turned of a dark yellow.

about to lie in, the husband took up his quarters in a side apartment, and sent to inquire about her twice a day. When the wife wished to visit her parents, she intimated her purpose through the matron. Inside the door of the harem, no liberty could be taken any more than with a reverend guest. Thus was the instruction of the people made to commence from the smallest matters, with a wonderful depth of wisdom!'

Ode 3. LAMENTING THE ABSENCE OF A CHERISHED FRIEND. Referring this song to T'ae-sz', Choo thinks it was made by herself. However that was, we must read it as if it were from the pencil of its subject.

St.1. L.1. 采, both by Maou and Choo, is taken as in I.3; the repetition of the verb denoting the repetition of the work; Tae Chin explains 采采 as='numerous, 'were many;' which also is allowable. There are many names for the 卷 (2d tone) 耳. Maou calls it the 芩耳; Choo, the 枲耳, adding that its leaves are like a mouse's ears, and that it grows in bunchy patches. The Pun-ts'aou calls it 苍耳, which, acc. to Medhurst, is the '*lappa minor.*' The Urh-ya yih (尔雅翼) says that its seed-

vessels are like a mouse's ears, and **prickly**, sticking to people's clothes.

L. 2. The 顷筐 was a shallow basket, of bamboo or straw, depressed at the sides, so that it could be easily filled. L.3. 我怀人=我之所怀者, 'the man (or men) of whom I think, whom I cherish in my mind.' Who this was has been variously determined ;—see on the Interpretation. L.4. 置 (now written 寘)=舍, 'to set aside.' 周行,—this phrase occurs thrice in the *she*. Here and in II. v. Ode IX., Choo explains it by 大道, 'the great or high way,' while Maou and his school make it =周之列位, ' the official ranks of Chow.' In II. i. Ode I., they agree in making it=大道 or 至道, meaning 'the way of righteousness.' Tae Chin takes 周=遍, and the whole line='I would place them everywhere in the official ranks.' Choo's explanation is the best here. There was anciently no difference in the sound of 行, however it might be applied. It would rhyme with 筐 in all its significations.

四章

陟彼砠矣。我马瘏矣。我仆痡矣。云何吁矣。

I will now take a cup from that rhinoceros' horn,
Hoping I may not have long to sorrow.

.4   I was ascending that flat-topped height,
But my horses became quite disabled,
And my servants were [also] disabled.
Oh! how great is my sorrow!

St 2. L.1. Choo, after Maou, gives 崔嵬 as 'a hill of earth, with rocks on its top,' whereas the Urh-ya gives just the opposite account of the phrase. The Shwoh-wăn explains 崔 by 'large and lofty,' and 嵬 by 'rocks on a hill'; and I have translated accordingly. L.2. 虺隤 is, with Maou, simply = 病, 'diseased.' Choo takes the phrase as in the translation, after Sun Yen (孙炎) of the Wei dyn. L.3. 姑 = 且, and 姑且 together, indicate a purpose to do something in the meantime, = 'now', 'temporarily'. The 罍 was made of wood, carved so as to represent clouds, and variously gilt and ornamented. L.4. 维 has here a degree of force, = 'only.' Followed by 以, they together express a wish or hope, = 庶几. 永 = 长, 'for long.' L.3. The 兕 is the rhinoceros, 'a wild ox, with one horn, of a greenish colour, and 1000 catties in weight;' and the 觥 was a cup made of the horn, very large, sometimes requiring, we are told, 3 men to lift it. L.4. 伤, 'to be wounded,'—here, to be pained by one's own thoughts.

St 3. L.2. 玄黄 is descriptive of the colour of the horses, 'so very ill that they changed colour.'

St.4. L.1. 砠 (Shwoh-wăn, with 山, instead of 石, at the side) is the opposite of 崔嵬, in st.1, 'a rocky hill, topped with earth.' Here, again, the Urh-ya and the critics are in collision. Ll.2,3. 瘏 and 痡 are both explained in the Urh-ya by 病, 'to be ill', 'sickness.' Horses and servants all fail the speaker. His case is desperate. L.4. 云 must be taken here, and in many other places, simply as an initial particle. Wang Yin-che calls it 发语词. Choo explains 吁—'to sigh sorrowfully.' Maou makes it simply—'to be sorrowful,' as if

it were formed from 心 and 于. The Urh-ya quotes the passage—云何吁矣, which Wang T'aou would still explain in the same way as Maou does his reading.

The rhymes are—in st. 1, 筐, 行 *, cat. 10: in 2, 嵬, 隤, 罍, 怀, cat. 15, t. 1: in 3, 冈, 黄, 觥 *, 伤, cat. 10: in 4, 砠, 瘏, 痡, 吁, cat. 5, t.1.

INTERPRETATION; AND CLASS. The old interpreters thought that this ode celebrated T'ae-sze for being earnestly bent on getting the court of Chow filled with worthy ministers; for sympathizing with faithful officers in their toils on distant expeditions; and for suggesting to king Wăn to feast them on their return. The 1st st. might be interpreted in this way, taking the 2d and 3d lines as='I sigh for the men I think of, and would place them in the official ranks of Chow.' They are quoted in the Tso Chuen (after IX. xv. 2), with something like this meaning, and by Seun K'ing (解蔽篇); though without any reference to T'ae-sze. To make the other stanzas harmonize with this, however, 我 must be taken, now as equal to 我君, 'my prince or husband,' and now as equal to 我使臣, 'my officers abroad on their commissions,' than which no interpretation could be more licentious. It is astonishing that the imperial editors should lean to this view;—on which the piece belongs to the allusive class. Choo ascribes the ode to T'ae-sze. Her husband, 'the man of her heart,' is absent on some toilsome expedition; and she sets forth her anxiety for his return, by representing herself, first as a gatherer of vegetables, unable to fill her basket through the preoccupation of her mind; and then as trying to drive to a height from which she might see her husband returning, but always baffled. All this is told in her own person, so that the piece is narrative. The whole representation is, however, unnatural; and when the baffled rider proceeds to console herself with a cup of spirits, I must drop the idea of T'ae-sze altogether, and can make nothing more of the piece than that some one is lamenting in it the absence of a cherished friend, —in strange fashion.

IV. *Këw muh.*

樛木

一章
南有樛木。葛藟累之。乐只君子。福履绥之。

二章
南有樛木。葛藟荒之。乐只君子。福履将之。

三章
南有樛木。葛藟萦之。乐只君子。福履成之。

1 In the south are the trees with curved drooping branches,
  With the dolichos creepers clinging to them.
  To be rejoiced in is our princely lady:—
  May she repose in her happiness and dignity!

2 In the south are the trees with curved drooping branches,
  Covered by the dolichos creepers.
  To be rejoiced in is our princely lady:—
  May she be great in her happiness and dignity!

3 In the south are the trees with curved drooping branches,
  Round which the dolichos creepers twine.
  To be rejoiced in is our princely lady:—
  May she be complete in her happiness and dignity!

Ode 4. CELEBRATING T'AE-SZE'S FREEDOM FROM JEALOUSY, AND OFFERING FERVENT WISHES FOR HER HAPPINESS. So far both the schools of interpreters are agreed on this ode, and we need not be long detained with it. The piece is allusive, supposed to be spoken or sung by the ladies of the harem, in praise of T'ae-szé, who was not jealous of them, and did not try to keep them in the back ground, but cherished them rather, as the great tree does the creepers that twine round it. The stanzas are very little different, the 3rd character in the 2d and 4th lines being varied, merely to give different rhymes.

St.1. L.1. For 'the south' we need not go beyond the south of the territory of Chow. K'ang-shing errs in thinking that the distant provinces of King and Yang, beyond the Këang, are meant. Trees whose branches curved down to the ground were designated 樛木. Such branches were easily laid hold of by creepers.

L.2. The 藟 was, probably, a variety of the 葛；累 is explained by 系, 'to be attached to.' L.3. 只 is another of the untranslateable particles; it occurs both in the middle and at the end of lines. The critics differ on the inter-

pretation of 君子. Maou and his school refer it to king Wăn, and construe the last two lines,—'She is able also to rejoice her princely lord, and make him repose in his happiness and dignity.' Choo refers it to T'ae-sze, and what follows is a good wish or prayer for her. He defends his view of the phrase by the designation of 小君, given to the wife of a prince, (Ana. XVI. xiv.), and of 内子, given to the wife of a great officer. The imperial editors allow his exegesis. It certainly gives a unity to the piece, which it does not have on the other view, and I have followed it. L.4. Choo, after the Urh-ya and Maou, takes 履 = 禄, 'emolument,' 'dignity.' Trying to preserve the proper meaning of 履, 'to tread on', 'footsteps', Yen Ts'an (严粲 ; Sung dyn.) and others say, 动冈不吉谓之福履, 'The movements all felicitous are what is meant by 福履.' 绥 = 安, 'to give repose to'

St.2. 荒＝奄, or 芘覆, 'to cover,' 'to overshadow.' The creepers send out their shoots,

V.　*Chung-sze.*

螽斯

一章

螽斯羽。诜诜兮。宜尔子孙。振振兮。

二章

螽斯羽。薨薨兮。宜尔子孙。绳绳兮。

1　Ye locusts, winged tribes,
　　How harmoniously you collect together!
　　Right is it that your descendants
　　Should be multitudinous!

2　Ye locusts, winged tribes,
　　How sound your wings in flight!
　　Right is it that your descendants
　　Should be as in unbroken strings!

and cover the branches of the tree. 将 is here best taken as＝ 大, 'to make great.'

St.3. 成 ＝ 就, 'complete'. The singers wish the happiness of T'ae-sz', 'from first to last, from the smallest things to the greatest', to be complete.

The rhymes are—in st. 1, 累．绥, cat.15, t.1: in 2, 荒, 将, cat. 10: in 3, 紫, 成, cat. 11.

Ode 5. THE FRUITFULNESS OF THE LOCUST; SUPPOSED TO CELEBRATE T'AE-SZE'S FREEDOM FROM JEALOUSY. The piece is purely metaphorical (比), T'ae-sze not being mentioned in it. The reference to her only exists in the writer's mind. This often distinguishes such pieces from those which are allusive. The locusts cluster together in harmony, it is supposed, without quarrelling, and consequently they increase at a wonderful rate; each female laying, some say 81 eggs, others 99, and others 100.

L.1. in all the stanzas. The 斯 in 螽斯 is by many disregarded, as being merely one of the poetical particles. We shall meet with it as such beyond dispute, and we find 螽 alone, frequently in the Ch'un Ts'ëw. Here, however, it would seem to be a part of the name, the insect intended being the same probably, as the 斯螽, in xv., Ode I. 5. Maou gives for it the synonym of 蚣 蝑, and Choo calls it 'one of the locusts (蝗 属).' But 蝗 will include crickets, grasshoppers, and locusts. We cannot as yet do more than approximate to an identification of the insects in the *She*. Williams calls the *chung-sze* one of the *truxalis* locusts; but

in descriptions and plates the length of the antennæ is made very prominent, so that the creature is probably to be found among the *achetidœ*. 羽 is to be taken as in the translation, ＝羽 虫, and not as meaning 'wings.' So, Ying-tah. The 'Complete Digest' says, 勿 作 翅 说．

L.3. Maou and his school make 尔 to be addressed to T'ae-sze; Choo refers it, better, simply to the locusts. Those who refer it to the lady try to find some moral meaning, in addition to that of multitude, in the concluding lines. The three second lines are all descriptive of the harmonious clustering of the insects. 诜 诜 is explained by Choo as the appearance of their 'collecting harmoniously,' and by Maou as meaning 'numerous'. The Shwoh-wăn gives it as 辛 with 多 at the side. We have the character in the text, the form of the Shwoh-wăn, 辛 with 羽 at the side, 先 with 马 at the side, and 生 with another 生 at the side;—all in binomial form with the same meaning. 薨 薨 is 'the sound of a crowd of locusts flying.' The bottom of the char. should be 羽, and not 死．

The last lines. 振振, is the 'appearance of their multitude;' Maou makes it＝'benevolent and generous.'' 绳绳,—'the appearance of uninter ᵣupted continuance;' Maou makes it＝ 'cautiᵒus,' or 'careful.' 蛰 蛰, is the ap-

三章
蟲斯羽。揖揖兮。宜尔子孙。蛰蛰兮。

3 Ye locusts, winged tribes,
 How you cluster together!
 Right is it that your descendants
 Should be in swarms!

VI. *T'aou yaou.*

桃夭
一章
桃之夭夭。灼灼其华。之子于归。宜其室家。

1 The peach tree is young and elegant;
 Brilliant are its flowers.
 This young lady is going to her future home,
 And will order well her chamber and house.

pearance of their being 'clustered together like insects in their burrows.' Maou makes it= 'harmoniously collected.'

The rhymes are—in st.1, 诜 *, 孙, 振 *, cat.13: in 2, 蘐, 绳, cat.6: in 3, 揖, 蛰, cat.7,t.3.

The idea of all the critics is that Wǎn's queen lived harmoniously with all the other ladies of the harem, so that all had their share in his favours, and there was no more quarrelling among them than among a bunch of locusts. All children born in the palace would be the queen's; and it was right they should increase as they did.— Surely this is sad stuff.

Ode 6. Allusive. PRAISE OF A BRIDE GOING TO BE MARRIED. The critics see a great deal more in the piece than this;—the happy state of Chow, produced by king Wǎn (acc. to Choo), or by T'ae-sze (acc. to Maou), in which all the young people were married in the proper season, *i.e.*, in the spring, when the peach tree was in flower, and at the proper age, *i. e.*, young men between 20 and 30, and girls between 15 and 20. It *was* a rule of the Chow dyn. that marriages should take place in the middle of spring (Chow Le, II. vi. 54). This marriage would be about that time, and the peach tree was in flower; but it was only the latter circumstance which was in the poet's mind.

St.1. L.1. 之 may be taken as the sign of the genitive, the whole line being='in the young and beautiful time of the peach tree.' Still, 之 is so constantly used throughout the *She* in the middle of lines, where we can only regard it as a particle, eking out the number of feet,

that it is, perhaps, not worth while to resolve such lines as this in the above manner. 夭夭 (Shwoh-wǎn, with 木 at the side) denotes 'the appearance of youth and elegance.' L.2. 灼灼 is descriptive rather of the brilliance of the flowers than of their luxuriance, as Choo has it. The young peach tree is allusive of the bride in the flush of youth, and its brilliant flowers of her beauty. L.3. 之=是, 'this;' 子='young lady.' Maou and Ch'ing take 于 as=往, 'to go to.' But it is better to regard it as a particle, as in Ode II.1. 归 here is used of the bride going to her husband's house. As Choo says, women speak of being married as going home (妇人 谓嫁曰归). Should we take 之子 in the singular or plural? Lacharme translates it by *puellæ nobiles*, and Heu Hëen (许 谦; Yuen dyn.) says, 'The poet saw the thing going on from the flowering of the peach tree till the fruit was ripe;—the young ladies were many.' This seems to me very unpoetical. L.4. 室 is the chamber appropriated to husband and wife; 家 is 'all within the door,'=our *house.* 室家 here, 家室 in st.2, and 家人 in st.3. convey the same idea, the terms being varied for the sake of the rhythm. Tso-she says that when a couple marry, the man has a 室, and the woman a 家; so that 室 家 are

二章
桃之夭夭。有蕡其实。之子于归。宜其家室。
三章
桃之夭夭。其叶蓁蓁。之子于归。宜其家人。

2　The peach tree is young and elegant;
　　Abundant will be its fruit.
　　This young lady is going to her future home,
　　And will order well her house and chamber.

3　The peach tree is young and elegant;
　　Luxuriant are its leaves.
　　This young lady is going to her future home,
　　And will order well her family.

VII.　*T'oo tseu.*

兔罝
一章
肃肃兔罝。椓之丁丁。赳赳武夫。公侯干城。

1　Carefully adjusted are the rabbit nets;
　　Clang clang go the blows on the pegs.
　　That stalwart, martial man
　　Might be shield and wall to his prince.

equivalent to husband and wife. Accordingly, Maou takes the line as meaning, 'Right is it they should be married without going beyond their proper years;' and in this view he is followed by K'ang-shing. But to this there are two objections. 1st, the antecedent to 其 is 之子, the girl, and the girl only. 2d, in the 4th line, 宜 must be construed as an active verb. So it is in the 'Great Learning,' Comm. ix.6, where the passage is quoted.

St.2. L.2. Choo says *fun* denotes the abundance of the fruit, intimating that the young lady would have many children. Maou makes the term='the appearance of the fruit,' intimating, that the lady had not beauty only, but also 'woman's virtue.' *Fun* is properly the seeds of hemp, which are exceedingly numerous; and hence it is applied to the fruit of other plants and trees to indicate its abundance. So, Lo Yuen (罗愿; Sung dyn.), Wang T'aou, and others.

St.3. L.2. *Ts'in-ts'in* sets forth the luxuriance of the foliage,—至 盛 貌.

The rhymes are—in st.1, 华 ⁎, 家 ⁎, cat. 5, t. 1 : in 2, 实, 室, cat. 12, t. 3; in 3, 蓁, 人, *ib.*, t. 1.

Ode 7.　Pʀᴀɪsᴇ ᴏꜰ ᴀ ʀᴀʙʙɪᴛ-ᴄᴀᴛᴄʜᴇʀ, ᴀs ꜰɪᴛ ᴛᴏ ʙᴇ ᴀ ᴘʀɪɴᴄᴇ's ᴍᴀᴛᴇ. Whether any particular individual was intended will be considered in the note on the interpretation. The generally accepted view is that the ode sets forth the influence of king Wăn (acc. to Choo), or of T'ae-sze (acc. to Maou), as so powerful and beneficial, that individuals in the lowest rank were made fit by it to occupy the highest positions.

St.1. L.1. 罝 is defined in the Urh-ya as 'a rabbit-net;' to which Le Seun, the glossarist, (李 巡 ; end of the Han dyn.), adds, that the rabbit makes paths underground for itself. Choo makes 肃肃 descriptive of the careful manner in which the nets were set; Maou, of the reverent demeanour of the trapper. It is difficult to choose between them. On Choo's view the piece is *allusive*; on Maou's, *narrative*.

二章
肅肅兔罝。施于中逵。赳赳武夫。公侯好仇。

三章
肅肅兔罝。施于中林。赳赳武夫。公侯腹心。

2 Carefully adjusted are the rabbit nets,
   And placed where many ways meet.
   That stalwart, martial man
   Would be a good companion for his prince.

3 Carefully adjusted are the rabbit nets,
   And placed in the midst of the forest.
   That stalwart, martial man
   Might be head and heart to his prince.

VIII. *Fow-e.-*

芣苢

一章
采采芣苢。薄言采之。采采芣苢。薄言有之。

1 We gather and gather the plantains;
   Now we may gather them.
   We gather and gather the plantains;
   Now we have got them.

L.2. 丁 (read *chǎng*) 丁 is intended to represent the sound of the blows (椓) on the pins or pegs (杙) used in setting the nets.

L.3. Both Maou and Choo give 赳赳 as—'martial-like,' while the Shwoh-wǎn defines the phrase by 輕勁有材力,'light, vigorous, able, and strong.' L.4. 公侯= 'duke and marquis;' together,—prince. We are to understand king Wǎn by the designation. At the time to which the ode refers, he was not yet styled king, and, indeed, Choo takes the phrase as one proof that Wǎn never assumed that title. Maou takes 干 = 扞, so that 干 城 go together,— 'defender,' or 'wall of defence;' probably after Tso-she, in his narrative appended to the 12th year of duke Ching. 'Shield and wall,' however, are suitable enough in the connection.

St.2. L.2. 施 is read *she*, 'to place,' 'to set.' 中 逵 and 中 林 below,—like 中 谷 in Ode II. 逵 = 九 达 之 道, a place from which 9 ways proceed.' I have asked Wang T'aou and other scholars, whether such a thoroughfare was not an unlikely place to catch rabbits in, and got no satisfactory answer. L.4. 仇 一 逑 in Ode I.

There is a difficulty as to the rhyming of 逵 and 仇. The latter is said to be here read, by poetical license, *k'e.* A better solution is to adopt the reading of 首 with 九 at the side, instead of 逵, for which there is some evidence.

St.3. L.4. 腹 心 = 'confidant and guide;' lit., 'belly and heart.' We do not use 'belly,' as the Chinese do.

The rhymes are—in st.1, 罝*, 夫, cat. 5. t. 1; 丁, 城, cat. 11: in 2, 罝, 夫; 逵*, 仇, cat. 3 t. 1 (this is a doubtful rhyme): in 3, 罝, 夫; 林, 心, cat. 7. t. 1. The alternate lines all rhyme, which is called 隔 句 韵.

二章
采采芣苢。薄言掇之。采采芣苢。薄言捋之。
三章
采采芣苢。薄言袺之。采采芣苢。薄言襭之。

2   We gather and gather the plantains;
     Now we pluck the ears.
    We gather and gather the plantains;
     Now we rub out the seeds.

3   We gather and gather the plantains;
     Now we place the seeds in our skirts.
    We gather and gather the plantains;
     Now we tuck our skirts under our girdles.

IX.   *Han kwang.*

汉广
一章
南有乔木。不可休息。汉有游女。不可求思。汉之广

1   In the south rise the trees without branches,
     Affording no shelter.
    By the Han are girls rambling about,
     But it is vain to solicit them.

INTERPRETATION. The ordinary view of this ode has been mentioned above. A special interpretation, however, which is worth referring to, has been put upon it. In the 2d of his chapters (尚贤，上), Mih Teih says that 'king Wăn raised from their rabbit nets Hwang Yaou and T'ae T'een.' We find both those names in the Shoo (V. xvi. 12) as ministers of Wăn. Kin Le-ts'eang (金履祥; Yuen dyn.) and other scholars think, therefore, that this ode had reference to them. This view seems very likely.

Ode 8. Narrative. THE SONG OF THE PLANTAIN-GATHERERS. We are supposed to have here a happy instance of the tranquillity of the times of Wăn, so that the women, the loom and other household labours over, could go out and gather the seeds of the plantain in cheerful concert. Why they gathered those seeds does not appear. From the Preface it appears that they were thought to be favourable to child-bearing. They are still thought in China to be helpful in difficult labours. Among ourselves, a mucilage is got from the seeds of some species of the plant, which is used in stiffening muslins.

St. 1. L. 1. 采采,—see on Ode III. The 芣苢 is one of the *plantaginaceæ*; probably our common ribgrass, as in the line of Tennyson, 'The hedgehog underneath the plantain bores.'

L. 2. 薄言,—both of these terms have been noticed, on Ode II., as untranslateable particles. Nothing more can be said of them, when they are found, as here, in combination.

Ll. 2, 4. 采之＝'let us go and gather them;' 有之,—'we have got them,' here they are. Maou, strangely, takes 有＝藏, 'to collect,' 'to deposit.'

St. 2. Ll. 2, 4. 掇＝拾, 'to gather,'—meaning the ears. 捋＝取, 'to take,'—meaning the seeds.

St. 3. 袺＝执 衽, 'to hold up the skirt,'—meaning as in the translation. 襭 ＝扱

矣。不可泳思。江之永矣。不可方思。

二章

翘翘错薪。言刈其楚。之子于归。言秣其马。汉之广

矣。不可泳思。江之永矣。不可方思。

> The breadth of the Han
> Cannot be dived across;
> The length of the Këang
> Cannot be navigated with a raft.

2　Many are the bundles of firewood;
　　I would cut down the thorns [to form more].
　　Those girls that are going to their future home,—
　　I would feed their horses.
　　The breadth of the Han
　　Cannot be dived across;
　　The length of the Këang
　　Cannot be navigated with a raft.

衽, 'to tuck the skirt under the girdle;' Medhurst says, 'round the waist.'

The rhymes are—in st. 1, 莒, 采, 苢, 有*, cat. 1, t. 2: in 2, 掇, 捋, cat. 15, t. 3: in 3, 袺, 襭, cat. 12, t. 3.

Ode 9. Allusive, and metaphorical. THE VIRTUOUS MANNERS OF THE YOUNG WOMEN ABOUT THE HAN AND THE KEANG. Through the influence of Wăn, the dissolute manners of the people, and especially the women, in the regions south from Chow, had undergone a great transformation.' The praise of the ladies in the piece, therefore, is to the praise of Wăn. So say both Choo and Maou, the 'Little Preface' ceasing here to speak of T'ae-sze. The first 4 lines of each stanza are allusive, the poet proceeding always from the first two lines to the things alluded to in them or intended by them. The last 4 lines are metaphorical, no mention being made of the poet's inner meaning in them. To bring that out, we should have to supply,— 'Those ladies are like.' See the remarks of Lëw Kin (刘 瑾 ; Yuen dyn.) appended to Choo's 'Collection of Comments,'—in the Yung-ching She.

St.1. L.1. The south here is difft. from that in Ode II. The connection makes us refer it to the States in Yang-chow and King-chow. 乔

木 means 'lofty trees with few or no branches

low down.' L.2. The 息 unites well enough with 休 of cognate meaning; but it can hardly be other than an error which has crept into the text, instead of 思, the particle with which all the other lines conclude, elsewhere found also at the end of lines. In those lofty trees, giving no shelter, we have an allusion to the young ladies immediately spoken of, virtuous and refusing their favours. L.3. The Han,—see the Shoo, III. i. Pt. ii. 8. L. 6. 泳 = 潜 行, 'to go hidden in the water,' to dive. L.8. Choo defines 方 (or 舫) by 栰, and Maou by 泭 ; these characters are synonyms, meaning a raft; here='to be rafted,' to be navigated with a raft. L.7. The Këang,—see the Shoo on III. i. Pt. ii. 9.—Rafts are seen constantly on the Këang. Does not the text indicate that in the time of the poet the people had not learned to venture on the mighty stream?

Stt. 2, 3. The first four lines in these stanzas are of difficult interpretation. 错 is explained by 杂, 'mixed,' 'made up of different components,' so that 错 薪='bundles of faggots of different kinds of wood, or of wood and grass or brushwood together.' 翘 翘 is given by Maou as indicating 'the appearance of the faggots;' but he does not say in what way. Choo

三章

翘翘错薪。言刈其蒌。之子于归。言秣其驹。汉之广矣。不可泳思。江之永矣。不可方思。

3   Many are the bundles of firewood;
I would cut down the southernwood [to form more].
Those girls that are going to their future home,—
I would feed their colts.
The breadth of the Han
Cannot be dived across;
The length of the Këang
Cannot be navigated with a raft.

X. *Joo fun.*

汝坟

一章

遵彼汝坟。伐其条枚。未见君子。惄如调饥。

1   Along those raised banks of the Joo,
I cut down the branches and slender stems.
While I could not see my lord,
I felt as it were pangs of great hunger.

says the phrase indicates 'the appearance of rising up flourishingly;' but how can this apply to bundles of faggots? Two other meanings of the phrase are given in the dict., either of which is preferable to this: viz., 'numerous (众),' which I have adopted; and 'high like (高貌).' 楚 is a species of thorn-tree (荆属); and 蒌 is a species of artemisia. It is also called 蒌 蒿 and 蒌 蒿, which last Medhurst calls 'a kind of southernwood.' It is described as growing in low places, and marshy grounds, with leaves like the mugwort, of a light green, fragrant and brittle. When young, the leaves may be eaten, and afterwards, they may be cooked for food. The reference to them in the text, however, is not because of their use for food, but, like the thorns, for fuel. The plant grows, it is said, several feet high; and even, with ourselves, the southernwood acquires a woody stem, after a few years. 秣 (Shwoh Wăn, 𩢸)='to feed.' 马, is a full-grown horse, 'six cubits high and upwards;' 驹, is a colt, a young horse, 'between 5 and 6 cubits high;' but stress cannot be laid on the specific differences in the meaning of such terms, which are employed

in order to vary the rhymes. But now, what relation was there between the piles of faggots, and cutting down the thorns and the southernwood? and how are the first two lines allusive of what is stated in the next two? Lacharme does not try to indicate this in his notes, and his translation is without Chinese sanction and in itself unjustifiable:—'*Ex virgultorum variis fasciculis spinas resecare* '(St. 3, *herbas silvestres avellere*) satagunt. *Puellæ matrimonio collocantur, et quærunt unde pascant equos suos* (St. 3, *pullos equinos*).' The nearest approach to a satisfactory answer to those questions that I have met with, is the following:—Cutting down the thorns and the southernwood was a toilsome service performed for the faggots, but such was the respect inspired by the virtuous ladies whom the speaker saw, that he was willing to perform the meanest services for them. This I have endeavoured to indicate in the translation, though the nature of the service done to the faggots is not expressed by any critic as I have done. See the 'Complete Digest' *in loc.*, and the various suggestions in the 'Collection of Opinions (集 说),' given in the imperial edition.

The rhymes are—in st.1, 休, 求, cat. 3, t. 1: in 2, 楚, 马 *, cat. 5, t 2: in 3, 蒌 *, 驹 *; cat. 4: in all the stanzas, 广, 泳 *, 永 *, 方, cat. 10.

二章
遵彼汝坟。伐其条肄。既见君子。不我遐弃。

三章
鲂鱼赪尾。王室如毁。虽则如毁。父母孔迩。

2 Along those raised banks of the Joo,
  I cut down the branches and fresh twigs.
  I have seen my lord;
  He has not cast me away.

3 The bream is showing its tail all red;
  The royal House is like a blazing fire.
  Though it be like a blazing fire,
  Your parents are very near.

Ode 10. Mainly narrative. THE AFFECTION OF THE WIVES OF THE JOO, AND THEIR SOLICITUDE ABOUT THEIR HUSBANDS' HONOUR. The royal House, in the last stanza, like a blazing fire, is supposed to be that of Shang, under the tyranny of Chow. The piece, therefore, belongs to the closing time of that dyn., when Wan was consolidating his power and influence. The effects of his very different rule were felt in the country about the Joo, and animated the wife of a soldier (or officer), rejoicing in the return of her husband from a toilsome service, to express her feelings and sentiments, as in these stanzas.

St. 1. L. 1. The Joo is not mentioned in the Shoo. It rises in the hill of T'een-seih (天息), in Joo Chow, Honan, flows east through that province, and falls into the Hwae, in the dep. of Ying-chow (颍州), Ngan-hwui. 坟 =大防, 'great dykes,' meaning the banks of the river, raised, or rising high, to keep the water in its channel. Some give the phrase 汝坟 a more definite meaning, and the site of an old city, which was so called, is pointed out, 50 *le* to the north east of the dis. city of Shëh (叶), dep. Nan-yang. L.2. 条 = 枝, 'branches.' 枚 = 'small trees.' The speaker must be supposed to have been cutting these branches and trees for firewood. L.3. 君子,—the speaker's 'princely man,'='her husband.' She longed to see him, but she did not do so yet (未). L.4. 怒 in the Urh-ya is explained both by 思, 'to think,' and by 饥, 'to be hungry.' Maou and Choo unite those definitions, and make it= 饥意, 'hungry thoughts.' 调 (*chow*), with Maou, = 朝, 'the morning,' so that the meaning is 'I feel like one hungry for the morning meal.' Much

better it is to adopt, with Choo, the reading of 辀, meaning 重. 'intense,' 'long-continued.'

St. 2. L 2. 肄 = 'fresh shoots;' a year had gone by. The branches lopped in the past par. had grown again, or fresh shoots in their place. The husband had long been away; but at length he has returned. So the 既 in l.3. intimates. L.4. 遐 = 远 = 'distant,' 'far.' 遐 弃, together,= 'to abandon.' 不我遐弃 = 不远弃我, 'has not abandoned me'; but whether this expression be='my husband is not dead,' as K'ang-shing and many others take it; or='he comes back, with all the affection of our original covenant,' it would be hard to say. On the latter view the stanza is *allusive*, and the husband has not yet returned. The fresh shoots awaken the speaker's emotion, and she exclaims, 'Another day, when I shall have seen my husband, perhaps he will not cast me off!' As Yen Ts'an puts it, 他日已见君子，庶几不远弃我也.

St.3. This stanza is metaphorical. L.1. The *fang* is the bream called also 鯟 and 鳊. 赪 = 赤, 'red.' The tail of the bream, we are told, is not naturally red like that of the carp; the redness in the text must be produced by its tossing about in shallow water. So was the speaker's husband toiled and worn out in distant service. The other 3 lines are understood to be an exhortation to the husband to do his duty to the royal House of Yin, notwithstanding the oppressiveness of Chow its Head. 毁 = 火 'a fire,' or to blaze as a fire. K'ang-shing and Ying-tah understand by 'parents' the husbands' parents, so that his wife's idea is that he should do his duty at all risks, and not disgrace his parents whom he should think of as always near him. Choo con-

XI. *Lin che che.*

麟之趾

一章
麟之趾。振振公子。于嗟麟兮。

二章
麟之定。振振公姓。于嗟麟兮。

三章
麟之角。振振公族。于嗟麟兮。

1   The feet of the *lin*:—
     The noble sons of our prince,
     Ah! they are the *lin!*

2   The forehead of the *lin*:—
     The noble grandsons of our prince,
     Ah! they are the *lin!*

3   The horn of the *lin*:—
     The noble kindred of our prince,
     Ah! they are the *lin!*

siders that the phrase is a designation of king Wăn, as the 'parent' of the people; and the wife exhorts her husband ever to think of him, serving the House of Yin loyally, and to copy his example. It may be the best way to accept the view of the old interpreters. 孔 = 甚, 'very.'

The rhymes are—in St. 1, 枚, 饥, cat. 15, t.1: in 2, 肄, 弃, *ib.* t.3: in 3, 尾, 毁 *, 毁 *, 逺 *, *ib,* t.2.

Ode 11. Allusive. CELEBRATING THE GOOD-NESS OF THE OFFSPRING AND RELATIVES OF KING WAN. The *lin* (Urh-ya, 麟) is the female of the *k'e* (麒), a fabulous animal, the symbol of all goodness and benevolence; having the body of a deer, the tail of an ox, the hoofs of a horse, one horn, the scales of a fish, &c. Its *feet* are here mentioned, because it does not tread on any living thing, not even on live grass; its *forehead* (定 = 题, Maou; = 额, Shwoh-wăn), because it does not butt with it; and its *horn*, because the end of it is covered with flesh, to show that the creature, while able for war, wills to have peace. The *lin* was supposed to appear, inaugurating a golden age; but the poet intimates that he considered the character of Wăn's family and kindred as a better auspice of such a time. Choo adopts here the explanation of 振振 given on Ode V.1 by Maou,—仁厚貌 'benevolent and generous-like,' while Maou, I know not for what reason, changes 仁 into 信, and makes the phrase= 'sincere and generous-like.' 公子 = the duke's sons.' 公

姓 = 公孙, 'the duke's grandsons.' The term 姓, 'surname,' is used for grandsons, because the grandson's descendants became a new clan, with the designation of his grandfather for a clan-name. By 公族 we are to understand all who could trace their lineage to the same 'high ancestor' as the duke.

The rhymes are—in st. 1, 趾, 子, cat. 1, t.2: in, 2, 定, 姓, cat. 11: iu 3, 角, 族, cat. 3, t.3: the 麟 at the end of each stanza is also considered as making a rhyme.

CONCLUDING NOTE. It is difficult for us to transport ourselves to the time and scenes of the pieces in this book. The Chinese see in them a model prince and his model wife, and the widely extended beneficial effects of their character and government. The institution of the harem is very prominent; and there the wife appears, lovely on her entry into it, reigning in it with entire devotion to her husband's happiness, free from all jealousy of the inferior inmates, in the most friendly spirit promoting their comfort, and setting them an example of frugality and industry. The people rejoice in the domestic happiness of their ruler, and in the number of his children, and would have these multiplied more and more. Among themselves, gravity of manners dignifies individuals of the meanest rank; and the rabbit-trapper is fit to be his prince's friend, guide, and shield. Purity is seen taking the place of licentiousness, both among women and men; and the wife is taught to prefer her husband's honour and loyalty to her own gratification in his society. The 4th Ode gives a pleasant picture of a bride, where yet her future work in her family is not overlooked; and the 8th, with its simple lines, shows to us a cheerful company of rib-grass-gatherers.

BOOK II. THE ODES OF SHAOU AND THE SOUTH.

I. *Ts'ëoh ch'aou.*

召南一之二

鹊巢

一章
维鹊有巢。维鸠居之。之子于归。百两御之。

二章
维鹊有巢。维鸠方之。之子于归。百两将之。

三章
维鹊有巢。维鸠盈之。之子于归。百两成之。

1 The nest is the magpie's;
   The dove dwells in it.
   This young lady is going to her future home;
   A hundred carriages are meeting her.

2 The nest is the magpie's;
   The dove possesses it.
   This young lady is going to her future home;
   A hundred carriages are escorting her.

3 The nest is the magpie's;
   The dove fills it.
   This young lady is going to her future home;
   These hundreds of carriages complete her array.

TITLE OF THE BOOK — 召南一之二, 'Shaou Nan, Book II. of Part I.' On the title of the last Book, it has been stated that king Wăn, on removing to Fung, divided the original Chow of his House into two portions, which he settled on his son Tan, the duke of Chow, and on Shih, one of his principal adherents, the duke of Shaou. The site of the city of Shaou was in dep. of Fung-ts'ëang, and probably in the dis. of K'e-shan. Shih was of the Chow surname of Ke (姬), and is put down by Hwang-poo Meih as a son of Wăn by a concubine; but this is uncertain. After his death, he received the honorary name of K'ang (康 公). On the overthrow of the Shang dyn., he was invested by king Woo with the principality of Yen, or North Yen (北 燕), having its capital in the pres. dis. of Ta-hing (大 兴), dep. of Shun-t'ëen, where his descendants are traced, down to the Ts'in dyn. He himself, however, as did Tan, remained at the court of Chow, and we find them, in the Shoo, as the principal ministers of king Ching. They were known as the 'highest dukes (上 公),' and the 'two great chiefs (二 伯),' Tan having charge of the eastern portions of the kingdom, and Shih of the western.

The pieces in this Book are supposed to have been produced in Shaou and the principalities south of it,—west from those that yielded the odes of the Chow-nan.

Ode 1. Allusive. CELEBRATING THE MARRIAGE OF A BRIDE,—A PRINCESS, TO THE PRINCE OF ANOTHER STATE. The critics will all have it, that the poet's object was to set forth 'the virtue of the lady,' and wherein they find the allusion to that will be seen below. For myself I do not see that the *virtue* of the bride was a point which the writer wished to indicate; his attention was taken by the splendour of the nuptials.

St. 1. L. 1. 维 ,—see on i. Ode II. 1. The *ts'eoh* is the magpie. It is common in China, and generally called *he-ts'eoh* (喜 鹊); it makes the same elaborate nest as with ourselves. L. 2. 鸠 is the general name for the dove; here, probably, the turtle dove, the *she-këw* (鸤 鸠). It has many local names. I do not know that it is a fact that the dove is to be found breeding in a magpie's nest, as is here assumed; but Maou K'e-ling vehemently asserts it, and says that any one with eyes may see about the villages a flock of doves contending with as many magpies, and driving the latter from their nests (续 诗 传 鸟 名 卷 一). The *virtue* of the bride is thought to be emblemed by the quietness and stupidity of the dove, unable to make a nest for itself, or making a very simple, unartistic one. The dove is a favourite emblem with all poets for a lady; but surely never, out of China, because of its 'stupidity.' But says Twan Ch'ang-woo (段 昌 武 , towards the end of the Sung dyn.), 'The duties of a wife are few and confined; there is no harm in her being stupid.'

L. 4. 两 = 一 车 , 'a carriage,' as being supported on two wheels (两 轮). 御 is

commonly read here *ya*, and generally when it has the signification of 'to meet.' But it rhymes here with *keu*, and the variation of its sound, according to its signification, is a device dating only from the Han dyn. The 100 carriages here are those of the bridegroom and his friends, who come to meet the lady, as she approaches the borders of his State.

St. 2. L. 2. 方 之 = 有 之 , 'has it.' Yen Ts'an quotes a sentence which ingeniously explains this use of 方 as a verb,— 方 之 以 为 其 所 也 . L. 4. 将 = 送 , to escort.' The carriages here are those of the bride and all her *cortége*.

St. 3. L. 2. The 'filling' of the nest alludes to the ladies accompanying the bride to the harem. She would be accompanied by two near relatives from her own State, and there would be three ladies from each of two kindred States, so that the prince of a State is described by Kung-yang as 'at once marrying 9 ladies (诸 侯 一 婆 九 女). L. 4. The 100 carriages here cover those of each of the previous stanzas. 成 之 ,—as in i. IV. 3.,= 'make her complete.'

The rhymes are—in st. 1, 居 , 御 , cat. 5. t. 1; in 2, 方 , 将 , cat. 10: in 3, 盈 , 成 , cat. 11.

NOTE ON THE INTERPRETATION. In his interesting essay on the poetry of the Chinese, (already referred to), Sir John Davis gives the following paraphrase of this ode :—

'The nest yon winged artist builds,
  The robber bird shall tear away:
—So yields her hopes the affianced maid,
  Some wealthy lord's reluctant prey.

'The anxious bird prepares a nest,
  In which the spoiler soon shall dwell:
—Forth goes the weeping bride constrained,
  A hundred cars the triumph swell.

'Mourn for the tiny architect;
  A stronger bird hath ta'en its nest:
Mourn for the hapless stolen bride,
  How vain the pomp to soothe her breast!'

This is paraphrased, he says, 'to convey the full sense of what is only hinted at in the original, and explained in the commentary.' He has made a little poem, more interesting than the original, but altogether away from the obvious meaning of that original, on a view of it not hinted at in any commentary.

II. *Ts'ae fan.*

采蘩
一章
于以采蘩。于沼于沚。于以用之。公侯之事。
二章
于以采蘩。于涧之中。于以用之。公侯之宫。
三章
被之僮僮。夙夜在公。被之祁祁。薄言还归。

1 She gathers the white southernwood,
  By the ponds, on the islets.
  She employs it,
  In the business of our prince.

2 She gathers the white southernwood,
  Along the streams in the valleys.
  She employs it,
  In the temple of our prince.

3 With head-dress reverently rising aloft,
  Early, while yet it is night, she is in the prince's *temple;*
  In her head-dress, slowly retiring,
  She returns *to her own apartments.*

Ode 2. Narrative. THE INDUSTRY AND RE-VERENCE OF A PRINCE'S WIFE, ASSISTING HIM IN SACRIFICING. Here we must suppose the ladies of a harem, in one of the States of the South, admiring and praising the way in which their mistress discharged her duties;—all, of course, add the commentators, through the transforming influence of the court of Chow. There is a view that it is not sacrificing that is spoken of, which I will point out in a concluding note.

St. 1. L. 1. Maou says 于＝於, which it is in the next line; but 于 以 cannot be so construed. K'ang-shing and Ying-tah, seeing this, made 于＝往, which would do in the 1st line, but not in the 3d. Our best plan is to take 于 and 以 together as a compound particle, untranslateable; so, Wang T'aou (于 以 犹 薄 言，皆 发 声 语 助 也). 蘩 is, no doubt, a kind of *artemisia*, and is defined as 白 蒿, after which Medhurst terms it 'white southernwood.' Its leaf is coarser than that of the other *haou*, with white hairs on it. It does not grow high, like some other varieties, but

thick. The *fan* was used both in sacrifices, and in feeding silkworms. L. 2. 沼 is a pool or natural pond, of irregular crooked shape, distinguished from 池, which is round. The general name for island is 洲 ; a small *chow* is called 渚 ; and a small *choo*, 沚. The *fan* is not a water plant, so that we must take 于 as ＝'by,' 'on.' L. 4. By 事 we must understand the business of sacrifice, *the* business, by way of eminence. The sacrifice intended, moreover, must be celebrated in the ancestral temple, within the precincts of the palace, as the lady could take no part in sacrifices outside those. 公 侯,—together, as in i. VII. The lady's husband might be a 公 or a 侯.

St. 2. 涧 is 'a stream in a valley (山 夹 水).' Here, however, the idea is more that of a valley with a stream in it. 宫＝庙, 'the ancestral temple;' so, often in the Ch'un Ts'ëw.

III. *Ts'aou-ch'ung.*

草虫

一章

喓喓草虫。趯趯阜螽。未见君子。忧心忡忡。亦既见
止。亦既觏止。我心则降。

二章

陟彼南山。言采其蕨。未见君子。忧心惙惙。亦既见

1 *Yaou-yaou* went the grass-insects,
   And the hoppers sprang about.
   While I do not see my lord,
   My sorrowful heart is agitated.
   Let me have seen him,
   Let me have met him,
   And my heart will then be stilled.

2 I ascended that hill in the south,
   And gathered the turtle-foot ferns.
   While I do not see my lord,
   My sorrowful heart is very sad.
   Let me have seen him,

St. 3. 被 is described as 首饰, 'an ornament for the head,' and as being made of hair plaited. It was probably the same with what is elsewhere called the 副, though Ying-tah identifies it with the 次. 僮僮 (written also without the 人 at the side) is defined by Maou, as= 竦敬, 'standing up high and reverently.' Then 祁祁, in l.3, is said to be 舒迟貌, 'the appearance of leisurely ease.' Both the predicates belong in the construction to the head-dress; in reality to the lady.— 夙夜 is not 'from morning till night,' as Lacharme takes it, but early in the morning, while it was yet dark (夙夜，非自夙至夜，乃夜之夙也，昧晦未分为夜，天光向辰为夙). The 公 in l.3 = 公所, 'the prince's place' the temple of last st. It must not be taken, says Choo, of 'the prince's private chamber.'

The rhymes are—in st. 1,虫 , 事 , cat.1, t.2; in 2,中, 宫, cat.9; in 3,僮 , 公, *ib.*; 祁, 归, cat. 15, t. 1.

NOTE ON THE INTERPRETATION. The interpretation of the ode above given is satisfactory enough. Choo mentions another, however, which would also suit the exigencies of the case pretty well;—that it refers to the duties of the prince's wife in his silk-worm establishment. The *fan* would be useful in this, as a decoction from its leaves, sprinkled on the silkworms' eggs, is said to facilitate their hatching. The imperial editors fully exhibit this view, but do not give it the preference. Le Kwang-te (李光地; of the pres. dyn.) adopts it in his 诗所, and takes no notice of the other.

Ode 3. Narrative. THE WIFE OF SOME GREAT OFFICER BEWAILS HIS ABSENCE ON DUTY, AND LONGS FOR THE JOY OF HIS RETURN. All the critics agree that the speaker is the wife of a great officer. According to Choo's view, she speaks as she is moved by the phænomena of the different seasons which she observes, and

止。亦既觏止。我心则说。

三章

陟彼南山。言采其薇。未见君子。我心伤悲。亦既见

止。亦既觏止。我心则夷。

    Let me have met him,
    And my heart will then be pleased.

3 I ascended that hill in the south,
    And gathered the thorn-ferns.
    While I do not see my lord,
    My sorrowful heart is wounded with grief.
    Let me have seen him,
    Let me have met him,
    And my heart will then be at peace.

gives expression to the regrets and hopes which she cherished. He compares the piece with the 3d and 10th of last Book. The different view of the older interpreters will be noticed in the concluding note.

St. 1. Ll. 1, 2. 喓 (the Shwoh-wăn does not give the character) 喓 is intended to give the sound made by the one insect; and 趯 趯 represents the jumping of the other. What specific names they should receive is yet to be determined. I have meanwhile, translated 草 虫 literally. It is described as 'a kind of locust, green and with a wonderful note.' The pictures of it are like the *locusta viridissima*. The 阜 螽 is, probably, the common grasshopper;—Seu Ting (徐 鼎 ; of the time of K'een-lung) says there can be doubt of it (蚱 蜢 无 疑 也). The Urh-ya calls it 蠜, and the former 负 蠜, or 'carrier of the *fan*.' These names arose from the belief that when the one gave out its note, the other leaped to it, and was carried on its back. 'They thus,' says K'ang-shing, 'sought each other like husband and wife.' This is the foundation of the old interpretation of the piece.

L. 4, in all the stanzas. 忡 忡 = 'to be agitated,' as if it were 冲 冲. The Shwoh-wăn explains both 忡 and 惙 by 忧. The predicates in all the three stanzas rise upon each other, as do those in the concluding lines. Ll. 5.—7. Of 亦 and 止 we can say nothing but that they are two particles untranslateable; one initial, the other final. So, Wang Yĭn-che.

The turn in the thought, indeed, makes 亦 = 'but.'

Stt. 2, 3. L. 2. 蕨 and 薇 are both ferns. Williams says on the former :—' An edible fern ; the stalks are cooked for food, when tender, and a flour is made from the root. The drawing of the plant resembles an *aspidium*.' Choo says, 'The *wei* resembles the *keueh*, but is rather longer; it has spinous points and a bitter taste. The people among the hills eat it.' The *keueh* is also called 鳖 and 鳖 脚, as in the translation.

The rhymes are—in st. 1, 虫, 螽, 忡, 降, cat. 9 : in 2, 蕨, 惙, 说, cat. 15, t. 3 : in 3, 薇, 悲, 夷, *ib.* t. 1.

NOTE ON THE INTERPRETATION. The old interpreters say, like Choo, that the subject of the ode is 'the wife of a great officer ;' but they make the subject of her distress, not the absence of her husband, but the anxiety incident to the uncertainty as to the establishment of her state as his acknowledged wife. According to the customs of those days, ladies underwent a probation of 3 months after their 1st reception by their husbands, at the end of which time they *might* be sent back as 'not approved.' The lady of the ode is supposed to be brooding during this period over her separation from her parents; and then anticipating the declaration of her husband's satisfaction with her, which would be an abundant consolation. I have noticed the *allusion* in the 1st two lines of the 1st st., whi h may be tortured into a justification of this view ; but the other stanzas have nothing analogous. The interpretation may well provoke a laugh. The imperial editors take no notice of it.

IV.   *Ts'ae pin.*

采蘋
一章
于以采蘋。南涧之滨。于以采藻。于彼行潦。
二章
于以盛之。维筐及筥。于以湘之。维锜及釜。
三章
于以奠之。宗室牖下。谁其尸之。有齐季女。

1   She gathers the large duckweed,
     By the banks of the stream in the southern valley.
     She gathers the pondweed,
     In those pools left by the floods.

2   She deposits what she gathers,
     In her square baskets and round ones;
     She boils it,
     In her tripods and pans.

3   She sets forth her preparations,
     Under the window in the ancestral chamber.
     Who superintends the business?
     It is [this] reverent young lady.

Ode 4. Narrative. THE DILIGENCE AND RE-
VERENCE OF THE YOUNG WIFE OF AN OFFICER,
DOING HER PART IN SACRIFICIAL OFFERINGS.
The ancient and modern interpreters are to some
extent agreed in their views of this ode. Wherein
they differ will be noticed under the 3d stanza.

St. 1. 于 以,—see on ode 2. The *p'in*
belongs to the same species of aquatic plants as
the 荇 菜 of i. I. The Pun-ts'aou says there
are three varieties of it:—the large, called *p'in*;
the small called 浮 萍; and the middle, called
荇 菜. Maou makes the *p'in* the large variety,
while Choo and some others make it the 3d.
Yen Ts'an observes that the *p'in* may be eaten;
but not the *fow p'ing*. If the *p'ing* could not be
eaten, it is not likely, he says, it would be gathered, like the plant here, to be used in sacrifice.
The *p'in* is, probably, the *lemna trisulca*. The
ts'aou is the tussel-pondweed,—*ruppia rostella-
ta*. Both by Maou and Choo it is called 聚 藻,
from the strings of tufts in which it grows. Williams erroneously translates 行 潦 by 'a tor-
rent.' 潦 is, primarily, the 'appearance of great

rain;' then 行 潦, is the rain left after a
heavy fall of it, and by the flooded streams, on
the roads and plains.
     St. 2. *K'wang* and *keu* are distinguished as
in the translation. They were both made of
bamboo. 湘 is defined by 烹 'to boil.' The
vegetables were slightly boiled and then pickled,
in order to their being presented as sacrificial
offerings. The 锜 is distinguished from the
釜, as 'having feet.'
     St. 3. 奠 = 置, 'to place,' 'to set forth.'
室 may be taken as = 宫, = 庙, so that 宗
室 simply = 'the ancestral temple.' More
particularly, however, the phrase may = 'the
ancestral chamber,' a room behind the temple,
specially dedicated to the 大 宗, or 'ancestor
of the great officer,' whose wife is the subject of
the piece. The princes of States were succeeded, of course, by the eldest son of the wife proper.
Their sons by other wives (庶 子) were called
'other sons (别 子).' The eldest son by the

V. *Kan t'ang.*

甘棠

一章
蔽芾甘棠。勿剪勿伐。召伯所茇。

二章
蔽芾甘棠。勿剪勿败。召伯所憩。

三章
蔽芾甘棠。勿剪勿拜。召伯所说。

1   [This] umbrageous sweet pear-tree ;—
Clip it not, hew it not down.
Under it the chief of Shaou lodged.

2   [This] umbrageous sweet pear-tree ;—
Clip it not, break not a twig of it.
Under it the chief of Shaou rested.

3   [This] umbrageous sweet pear-tree ;—
Clip it not, bend not a twig of it.
Under it the chief of Shaou halted.

wife proper of one of them became the 大宗 宗室 of the clan descended from him, and the 宗室 was an apartment dedicated to him. The old interpreters, going upon certain statements as to the training of the daughters in the business of sacrifices in this apartment, for 3 months previous to their marriage, contend that the lady spoken of was not yet married, but that the piece speaks of her undergoing this preparatory education. The imperial editors mention their view with respect, but think it better to abide by that of Choo. The door of the 室 was on the east side of it, and the window on the west; and by the 牖 下 is to be understood the south corner beyond the window, which was the most honoured spot of the apartment. In l.3, 尸=主, 'to superintend.' The 其 is little more than a particle. In cases like the text, Wang Yin-che calls it 拟 议 之 词, 'a term or particle of deliberative inquiry.' The wife presided over the arrangement of the dishes in sacrifice, and the filling them with the vegetables and sauces. 齐 (read *chae*)＝敬, 'to respect,' 'reverent.' 季＝少, 'young.' This term gives some confirmation to the old interpretation of the ode.

The rhymes are—in st.1, 蘋, 滨, cat.12, t.1; 藻, 潦, cat.2; in 2, 筥, 釜, cat.5, t.2; in 3, 下 *, 女, *ib.*

Ode. 5. Narrative. THE LOVE OF THE PEOPLE FOR THE MEMORY OF THE DUKE OF SHAOU MAKES THEM LOVE THE TREES BENEATH WHICH HE HAD RESTED. 召伯 might be translated 'Shaou, the chief;'—see note on the title of the Book. The nobleman is called *pih*, not as lord or duke of Shaou, but as invested with jurisdiction over all the States of the west. In the exercise of that, he had won the hearts of the people, and his memory was somehow connected with the tree which the poet had before his mind's eye, who makes the people therefore, as Tso-she says (XI. ix. under p. 1), 'think of the man and love the tree.' Stories are related by Han Ying and Lëw Heang of the way in which the chief executed his functions in the open air; but they owed their origin probably to the ode. We do not need them to enable us to enter into its spirit.

The *kan-t'ang* is, no doubt, a species of pear-tree. Maou identifies it with the *too* (杜), after the Urh-ya; others distinguish between them, saying that the fruit of the *t'ang* was whitish and sweet, while that of the *too* is red and sour. Maou makes 蔽芾＝'small-like;' much better seems to be Choo's view of the phrase, which I have followed. 伐=击, 'to strike' the tree, 'hew it down;' 败, acc to Choo,＝折, 'to break it;' and 拜＝屈, 'to bend it,'—as the body is bent in bowing. The tree becomes dearer, the more the poet keeps it before him. The concluding characters of the stanzas have nearly the same meaning. 茇 is explained by 草 舍, 'to halt among the grass;' 说 (read *shwuy*; *al.* 税), simply by 舍, 'to halt,' 'to lodge;' and 憩 (*al.* 愒), by 息, 'to rest.'

VI.   *Hing loo.*

行露

一章

厌浥行露。岂不夙夜。谓行多露。

二章

谁谓雀无角。何以穿我屋。谁谓女无家。何以速我

狱。虽速我狱。室家不足。

三章

谁谓鼠无牙。何以穿我墉。谁谓女无家。何以速我

1   Wet lay the dew on the path:—
   Might I not [have walked there] in the early dawn?
   But I said there was [too] much dew on the path.

2   Who can say the sparrow has no horn?
   How else could it bore through my house?
   Who can say that you did not get me betrothed?
   How else could you have urged on this trial?
   But though you have forced me to trial,
   Your ceremonies for betrothal were not sufficient.

3   Who can say that the rat has no molar teeth?
   How else could it bore through my wall?

The rhymes are—in st. 1, 伐, 芨, cat. 15, t. 3; in 2, 败, 憩, *ib.*: in 3, 拜, 说, *ib.*

Ode 6. Narrative; and allusive. A LADY RESISTS AN ATTEMPT TO FORCE HER TO MARRY, AND ARGUES HER CAUSE. The old interpreters thought that we have here a specimen of the cases that came before the duke of Shaou; and Choo does not contradict them. Lëw Heang (列女传, 贞顺篇) gives this tradition of the origin of the piece:—A lady of Shin was promised in marriage to a man of Fung. The ceremonial offerings from his family, however, were not so complete as the rules required; and when he wished to meet her and convey her home, she and her friends refused to carry out the engagement. The old party brought the case to trial, and the lady made this ode, asserting that, while a single rule of ceremony was not complied with, she would not allow herself to be forced from her parents' house.

St. 1. *Yeh-yih* conveys the idea of 'being wet.' 行＝道, 'way,' 'path.' 夙夜,—see on II.3. The difficulty in interpreting and translating this stanza arises from the 岂不 'How not,' which must be supplemented in some

way. Maou takes the characters as 有是, 'there was this;' meaning, acc. to K'ang-shing, that she might have been married at this dewy season of the year in the early morning. But on this allusive view, I cannot understand the last line, and hold, therefore, that the lady is here simply giving an illustration of the regard for her safety and character which she was in the habit of manifesting.

Stt. 2, 3 contain the argument. Appearances were against the lady; but to herself she was justified in her course. People would infer from seeing the hole made by a sparrow, that it was provided with a horn, though in reality it has none. Her 2d illustration is defective, if we take 牙 to mean, as is commonly said, only 'the grinders,' in opposition to 齿, the front or incisor teeth, for the rat has both incisors and molars, wanting only the intermediate teeth. But by 牙 is probably to be understood all the other teeth but the incisors. People might infer from seeing what it did, that its mouth was full of teeth, which is not the case. So they might infer, from her being brought by her prosecutors to trial, that their case was complete; but in reality it was not so. The 3d line is very perplexing,— 女 (＝汝, 'you') 无家; but

讼。虽速我讼。亦不女从。

Who can say that you did not get me betrothed?
How else could you have urged on this trial?
But though you have forced me to trial,
I will still not follow you.

VII. *Kaou yang.*

羔羊

一章
羔羊之皮。素丝五绌。退食自公。委蛇委蛇。

二章
羔羊之革。素丝五绒。委蛇委蛇。自公退食。

1   [Those] lamb-skins and sheep-skins,
     With their five braidings of white silk!
     They have retired from the court to take their meal;
     Easy are they and self-possessed.

2   [Those] lamb-skins and sheep-skins,
     With their five seams wrought with white silk!
     Easy are they and self-possessed;
     They have retired from the court to take their meal.

a'l the critics agree that we are to understand by 家 all the formalities of engagement and be rothal (以 媒 聘 求 为 室 家 之 礼). We must take 室 家 in the last line of st. 2 in the same way. 速 = 召 致, 'to summon and bring to.' 狱 and 讼 are both =‘trial.’ Maou gives for the former 埆, which should be, as in the Shwoh-wăn, 确, the place where the defendant was confined while the case was pending.

The rhymes are—in st. 1, 露, 夜 ，, 露, cat. 5, t. 1: in 2. 角, 屋, 狱, 狱, 足, cat. 3, t. 3: in 3, 牙 ，, 家 ，, cat. 5, t. 1; 埇, 讼, 讼, 从, cat. 9.

Ode. 7. Narrative. THE EASY DIGNITY OF THE GREAT OFFICERS OF SOME COURT. The structure of the piece is very simple, the characters and their order in the lines, and the order of the lines themselves, being varied for the sake of the rhythm. By the ‘lamb-skins and sheep-skins’ we are to understand the officers wearing such furs. It is better to do so than to take the piece as allusive.

革, in st. 2, is to be taken as= 皮. We cannot give it its proper signification of ‘the hide, with the hair taken off.’ Great officers wore such furs;—some say, in court; others, as both Maou and Choo, in their own families. It is not worth while entering here on a discussion of the point. They were often dyed black, and being seamed together with white silk, the hems were conspicuous. 绌, 绒, and 总 all refer to the same thing,—the seams of the furs of which the robes were made. Choo acknowledges that he does not understand 绌 and 总, and Maou explains them both by 数, which is unintelligible. The meaning of 绌 which I have followed is that given by K'oh King (郝 敬; Ming dyn.):—织 素 丝 为 组, 掩 其 缝 际,

三章
羔羊之缝。素丝五总。委蛇委蛇。退食自公。

3   The seams of [those] lamb-skins and sheep-skins,
    The five joinings wrought with white silk!
    Easy are they and self-possessed;
    They have retired to take their meal from the court.

VIII.   *Yin k'e luy.*

殷其雷
一章
殷其雷。在南山之阳。何斯违斯。莫敢或遑。振振君

子。归哉归哉。
二章
殷其雷。在南山之侧。何斯违斯。莫敢遑息。振振君

1   Grandly rolls the thunder,
    On the south of the southern hill!
    How was it he went away from this,
    Not daring to take a little rest?
    My noble lord!
    May he return! May he return!

2   Grandly rolls the thunder,
    About the sides of the southern hill!
    How was it he went away from this,

日绖; and for that of 总, I am indebted to Hoo Yih-kwei (胡一桂; Yuen dyn.);—合二为一谓之总 Maou says 绒 is the same as 缝,—after the Urh-ya.

委蛇 (*al.* 佗)＝自得之貌, 'the app. of self-possession.' Maou says it denotes 'the straight and equal steps with which the officers walked.' 公＝公门, 'the duke's gate,' or generally 'the court.'

The rhymes are—in st. 1, 皮 *, 绖, 蛇 *, cat. 17: in 2, 革, 绒·食 , cat. 1, t. 3: in 3, 缝, 总, 公. cat. 9.

Ode. 8. Allusive. A LADY'S ADMIRATION OF HER HUSBAND ABSENT ON PUBLIC SERVICE, AND HER LONGING FOR HIS RETURN. The lady, it must be supposed, is the wife of a great officer.

She hears the rolling of the thunder, and is led to think of her absent husband. Yen Ts'an observes that the piece is simply allusive, without any metaphorical element (兴之不兼比者); but K'ang-shing and others torture the first two lines into symbols of the officer on his commission. The rhythmical variations in the stanzas are, it will be seen, very small.

L. 1. 殷 (sometimes doubled) represents the *solemn* sound of thunder, heard rolling at some considerable distance off. 其 is the demonstrative,—'the,' or 'that.' 雷 has now given place to the less complicated 靁. L. 2. 'The southern hill' must be one of the hills in the south of the territory of Chow. The southern side of a hill is called 阳. L. 3. The 1st 斯＝斯人. So, Maou and Choo; better than Yen Ts'an, who makes it＝斯时, 'at this time.' The

子。归哉归哉。

三章

殷其雷。在南山之下。何斯违斯。莫敢遑处。振振君

子。归哉归哉。

        Not daring to take a little rest?
        My noble lord!
        May he return! May he return!

3   Grandly rolls the thunder,
        At the foot of the southern hill!
        How was it he went away from this,
        Not remaining a little at rest?
        My noble lord!
        May he return! May he return!

              IX.   *P'eaou yew mei.*

摽有梅

一章

摽有梅。其实七兮。求我庶士。迨其吉兮。

二章

摽有梅。其实三兮。求我庶士。迨其今兮。

1   Dropping are the fruits from the plum-tree;
    There are [but] seven [tenths] of them left!
    For the gentlemen who seek me,
    This is the fortunate time!

2   Dropping are the fruits from the plum-tree;
    There are [but] three [tenths] of them left!
    For the gentlemen who seek me,
    Now is the time.

2nd=斯所, 'this place.' 违=去, 'to go away from,' 'to leave.' L. 4. 遑=暇, 'leisure.' The Urh-ya has 偟, but the oldest reading was simply 皇, in the same sense. Wang T'aou, Wang Yin-che, and many others, take 或 here=有, so that the line=不敢有暇. I prefer, however, the construction of Yen Ts'an:—或者间或之义，不敢或遑，则无一时之暇矣. In the other stanzas 遑 is used adverbially. L. 5. 振振,—see on i. XI. L. 6. The repetition of 归哉 is understood to express a wish for the husband's return, but with submission to his absence so long as duty required it.

    The rhymes are—in st. 1, 阳, 遑, cat. 10: in 2, 侧, 息, cat. 1, t. 3: in 3, 下 ,, 处, cat. 5, t. 2. In addition to the above, the 1st, 3rd, 5th, and 6th lines of the three stanzas are supposed to rhyme with one another.

三章

摽有梅。頃筐墍之。求我庶士。迨其謂之。

3 Dropt are the fruits from the plum-tree;
  In my shallow basket I have collected them.
  Would the gentlemen who seek me
  [Only] speak about it!

X. Sëaou sing.

小星

一章

嘒彼小星。三五在東。肅肅宵征。夙夜在公。寔命

1 Small are those starlets,
  Three or five of them in the east.
  Swiftly by night we go;
  In the early dawn we are with the prince.
  Our lot is not like hers.

Ode 9. Narrative. ANXIETY OF A YOUNG LADY TO GET MARRIED. It is difficult for a foreigner to make anything more out of the piece. The critics, however, all contend that it is not the desire merely to be married which is here expressed, but to be married in accordance with propriety, and before the proper time was gone by. They mix up two things:—the age when people should be married, males before 30, and females before 20; and the season of the year, most proper for marriages,—the season of spring. We can see an allusion to the latter, in the stanzas, but none to the former.

L. 1, 摽 = 落, 'to fall.' It is difficult to construe the 有, which has no more force than the 其 in the last ode. See under 有 in the 3d index to the Shoo, where this peculiarity of the usage of 有 is pointed out. None of the critics say a word about it here. The mei is the general name for the plum tree; here a species, whose fruit is rather small and sour, and which ripens earlier than the peach. The falling of the plums makes the lady think of her own ripeness, and that it was time she should be plucked and married.

L. 2. Are we to understand 七 and 三 of 7 plums and 3 plums left on the tree, or as in the translation? Maou, Choo, and the commentators generally understand the single plums; Ying-tah adopts the proportional view (十分之中, 尚在樹者七). I agree with him because of the last stanza, for what need would there be of a basket to gather 3 plums?

Ll.3.4. The freedom of the lady's expressions in these lines have been a stumbling-block to many. Ying-tah says, 'We are not to understand that the lady is speaking in her own person (非女自我), but that the poet personates any marriageable young person.' Hwang Chin (黃震; end of the Sung dyn.) hears in the words the language of a go-between, expressing the desire of the parents. But the 我 cannot be thus explained away. 迨及,—'till.' It is here=our 'while.' As Choo expands the line, 其必有及此吉日而來, 'they must come up to (=while it is now) this fortunate time.'

In st. 3, 頃筐,—see i.III. 墍 (al. 慨)= 取, 'to take,' 'gather.' 迨其謂之—'if they would but come to the speaking about it;' as Lacharme has it, 'diem dicat ille.' The lady is prepared to dispense with all previous formalities (但相告語而約可定).

The rhymes are—in st. 1, 七, 吉, cat.12, t.3: in 2, 三 *, 今, cat. 7, t.1: in 3, 墍, 謂, cat.15, t.3.

Ode 10. Allusive. THE THANKFUL SUBMISSION TO THEIR LOT OF THE INFERIOR MEMBERS OF A HAREM. We must suppose that we have here the description by one of the concubines of the lot of herself and her companions. It is the early dawn, and she is returning from her visit to the prince's chamber, which had been allowed

不同。

二章

嘒彼小星。维参与昴。肃肃宵征。抱衾与裯。寔命

不犹。

2　　Small are those starlets,
　　　And there are Orion and the Pleiades.
　　　Swiftly by night we go,
　　　Carrying our coverlets and sheets.
　　　Our lot is not as hers.

XI.　*Keang yew sze.*

江有汜

一章

江有汜。之子归。不我以。不我以。其后也悔。

1　　The Këang has its branches, led from it and returning to it.
　　　Our lady, when she was married,
　　　Would not employ us.
　　　She would not employ us;
　　　But afterwards she repented.

her by his wife. Only the wife could pass the whole night with her husband. The other members of the harem were admitted only for a short time, and must go and return in the dark. But so had the influence of king Wăn and T'ae-sze wrought, that throughout Shaou and the south the wives of the princes allowed their ladies freely to share the favours of their common lord, only subject to the distinctive conditions belonging to her position and theirs. Hence as *they* were not jealous, *the others* were not envious. Such is the interpretation given to this piece; but there are difficulties, it will be seen, with some of the lines.

L.1. 嘒＝小貌, 'small-like.' L.2. 三五 are best translated literally, meaning a few. So, Choo. Maou makes them out to be certain stars in Scorpio and Hydra; but it seems decisive against him that those stars are not visible together in the morning, in the same month. There can be no doubt, however, as to the identification of 参 and 昴 in st.2; but we must not seek, in the 1st line, a special allusion to the mass of the concubines, and in the 2d to those of higher rank among them. L.3. Maou explains 肃肃 as 'the app. of rapidity,' to which Choo would add that of 'reverence.' 征＝往, 'to go.' 宵＝夜, 'at night.' The difficulty to me is with the 4th line. If 宵 denote the

time of the concubines' going, and 夙夜 the time of their return, then they have been the night with the prince. It seems to me that 宵 and 夙夜 must have nearly the same meaning, and that 宵 should be translated—'in the dark.' 在公 is inconsistent with the 4th line's speaking of the return of the ladies. K'ang-shing's view, that 夙夜＝或早或夜, 'some early, some late,' and that this and the next line set forth the different times at which different ladies were received, ought not to be entertained. It is a strange picture which the 4th line of st.2 gives us, of the concubines carrying their sheets with them to the prince's chamber. L 5. This line expresses the acquiesence of the concubines with their lot. 实 or, 寔 may be taken as＝是, 'to be,' 'it is.' The use of 犹 as an adjective is to be noted.

The rhymes are—in st. 1, 星, 征, cat. 11; 东, 公, 同. cat. 9: in 2, 星, 征; 昴, 裯, 犹, cat. 3, t. 2.

Ode 11. Allusive. JEALOUSY CURED. THE RESTORATION OF GOOD FEELING IN A HAREM. Acc. to the little Preface, with which Choo in the main agrees, the bride of some prince in the

二章
江有渚。之子归。不我与。不我与。其后也处。
三章
江有沱。之子归。不我过。不我过。其啸也歌。

2　The Këang has its islets.
　　Our lady, when she was married,
　　Would not let us be with her.
　　She would not let us be with her;
　　But afterwards she repressed [such feelings].

3　The Këang has the T'o.
　　Our lady, when she was married,
　　Would not come near us
　　She would not come near us;
　　But she blew that feeling away, and sang.

south had refused to allow her cousins, who by rule should have accompanied her, to go with her to the harem; but afterwards, coming under the influence of the govt. of king Wăn and the character of T'ae-sze, she repented of her jealousy, sent for them, and was happy with them. Such is the traditional interpretation of the piece, and the lines suit it tolerably well.

L. 1, in all the stanzas. 汜 is the name for streams derived from larger rivers, flowing through a tract of country, and then conveyed into their mother stream again. From the definition of the term in the Urh-ya, 水决复入为汜, it would appear that such streams were made in the 1st place artificially. 渚 is 'a small islet.' Rising in the stream, it divides its waters which again unite at the other end of it. 沱 was the name of rivers issuing from the Këang, pursuing a different course from the main stream, but ultimately rejoining it. Two T'os are mentioned in the Shoo (III. i. Pt. i. 64; Pt. ii. 9): These lines contain the allusive portion of the ode, giving, all of them, the ideas of separation and reunion.

L. 2. The 之子 is, of course, the wife that is spoken of, and in the connection 之子归 = 此子向者于归之时, 'this lady, formerly, when she went to her home.'

Ll. 3, 4. These lines all describe the early conduct of the wife, though it is perhaps too

much to infer, with the critics, from the words, that she left her cousins in their native State. There is nothing in the terms which would not be satisfied with their having in the first place accompanied her to the harem, and then been kept by her in the background. 以 is to be taken in the sense of 用, 'to employ.' 与 is not distinguished by Choo from 以. We may explain it by 'to be with,' 'to associate with.' We hardly know what to make of 过. Choo says, 过谓过我而与俱也, 'to pass close to us, and then to be together with us.' L. 5. describes the wife's subsequent conduct. I cannot follow Choo in his account of 处,一安也, 得其所安也. Maou explains it by 止, 'to stop,' 'to desist;' which K'ang-shing enlarged to 自止, 'she repressed herself.' 啸 is 'to purse up the mouth and emit a sound,' = 'to blow,' 'to whistle.' Morrison quotes the line under the character, saying, 'K'e seaou yay ko, "whistled and sang," to divert the mind from what vexed it;' but the whistling and singing was an expression rather of relief and satisfaction.

The rhymes are—in st. 1, 汜 以, 以, 悔 *, cat. 1, t.2: in 2, 渚, 与, 与, 处, cat. 5, t.2: in 3, 沱, 过, 过, 歌, cat. 17.

XII. *Yay yew sze keun.*

野有死麕

一章
野有死麕。白茅包之。有女怀春。吉士诱之。

二章
林有朴樕。野有死鹿。白茅纯束。有女如玉。

三章
舒而脱脱兮。无感我帨兮。无使尨也吠。

1   In the wild there is a dead antelope,
    And it is wrapped up with the white grass.
    There is a young lady with thoughts natural to the spring,
    And a fine gentleman would lead her astray.

2   In the forest there are the scrubby oaks;
    In the wild there is a dead deer,
    And it is bound round with the white grass.
    There is a young lady like a gem.

3   [She says], Slowly; gently, gently;
    Do not move my handkerchief;
    Do not make my dog bark.

Ode. 12. A VIRTUOUS YOUNG LADY RESISTS THE ATTEMPTS OF A SEDUCER. The little Preface says that the piece teaches disgust at the want of proper ceremonies, and belongs to the close of Chow's reign, when the influence of king Wǎn was gradually prevailing to overcome the lust and license, through which the Shang dynasty was extinguished. A lady is sought to be won by insufficient ceremonies, yet they were better than none, and showed that the times were mending; and she is willing. He must be clear-sighted who can see traces of all this in the ode. The view which I take of it is substantially the same as Choo's, who inclines to look on it as an allusive piece, but at the same time allows it may be taken as narrative. It is not worth while to enter on this question.

St. 1. Ll 1,2. 野 denotes 'the open country, beyond the suburbs,' not yet brought under cultivation. 麕, written also with 君 and with 禾 under the 鹿, is said to be the same as the *chang* (鹿 with 章 under it), which Medhurst calls a kind of musk deer, and Williams, a kind of gazelle. Choo says it is hornless, and Williams thinks therefore it may be the *antilope gutturosa*, the doe of which has no horns. The figure of the creature, however, in Seu Ting's plates, has short horns. It has yet to be identified. 茅 is a name both of a grass and a rush; here apparently, designating the former. We are told that 'it is very common, with a large leaf, soft and white, the lines on it quite straight.' L. 3. We have already seen that the spring was the favourite time for marriages. The ancient legislators of China would have the pairing time of the lower creatures to be also the nuptial season in human societies; 怀春, 'cherishing the spring,' therefore = thinking of marriage. L. 4. 吉 = 美 'fine' 'elegant;' but we must understand the epithet to be applied ironically. So, Yen Ts'an. I do not see how 诱 can have any other meaning than that given to it in the translation. Maou's explanation of it by 道, so that 诱之 = 谓之, in IX. 3, is inadmissible.

St. 2. Ll. 1,3. All that we learn from Maou and Choo about the *p'uh-suh* is that it is 'a small tree.' The figure of it in the Japanese plates to the *She* leaves no doubt that it is a kind of oak. An able botanist in Yokohama to whom it was submitted, pronounced it the *quercus serrata*. I have ventured, therefore, to translate the name 'by scrubby oaks.' 鹿 is the

XIII. *Ho pe nung.*

何彼秾矣

一章

何彼秾矣。唐棣之华。曷不肃雍。王姬之车。

二章

何彼秾矣。华如桃李。平王之孙。齐侯之子。

1 How great is that luxuriance,
Those flowers of the sparrow-plum!
Are they not expressive of reverence and harmony,—
The carriages of the king's daughter?

2 How great is that luxuriance,
The flowers like those of the peach-tree or the plum!
[See] the grand-daughter of the tranquillizing king,
And the son of the reverent marquis!

general name for the deer tribe; specially, it is figured as the spotted axis. 纯 (*t'un*) 束, 'to tie up in a bundle,'—the 包 之 of last stanza. L. 4. Choo says that 如 玉 intimates the girl's beauty. I think, with Maou, that the poet would represent as it her virtue rather. St. 3. We must take these lines as the language of the young lady, warning her admirer away. Her meaning gleams out indeed but feebly from them, but I have met with no other exposition of the stanza, which is not attended with greater difficulties. The 而, in 舒 而 —如, so that the phrase='slow-like,' 'slowly;' much the same is the meaning of 脱 (*chwae*) 脱 感 ='to move,' 'to touch;' as if the character were 撼. The napkin or handkerchief (帨, 拭 物 之 巾) was worn at the girdle. 'This 2nd line,' says Hoo Yih-kwei, 'warns the man away from her person, as the next warns him from her house.' The Shwoh-wăn defines 尨, as 'a dog with much hair,'=a tyke; but we may take it with Choo as simply a synonym of 犬. The student will do well to refer to the application which is made of this line in the 1st narrative subjoined by Tso-she to par. 3 of XI. i., in the Ch'un Ts'ëw.

The rhymes are—in st. 1, 麛 *，春, cat. 13; 包 *，诱, cat. 3, t. 2: in 2, 楸, 麛, 束, 玉 *，t. 3: in 3, 脱, 帨, 吠, cat. 15, t. 3.

Ode 13. Allusive. THE MARRIAGE OF ONE OF THE ROYAL PRINCESSES TO THE SON OF ONE OF THE FEUDAL NOBLES. The critics, of course, all see a great deal more in the piece than this, and think that it celebrates the wifely dignity and submissiveness of the lady. Whether anything can be determined as to who she was will be considered on the 2d stanza.

Stt. 1, 2. Ll. 1, 2. 秾 (or in Maou, with 衣 at the side) denotes 'the appearance of abundance.' There are great differences of opinion about the tree called *t'ang-te*. Maou, after the Urh-ya, calls it the e (栘), and is followed by Choo, who adds that it is like the white willow (白杨). Descriptions are given of the constant motion and quivering of its leaves, which would make us identify it with the aspen, a species of the poplar. But the flowers of the tree are what the writer has in view, and this forbids our taking it for a willow or a poplar. Wang T'aou argues moreover that the 栘 in the Urh Ya and Maou is a mistake for 棣. Evidently, from the 2d line of st. 2, the tree in the ode is akin to the peach and the plum. And so say many commentators. Luh Ke (陆 玑; during the time of the 'Three Kingdoms') makes it out to be the same as the *yuh li* (薁 李), called also the 'sparrow's plum,' and other names. The flowers of this are both white and red, and the fruit is distinguished in the same way. I suspect the tree here is the white cherry.

Ll. 3, 4. 肃 is explained by 敬, 'to be reverent' and 雍 by 和, 'to be harmonious.' And say the critics, 'reverence and harmony

三章
其钓维何。维丝伊缗。齐侯之子。平王之孙。

3   What are used in angling?
Silk threads formed into lines.
The son of the reverent marquis,
And the grand-daughter of the tranquillizing king!

XIV.   *Tsow-yu.*

驺虞
一章
彼茁者葭。壹发五豝。于嗟乎驺虞。
二章
彼茁者蓬。壹发五豵。于嗟乎驺虞。

1   Strong and abundant grow the rushes ;
He discharges [but] one arrow at five wild boars.
Ah! he is the Tsow-yu!

2   Strong and abundant grows the artemisia;
He discharges [but] one arrow at five wild boars.
Ah! he is the Tsow-yu!

are the chief constituents of wifely virtue.' What there was about the carriages to indicate these virtues in the bride, we are not told. She is called a royal *Ke*, 姬 being the surname of the House of Chow. Evidently she was a king's daughter. Most naturally we should translate the 2d and 3d line of st. 2,

'The grand-daughter of king P'ing, And the son of the marquis of Ts'e;'

but, so taken, the piece must be dated about 400 years after the duke of Shaou, and is certainly out of place in this Book of the She. Choo, indeed, is not sure but they may be correct who find here king P'ing and duke Seang of Ts'e; but the imperial editors sufficiently refute that view. We must take 平 and 齐 as two epithets, the former designating, probably, king Wăn, and the latter some one of the feudal princes.

St. 3. L. 2. 伊 has no more force here than the 维. Yin-che says it is synonymous with 维, but the examples he adduces have the sense of 'but,' 'only.' The case in the text is sufficient to show that the two particles are synonymous only when they have that sense.

缗=纶, 'a cord' 'a string.' The allusion in the silk twisted into fishing lines would seem to be simply to the marriage—the union—of the princess and the young noble. I cannot follow Maou and his school, when they make it out to be to the lady's 'holding fast of wifely ways to complete the virtues of reverence and harmony.'

The rhymes are—in st. 1, 缗, 雍, cat. 9; 华 ∗, 东 ∗, cat. 5, t. 1: in 2, 矣, 李, 子, cat. 1, t. 2: in 3, 缗 ∗, 孙, cat. 13.

Ode 14. Narrative. CELEBRATING SOME PRINCE IN THE SOUTH FOR HIS BENEVOLENCE. There is a general agreement as to the object of this short piece, though there are great differences, as we shall see, in the explanation of it in detail. Its analogy to the concluding ode in the 1st Book is sufficiently evident, and must be allowed to have the turning weight in settling the interpretation.

Ll. 1. 苗 expresses the fresh, vigorous appearance of plants, as they first rise above the ground. 葭 is another name for 芦, which Williams calls—' high rushes along river courses.' When full-grown and flowered, they are called 苇.

We must suppose that the prince, who is the subject of the ode, is hunting in spring, by some lake or stream where such rushes were common. Maou and Choo say nothing more about 蓬 than that it is the name of a grass. According to the Shwoh-wǎn, it should be a kind of artemisia. One account of it says that its flowers grow like the catkins of the willow, and fly about in the wind, like hair.

Ll. 2. Maou gives 豝 as 'the female of the swine;' and in the connection we must understand the wild animal. Choo makes it just the opposite,—the male, Maou took his account from the Urh-ya; but in both cases I imagine there is an error of the text,—牝 for 牡. To shoot female animals would be inconsistent with the benevolence which the piece is understood to celebrate. The Kwang-ya, wi hout reference to the sex, says, 'the *pa* is a pig two years old,' and all authorities agree in taking *ts'ung*, as one, 'one year old.' But we cannot suppose that the poet laid any stress on these special distinctions of the terms. He varied them to suit his rhymes merely. 一发 ='by one discharge,' *i.e*, of his arrows, acc. to Choo. The prickers, it is understood, had driven together a herd of the animals; but the noble would not kill them all. He contented himself with discharging the four arrows, which constituted what we may call *a round*. But could he kill 5 boars with 4 arrows? Choo supposes that one of the arrows transfixed two of them. This does not seem very likely; and I am inclined to adopt the view of K'ang-shing, as expounded by Ying-tah, that out of 5 boars driven together the prince would shoot only one (君 止 一 发，必 翼 五 豝 者，中 则 杀 一 而 已。)

Ll. 3. The great battle of the ode, however, is over 驺 虞. Maou and Choo, after him, take these terms as the name of a wild beast, 'a righteous beast; a white tiger, with black spots, which does not tread on live grass, and does not eat any living thing, making its appearance when a State is ruled by a prince of perfect benevolence and sincerity. Being a tiger, it might be expected to kill animals, like other tigers, but it only eats the flesh of such as have died a natural death.' This view of the terms was not challenged till Gow-yang Sëw of the Sung dyn., who contended that we are to understand by them the huntsmen of the prince's park. Since his time this interpretation has been variously enlarged and insisted on. One of the ablest assertors of it is Yen Ts'an, who appeals to the fact that the Urh-ya says nothing of the fabulous animal, as a proof that it was not heard of before Maou. The imperial editors, however, refute this statement, and I agree with

them that the old view is not to be disturbed. The analogy of the *Lin che che* is decisive in its favour. 于 嗟 乎 here = 于 嗟… 兮 of that ode.

The rhymes are—in st. 1, 葭 *, 豝 *, 虞, and 虞 of st. 2, cat. 5, t. 1: in 2, 蓬, 豵, cat. 9.

Concluding Note. Confucius once (Ana. XVII. x.) told his son to study the Chow-nan and Shaou-nan, adding that 'the man who has not done so is like one who stands with his face right against a wall.' Like many more of the sayings of the sage, it seems to tell us a great deal, while yet we can lay hold of nothing positive in it.

Choo He says, 'The first four odes in this 2d Book speak of the wives of princes and great officers, and show how at that time princes and great officers had come under the transforming influence of king Wǎn, so that they cultivated their persor s and regulated rightly their families. The other pieces show how the chief prince among the States spread abroad the influence of king Wǎn, and how other princes cultivated it in their families and through their States. Though nothing is said in them about king Wǎn, yet the wide effects of his brilliant virtue and renovation of the people appear in them. They were so wrought upon, they knew not how. There is only the 13th piece which we are unable to understand, and with the perplexities of which we need not trouble ourselves.' One of the Ch'ings says, 'The right regulation of the family is the first step towards the good govt. of all the empire. The two *Nan* contain the principles of that regulation, setting forth the virtues of the queen, of princesses, and the wives of great officers, substantially the same when they are extended to the families of inferior officers and of the common people. Hence these odes were used at courts and village gatherings. They sang them in the courts and in the lanes, thus giving their tone to the manners of all under heaven.'

These glowing pictures do not approve themselves so much to a western reader. He cannot appreciate the institution of the harem. Western wives cannot submit to the position of T'ae-sze herself. Western young ladies like to be married 'decently and in order,' according to rule, with all the ceremonies; but they want other qualities in their suitors more important than an observance of formalities. Where purity and frugality in young lady and wife are celebrated in these pieces, we can appreciate them. The readiness on the part of the wife to submit to separation from her husband, when public duty calls him away from her, is also very admirable. But upon the whole the family-regulation which appears here is not of a high order, and the place assigned to the wife is one of degradation.

BOOK III.   THE ODES OF P'EI.

I.   *Pih chau.*

邶一之三

柏舟

一章

泛彼柏舟。亦泛其流。耿耿不寐。如有隐忧。微我无
酒。以敖以游。

二章

我心匪鉴。不可以茹。亦有兄弟。不可以据。薄言往
愬。逢彼之怒。

1 It floats about, that boat of cypress wood;
  Yea, it floats about on the current.
  Disturbed am I, and sleepless,
  As if suffering from a painful wound.
  It is not because I have no wine,
  And that I might not wander and saunter about.

2 My mind is not a mirror;—
  It cannot [equally] receive [all impressions].
  I, indeed, have brothers,
  But I cannot depend on them.
  If I go and complain to them,
  I meet with their anger.

TITLE OF THE BOOK.—邶, 一之三 'P'ei, Book III. of Part I.' Of P'ei which gives its name to this Book, and of Yung which gives its name to the next, we scarcely know anything. Long before the time of Confucius, perhaps before the date of any of the pieces in them, they had become incorporated with the State of Wei, and it is universally acknowledged that the odes of Books III., IV., and V. are odes of Wei. Why they should be divided into three portions, and two of them assigned to P'ei and Yung is a mystery, which Choo declares it is impossible to understand. It would be a waste of time to enter on a consideration of the various attempts which have been made to elucidate it. In the long narrative which is given by Tso-she under p.8 of the 29th year of duke Seang, they sing to Ke-chah, their visitor from Woo at the court of Loo, the odes of P'ei, Yung, and Wei, and that nobleman exclaims, 'I hear and I know:— it was the virtue of K'ang-shuh and of duke Woo, which made these odes what they are,— the odes of Wei,' This was in B. C. 543, when Confucius was 8 years old. Then there existed the division of these odes into 3 Books with the names of different States, all, however, acknowledged to be odes of Wei.

When king Woo overthrew the dynasty of Shang, the domain of its kings was divided by

三章

我心匪石。不可转也。我心匪席。不可卷也。威仪棣

棣。不可选也。

3　My mind is not a stone;—
It cannot be rolled about.
My mind is not a mat;—
It cannot be rolled up.
My deportment has been dignified and good,
With nothing wrong which can be pointed out.

him into three portions. That north of their capital was P'ei; that south of it was Yung; and that east of it was Wei. These were constituted into three principalities; but who among his adherents were invested with P'ei and Yung has not been clearly ascertained. Most probably they were assigned to Woo-kăng, the son of the last king of Shang, and the 3 brothers of king Woo, who were appointed to oversee him. What was done with them, after the rebellion of Woo-kăng and his overseers, is not known; but in process of time the marquises of Wei managed to add them to their own territory.

The first marquis of Wei was K'ang-shuh, a brother of king Woo, of whose investiture we have an account in the Shoo, V. ix., though whether he received it from Woo, or in the next reign from the duke of Chow, is a moot point. The first capital of Wei was on the north of the Ho, to the east of Ch'aou-ko, the old capital of Shang. There it continued till B. C. 659, when the State was nearly extinguished by some northern hordes, and duke Tae (戴公) removed across the river to Ts'aou (漕邑); but in a couple of years, his successor, duke Wăn (文公), removed again to Ts'oo-k'ëw (楚邱) —in the pres dis. of Shing-woo (城武) dep. Ts'aou-chow, Shan-tung. The State of Wei embraced the territory occupied by Hwae k'ing, Wei-hwuy, Chang-teh,—all in Ho-nan, and portions of the depp. of K'ae-fung in the same province, of Ta-ming in Chih-le, and of Tung-chang in Shan-tung.

Ode 1. Mostly narrative. AN OFFICER OF WORTH BEWA LS THE NEGLECT AND CONTEMPT WITH WHICH HE WAS TREATED. Such is the view taken of the piece by Maou, who refers it to the time of duke K'ing (顷公: B.c. 866— 854); of the difft. view of Choo I will speak in a concluding note.

St. 1. Ll. 1, 2. 泛 denotes 'the app. of floating about.' 柏 is the cypress, whose wood is said to be good for building boats. The two lines are, by the school of Maou, understood to be allusive, representing the 'state of the officer unemployed, like a boat floating uselessly about with the current.' Yen Ts'an thinks the allusion is to the sad condition of the State left to go to ruin, as a boat must do with no competent person in it to guide it. Choo takes the lines as metaphorical. Ll. 3, 4. Maou takes 耿耿 as = 儆儆, meaning 'restless,' 'disturbed.' 隐 = 痛, 'a pain.' Ll. 5, 6, 微 = 非 'not,' 'it is not that.' The two lines are construed together,—as Choo explains them, 非为无酒可以遨游而解之也,' 'It is not because I have no spirits, or that I could not dissipate my grief by wandering about.' To the same effect Yen Ts'an:—'This sorrow is not such as can be relieved by drinking or by rambling.' Lacharme quite mistakes the meaning: —ego deambulo, ego iter facio, non quia vino careo.

St. 2. Ll. 2. The difficulty in these lines is with 茹, which both Maou and Choo explain here by 度, 'to estimate,' 'to measure,' as if the meaning were, 'A glass can only shew the outward forms of things; but there is more than what appears externally in my case, and the causes of my treatment are too deep to be examined by a glass.' I must adopt another meaning of 茹, which is also found in the dict.,—that of 受 or 容, 'to receive,' 'to admit.' A glass reflects all forms submitted to it, with indifference; but the speaker acknowledged only the virtuous. Bad men he rejected, and would have nothing to do with them.

Ll. 3—6. Here, and in st. 1, we can allow some connective force to 亦' By 'brothers'

四章
忧心悄悄。愠于群小。觏闵既多。受侮不少。静言思
之。寤辟有摽。

五章
日居月诸。胡迭而微。心之忧矣。如匪浣衣。静言思
之。不能奋飞。

4 My anxious heart is full of trouble;
I am hated by the herd of mean creatures;
I meet with many distresses;
I receive insults not a few.
Silently I think of my case,
And, starting as from sleep, I beat my breast.

5 There are the sun and the moon,—
How is it that the former has become small, and not the latter?
The sorrow cleaves to my heart,
Like an unwashed dress.
Silently I think of my case,
But I cannot spread my wings and fly away.

we must understand 'officers of the same surname with the speaker (同姓臣).' Choo's view of the ode enables him to take 兄弟 in its natural meaning. 据=依, 'to rely, or be relied, on.' 薄言,—as in i. VIII.

St. 3. In the first 4 lines, the speaker says his mind was firmer than a stone, and more even and level than a mat. 威仪 denotes his whole manner of conducting himself. 棣棣 (read tae)='the app. of complete correctness and long practice.' 选 = 'to select.' The meaning is that nothing in the speaker's deportment could be picked out, and made the subject of remark.

St. 4. 悄悄 denotes 'the app. of sorrow.' The 于 after 愠 gives to that term the force of the passive voice. 群小, 'the herd of small people,' denotes all the unworthy officers who enjoyed the ruler's favour. 闵=病 'distress;' here probably meaning blame or slander. In l. 5, 言 is the particle, so frequent in the She. L. 4, 辟 is explained by 拊 心, 'to lay the hand on the heart,' or 'to beat

the breast,' and 摽, as 'the app of doing so.' In this acceptation the 有 may have its meaning of 'having'; but it rather has a descriptive power, making the word that follows very vivid, as if it were repeated.

St 5. Ll. 1, 2. 居 and 诸 are used as particles which we cannot translate, unless we take them as=乎, and render,—'O sun,' 'O moon.' So, Choo on ode 4, where he says, 日居月 诸, 呼而诉之也. 迭=更, 'to change,' 'in altered fashion.' The meaning seems to be:—The sun is always bright and full, while the moon goes through regular changes, now full, and now absent from the heavens. In Wei the ruler was at this time obscured by the unworthy officers who abused his confidence and directed the govt. The sun had become small, and the moon had taken its place.

The rhymes are—in st.1, 舟, 流, 忧, 游, cat.3, t.1; in 2, 茹, 据, 愬, 怒, cat.5. t.2; in 3, 石*, 席*, ib., t.9; 转, 卷, 选, cat. 14; in 4, 悄, 小, 少, 摽, cat.2; in 5, 微, 衣, 飞, cat. 15, t.1.

II. *Luh' e.*

绿衣

一章

绿兮衣兮。绿衣黄里。心之忧矣。曷维其已。

二章

绿兮衣兮。绿衣黄裳。心之忧矣。曷维其亡。

1　Green is the upper robe,
　　Green with a yellow lining!
　　The sorrow of my heart,—
　　How can it cease?

2　Green is the upper robe;
　　Green the upper, and yellow the lower garment!
　　The sorrow of my heart,—
　　How can it be forgotten?

NOTE ON THE INTERPRETATION. Choo He, in his Work on the *She*, contends that we have in this ode the complaint of Chwang Këang, the wife of one of the marquises of Wei, because of the neglect which she experienced from her husband;—as will be explained on the next ode. He was preceded in the view that the subject of the ode was a lady by Han Ying and Lëw Heang; but they referred it to Seuen Këang, the circumstances of whose history, as related by Tso-she under the 11th year of Chwang, p.5, and the 2d year of Min, p.7, would not harmonize with the spirit of this piece. Choo, therefore, discarded her, adopted Chwang Këang, and argues at great length, in his notes on the 'Little Preface,' against Maou's view. His work on the *She* was published A. D. 1,177; but in his work on the 'Four Books,' completed about 12 years afterwards, he seems to have returned to the view of the older school. See his remarks on the first two lines of st. 4, in Mencius, VII. Pt. ii. XIX. Mencius at any rate, by applying those lines to Confucius, sanctions the view of the ode which regards it as the complaint of a worthy officer, neglected by his ruler, and treated with contempt by a host of mean creatures.

Ode 2. Metaphorical. THE COMPLAINT, SAD BUT RESIGNED, OF A NEGLECTED WIFE. We said that the last piece was explained by Choo of Chwang Këang, one of the marchionesses of Wei. This ode and several others are, by the unanimous consent of the critics, assigned to her, though it is only in ode 3 that we have internal evidence of the authorship, or subject at least, that is of weight.

The marquis Yang (扬), or duke Chwang (庄), succeeded to the State of Wei in B.C. 756. In that year, he married a Këang, a daughter of the House of Ts'e,—the Chwang Këang of history. She was a lady of admirable character,

and beautiful; but as she had no child, he took another wife, a Kwei (厉妫) of the State of Ch'in. She had a son, who died early; but a cousin who had accompanied her to the harem, called Tae Kwei (戴妫), gave birth to Hwan (完), whom the marquis recognized as destined in due time to succeed him. At his request, and with her own good will, Chwang Këang brought this child up as her own. Unfortunately, however, another lady of the harem, of quite inferior rank, bore the marquis a son, called Chow-yu (州吁), who became a favourite with him, and grew up a bold, dashing, unprincipled young man. The marquis died in 734, and was succeeded by his son Hwan, between whom and Chow-yu differences soon arose. The latter fled from the State; but he returned, and in 718 murdered the marquis, and attempted, without success, to establish himself in his place.—The above details we have from Sze-ma Ts'ëen, and from Tso-she under the 3d and 4th years of duke Yin. The odes lead us further into the harem of Wei, and show us the dissatisfactions and unhappiness which prevailed there.

Stt. 1, 2. Ll. 1. 2. 'Yellow' is one of the 5 'correct' colours of the Chinese (see on Ana. X. vi.), and 'green' is one of the 'intermediate,' or colours that are less esteemed. Here we have the yellow used merely as a lining to the green, or employed for the lower and less honourable part of the dress;—an inversion of all propriety, and setting forth how the concubine, the mother of Chow-yu, had got into the place of the rightful wife, and thrust the latter down. The old interpreters take the lines as allusive, while with Choo they are metaphorical; but they understand them in the same way. Choo's view seems the preferable:—'Like a green robe with

三章
绿兮丝兮。女所治兮。我思古人。俾无讹兮。

四章
绤兮绤兮。凄其以风。我思古人。实获我心。

3 [Dyed] green has been the silk;—
It was you who did it.
[But] I think of the ancients,
That I may be kept from doing wrong.

4 Linen, fine or coarse,
Is cold when worn in the wind.
I think of the ancients,
And find what is in my heart.

III.   *Yen-yen.*

燕燕

一章
燕燕于飞。差池其羽。之子于归。远送于野。瞻望弗

1 The swallows go flying about,
With their wings unevenly displayed.
The lady was returning [to her native state],
And I escorted her far into the country.

yellow lining, &c, *so is the state of things with us.*
Ll.3.4 describe Chwang Këang's feelings. 已
＝止, 'to stop;' 亡 is equivalent to 忘, 'to
forget,' 'to be forgotten.'

St.3. The green garment was originally so
much silk on which the colour had been su-
perinduced by dyeing;—intimating how the
marquis had put the concubine in the place of
the wife. 女＝汝, 'you,' referring to the
marquis or husband. So, Choo;—better than
K'ang-shing, who takes 女＝女人. 治 has
the meaning of 'to do,' 'to bring about.' The
'ancients' are wives of some former time, who
had been placed in similarly painful circumstances, and set a good example of conduct in
them. K'ang-shing makes them out to be simply
the ancient authors of the rules of propriety,
with whom Chwang Këang was in accord, while
the marquis had turned those rules upside down.
讹＝尤, 'extraordinary,' 'to go beyond what
is right.'

St.4. 绤 and 绤,—see on i.II.2. 'Linen'
in the translation is not quite accurate, as this
cloth was made of dolichos fibre. 凄, is the

rec. text; but we should read 凄, meaning
'cold'; 凄 denotes 'the app. of clouds rising.'
See K'ang-shing, as quoted by Yen Ts'an *in loc.*
It is not easy to construe the 2nd line. Wang
T'aou would take both 其 and 以 as particles; but we might give it literally:—'cold is it
because of the wind.' The speaker represents
herself as wearing a cold dress in cold weather,
when she should be warmly clad. All things
are against her. 实（＝是）获我心, 'and
get my mind'; meaning apparently, that, by her
study of the examples of antiquity, Chwang
Këang, found herself strengthened to endure, as
she was doing, her own painful experience.'

The rhymes are—in st. 1, 里, 已, cat. 1,
t. 2; in 2, 裳, 亡, cat. 10: in 3, 丝, 治,
讹 *, cat.1, t.1; in 4, 风 *, 心, cat. 7, t. 1.

Ode 3. Narrative and allusive. CHWANG KEANG
RELATES HER GRIEF AT THE DEPARTURE OF TAE
KWEI, AND CELEBRATES THAT LADY'S VIRTUE.
It has been related on the last ode, how Tae Kwei
bore Hwan to duke Chwang of Wei; and how
he was brought up by Chwang Këang and final-

及。泣涕如雨。

二章

燕燕于飞。颉之颃之。之子于归。远于将之。瞻望弗

及。伫立以泣。

三章

燕燕于飞。下上其音。之子于归。远送于南。瞻望弗

及。实劳我心。

I looked till I could no longer see her,
And my tears fell down like rain.

2　The swallows go flying about,
Now up, now down.
The lady was returning [to her native state],
And far did I accompany her.
I looked till I could no longer see her,
And long I stood and wept.

3　The swallows go flying about;
From below, from above, comes their twittering.
The lady was returning [to her native state],
And far did I escort her to the south.
I looked till I could no longer see her,
And great was the grief of my heart.

ly succeeded to his father. In B. C. 718, he—duke Hwan, 桓 公 —was murdered by his half brother Chow-yu, and his mother then returned—was obliged, probably, to return—to her native State of Ch‘in Chwang Këang continued in Wei, the marchioness-dowager: and she is understood to bewail, in this piece, her sorrow at the departure of her cherished and virtuous companion.

Stt. 1, 2, 3. Ll. 1, 2. 燕 is still the common name in China for the swallow. Maou and Choo take the reduplication of the character here as still singular;—after the Urh-ya. It seems more natural, however, to take it as plural. So, Yen Ts‘an, and others. The figure of the creature in illustrations of the *She* is that of the *Hirundo daurieus*. Synonyms of 燕 are 鳦 and 玄 鸟. 差 (read as in i. I.) 池 = 'the app. of being uneven.' To the spectator, the wings of the swallow, in its rapid and irregular flight, often present this appearance. 颉 颃 (*al.*, with 羽 on the right) denote the app. of the birds in flying, their darting upwards being specially signified by the former character, and their sudden turns downwards by the latter. So

says Maou, 飞 而 上 曰 颉 , 飞 而 下 曰 颃. Wang T‘aou, however, calls attention to an argument of Twan Yuh-tsae, that 上 and 下 should here change places. ‘颉,’ he says, ‘takes its meaning from 页,＝头, “the head,” and 颃 its meaning from 亢＝颈, “the neck.” When a bird is flying downwards, we see its head; when it is rising in the air, we see its neck. And moreover, that it is the downward flight which is first described appears from the 下 上 of the next stanza.’ It is not worth while to try and settle the point. The migratory habits of the swallow, probably, lie at the basis of the allusion. Chwang Këang and Tae Kwei had been happy together as two swallows, and now one of them was off to the south, and the other was left alone.

Ll. 3, 4. 归 is here ‘the great return (大归)’; not the visit of a wife to see her parents, but her return for good to her native State. 之子;—子 is here ‘a lady,’ one who was a widow

四章
仲氏任只。其心塞渊。终温且惠。淑慎其身。先君之

思。以勖寡人。

4　Lovingly confiding was the lady Chung;
　Truly deep was her feeling.
　Both gentle was she and docile,
　Virtuously careful of her person.
　In thinking of our deceased lord,
　She stimulated worthless me.

IV.　*Jeh yueh.*

日月
一章
日居月诸。照临下士。乃如之人兮。逝不古处。胡能

有定。宁不我顾。

1　O sun; O moon,
　Which enlighten this lower earth!
　Here is this man,
　Who treats me not according to the ancient rule.
　How can he get his mind settled?
　Would he then not regard me?

In 于 归, 于 将, 于 is the particle. 将 = 送, 'to escort.' Ch'in lay south from Wei, and therefore we have 于 南.

Ll. 5, 6. We must take 泣 and 涕 together as = 'to weep'; though 泣 is defined as 'the emission of tears without any sound.' 仁 = 久, 'a long time.'

St. 4. By 仲氏, 'the lady Chung,' we are to understand Tae Kwei. She was called 仲, as the 2d of sisters or of cousins, to distinguish her in the family and the harem; and the designation becomes here equivalent to a surname. 只 occurred before, an untranslateable particle, in i. IV., in the middle of a line; here it is at the end. We find it with 尺 and 车 at the side, used in the same way, and also interchanged with 旨. 任 has the meaning in the translation. One definition of it is—信 于 友 道.

'sincere in the ways of friendship.' 塞 = 实, 'really.' Throughout the She, 终, followed by 且, is merely = 既, and may be translated by 'both.' We must not give it the sense of 'ever.' By 先君 is intended duke Chwang. Considering all the evils which he had brought on the two ladies, it is matter of astonishment that they should be able to think of him with any feeling but that of detestation. But, according to Chinese ideas, though the husband have failed in every duty, the wife must still cherish his memory with affection.

The rhymes are—in st. 1, 羽, 野 *, 雨, cat. 5, t. 2: in 2, 顽, 将, cat. 10; 及, 泣, cat. 7, t. 3: in 3, 音, 南 *, 心, *ib.*, t. 1: in 4, 渊, 身, 人, cat. 12, t. 1. 飞, 归 make a rhyme also in stt. 1—3, cat. 15, t. 1.

Ode 4. Narrative. CHWANG KĔANG COM-PLAINS OF AND APPEALS AGAINST THE BAD TREATMENT SHE RECEIVED FROM HER HUSBAND. Both the old interpreters and Choo give this

二章

日居月诸。下土是冒。乃如之人兮。逝不相好。胡能

有定。宁不我报。

三章

日居月诸。出自东方。乃如之人兮。德音无良。胡能

有定。俾也可忘。

2   O sun, O moon,
Which overshadow this lower earth!
Here is this man,
Who will not be friendly with me.
How can he get his mind settled?
Would he then not respond to me?

3   O sun, O moon,
Which come forth from the east!
Here is this man,
With virtuous words, but really not good.
How can he get his mind settled?
Would he then allow me to be forgotten?

interpretation of the piece; but the former refer it to the time when she was suffering from the usurpation and oppressive ways of Chow-yu, long after the death of duke Chwang. To this view Choo very properly objects; the individual of whom the piece complains is evidently still alive, and a faint hope is intimated that he would change his course. It is strange that critics like Yen Ts'an should still hold to the opinion of Maou. Choo is also correct in saying that the whole is narrative. There is no allusion, as the old school thinks, in the sun and moon to the marquis and his wife. The suffering lady simply appeals to those heavenly bodies, as if they were taking cognizance of the way in which she was treated. As well might it be said that there is a similar allusion in her appeal to her parents in the last stanza.

Ll. 1, 2, in all the stt. 居 and 诸,—see on I. 5. I have not translated 临, but it has its meaning of 'a superior's regarding those below him.' 冒 = 覆, 'to cover,' 'to overshadow.' In stt. 3, 4, the writer is thinking of the sun as it rises daily in the east, and of the moon as it does so when it is full. Obs. how in st. 4 the 自 follows the noun which it governs.

Ll. 3, 4. 乃 如 must be taken as a compound conjunction, nearly equivalent to our 'but.' 乃 alone has often this meaning, indicating 'a turn in the narration or discourse (乃, 转 语 词 也)'; and Wang Yin-che takes 乃 如, here and elsewhere, in the same way (乃 如, 亦 转 语 词 也). So, he adds, 乃 若 in Mencius, IV. Pt. ii. XXVIII. 7, et al., though the characters are also found at the beginning of paragraphs. 之 人,—之 = 此 or 是, 'this.' 逝 by Choo and Wang Yin-che, is taken as simply an initial particle. This is better than to try, with Maou and Wang T'aou, to explain it by 逮 or 及. Instead of 逝 we also find 噬 and 遾, used in the same way. Choo acknowledges that he does not understand 古 处, but he gives the explanation of some other critic— 以 古 道 相 处, as in the translation;—which is the best that can be made of it. Chwang Këang was not treated as the ancient rules laid down that a wife should be. In 德 音, the 音 = 言 语, 'words.' So, Choo and Yen Ts'an. Wang T'aou prefers to take the phrase in the sense, which it sometimes has, of 令 名, 'a good name, or reputation.' In 畜 我 不 卒, 畜 = 养, 'to nourish;' and 卒 = 终, 'end,' or 'conclusion.' The 'Complete

四章

日居月诸。东方自出。父兮母兮。畜我不卒。胡能有

定。报我不述。

4   O sun, O moon,
From the east which come forth!
O father, O mother,
There is no sequel to your nourishing of me.
How can he get his mind settled?
Would he then respond to me, contrary to all reason?

V.   *Chung fung.*

终风

一章

终风且暴。顾我则笑。谑浪笑敖。中心是悼。

1   The wind blows and is fierce.
He looks at me and smiles,
With scornful words and dissolute,—the smile of pride.
To the centre of my heart I am grieved.

Digest' expands the line very well:—今我中道见弃, 何父母养我不终也.

Ll. 5,6. Both 胡 and 宁 have the sense of 何, 'how.' So, Choo. Maou explains 胡 in the same way by 何; but he says nothing of 宁. Wang Yin-che takes 宁 here in the sense of 乃 or 曾, denoting 'a turn in the discourse'; but the meaning comes to the same thing, the 5th and 6th lines being construed closely together. The mind of the marquis was all perverted; could it but get settled as it ought to be, he would treat the speaker differently. To quote again from the 'Complete Digest:'—心志回惑, 亦胡能有定哉, 使其有定, 则古道之善, 宜知之也, 何为独不我顾也. 报 = 答, 'to respond to.' The speaker did her duty as a wife. She longed for the marquis to respond to her with the duty of a husband. The last line in st. 3 is difficult to construe. It is still interrogative like those of the preceding stanzas:—' would it be given to me to be forgotten?' As Choo expands it:—何独使我为可忘者耶. So also the last line in st. 4 may be regarded as interrogative, though we are able to translate it as it stands. 述 = 循, 'to be in accordance with,' *i. e.*, with the principles of reason. So, both Maou and Choo. According to Choo's interpretation of this ode and the next, which I believe to be correct, they ought to take precedence of the last.

The rhymes are—in st. 1, 土, 处, 顾, cat. 5, t. 2: in 2, 冒 *, 好 *, 报 *, cat. 3, t. 2: in 3, 方, 良, 忘, cat. 10: in 4, 出, 卒, 述, cat. 15, t. 3.

Ode 5. Metaphorical. CHWANG KEANG BE-MOANS THE SUPERCILIOUS TREATMENT WHICH SHE RECEIVED FROM HER HUSBAND. The old interpreters think the lady is bemoaning the cruel treatment which she received from Chow-yu. The imperial editors approve of Choo's view, but have in their edition preserved also the earlier. If Choo's interpretation be correct, the ode should, like the last, be placed before the 3d; 'he did not venture,' say the editors, 'to alter the existing order of the pieces;'—because to do so would have brought him into collision with the authority of Confucius.

二章
终风且霾。惠然肯来。莫往莫来。悠悠我思。

三章
终风且曀。不日有曀。寤言不寐。愿言则嚏。

四章
曀曀其阴。虺虺其雷。寤言不寐。愿言则怀。

2　The wind blows, with clouds of dust.
　　Kindly he seems to be willing to come to me;
　　[But] he neither goes nor comes.
　　Long, long, do I think of him.

3　The wind blew, and the sky was cloudy;
　　Before a day elapses, it is cloudy again.
　　I awake, and cannot sleep;
　　I think of him, and gasp.

4　All cloudy is the darkness,
　　And the thunder keeps muttering.
　　I awake and cannot sleep;
　　I think of him, and my breast is full of pain.

Maou treats the piece as allusive; it seems better to understand with Choo that the stanzas all begin with a metaphorical description of the harassing conduct of duke Chwang.

Stt. 1. 2. Ll. 1. Maou and Choo both explain 终风 by 终日风, 'wind through all the day.' Wang Yin-che, as has already been observed, takes 终 here, and generally in the *She*, as = 既; which is ingenious, and probably correct. 暴 = 疾, 'rapid,' 'fierce.' The Urh-ya says, 风而雨土为霾 'wind after which the dust descends like rain is 霾.'

Stt. 3, 4. Ll. 1, 2. 曀 denotes 'dark and windy';—the wind blowing, and clouds at the same time obscuring the sun. In 不日有曀, the 有 = 又, 'further,' 'again.' I translate the 1st line of st. 3 in the past tense. We are then led to think of the sky clearing for a time; but before a day elapses (不日), it is again overcast. The reduplication of 曀 in st. 4 denotes 'the app. of the darkness or cloudiness,' and 虺虺 signifies, acc. to Choo, the

muttering of thunder before it bursts into a crash, while Maou makes it the crash itself.

Stt. 1, 2. Ll. 2—4. The 2d line describes some fitful gleams of kindness shown by duke Chwang; and the 3d line, how they were only deceitful and mocking. 谑 = 戏言, 'sportive, or scornful words.' 浪 = 放荡, 'dissolute,' 'unlicensed,' The Urh-ya explains 谑浪笑敖 all together by 戏谑. 莫往莫来 express the uncertainty and changeableness of duke Chwang's moods. He would neither go nor come; was neither one thing nor another. Maou's explanation of the line is very far-fetched.— 'Chow-yu did not come as a son to serve Chwang Këang, and she could not go and show to him the affection of a mother.' 悼 = 伤, 'to be wounded,' *i. e.*, with grief. 悠悠,—see on i. I.

Stt. 2, 3, 4, Ll. 3, 4. 言 must be treated simply as a particle. Here it is in the middle of the line as in ode I., stt. 4, 5. Taking 言 as a particle, we cannot explain 愿 by 'to wish.' Maou says nothing about it, but Choo defines it

VI. *Keih koo.*

击鼓

一章

击鼓其镗。踊跃用兵。土国城漕。我独南行。

二章

从孙子仲。平陈与宋。不我以归。忧心有忡。

1 Hear the roll of our drums!
 See how we leap about, using our weapons!
 Those do the fieldwork in the State, or fortify Ts'aou,
 While we alone march to the south.

2 We followed Sun Tsze-chung,
 Peace having been made with Ch'in and Sung;
 [But] he did not lead us back,
 And our sorrowful hearts are very sad.

by 思, 'to think.' There is a difficulty with *te*, which means 'to sneeze;' and Morrison. under the character, translates the line,—'I think with anxiety, till indisposition makes me sneeze.' We must cast about surely for some other meaning. Now Maou has 疐 without the 口 by the side, and it would appear that this was the reading till the time of Wăn-ts'ung (文宗) of the T'ang dynasty (A.D. 827-840), when 嚏 got into the stone tablets of the classics which were then cut. Maou further explains 疐 by 跲, or, acc. to Luh Teh-ming, by 欱 meaning 'to open the mouth wide,' 'to gape.' I venture, therefore, to give the meaning in the translation.

Maou explains 怀 by 伤, 'to be pained'; and Choo, by 思, 'to think.' The speaker cherished her husband despairingly in her thoughts.

The rhymes are—in stt. 1, 暴, 笑, 敖, 悼, cat. 2: in 2, 霾 *, 来, 来, 思, cat. 1, t. 1: in 3, 曀 *, 曀 *, 疐 *, cat. 12, t. 3: in 4, 雷, 怀, cat. 15, t. 1.

Ode 6. Narrative. SOLDIERS OF WEI REPINING BITTERLY OVER THEIR SEPARATION FROM THEIR FAMILIES, AND ANTICIPATING THAT IT WOULD BE FINAL. We read in the Ch'un Ts'ew (I. iv. 4,5) that, in B. C. 718, Wei twice joined in an expedition against Ch'ing. Chow-yu had just murdered duke Hwan, and the people were restless under his rule. He thought it would divert their minds, and be acceptable to other States, if he attacked Ch'ing; and having made an agreement with Sung, Ch'in and Ts'ae, a combined force marched against that State. Its operations lasted only 5 days; but very soon, in autumn, the troops, having been joined by a body of men from Loo, returned to the south, and carried off all the grain of Ch'ing from the fields.—It is supposed that it is to these operations that the ode refers, and I would assign it to the period of the second expedition. The soldiers had hoped to return to their families at the conclusion of the former service; and finding that another was to be performed, they gave vent to their aggrieved feelings in these stanzas. We must bear in mind, however, that this interpretation of the piece is only traditional.

St.1. 镗 denotes the sound of the drums. The line is twice quoted in the Shwoh-wăn, and once we have this character with 鼓 instead of 金;—probably the more correct form. The demonstrative force of the 其 justifies the translation 'Hear!' 兵 denotes sharp, pointed weapons. The drum gave the signal for action or advance. The troops are here represented as bestirring themselves on hearing it. 土 = 土功, 'field labour' 国 = 国中 'in the State.' 漕 was the name of a city of Wei, to which duke Tae removed the capital for a short time in B. C. 659, as mentioned in the note on the title of the Book. It was in the pres. dis. of Hwah (滑), dep. Wei-hwuy. The 独 in the last line leads us to refer this 3d line away from the troops which were in march southwards to Ch'ing. to the rest of the people.

三章

爱居爱处。爱丧其马。于以求之。于林之下。

四章

死生契阔。与子成说。执子之手。与子偕老。

五章

于嗟阔兮。不我活兮。于嗟洵兮。不我信兮。

3　Here we stay; here we stop;
　　Here we lose our horses;
　　And we seek for them,
　　Among the trees of the forest.

4　For life or for death, however separated,
　　To our wives we pledged our word.
　　We held their hands;—
　　We were to grow old together with them.

5　Alas for our separation!
　　We have no prospect of life.
　　Alas for our stipulation!
　　We cannot make it good.

As the 'Complete Digest' expands it,— 顾彼 卫国之民，或役土功于国， 或筑城于漕. They were toiled too, but not to the peril of their lives, as the troops were.

St. 2. Sun Tsze-chung was the name of the commander. Maou, in his introductory note on the ode, says he was the Kung-sun Wán-chung. There was a noble family in Wei having the surname of Sun, of which we read much in the Ch‘un Ts‘ëw. L. 2. See the note above, on the interpretation of the piece. L. 3, 以 is here explained by 与, 'with.' See the same note. L. 4. Maou explains 有忡 by 忡忡然, 'very sad-like.' It is another of the many instances where 有 makes the word that follows it vividly descriptive.

St. 3. 爰 is defined by Choo by 于, which he immediately expands to 于是, 'here.' We must take it as a particle, = 于, which takes the place of it in the 3d line. So, Wang Yin-che. 于以,—see on ii. II. 1, 2. This stanza sets forth, acc. to Choo, the disorder in the ranks

of the troops, who had no heart to fight. **Wang Suh** (王肃; of the kingdom of Wei) considered that in this and the two next stanzas we had the words of the farewell taken by the soldiers of their families:—'We shall not return from this expedition. We know not where we shall finally rest ourselves, nor where we shall lose our horses. You will have to look for us and them in the forests.'

St. 4. The soldiers think here of their engagements with their wives at the time of their marriage, and go on, in the next stanza, to mourn because they cannot now be carried out. 契 (read k‘ëeh) 阔 express the idea of separation. Maou explains the phrase by 勤苦, 'toil and suffering.' The dict., on 契, gives both this meaning of the phrase and that which I have adopted. 与子, 子 must refer to their wives. The last two lines seem to necessitate this. K‘ang-shing, very unnaturally, refers it to the 'comrades' of the speakers, (从军之士，与其伍约云云). Perhaps this was the idea of Maou, who explains 说 by 数, as if the 与子成说 = 'with you we will

VII.　*K'ae fung.*

凯风
一章
凯风自南。吹彼棘心。棘心夭夭。母氏劬劳。
二章
凯风自南。吹彼棘薪。母氏圣善。我无令人。

1　The genial wind from the south
　　Blows on the heart of that jujube tree,
　　Till that heart looks tender and beautiful.
　　What toil and pain did our mother endure!

2　The genial wind from the south
　　Blows on the branches of that jujube tree,
　　Our mother is wise and good;
　　But among us there is none good.

complete the number in our ranks.' 成 说 =
'we pledged our word.'

St. 5. 不 我 活,—'there is now no living
for us.' 洵,—'to be true.' It is often used
adverbially, and here it has a substantive meaning, referring to the engagements in the previous
stanza. 信 = 伸, 'to stretch out,' 'to make
good;'—an established usage of the term. 于
嗟,—as in i. XI.

The rhymes are—in st. 1, 镗, 兵 *, 行 *,
cat. 10: in 2, 仲, 宋, 忡, cat. 9: in 3, 处,
马 *, 下 *, cat. 5, t. 2: in 4, 阔, 说, cat. 15,
t. 3; 手, 老 *, cat. 3, t. 2: in 5, 阔, 活, cat.
15, t. 3; 洵, 信, cat. 12, t. 1.

Ode 7. Metaphorical and allusive. SEVEN
SONS OF SOME FAMILY IN WEI BLAME THEMSELVES
FOR THE RESTLESS UNHAPPINESS OF THEIR MO-
THER. The 'Little Preface' says that the mother could not rest;—we must suppose in her
state of widowhood, and wanting to marry a
second time; and that her sons, by laying the
blame of her restlessness upon themselves, recalled her to a sense of duty. There is nothing
in the ode, as Choo says, to intimate that the
mother was thus wrought upon; and he might
have added that there is nothing in it to suggest
that it was her wish to marry again which
troubled the sons. However, he accepted the
traditional interpretation so far. Mencius, VI.

Pt. ii. III., alludes to the ode, but he merely
says that the fault of the parent referred to in
it was small, and it was proper therefore that
the dissatisfaction with her expressed by the
sons should be slight.

St. 1, 凯 风, 'the triumphant or pleasant
wind,' is a name given to the south wind from
its genial influence on all vegetation.　By the
kih we are, probably, to understand the *zizyphus
jujuba*, a small thorny tree, bearing a fruit the
size of a cherry, which is mealy and eatable, and
goes among foreigners by the name of the Chinese date. The name of this is generally written
枣; but Heu Shin says that 棘 is applied to
a smaller variety of the tree or shrub, whose
fruit is more acid. By the 'heart' of the tree
are intended the inner and hidden shoots, which
it is more difficult for the genial influence to
reach. 夭 夭,—see i. VI.　母 氏,—氏 is
used much as in III. 4. We cannot translate
it, and say 'our mother, of such and such a
surname.'　劬 劳 = 病 苦, 'to have dis-
tress and toil.' In this 4th line, the sons, acc.
to Choo, refer to their mother's toil in their nur-
ture and upbringing.—He makes this stanza to
be metaphorical, agreeing with the old interpreters in regard to the allusive character of
the others. See in justification of this, the
remarks of Lëw Kin on the next stanza.

St. 2. Maou explains 薪 of the shoots of
the tree, now grown into branches (其 成 就
者). They might be used for firewood.　圣

三章
爰有寒泉。在浚之下。有子七人。母氏劳苦。

四章
睍睆黄鸟。载好其音。有子七人。莫慰母心。

3　There is the cool spring
　　Below [the city of] Tseun.
　　We are seven sons,
　　And our mother is full of pain and suffering.

4　The beautiful yellow birds
　　Give forth their pleasant notes.
　　We are seven sons,
　　And cannot compose our mother's heart.

VIII. *Heung che.*

雄雉

一章
雄雉于飞。泄泄其羽。我之怀矣。自诒伊阻。

1　The male pheasant flies away,
　　Lazily moving his wings.
　　The man of my heart!—
　　He has brought on us this separation.

一 叡, 'wise.' 善 and 令 are synonyms. Lëw Kin (刘 瑾 ; Yuen dyn.) says:—'The former stanza speaks of the genial wind, and the heart of the jujube tree, but afterwards does not mention what was in the poet's mind corresponding to these things, so that the verse is metaphorical. This stanza speaks of the wind and jujube tree, and then mentions the mother and the sons which correspond to these, so that it is allusive. There is a similarity between the two, but they are not of the same character.'

St. 3. 爰,—see on st. 3 of last ode. Tseun was a city of Wei,—in the pres. Puh Chow, dep. Ts‘aou-chow, Shan-tung. Near it was a famous spring, to the virtue of which the sons refer as a contrast to their own uselessness. The spring refreshed the people of Tseun, while they could not keep their mother from trouble and pain.

St. 4. 睍 睆 is explained by Maou as meaning 好 貌, 'good-like.' Choo understands the phrase of the notes of the orioles, 'clear and twirling.' It may be doubted if either of them have brought out the meaning correctly. One would expect some description of the eyes in the characters. 载 must be taken simply as a particle. Wang Yin-che explains it by 则, but there is not that force of meaning in it. The birds were useful in their way, contributing to the pleasure of men; but the sons failed to comfort their mother's heart. The old interpreters have a great deal more to say on the allusion; but it would be a waste of time and space to dwell on their views.

The rhymes are—in st. 1, 南 *, 心, cat. 7, t. 1; 天, 劳, cat. 2: in 2, 薪, 人, cat. 12: in 3, 下 *, 苦, cat. 5, t. 2: in 4, 音, 心, cat. 7, t. 1.

Ode 8. Allusive and narrative. A WIFE DEPLORES THE ABSENCE OF HER HUSBAND, AND CELEBRATES HIS VIRTUE. The 'Little Preface' says that this ode was composed by the people of Wei against duke Seuen,—the marquis (晋), called to the rule of the State on the death of Chow-yu (B.C. 718—699). His dissoluteness and constant wars distressed and widowed the people, till they expressed their resentment in this ode.

二章
雄雉于飞。下上其音。展矣君子。实劳我心。

三章
瞻彼日月。悠悠我思。道之云远。曷云能来。

四章
百尔君子。不知德行。不忮不求。何用不臧。

2   The pheasant has flown away,
     But from below, from above, comes his voice.
     Ah! the princely man!—
     He afflicts my heart.

3   Look at that sun and moon!
     Long, long do I think.
     The way is distant;
     How can he come to me?

4   All ye princely men,
     Know ye not his virtuous conduct?
     He hates none; he covets nothing;—
     What does he which is not good?

Choo well observes that there is nothing in the piece about the dissoluteness of duke Seuen, or to indicate that it was made in his time; that we ought not to hear in it the voice of the people, but of a wife deploring the absence of her husband. The imperial editors in this case fully agree with him.

Stt. 1, 2, Ll. 1, 2. 于 is the particle. 泄泄 describes the slow flight of the pheasant moving, not under alarm, from one place to another. So, l. 2 in st. 2, is understood to shew the feeling of security enjoyed by the bird. Yen Ts'an observes that here, in v. VL., and some other odes, where the subject is an officer engaged on military duty, the male pheasant is introduced, because of the well-known fighting character of that bird. It may be so; but here it is the contrast between the ease and security of the pheasant and the toils and danger of her husband, which is in the speaker's mind. 我之怀＝我怀人 in I.i. III. 1 伊 is the particle. K'ang-shing says it should be 繄, and explains it by 'this;'—which is unnecessary. 阻 means 'to hinder,' 'to obstruct;' hence 'an impediment,' that by which communication is prevented. Here Choo explains it by 隔, 'to be separated.' This is better than Maou's 难, 'difficulty,' 'hardship.' 诒＝遗, simply ＝'to occasion.' There is some difficulty with the 自. Yen Ts'an's reference of it to the speaker—the wife—is inadmissible. 'She attributes,' says Foo K'wang, 'their separation to her husband, not wishing to blame others for it.' 君子 denotes the husband,—as in i. X., et al. 展＝诚, 'sincere,' 'sincerely.' Choo observes that the 展 and 实 give strong emphasis to these lines of st. 2.

Stt. 3, 4. These are simply narrative. The sun and moon are spoken of as the measurers of time. Many revolutions had they performed since the husband went away. The 云 in ll. 3 and 4 is merely a particle. It is found both at the beginning and in the middle of lines. Wang Yin-che says on this passage, 云,语中助词也,诗雄雉曰,道之云远,曷云能来,言道之远,何能来也. Lacharme, endeavouring to translate the 云, has,—' Viam longam esse aiunt; quid igitur memorant eum advenisse posse!' The

IX.   *P‘aou-yew-koo-yeh.*

飽有苦叶
一章
飽有苦叶。济有深涉。深则厉。浅则揭。
二章
有弥济盈。有鷕雉鸣。济盈不濡轨。雉鸣求其牡。

1　The gourd has [still] its bitter leaves,
　And the crossing at the ford is deep.
　If deep, I will go through with my clothes on ;
　If shallow, I will do so, holding them up.

2　The ford is full to overflowing ;
　There is the note of the female pheasant.
　The full ford will not wet the axle of my carriage ;
　It is the pheasant calling for her mate.

君子 in st. 4 must be taken as addressed to the brother officers of the husband, who is described, though he is not named explicitly, in the 3d and 4th lines. The 2d line is taken interrogatively. The last 2 lines are quoted by Confucius (Ana. IX. xxvi), as illustrated in the character of Tsze-loo. Le Hung-tsoo (李闳祖; Sung dyn.) distinguishes the force of 恶 and 求 ingeniously :—'恶 indicates hatred of men because of what they have ; 求, shame, because of what we ourselves have not.' 用=行 or 为, 'to do.'

The rhymes are—in st. 1, 羽, 阻, cat. 5, t. 2: in 2, 音, 心, cat. 7, t. 1: in 3, 思, 来, cat. 1, t. 1: in 4, 行 *, 臧, cat. 10.

Ode 9. Allusive and narrative. AGAINST THE LICENTIOUS MANNERS OF WEI. According to the 'Little Preface,' the piece was directed against duke Seuen, who was distinguished for his licentiousness, and his wife also. Choo demurs to its having this particular reference, which, however, the imperial editors are inclined to admit. Duke Seuen was certainly a monster of wickedness. According to Tso-she (on p. 5 of the 16th year of duke Hwan), his first wife was a lady of his father's harem, called E Këang (夷姜), by an incestuous connection with whom he had a son called Keih-tsze (急子), who became his heir-apparent. By and by he contracted a marriage for this son with a daughter of Ts‘e, known as Seuen Këang (宣姜);

but on her arrival in Wei, moved by her youth and beauty, he took her himself, and by her he had two sons,—Show (寿) and Soh (朔). E Këang hanged herself in vexation, and the duke was prevailed on, in course of time, by the intrigues of Seuen Këang and Soh, to consent to the death of Keih-tsze, Show peristing in a noble, but fruitless, attempt to preserve his life. In the next year, the duke died, and was succeeded by Soh, when the court of Ts‘e insisted on Ch‘aou-peh (昭伯), another son of Seuen, marrying Seuen Këang. From this connection sprang two sons, who both became marquises of Wei, and two daughters, who married the rulers of other States ;—see Tso-she on p. 7 of the 2d year of duke Min.

When such was the history of the court of Wei, we can well conceive that licentiousness prevailed widely through the State. The particular reference of the ode to duke Seuen must remain, however, an unsettled question. The explanation of the different stanzas is, indeed, difficult and vexatious on any hypothesis about the ode that can be formed.

St. 1. The p‘aou is no doubt, the bottle gourd, called also 葫, or 壶, 芦. When the fruit has became thoroughly hard and ripe, the shell, emptied of its contents, can be used as a bladder. We often see one or more tied to boat-children on the Chinese rivers, to keep them afloat, should they fall into the water, till they can be picked up. The gourd in the text had still its leaves on it ; the fruit was not yet hard enough to serve the purpose of a bladder in crossing a stream. 济＝渡处, 'a ford or ferry.' So, both Maou and Choo. Le Kwang-te takes the character as the name of the river Tse. 涉 means 'to wade,' to cross the ford on foot.

三章
雝雝鳴雁。旭日始旦。士如歸妻。迨冰未泮。
四章
招招舟子。人涉卬否。人涉卬否。卬須我友。

3　The wild goose, with its harmonious notes,
At sunrise, with the earliest dawn,
By the gentleman, who wishes to bring home his bride,
[Is presented] before the ice is melted.

4　The boatman keeps beckoning;
And others cross with him, but I do not.
Others cross with him, but I do not;—
I am waiting for my friend.

In st. 4, however, we must take it differently. 厲 means to go through the water, without taking one's clothes off; while 揭 (*k'e*) denotes to go through, holding the clothes up. The Urh-ya says that when the water only comes up to the knees, we may *k'e* it; when it rises above the knees, we can wade it (涉); but when it rises above the waist, we must *le* it. The 3d and 4th lines are quoted in the Ana. XIV. xiii. to illustrate, apparently, the propriety of acting according to circumstances; and so Maou and Choo try to explain them here. Yen Ts'an, however, seems to me to take them more naturally. The first two lines are intended to show the error of licentious connections. The ford should not be attempted, when there are not the proper appliances for crossing it. The last two lines show the recklessness of the parties against whom the piece is directed. They are determined to cross in one way or another.

St. 2. 瀰 denotes 'the full or swollen appearance of the water.' 有 is used as in 有帊, in VI. 2. It gives a vivid or descriptive force to the character that follows it,—as in the reduplication of adjectives which is so common. 有鷕 in the same way denotes the note of the female pheasant. 軌 is here the axle of the carriage; not as Choo says, the rut or trace of the wheel. The character should be 輒. Both Maou and Choo take 牡 as= 'a male quadruped,' saying that the male and female of birds are expressed by 雄 and 雌, while for quadrupeds we have 牡 and 牝; but this distinction is not always observed. We have in the She itself 雄狐 for 'a male fox,' and in the Shoo, 牝鷄 for 'a female fowl.'

To suppose that the female pheasant is here calling to her a male quadruped is too extravagant.—The explanation of the stanza is substantially the same as that of the preceding.

St. 3. This stanza is of a different character, and indicates the deliberate formal way in which marriages ought to be contracted,—in contrast with the haste and indecencies of the parties in the poet's mind. When the bridegroom wanted to have the day fixed for him to meet his bride and conduct her to his house, he sent a live wild goose, at early dawn, to her family. Why that bird was employed, and why that early hour was selected for the ceremony, are points on which we need not here enter. This was done, it is said, 'before the ice was melted' implying that the concluding ceremony would take place later. The meaning is that no forms should be omitted, and no haste shown in such an important thing as marriage.

According to this view, the stanza is parenthetical and explanatory. 雝雝 denotes 'the harmony of the goose's notes,' which may be doubted. 雁, from the pictures of it, should be the Bean goose, *Anser segetum*. 旭 is 'the appearance of sunrise.' 如 = 'if,' almost = our 'when.' 歸妻 = 'to bring his wife home.' (使之來歸于已). 迨,—as in ii. IX.

St. 4. 招 is 'to beckon,' 'to call with the hand.' The repetition of it vividly represents the calling. 舟子, 'boat-son,' = the master of the ferry boat. 涉 is here to cross the ferry in the boat, and not to wade through it on foot. Yen Ts'an keeps here, indeed, the latter meaning of the term, which is the only one given in the dict.; but to do so, he is obliged to construe the first line,—'I keep beckoning to the boatman,' in which it is impossible to agree with him. 卬

X. *Kuh fung.*

谷风
一章
习习谷风。以阴以雨。黾勉同心。不宜有怒。采葑采

菲。无以下体。德音莫违。及尔同死。

二章
行道迟迟。中心有违。不远伊迩。薄送我畿。谁谓荼

1   Gently blows the east wind,
With cloudy skies and with rain.
[Husband and wife] should strive to be of the same mind,
And not let angry feelings arise.
When we gather the mustard plant and earth melons,
We do not reject them because of their roots.
While I do nothing contrary to my good name,
I should live with you till our death.

2   I go along the road slowly, slowly,
In my inmost heart reluctant.
Not far, only a little way,
Did he accompany me to the threshold.

一我, 'I.' The meaning of the stanza is, that people should wait for a proper match, and not hurry on to form licentious connections.

The rhymes are—in st. 1, 叶 *, 涉, cat. 8, t. 3; 厉, 揭, cat. 15, t. 3: in 2, 盈, 鸣, cat. 11; 轨 (prop. 厬, cat. 7), 牡 *, cat. 3, t. 2: in 3, 雁, 旦, 泮, cat. 14: in 4, 子, 否 *, 否 *, cat. 1, t. 2.

Ode 10. Metaphorical, allusive, and narrative. THE PLAINT OF A WIFE REJECTED AND SUPPLANTED BY ANOTHER. Thus much we learn from the ode itself. There can be no doubt that the manners of the court of Wei injuriously affected the households of the State; but this does not appear in the piece, though Maou seems to say that it does.

St. 1. Maou and Choo take 习习 as describing the 'gentle breath' of the wind. 谷风 is taken by them, after the Urh-ya, as meaning 'the east wind.' This brings clouds and rain, and all genial influences. Ying-tah explains 谷 as if it were 榖, 'living.' We may take these

two lines either as metaphorical or allusive, referring to what the harmony and happiness of the family should be. Yen Ts'an explains them very differently, as referring to the angry demonstrations of the husband, like gusts of wind coming constantly (习习=连续不断), from great valleys, and bringing with them gloom and rain. Who shall decide on the comparative merits of the two views thus conflicting? 黾勉 = 勉勉, 'to exert one's self.' Maou gives 黾 with 人 at the side, which is also found in the same sense. 葑 and 菲 are, probably, two species of Brassica; Williams calls 葑, 'vegetables resembling mustard.' Maou says it is the *seu* (须) and Choo the *man-tsing* (蔓菁); others make it the *woo-tsing* (芜菁); and others again the *keae* (芥), or mustard plant. These are but different names for varieties of the same plant. In the Japanese plates, the figure of the *fung* is that of a sorrel or dock,— *rumex persicariodes;* and the author says he does

苦。其甘如荠。宴尔新婚。如兄如弟。

三章

泾以渭浊。湜湜其沚。宴尔新婚。不我屑以。母逝我

梁。母发我笱。我躬不阅。遑恤我后。

> Who says that the sowthistle is bitter?
> It is as sweet as the shepherd's purse.
> You feast with your new wife,
> [Loving] as brothers.

3   The muddiness of the King appears from the Wei,
     But its bottom may be seen about the islets.
     You feast with your new wife,
     And think me not worth being with.
     Do not approach my dam,
     Do not move my basket.
     My person is rejected ;—
     What avails it to care for what may come after?

not know the *fei*. After the Urh-ya, Maou calls *fei* the *wuh* (葹) 'a sort of turnip, the flower of which is purple.' The root is red. It is, no doubt, a kind of radish; but Kwoh Poh calls it 'the earth melon (土瓜);' and so I have translated it. The leaves, stalk, and root of the *fung* and *fei* are all edible; and if sometimes the root or lower part— 下体 —be bad, yet the whole plant is not on that account thrown away. From this the wife argues that though her beauty might in some degree have decayed, she should not on that account have been cast off. 德音 is explained by Choo by 美誉, 'admirable praise,'=good character or name. K'angshing and Yen Ts'an, however, take the phrase here as in IV. 3 ;—'Husband and wife should speak kindly to each other.' Choo's view suits the connection best.

St. 2. The first 4 lines describe the cold manner in which the wife was sent away, and her reluctance to go. The 2d line says that while her feet went slowly on the way, her heart was all the while rebelling, and wished to turn back. 伊 = 惟, almost='only.' Both Maou and Choo explain 畿 by 门内, 'the inside of the door.' The word is used in the sense of 限, a limit or boundary, which, from the 3d line, we infer would here be the threshold.

The last 4 lines describe the bitterness of the wife's feelings at seeing herself supplanted. Medhurst is probably correct in calling the *t'oo* the sowthistle. I was inclined, from the descriptions of it, to call it a sort of lettuce. 'Its leaf exudes a white juice, which is bitter. Its flowers are like those of an aster. It is edible but bitter.' The pictures of the *tse* are those of the shepherd's purse. They say that the seeds of it are sweet. 婚 is used for a marriage, because it was in 'the dark,' at night, that the wife was brought home. Here it= 妻, 'wife.'

St. 3. The King and the Wei ;—see the Shoo, on III. Pt.i.73, Pt.ii.12. 湜湜 ='clear-looking.' The Shwoh-wăn defines the term as 'clear water, where the bottom can be seen.' 'The waters of the King,' says Choo, 'are muddy, and those of the Wei are clear, and the muddiness of the King appears more clearly after its junction with the Wei ; yet where its channel is interrupted by islets, and the stream flows more gently, it is not so muddy but that the bottom may be seen. So, with the rejected and the new wife. The former was thrown into the shade by the latter. Yet if the husband would only think, he might know that she still had her good qualities.' Yen Ts'an here again construes differently. With him the new wife is the King, well known for its muddiness, representing her, the clear Wei, to be muddy ;—a misrepresentation which inspection or reflection would readily refute. In l. 4 不屑,='you

四章
就其深矣。方之舟之。就其浅矣。泳之游之。何有何

亡。黾勉求之。凡民有丧。匍匐救之。

五章
不我能慉。反以我为仇。既阻我德。贾用不售。昔育

4 Where the water was deep,
  I crossed it by a raft or a boat.
  Where it was shallow,
  I dived or swam across it.
  Whether we had plenty or not,
  I exerted myself to be getting.
  When among others there was a death,
  I crawled on my knees to help them.

5 You cannot cherish me,
  And you even count me as an enemy.
  You disdain my virtues,—
  A pedlar's wares which do not sell.

do not think it right to demean yourself to.' See, by help of the index, the use of 不屑 in Mencius. Both by Maou and Choo, 屑 is correctly explained by 洁, 'pure;' but Choo is wrong when he construes 不我屑,—不以我为洁, 'you do not consider me to be pure;' such is not the usage of 不屑 We must, then, look out for a substantive meaning to the concluding 以. K'ang-shing explains it by 用, 'to employ,' which is allowable. It is better, however, to take it, with Choo, as = 与, 'with,' 'to associate with.' Though he errs with the 不屑, his expansion of the whole line is not far wrong:—不以我为洁而与之. Chaou K'e on Mencius, II. Pt.i.IX., quotes the line as 不我屑已; but we cannot argue from that. 梁 is a stone dam in the stream, with open spaces, through which the fish might pass, or where they might be taken by means of baskets (筍). 逝 = 之, 'to go to,' 'to approach.' The wife is suddenly excited to address her enemy, and order her away from her place and her property; but she as suddenly checks herself. Her person rejected, she could hereafter have no interest in anything that had belonged to her. 阅 is explained by 容, 'to bear, be borne, with;' 遑, 'leisure,' is, as often, taken interrogatively:—'what leisure have I to—,' or 'of what use will it be to.—' 我后=我已去之后, 'what will happen after I am gone.'

St.4. The wife here sets forth how diligent and thoughtful she had been in her domestic affairs, ever consulting for the prosperity of her husband.

方 and 泳,—see on i. IX.1. 之 after these characters, and also 舟 and 游,—as in 颙之,颙之, in III.2. 何有.何亡=不论贫富, 'without regard to our being rich or poor.' 'If they had plenty,' says K'ang-shing, 'she sought that they might have more; if they wanted, she sought that they might have enough.' And not in her own family only was she thus sedulous. She was ever ready to help in the need of her neighbours, thus consulting for her husband's popularity and comfort.

St.5. The wife dwells on her husband's hostile feeling to her in his prosperity, in contrast with what had been her interest in his early struggles. We may accept Ying-tah and Choo's explanation of 慉 by 养, 'to nourish.' 阻 = 'to hinder

恐育鞠。及尔颠覆。既生既育。比予于毒。

六章

我有旨蓄。亦以御冬。宴尔新婚。以我御穷。有洸有

溃。既诒我肄。不念昔者。伊余来塈。

Formerly, I was afraid our means might be exhausted,
And I might come with you to destitution.
Now, when your means are abundant,
You compare me to poison.

6 My fine collection of vegetables
Is but a provision against the winter.
Feasting with your new wife,
You think of me as a provision [only] against your poverty.
Cavalierly and angrily you treat me;
You give me only pain.
You do not think of the former days,
And are only angry with me.

or impede.' Choo explains it here by 却, 'to reject.' The idea is that of an impediment or obstruction between the wife's virtues and the husband's mind, so that he would give no recognition of them. 贾 is read *koo*, 'a shopman' 'a trader.' 用 may be taken as = 以 or 因, and the whole line is—'The trader therefore does not sell his wares.'

In the last 4 lines, there is a difficulty with the two 育 in l. 5 and 既 生 既 育 in l. 7. Yen Ts'au thinks the former 育 refers to the business of child-bearing, after the marriage of the parties, when the wife was always fearing that the number of mouths would be more than they could feed, and the 7th line says that that business was all over;—the children were grown up and there was prosperity. Few will be inclined to accept this exegesis, and I can make nothing out of Maou, who explains 育 by 长. We must be content to accept the construction of of Choo. The 1st 育 is the struggle for a livelihood, and the 2nd is the means of that livelihood. Then 既 生 既 育 expresses the idea that that livelihood has been abundantly secured. 鞠 = 穷, 'to be exhausted.' 颠

覆 means 'to be overthrown;' here == to come to destitution. Yen Ts'an and Ying-tah are both obliged to force upon the terms the meaning of 'did my utmost.'

St. 6. The wife repeats the plaint of last stanza, and concludes by deploring her husband's angry mood. 蓄 is understood to be 'the collection,' of vegetables which the wife has made against (御 = 禦 or 当) the winter. In the spring, when new vegetables were produced, she would not need it. So she herself had been cherished by her husband only when he had need of her in his poverty. The text has thus to be supplemented considerably in order to get a meaning out of it. 有 洸 = 'fierce-like.' 有 溃 = 'angry-like.' 肄 = 劳, 'pain,' 'toil.' Both Maou and Choo take 塈 in the sense of 息 'to rest,' so that the 7th and 8th lines = 'you do not think of the former days, when I came to rest.' Much better is the exegesis of Wang Yin-che, which I have followed. He explains 伊 by 惟, 来 by 是, and 塈 by 忾,—'to be angry.' This usage of 来 is not infrequent.

XI.　*Shih Wei.*

式微

一章

式微式微。胡不归。微君之故。胡为乎中露。

二章

式微式微。胡不归。微君之躬。胡为乎泥中。

1　Reduced! Reduced!
　Why not return?
　If it were not for your sake, O prince,
　How should we be thus exposed to the dew?

2　Reduced! reduced!
　Why not return?
　If it were not for your person, O prince,
　How should we be here in the mire?

XII.　*Maou-k'ew.*

旄丘

一章

旄丘之葛兮。何诞之节兮。叔兮伯兮。何多日也。

1　The dolichos on that high and sloping mound;—
　How wide apart are [now] its joints!
　O ye uncles,
　Why have ye delayed these many days?

The rhymes are—in st. 1, 风 *, 心, cat. 7, t. 1; 雨, 怒, cat. 5, t. 2; 菲, 体, 死 cat. 15, t. 2: in 2, 迟, 违, 畿, *ib.*, t. 1; 荑, 弟, *ib.*, t. 2: in 3, 泚, 以, cat. 1, t. 2; 笱, 后, cat. 4, t. 2; in 4, 舟, 游, 求, 救, cat. 3, t. 1: in 5, 惵, 仇, 售, cat. 3, t. 2; 鞠, 覆, 育, 毒, *ib.*, t. 3: in 6, 冬, 穷, cat. 9; 溃, 肆, 墍, cat. 15, t. 3.

Ode 11. Narrative. THE OFFICERS OF SOME STATE WHO WERE REFUGEES AND IN DISTRESS IN WEI, EXHORT THEIR RULER TO RETURN HOME WITH THEM. The 'Little Preface' says that the prince addressed was the marquis of Le (黎侯), a State adjoining Wei, who had taken refuge from the Teih, in the time of duke Seuen. His officers feel themselves in very reduced circumstances, and advise their ruler to return with them.

In l. 1, 式, is an initial particle. 微＝衰, 'to be decayed.' The repetition shows the extent of the decay. Comp. 悠 哉 悠 哉, in i. I. 2. The parties had come refugees to Wei, and there perhaps they were slighted, and little cared for. The 微 in l. 3, ＝无, 'but for.' It is difft. from 微＝非, in l. 1. In l. 4, 中 露 ＝ 露 中, like 泥 中 in the 2d st. Maou says Chung-loo and Ne-chung were two towns of Wei that had been assigned to the refugees. Even the imperial editors allow that it is better to take the characters as I have done.

The rhymes are—in st. 1, 微, 归, cat. 15, t. 1; 故, 露, cat. 5, t. 1: in 2, 微, 归; 躬, 中, cat. 9.

二章
何其处也。必有与也。何其久也。必有以也。

三章
狐裘蒙戎。匪车不东。叔兮伯兮。靡所与同。

四章
琐兮尾兮。流离之子。叔兮伯兮。褎如充耳。

2   Why do they rest without stirring?
It must be they expect allies.
Why do they prolong the time?
There must be a reason for their conduct.

3   Our fox-furs are frayed and worn.
Came our carriages not eastwards?
O ye uncles,
You do not sympathize with us.

4   Fragments, and a remnant,
Children of dispersion [are we]!
O ye uncles,
Notwithstanding your full robes, your ears are stopped.

Ode 12. Allusive and narrative. COMPLAINT OF THE MINISTERS OF LE AGAINST THOSE OF WEI FOR NOT ASSISTING THEM. The piece, acc. to the 'Little Preface' is directed against the marquis of Wei, though only his officers are spoken of. In this interpretation of it both the old school and the new agree. We shall find, however, that Maou and Choo differ considerably in their explanations of many of the lines.

St.1. In the Urh-ya 旄丘 is defined as 'a mound, the front of which is high;' and the current definition now is—'a mound high in front, and low behind.' It is said that the very mound thus described is to be recognized in K'ae-chow (开 州), dep. Ta-ming, Chih-le. The speakers in the ode refer to the length of the joints of the koh, to show how long they had been waiting in vain in Wei. We need not, like Maou, seek in the intertwining of the creepers the chose alliance which should subsist between the different States. 诞 = 阔, 'wide apart.' 节 is 'the joints' of the creeping plant. By 叔伯 'uncles,' we are to understand the ministers of Wei, thus honourably designated by those of Le. The complaint against them is in reality intended for their ruler. 何多日 也 = 何其久而不见救乎, 'How is it that we are left unhelped so long?'

St.2. The officers of Wei are spoken of, if not directly addressed; and the speakers seem to be trying to account for their dilatoriness, in itself so strange and unworthy. 处 = 安处, 'to dwell quietly,' i.e., to make no movement in favour of Le. 与 = 与国, 'cooperating States,' i.e., allies who would act with them. 以, = 'a reason,' something by which their conduct was regulated. Maou says that 与 denotes 'benevolence and righteousness' and 以, 'serviceable kindness (功 德);'—which is surely wide of the mark. Attempting to show the application of these interpretations, K'ang-shing takes the stanza as addressed to the marquis of Le:—'Why do you stay here? You must be [vainly] thinking that Wei has benevolence and righteousness;' &c.

St.3. The speakers advance here to a charge against the officers of Wei of a want of sympathy with their distress. They had long been waiting;—so long that their fox-furs, were worn out. 蒙 戎 denotes 'the appearance of disorder,' i.e., says Choo, 'of being worn out.' Le was on the west of Wei, and they had come east in their carriages, imploring help. 靡所与同 = 'have nothing (no feeling) in common with us.' The old interpreters consider all the stanza as

XIII. *Kёen he.*

简兮
一章
简兮简兮。方将万舞。日之方中。在前上处。
二章
硕人俣俣。公庭万舞。有力如虎。执辔如组。

1　Easy and indifferent! easy and indifferent!
　　I am ready to perform in all dances,
　　Then when the sun is in the meridian,
　　There in that conspicuous place.

2　With my large figure,
　　I dance in the ducal courtyard.
　　I am strong [also] as a tiger;
　　The reins are in my grasp like ribbons.

spoken of the officers of Wei, whose disordered dresses were an emblem of their disordered minds, and who had carriages in which they might have come eastwards to the help of Le; but they were not so inclined. That Le was on the west of Wei is a sufficient refutation of this view.

St. 4. The 1st two lines describe the piteous condition of the officers of Le. 琐＝细, 'anything small,' a fragment. 尾, 'the tail ＝末,' 'the end,' or last, of anything. 流离之子＝children carried by a current and dispersed. Again Maou takes these lines of the officers of Wei. 琐尾 is with him 'the app. of being good-looking when young.' Then 流离 is the name of a bird, a kind of owl (枭), which is beautiful when young, and ugly when grown. So had Wei falsified its promises. Wang T‘aou spends pages in vindicating this absurd explanation. 褎 is defined by Choo 多笑貌, 'the app. of many smiles.' K‘ang-shing seems to justify this definition, taking 如充耳＝'like a deaf man.' 'Such a person,' he says, 'not hearing what you say, generally answers with a smile.' This account of the term, however, cannot be supported, and the dict. does not recognize it. We must take 褎 (yew) and 如 together (see Wang Yin-che on 如), as meaning 'the app. of being in full dress.' 充,—'to fill up,' meaning to stop.

The rhymes are—in st. 1, 葛 (prop cat. 15), 节, 日, cat. 12, t. 3; in 2, 处, 与, cat. 5,

t. 2; 久 *, 以, *, cat. 1, t. 2: in 3, 戎, 东, 同, cat. 9: in 4, 子, 耳, cat. 1, t. 2.

Ode 13. Narrative and allusive. HALF IN SCORN, HALF IN SORROW, AN OFFICER OF WEI TELLS OF THE MEAN SERVICE IN WHICH HE WAS EMPLOYED. The 'Little Preface' says the piece censures Wei for not giving offices equal to their merit to its men of worth, but employing them as dancers. This is a correct view of the scope of the piece; but in bringing out the meaning of the different stanzas of it Maou and Choo are wide apart. The imperial editors do not touch upon their differences, and only call attention to Maou's peculiar interpretations in a portion of the 2d stanza, intimating in this way their opinion that they may without loss be consigned to oblivion. I shall copy their example, and make little reference to the old school in the notes. I believe with Le Kwang-te that in this instance, 'only Choo has caught the spirit of the ode.'

St. 1. 简 简＝简 易, giving the idea of taking things easily. 万 is 'a general name for dancing,' or posture-making, for such the dancing of the Chinese was and is. There were the civil and the military dances, 万 being applied more expecially to the latter, when it and 舞 are contrasted. 方 in l. 2 can hardly be translated. K‘ang-shing says that 方将＝方且, which Williams translates—'about to do,' 'just then.' The phrase is in accordance with the idea of the speaker's indifference, which the 1st line gives. In l. 3, 方 has the sense of 今, 'now.' Shin Le-lung (沈 李 龙, pres. dyn.) observes that

三章

左手执籥。右手秉翟。赫如渥赭。公言锡爵。

四章

山有榛。隰有苓。云谁之思。西方美人。彼美人兮。

西方之人兮。

3   In my. left hand I grasp a flute;
     In my right I hold a pheasant's feather.
     I am red as if I were rouged;
     The duke gives me a cup [of spirits].

4   The hazel grows on the hills,
     And the liquorice in the marshes.
     Of whom are my thoughts?
     Of the fine men of the west.
     O those fine men!
     Those men of the west!

the 3d and 4th lines are to be taken together, as indicating that the speaker would dance in a conspicuous place, and not as describing the former the time and the latter the place of his performance. 前上处 is, lit., 'the' high place in front.'

St. 2. 硕＝大, 'large.' There is no idea of 'virtue' in it, as Maou says. 俣 俣＝'stout-like.' 公 庭,—the open court of the duke or marquis. Here, and often elsewhere, we might render 公 by palace;—as in Ana. X. 4. The speaker, in this stanza, is merely describing his various qualities which might have attracted the attention of the marquis of Wei, and made him aware of his abilities. The old school got great mysteries out of the last two lines, that the neglected officers of Wei had great military vigour and great civil capacity. This civil capacity is indicated, they thought, in the warp and woof of the ribbons to which the reins are compared!

St. 3. 籥, acc. to Williams, is 'a reed or pipe with 3 or more holes, resembling a flageolet.' It is more like a flute. 翟＝雉 羽, 'a pheasant's feather.' The flute and the feather were carried in the hand in the civil dances (文 舞). 赭 is the name of red ochre. Here, however, Choo defines it as simply＝赤 色 'a red colour.' The speaker's countenance was red and flushed as if rouged with some red pig-

ment;—with the spirits given him by the marquis, says Le Kwang-te. Rather, we may say, with his exercise in dancing, which the marquis rewarded with a cup. 渥—'to moisten,' 'to be moistened.'

St. 4. The 榛 is described as a small tree, like the chestnut. Lacharme, however, translates the term by corylus arbor. It may, however, be a small variety of the castanaceæ. The 苓, acc. to the Pun-ts'aou, which is followed by Choo, is the 甘 草 'sweet grass,' or liquorice. Maou calls it 大 苦, 'the great bitter,' which Seu Ting thinks may, notwithstanding the dissonance, be another name for the same plant. The hazel and the liquorice were to be found in the places proper to them; but it was not so with the speaker.

The last 4 lines show us the true character of all that precedes. The dancer might speak jestingly of his position, but he felt the degradation of it. He passes in thought from Wei to the early seat of the House of Chow, and from the incapable ruler who neglected him to the chiefs of that western region, who sought out merit, appreciated and rewarded it.

The rhymes are—in st. 1, 舞, 处, cat. 5, t. 2: in 2, 俣, 舞, 虎, 组, ib.: in 3, 籥 *, 翟 *, 爵 *, cat. 2: in 4 榛, 苓 *, 人, 人, 人, cat. 12, t. 1.

XIV.　*Ts‘euen shwuy.*

泉水

一章

毖彼泉水。亦流于淇。有怀于卫。靡日不思。娈彼诸

姬。聊与之谋。

二章

出宿于沛。饮饯于祢。女子有行。远父母兄弟。问我

诸姑。遂及伯姊。

1　How the water bubbles up from that spring,
　　And flows away to the K‘e!
　　My heart is in Wei;
　　There is not a day I do not think of it.
　　Admirable are those, my cousins;
　　I will take counsel with them.

2　When I came forth, I lodged in Tse,
　　And we drank the cup of convoy at Ne.
　　When a young lady goes [to be married],
　　She leaves her parents and brothers;
　　[But] I would ask for my aunts,
　　And then for my elder sister.

Ode 14. Allusive and narrative. A DAUGHTER OF THE HOUSE OF WEI, MARRIED IN ANOTHER STATE, EXPRESSES HER LONGING TO REVISIT WEI. The 'little Preface' does not say who this princess was, nor into what State she married; but it assumes that her parents were dead. It would have been allowable for her, according to the custom at least which prevailed in the Ch‘un Ts‘ew period, to visit them at stated times, so long as they were alive.

St. 1. 毖 (*al.* 必 with 水, 示, and 目 at the side) denotes 'the app. of water issuing from a spring.' 泉水 is taken by K‘ang-shing and Choo as the name of a stream,—the 'Hundred springs (百 泉)' of the pres. day. But it is better to take the characters as in the translation. Those waters, wheresoever they rose, flowed into the K‘e, and so traversed Wei. The speaker, debarred from Wei, could have wished that her lot had been theirs. I can make out no reasonable allusion to her condition in the fact of one river of Wei running into another. The K‘e was a famous river of Wei, rising at the hill of Ta-haou (大 号), and flowing eastwards from the pres. dis. of Lin (林). dep. Chang-tih.

The Shwoh-wăn says it fell into the Ho, but it now pursues a difft. course to the sea. 有 怀, —'I have my cherishings,' *i.e.*, my affections. 娈 = 'good-like' and may be used with reference to the body or mind. 诸 姬,—'all the Ke.' The lady herself was a *Ke*, for that was the surname of the House of Wei. By 'all the Ke' she means her cousins, and the other ladies from States of the same surname, who had accompanied her to the harem. 聊 is explained by Maou by 愿, 'to wish.' Its meaning is not so substantive. K‘ang-shing calls it 且 略 之 辞, 'a particle lightly indicating a purpose.' The lady will consult with her cousins on the subject of her wish to revisit Wei.

St. 2. K‘ang-shing says that *Tse* and *Ne* were places in the State where the lady was married. Rather we may think, with Choo, that they were in Wei, not far from its capital city, and that the speaker is referring to her departure from her native State. People going on a journey offered a sacrifice to the spirit of the way, and when that was concluded, the friends who had escort-

三章

出宿于干。饮饯于言。载脂载舝。还车言迈。遄臻于

卫。不瑕有害。

四章

我思肥泉。兹之永叹。思须与漕。我心悠悠。驾言出

游。以写我忧。

3　I will go forth and lodge in Kan,
　　And we will drink the cup of convoy at Yen.
　　I will grease the axle and fix the pin,
　　And the returning chariot will proceed.
　　Quickly shall we arrive in Wei;—
　　But would not this be wrong?

4　I think of the Fei-ts'euen,
　　I am ever sighing about it.
　　I think of Seu and Ts'aou,
　　Long, long, my heart dwells with them.
　　Let me drive forth and travel there,
　　To dissipate my sorrow.

ed them so far, drank with them, and feasted them close by. This was called 饮饯. 行 = 出嫁, 'to go or come forth to be married.' There is a difficulty with the 4th line, and to see its connection with the whole piece, we must supplement it by the assumption which I have noticed above, that the speaker's parents were dead. Thus Choo explains, and adds:—'When I came here to be married, I left my parents and brothers; how much more can this be said, now that my parents are dead? Can I in this case return to Wei again?' He then takes the last two lines as equivalent to the last two of the prec. stanza. The aunts and the elder sister here are the same, he says, as the cousins there. It is impossible to agree with him in this. From Tso-she's narrative on p. 6 of the 2d year of duke Wăn, we see that he understood 姑 and 姊 as really meaning 'aunts and sisters.' We cannot suppose that any of these had accompanied the lady to the harem. As the imperial editors say, Choo can adduce no usage of terms in support of his view. We must then take 问 not in the sense of 'asking and consulting with,' but of 问安, 'asking about their welfare.' The lady allows that she cannot see her parents and brothers; but there are aunts remaining and her sister. May she not go to Wei and see them?

St.3. The lady supposes now that she can accomplish her purpose, and is on the way to Wei,

her departure to it escorted as that from it had been. *Kan* and *Yen* are two places outside the capital of the State where she was married. 舝 is the iron ends of the axle, that enter the nave of the wheels. If we suppose that only one act is described in the 3d line, the lady says that she will grease the ends of the axle. If there are two acts in it, as the repetition of the particle 载 suggests, the meaning must be that which I have given. 还车,—K'ang-shing and Choo supposes that the carriage is called 'returning.' because the lady purposed to go back to Wei in the same carriage that she had come from it in. This does not seem to be necessary. 迈 = 行, 'to go,' 'to proceed.' 遄 = 疾, 'rapidly.' 臻 = 至, 'to come to.' The last line has greatly vexed the critics. Maou took 瑕 in the sense of 远 'to be far from,' as if the meaning were—'For me thus to go back to Wei will not be anything so injurious as going far from what is right.' Ying-tah also adduces Wang Suh in support of this view; but it is too strained. Choo takes 瑕 as = 何, 'how,' and makes the moral value of the whole ode then turn on the line, The lady has in fancy arrived in Wei, but she suddenly arrests her thoughts and says to herself,—'But would not this be injurious to—contrary to—right and reason?' And so she will not think seriously any more of going back to

XV. *Pih mun.*

北门
一章
出自北门。忧心殷殷。终窭且贫。莫知我艰。已焉

哉。天实为之。谓之何哉。
三章
王事适我。政事一埤益我。我入自外。室人交遍谪

1   I go out at the north gate,
With my heart full of sorrow.
Straitened am I and poor,
And no one takes knowledge of my distress.
So it is !
Heaven has done it ;—
What then shall I say ?

2   The king's business comes on me,
And the affairs of our government in increasing **measure**.
When I come home from abroad,

Wei. K'ang-shing took 瑕 in its ordinary sense of 'a flaw,' 'a fault'; and though his explanation of the line (taking 害＝何) is otherwise inadmissible, he probably suggested to Yen Ts'an a view of it, according to which we should translate,

'It would not be wrong with any harm in it.'

The difficulty, however, with this is that we cannot so translate the same words elsewhere, as in XIX. 2, where we are forced to take 不瑕 as＝何不, a question, expressing a doubt in the mind. So Wang Yin-che, on the term 遐.

St.4. In this the lady repeats her longing desire to revisit Wei ; and we cannot say from it positively whether her desire was gratified or not. The *Fei-ts'euen* was a river of Wei, which she had crossed, probably, on her departure from it. Many identify it with what is now called 'the Water of a hundred streams.' The account of it given by Maou, from the Urh-ya, is all but unintelligible; and does not affect our understanding of the ode. 兹＝此;— 'this is what I am ever sighing for.' *Seu* and

Ts'aou were two cities of Wei which the lady had passed on her leaving. Ts'aou—see on VI.1. 驾,—'to yoke,' 'to put the horses to the carriage.' 写,—lit., 'to overturn,' as a vessel, and so empty it of its contents,＝'to remove,' 'to dissipate.'

The rhymes are—in st.1, 淇．思．姬．谋 *,, cat.1, t 1 · in 2, 沛，祢，弟，姊, cat.15, t.2 ; in 3, 干，言, cat.14; 瀳，迈，卫，害, cat.15, t.3: in 4, 泉，叹 cat.14; 漕 *,, 悠，游，忧, cat.3, t. 1.

Ode 15. Metaphorical and narrative. An OFFICER OF WEI SETS FORTH HIS HARD LOT, AND HIS SILENCE UNDER IT IN SUBMISSION TO HEAVEN. The object of the piece, acc. to Maou, is to expose the government of Wei, which neglected men of such worth.

St. 1. The south is the region of brightness, and the north of darkness; and so the officer here represents himself as passing from light to darkness. So, Maou and Choo. If we suppose, with Yen Ts'an and others, that the speaker had quitted the capital by the north gate on

我。已焉哉。天实为之。谓之何哉。

三章
王事敦我。政事一埤遗我。我入自外。室人交遍摧

我。已焉哉。天实为之。谓之何哉。

The members of my family all emulously reproach me.
So it is!
Heaven has done it;—
What then shall I say?

3　The king's business is thrown on me,
And the affairs of our government are left to me more and more.
When I come home from abroad,
The members of my family all emulously thrust at me.
So it is!
Heaven has done it;—
What then shall I say?

some public service, then the ode is all narrative. 股 股 = 忧, 'sorrowful'; it denotes 'the app. of grief.' 终,—see on V. 1. This line should be decisive as to the meaning of 终 in the *She* when followed by 且. 窶 and 贫 are of cognate signification. The critics try to distinguish between them here, and say that the former denotes 'the want of money to make presents,' and the latter, 'the want of it to supply one's own wants.' In 1.4 the ruler of Wei may be specially intended; but the terms are quite general. 已 焉 哉 = 既 然 哉, 'it is so!' or 'since it is so.' The 'Complete Digest' says, 'Take care and not make Heaven here equivalent to Fate;' but it does not say what the word really indicates. The idea is our 'Providence.' 谓 in 1.7 = 如, as often.

St. 2. 王 事 = 王 所 命 之 事, 'affairs ordered by the king,'—committed by him to Wei for execution. 政 事 refers to the affairs of the government of Wei. We must suppose, however, that they are not great affairs which are intended, but vexatious and trivial

matters. The speaker would not have been in such poverty if he had been high in office. 适 = 至, 'to go or come to.' —— both by Choo and Wang Yin-che, is explained by 皆, 'all.' Wang T'aou prefers the meaning of 乃, 'are,' which —— also has. 埤 = 厚 or 增, as in the translation. 室 人 = 家 人, 'the members of the family.' 交,—as in Mencius I. Pt. i. I. 4. 谪 = 责, 'to reproach.'

St. 3. Choo follows K'ang-shing in reading 敦 *tuy*, and explaining it by 投 掷,—as in the translation. Maou's 敦 *(tun)*, = 厚, is not so appropriate. 遗, 'to be left to,' = 加, 'to be laid upon.' 摧, both by Maou and Choo is explained by 沮, 'to repress.' The word means 'to press upon,' 'to throw down,' 'to push.'

The rhymes are—in st. 1, 门, 股 *, 贫 *, 艰 *, cat. 13; in 2, 适, 益, 谪, cat. 15, t. 3; in 3, 敦 (prop. cat. 13), 遗, 摧, cat. 15, t. 1: in all the stt., 哉 之, 哉, cat. 1, t. 1.

XVI. *Pih fung.*

北风

一章
北风其凉。雨雪其雱。惠而好我。携手同行。其虚其

邪。既亟只且。

二章
北风其喈。雨雪其霏。惠而好我。携手同归。其虚其

邪。既亟只且。

1   Cold blows the north wind ;
     Thick falls the snow.
     Ye who love and regard me,
     Let us join hands and go together.
     Is it a time for delay?
     The urgency is extreme!

2   The north wind whistles;
     The snow falls and drifts about.
     Ye who love and regard me,
     Let us join hands, and go away for ever.
     Is it a time for delay?
     The urgency is extreme!

Ode. 16. Metaphorical. SOME ONE OF WEI PRESSES HIS FRIENDS TO LEAVE THE COUNTRY WITH HIM AT ONCE, IN CONSEQUENCE OF THE PRE-VAILING OPPRESSION AND MISERY. St. 1. 雱 is the 'app. of much snow.' The first two lines in all the stanzas are a metaphorical description of the miserable condition of the State. Choo explains 惠 by 爱, 'to love.' K'ang-shing makes it='ye who are of a loving nature.' Yen Ts'an well explains the line by 以 恩 惠 相 与 者, 'ye who have kindly intercourse with me.' We might translate the whole by 'O friends.' 携 is 'to lead by the hand'; 携 手 here, 'to take one another by the hand.' The 5th line is the difficulty of the ode. The 其 is both graphic and interrogative, which decides against the explanation of K'ang-shing:—'The forbear-ing and good all think things have come to a climax, and that they should leave. We also ought to go.' The Urh-ya quotes the line as 其 虚 其 徐, and so 邪 is here read. How it comes to have that pronunciation and mean-ing—'slow,' 'leisurely'--is a point on which pages are written. But 邪 being taken in this sense, we are led to give a cognate one to 虚, and Choo, after one of the Ch'ings, explains it by 宽 貌, 'forbearing-like.' I have no doubt the translation gives the idea of the line correctly. Lacharme has *nullus moræ datur locus.* 既 = 已, in last ode. 亟 = 急, expressing 'extreme urgency.' 只 且 (*tseu*) go together, particles untranslateable.

St. 2. 喈,—see i. II. 1. It here represents the rapid whistling of the wind, which is the reason, probably, that it is made to rhyme with 霏 and 归. 霏 denotes 'the app. of the falling snow, scattered about.' Choo takes 归 here in the sense of 大 归, 'going away for good.'

三章

莫赤匪狐。莫黑匪乌。惠而好我。携手同车。其虚其

邪。既亟只且。

3　Nothing red is seen but foxes,
　　Nothing black but crows.
　　Ye who' love and regard me,
　　Let us join hands, and go together in our carriages.
　　Is it a time for delay?
　　The urgency is extreme!

XVII.　*Tsing neu.*

静女

一章

静女其姝。俟我于城隅爱而不见。搔首踟蹰。

1　How lovely is the retiring girl!
　　She was to await me at a corner of the wall.
　　Loving and not seeing her,
　　I scratch my head, and am in perplexity.

St. 3. Foxes and crows were both creatures of evil omen. Every thing about Wei was of evil auspice. 莫 赤 匪 狐，＝无 有 赤 而 非 狐, ' there is nothing red which is not a fox.'

The rhymes are—in st. 1, 凉, 雩, 行 *, cat. 10: in 2, 嗜, 霍, 归, cat. 15, t. 1: in 3, 狐, 乌, 车, *, cat. 5, t. 1: in all the stanzas, 邪 *, 且 *, *ib.*

Ode 17. Narrative. A GENTLEMAN DEPLORES HIS DISAPPOINTMENT IN NOT MEETING A LADY ACCORDING TO ENGAGEMENT, AND CELEBRATES HER GIFTS AND BEAUTY. This is the first of many odes, more or less of a similar character, in the interpretation of which the new and old schools greatly differ. Acc. to Maou, it describes the virtues of a correct and modest lady, who would make a good mate for a prince; acc. to Choo, it refers to a licentious connection between two young persons. The account of it in the 'little Preface' may be made to agree with either interpretation. All that is there said is that ' the piece is directed against the age. The marquis of Wei had no principle, and the marchioness no virtue.' On Choo's view we have only to say, 'Like rulers, like people.' On Maou's that we have a description of what the marchioness should have been.

The imperial editors give both views in their notes, inclining themselves to maintain that of Maou. It will be seen from the notes below that I do not agree with them. It is allowed on all hands that Choo's interpretations are the most natural deductions from the words of the odes; but it is alleged that he is superficial, and that the deeper we dig, the more do we find to support the older views. Here and elsewhere I have tried to follow Maou and his advocates in all their researches; but it is often impossible to assent to their conclusions without the entire surrender of one's own judgment.

St. 1. 静 means 'still,' 'quiet,' 'retiring.' The idea which it conveys is of one who is modest and correct; and this is held to be inconsistent with Choo's view. Still, the speaker would not be likely to give a bad character to the lady, who was bestowing her favours on him. Ts'aou Suy-chung (曹 粹 中; Sung dyn.) distinguishes between 静 女 and 游 女, or 'the rambling girls' of i.IX. The latter were girls of the common people, whose circumstances did not allow them to keep themselves immured in the harem, whereas the former were daughters of officers' families, who could and did keep themselves so retired. On this view 静 in the text need not say anything of the character of the lady. 姝 ＝美 色, 'beautiful.' 城 隅,—'a corner of the city wall.' 踟 蹰, denotes the 'app. of a man stopping as he walks,' and hence is used to signify ' irresolute,' ' perplexed.'—Morrison quotes the stanza under 姝, and remarks on

二章

静女其娈。贻我彤管。彤管有炜。说怿女美。

三章

自牧归荑。洵美且异。匪女之为美。美人之贻。

2   How handsome is the retiring girl!
She presented to me a red tube.
Bright is the red tube;—
I delight in the beauty of the girl.

3   From the pasture lands she gave me a shoot of the white grass,
Truly elegant and rare.
It is not you, O grass, that are elegant;—
You are the gift of an elegant girl.

the last line:—‘It is curious to mark the similarity which exists among men of every clime and every age. Man, when vexed and embarrassed, scratches his head with his hand, in China as in Europe, both in ancient and modern times.’

Let us see what Maou makes of the stanza. ‘静 denotes correct and quiet. When a lady's virtue is correct and quiet, and she acts according to law and rule, she is one to be pleased with. 姝 means beautiful; 俟 means to wait. We have “a corner of the city wall” to express what was high and could not be passed over.’ This is all we have from Maou. Expanding and explaining his view, Ying-tah says, ‘The meaning is, There is a correct and modest girl, who is beautiful, and could be submissive and obedient to her husband, waiting till she is assured of its propriety before doing anything, guarding herself as by a city wall, which is high and cannot be passed over. Such is her virtue, and therefore I love her, and wish she were the ruler's mate. Since I love her in my heart, and cannot see her, I scratch my head, and look perplexed.’ I am persuaded the student who cares to read this with attention will pronounce it to be *mere drivelling*. The meaning which it is thus attempted to force on the 2d line is simply ridiculous.

St. 2. 娈,—as in XIV. 1. 贻 —‘to present to.’ 彤 管 is ‘a red reed or tube;’ but what article is denoted by it, we of course, cannot tell. The bamboo tubes, with which pencils are now made, are called 笔 管. There might

be many things of small tubes, painted or varnished red, among a young lady's possessions, one of which she might present to a friend or admirer. Maou makes the ‘red reed’ to have been an instrument used by a literate class of ladies in the harem, who acted as secretaries to the mistress, and recorded the rules and duties for all the inmates; and then he says that the presenting the red reed is equivalent to acquainting the speaker with the exact obedience she paid to the ancient regulations of the harem! The mere statement of this view is its refutation. Choo says that 炜 means ‘red-like;’ but it is the brilliance of the colour, and not the colour itself, which is intended. 说, (=悦) and 怿 are cognate in meaning, ‘to be pleased with,’ ‘to delight in.’ 女 美=女 之 美, ‘the beauty of the girl.’

St. 3. 牧=牧 地, ‘pasture grounds.’ 归 =贻, ‘to give,’ or ‘to send to;’—as in Ana. XIII. i. 1. 荑 means ‘a plant just sprouting.’ It is accepted, here, that the plant was the 茅, or ‘white grass’ of ii. XII. 洵,—here, as often, an adverb, meaning ‘truly.’ 女 = 汝, ‘you,’ addressed to the grass. 匪,= 非, ‘it is not,’ not simply=不, ‘not,’ as frequently.

The rhymes are—in st. 1, 姝 ∗, 隅 ∗, 蹰 ∗, cat. 4, t. 1; in 2, 娈, 管, cat. 14; 炜, 美, cat. 15, t. 2: in 3, 异, 贻, cat. 1, t. 1.

XVIII.　*Sin-t'ae.*

新台

一章
新台有泚。河水弥弥。燕婉之求。籧篨不鲜。

二章
新台有洒。河水浼浼。燕婉之求。籧篨不殄。

三章
鱼网之设。鸿则离之。燕婉之求。得此戚施。

1　Fresh and bright is the New Tower,
　　On the waters of the Ho, wide and deep.
　　A pleasant, genial mate she sought,
　　[And has got this] vicious bloated mass!

2　Lofty is the New Tower,
　　On the waters of the Ho, flowing still.
　　A pleasant, genial mate she sought,
　　[And has got this] vicious bloated mass!

3　It was a fish net that was set,
　　And a goose has fallen into it.
　　A pleasant, genial mate she sought,
　　And she has got this hunchback.

Ode 18. Narrative and allusive. SATIRIZING THE MARRIAGE OF DUKE SEUEN AND SEUEN KEANG. In the introduction to the notes on ode 9, it has been stated how duke Seuen took to himself the lady who had been contracted to marry his son Keih. It is only necessary to add here, that to accomplish his purpose, he caused a tower to be built on the Ho, where he received the lady on her way from Ts'e and forced her. The general opinion of scholars is that the tower was in the pres. dis. of Kwan-shing (观 城), dep. Ts'aou-chow, Shan-tung.

St. 1. 泚 = 鲜明, 'fresh and bright.' The Shwoh-wăn quotes the line with 玼, which is, probably, the more correct reading. 弥 弥 denotes 'the full appearance of the stream.' 燕 婉 is explained by 安 顺, 'quiet and docile,' and is understood as descriptive of Keih-tsze, whom Seuen Këang should have married. Two meanings are given in the dict. to 籧 篨. The first is, 'a coarse bamboo mat;' the 2d, 'an ugly disease,' which is said to prevent its subjects from stooping down. Choo observes that if you roll up a bamboo mat, so as to form a sort of grain-barrel, it presents the appearance of a man bloated and swollen, so that he cannot stoop down, and hence the characters were used as a designation of that disease. However we may account for the applications of the terms. they were so employed,—so long ago. The disease must have been dropsy. We are not to suppose that duke Seuen did suffer from this; he is here spoken of as doing so, to indicate his loathsomeness. Choo explains 鲜 by 少, 'few;' but I do not see how the word can here be construed with that meaning. I take it, with K'ang-shing, as = 善, 'good.'

St. 2. 洒 = 高峻, 'lofty.' 浼 浼 denotes 'the app. of a stream flowing quietly.' Yen Ts'an accepts the account of it as the ·app. of a muddy stream.' Such should be its signification if the character be read *mei*; but the pronunciation here is *mëen*; 殄 means 'to cut off,' 'to exterminate,'—a meaning which is inapplicable here. I must again agree with K'ang-shing, who thinks 殄 was an old form of 腆. = 善, 'good.'

XIX. *Urh-tsze.*

二子乘舟
一章
二子乘舟。泛泛其景。愿言思子。中心养养。
二章
二子乘舟。泛泛其逝。愿言思子。不暇有害。

1   The two youths got into their boats,
    Whose shadows floated about [on the water].
    I think longingly of them,
    And my heart is tossed about in uncertainty.

2   The two youths got into their boats,
    Which floated away [on the stream].
    I think longingly of them;—
    Did they not come to harm?

St.3. The *hung* is described as a large species of the *yen* (雁); see on IX.3. 离 = 遇, 'to meet with;' here='to come or fall into.' 戚 施 is the name for another 'ugly infliction' of an opposite nature to that denoted by *k'euch'oo*. That prevents a man from bending down; this prevents him from standing up straight. It is what is now called 驼背, or hunch-back. The 得此 shows how we should supplement the last line of the other stanzas.

The rhymes are—in st.1, 泚 *, 弥 *, 鲜 * (prop. cat.14), cat.15, t.2: in 2, 洒 *, 浼 *, 殄 *, cat. 13: in 3, 离 *, 施 *, cat.17.

Ode 19. Narrative. SURMISES AS TO THE DEATH OF TWO SONS OF DUKE SEUEN. See again the introductory note to ode 9. Seuen Këang and Soh, one of her sons, had long plotted to get rid of Keih-tsze, the duke's son by E Këang, to clear the way for Soh's succession to the State; and at last the duke was prevailed on to send him on a mission to Ts'e, having arranged beforehand that he should be waylaid by ruffians and murdered, soon after he landed on the northern bank of the Ho. Show, Seuen Këang's other son, became aware of this design, and as there was a close, brotherly, intimacy between him and Keih-tsze, he told him of it, and exhorted him to make his escape to another State. Keih-tsze being resolved to meet his fate

rather than run away, the other made him drunk, took his boat, personated him, and was murdered by the ruffians;—thus endeavouring by the sacrifice of himself to save his brother. When Keih-tsze recovered from the effects of his intoxication, and found that Show was gone, he divined his object, and followed after him in another boat. It was too late. He approached the spot, crying out in language which must always recal to a western reader the words of Nisus,

' *Me, me! adsum qui feci ; in me convertite ferrum.*'

But Show was already murdered, and the ruffians, 'that they might make no mistake,' put Keih-tsze to death also.

The duke gave out that his sons had been killed by bandits, but the people had their suspicions, and they are supposed to have expressed them enigmatically in the two verses of this ode.

St. 1. The 二 子 are Show and Keih-tsze. 泛, see on I. i. The repetition of the term sets the vessels vividly before us, floating on the water. The idea of 'floating about,' without direction, which 泛 is said to express, does not apply, however to the 2d l. of the next stanza. 景 is the old form of 影, 'a shadow.' The 彡 was first added by Koh Hung (葛 洪) of the Tsin dynasty. 愿 言,—as in V. 3, 4; but the 则 there makes us look more for a substantive meaning in 愿. In this and many other places 愿 言 appears to me to have no more meaning than 薄 言. 每,—'every time,' 'whenever.' 养 养 is explained as 'the app. of sorrow and perplexity.' Choo says the characters are equivalent to 漾 漾. Others would read 恙 恙, and 洋 洋.

St. 2. 逝 = 往, 'to go,' 'to proceed to.' 不 暇 有 害,—see on XIV. 3. The 害 indeed in that case is said of wrong,—what is injurious to the right; in this 'of harm,'—what is injurious to the person. No better meaning, however, can be drawn out of the line.

The rhymes are—in st. 1, 景,∗ 养, cat. 10: in 2, 逝, 害, cat. 15, t. 3.

CONCLUDING NOTE ON THE BOOK. The odes of Wei have the 1st place in those which are styled 'Lessons of Manners, Degenerate (变 风).' Certainly they are of a different character from those of the two former Books, which contain the 'Lessons of Manners, Correct.' The influence of king Wăn and his queen, and of the dukes of Chow and Shaou, had left no very beneficial effects in Wei. And yet, the horrible licentiousness and atrocious crimes which disgraced the State of Wei were mainly the fruit of the polygamy which the founders of the Chow dynasty approved and exemplified.

Lëw Kin observes that as the odes of Wei occupy the first place in the 'Lessons, Degenerate,' so that division of them which is assigned to P'ei takes precedence of the others, because no disorders of the social state, and no neglect of the principles of good government, greater than what appear in them, could be found.

BOOK IV. THE ODES OF YUNG.

I. *Peh chow.*

鄘一之四

柏舟

一章

泛彼柏舟。在彼中河。髧彼两髦。实维我仪。之死矢

靡他。母也天只。不谅人只。

1   It floats about, that boat of cypress wood,
There in the middle of the Ho.
With his two tufts of hair falling over his forehead,
He was my mate;
And I swear that till death I will have no other.
O mother, O Heaven,
Why will you not understand me?

TITLE OF THE BOOK.—鄘 一 之 四, 'Yung; Book IV. of Part I.' There is little to be said here beyond what has been stated on the title of the last Book. The statistical account of the pres. dynasty says that the capital of Yung was in the north-east of the pres. dis. of Keih (汲), dep. Wei-hwuy. Some writers refer it to the south-west of the dis. of Sin-heang (新 乡), which would bring us to about the same spot.

Ode 1. Allusive. PROTEST OF A WIDOW AGAINST BEING URGED TO MARRY AGAIN. Acc. to the 'Little Preface,' this ode was made by Kung Këang, the widow of Kung-peh, son of the marquis He (僖 侯; B.C. 854—813). Kung-peh dying an early death, her parents (who must have been the marquis of Ts'e and his wife or one of his wives) wanted to force her to a second marriage;—against which she here protests. Choo says this account rests on the sole authority of the Preface, but he is content to follow

it. It is not, however, without its difficulties. Acc. to Sze-ma Ts'ëen, Kung-peh was attacked at their father's grave by his younger brother Ho (和), and killed himself. Ho then took his place, and had a very long rule in Wei of 55 years (he is known as duke Woo;—武公), dying at the age of 95;—see the 'Narratives of the States,' VI. Pt.i.6. Duke Woo then must have been 40. when he came to the marquisate, and Kung-peh must have been older. If the reference in the ode be to him, the Preface is incorrect, when it says that 'he died an early death.'

In both stt., ll.1,2. See on III. i. and xix. 'The middle of the Ho,' and 'the side of the Ho,' are simply rhythmical variations. The allusion is probably to the speaker's widowhood, which left her like 'a boat floating about on the water.' K'ang-shing interprets it rather differently:— 'A boat on the river is like a wife in her husband's family;—each is in the proper place.'

二章

泛彼柏舟。在彼河側。髧彼两髦。实维我特。之死矢
靡慝。母也天只。不谅人只。

2　It floats about, that boat of cypress wood,
　　There by the side of the Ho.
　　Wi⁺h his two tufts of hair falling over his forehead,
　　He was my only one；
　　And I swear that till death I will not do the evil thing.
　　O mother, O Heaven,
　　Why will you not understand me?

II. *Ts'ëang yew ts'ze.*

墙有茨

一章

墙有茨。不可埽也。中冓之言。不可道也。所可道
也。言之丑也。

1　The tribulus grows on the wall,
　　And cannot be brushed away.
　　The story of the inner chamber
　　Cannot be told.
　　What would have to be told
　　Would be the vilest of recitals.

Ll. 3, 4. 髧 denotes 'the app. of the hair hanging down or forward;' 髦 describes the mode in which the hair was kept, while a boy or young man's parents were alive, parted into two tufts from the *pia mater*, and brought down as low as the eyebrows on either side of the forehead. Both Maou and Choo take 仪 as＝匹, 'mate;' thus making both the lines refer to the deceased husband. Similarly they explain 特 also by 匹. Han Ying read 值,＝'the price or equivalent of.' The term indicates that which stands out alone, and, as Hwang Tso (黄佐; Ming dyn.) says, is appropriately used by a wife of her husband. Yen Ts'an understands these two lines of the lady herself, wearing her hair this way, in token of her widowhood. 仪 would suit this view, if it were otherwise tenable; but 特 must be strained to comport with it.

Ll. 4, 5. 之＝至, 'to,' 'till;' 矢＝誓, 'to swear.' 也 and 只 must both be taken as particles of exclamation. Maou says that by 'Heaven' the father is intended, while Choo says that the mother is here called Heaven by the distressed lady, and supposes that her father may have been dead. Why may we not suppose that she really appeals to Heaven? 谅 is hardly sufficiently exhausted by the 信, 'to believe,' of Maou and Choo. Its meaning is 'to believe and sympathize with,'—our 'to understand.' 慝＝邪, 'that which is evil or depraved.' In thus characterizing a second marriage, the lady expresses her abhorrence of such a thing in the strongest way; and Confucius, it is said, preserved such an instance of virtue, as an example to all future ages. One of the Ch'ings gives his opinion on the point thus:—'It may be asked whether a widow left solitary and poor, with none to depend on, may not marry again, to which I reply that such is

二章

墙有茨。不可襄也。中冓之言。不可详也。所可详

也。言之长也。

三章

墙有茨。不可束也。中冓之言。不可读也。所可读

也。言之辱也。

2   The tribulus grows on the wall,
     And cannot be removed.
     The story of the inner chamber
     Cannot be particularly related.
     What might be particularly related
     Would be a long story.

3   The tribulus grows on the wall,
     And cannot be bound together, [and taken away].
     The story of the inner chamber
     Cannot be recited.
     What might be recited
     Would be the most disgraceful of things.

the suggestion of subsequent times through fear of want and starvation. But to die of want is a very small matter, while the loss of chastity is a very great matter!' But why should Chinese moralists mete out different measures for the widow and the widower?

The rhymes are—in st. 1 舟, 毳 (prop. cat. 2), cat. 3, t. 1; 河, 仪 *, 他, cat. 17; 天 人, cat. 12, t. 1: in 2, 舟, 毳; 侧 特, 慝, cat. 1, t. 3; 天, 人.

Ode 2. Allusive. Tʜᴇ ᴛʜɪɴɢs ᴅᴏɴᴇ ɪɴ ᴛʜᴇ ʜᴀʀᴇᴍ ᴏғ ᴛʜᴇ ᴘᴀʟᴀᴄᴇ ᴏғ Wᴇɪ ᴡᴇʀᴇ ᴛᴏᴏ sʜᴀᴍᴇ-ғᴜʟ ᴛᴏ ʙᴇ ᴛᴏʟᴅ. This piece is supposed, on the authority of the 'Little Preface,' to have reference to the connection between Ch'aou-peh, or duke Seuen's son Hwan (顽), and Seuen Këang, which has been mentioned on the 9th ode of last Book.

In all the stt., ll. 1, 2. The *tsze* is said in the Urh-ya, to be the *tsih-le* (蒺 藜), which Williams simply calls a 'very spinous plant.' Medhurst says it is the 'tribulus terrestris,' which is probably a correct identification. It is described as a creeper, growing along the ground, with a small leaf, and triangular seeds or seed-vessels, armed with prickles. There are two varieties of it: one bearing a small yellow flower; the other having a purple flower. From the picture of the plant in the Japanese plates, the botanist whom I have already referred to, judged

that it was the *trapa bicornis;* but that is an aquatic plant, and would not be spoken of as 'growing on a wall.' 扫 is interchanged with 扫 'to brush or sweep away.' 襄＝除, 'to remove.' 束＝束 而 去 之,—as in the translation. A plant like the tribulus on the wall was unsightly and injurious to it; but the attempt to remove it would be still more injurious, and it is therefore let alone. So with the deeds done in the harem, vile and disgusting, so that it was better not to speak of them openly.—The allusive portion of the stanzas is thus explained.

Ll. 3, 4. All that Maou says of 中 冓 is 内冓, leaving 冓 unexplained. K'ang-shing tries to explain the phrase by taking the term as＝构,＝成, 'to complete,' 'to do.' The Shwoh-wăn seems to make it the name of the couples of a roof, or of all its wooden structure (中 冓 交 积 材). Whatever difficulty there may be with the term, the phrase is acknowledged to mean the inside of the palace, in opposition to the wall, and not only so, but the most secret and retired part of the interior, —the harem. 言 is not to be taken of the words spoken in the harem, but of the deeds done there, put into words and told. Yen Ts'an says well:—中 冓 之 言, 但 谓 闺 门

III. *Keun-tsz' këae laou.*

君子偕老

一章

君子偕老。副笄六珈。委委佗佗。如山如河。象服是

宜。子之不淑。云如之何。

二章

玼兮玼兮。其之翟也。鬒发如云。不屑髢也。玉之瑱

1   The husband's to their old age;
    In her headdress, and the cross-pins, with their six jewels;
    Easy and elegant in her movements;
    [Stately] as a mountain, [majestic] as a river,
    Weil beseeming her pictured robes :—
    [But] with your want of virtue, O lady,
    What have you to do with these things?

2   How rich and splendid
    Is her pheasant-figured robe!

之事，不必以为顽与夫人淫昏之言．道＝言, 'to speak about.' 详, ＝'to speak about particularly.' 读, 'to read,' here = 'to recite.' Maou explains the term by 抽, which K'ang-shing explains again by 出, 'to give forth,' 'to publish.'

Ll. 5, 6. 所可道,—可 has to be taken in the conditional mood, past complete tense,— 'what would have to be told.' 言之长,— 'would be the longest of stories.' 'The speaker,' says Choo, 'does not wish to enter on the story, and so he excuses himself by saying that if he once began, it would be difficult for him to end.'

The rhymes are—in st. 1, 埽 *, 道 *, 道 *, 且, cat. 3, t. 2: in 2, 襄, 详, 详, 长, cat. 10: in 3, 束, 读, 读, 辱, cat. 3, t. 3.

Ode 3. Narrative. CONTRAST BETWEEN THE BEAUTY AND SPLENDOUR OF SEUEN KEANG, AND HER VICIOUSNESS. This piece like the last is supposed to be directed against Seuen Këang, the true spirit and meaning of it coming out in the last two lines of the 1st stanza.

St. 1. 君子 is here, as often, the designation of 'the husband.' 偕老, see iii. VI. 4.

We must understand an 与 before 君子. The subject of the line is the lady of whom the ode speaks, though she does not directly appear in it till the 6th line. 'Woman is born,' says Choo He,' for the service of the man with her person, so that the wife draws out her life with her husband, and should die with him. Hence

when her husband dies, she calls herself "The person not yet dead." She henceforth is simply waiting for death, and ought not to have any desire of becoming the wife of another.' 副 *(fow)* was the head-dress worn by the queen or the princess of a State, when taking part in sacrifices. It was made of hair. 笄 was 'a hair-pin;' here a special article of the kind, used in connection with the *fow*, and adorned with six gems (珈＝玉之加, gems attached). To the end or head of the pin was attached the string of the ear-plug, and hence I imagine we must take 笄 in the plural, a pin crossing from each side of the head. 委委 is referred by Maou to the elegance of the lady's movements, and 佗佗 to her virtuous appearance. The Urh-ya makes the whole line to mean 'elegant,' or 'beautiful' (美). Comp. 委蛇 in ii. VII. 象服,—see on the Shoo, II. iv. 4; and the 2d line of next stanza. 子 is to be taken as addressed to Seuen Këang. Notwithstanding the splendour of her array and the elegance of her carriage, she was 不淑 'not good.' Yen Ts'an directs attention to v. III. and to viii. XI., as two odes constructed on the same model as this, in which the spirit and design of the piece comes out in a single line, 'one or two words coolly interjected.'

St. 2. 玼 denotes what has a rich lustre. 翟 is what is called 'the Tartar pheasant.' Here the term denotes the robe of the princess used in sacrificing, which had such a pheasant

也。象之揥也。扬且之皙也。胡然而天也。胡然而

帝也。

三章

瑳兮瑳兮。其之展也。蒙彼绉绤。是绁袢也。子之清

Her black hair in masses like clouds,
No false locks does she descend to.
There are her ear-plugs of jade,
Her comb-pin of ivory,
And her high forehead, so white.
She appears like a visitant from heaven!
She appears like a goddess!

3　How rich and splendid
　Is her robe of state!
　It is worn over the finest muslin of dolichos,
　The more cumbrous and warm garment being removed.

brilliantly represented upon it. 鬒＝黑, 'black.' 不 屑,—see on iii. X. 3. 髢 is defined in the Shwoh-wăn by 益发, 'an increase of the hair.' It is our 'false hair.' 瑱＝塞耳, 'ear-stoppers.' We shall speak of them hereafter. The 揥 is described by Williams as 'a hair-pin, which was used to secure the hair in a knot.' But it was not used to secure the hair at all, but 'to scratch the head (搔 首).' It was, in fact, a rudimentary comb, consisting of a single tooth, and is said therefore to correspond to 'the present comb (若 今 之 篦 儿).' Being elegantly made of ivory (象＝ 象 骨), it was worn in the hair, as an ornament. 扬 is given in the dict. as meaning 'the space above and below the eyebrows,' but Maou, who is followed by Choo, simply calls it 眉 上 广, 'being broad or high above the eyebrows.' 且 is taken by Choo as the particle. Yen Ts'an says it is the conjunction 'and;' but I cannot follow him in his explanation of 扬 on that view. Wang Yin-che and Wang T'aou also say that 之, in this and the other lines of the stanza, is merely 'a helping particle;' and it is better to rest in that view, than to try

to keep its common meaning;—'The whiteness of her high forehead!' In the last two lines, 而＝如, 'as.' This may be said to be universally acknowledged, and there is also a general agreement as to the meaning, though it is variously expressed without an attempt to define the force of the other terms. Choo says 一见 者惊, 犹鬼神也, 'Beholders are struck with awe, as if she were a spiritual being.' Heu Heen (许 谦; Yeen dyn.) says, 'With such splendour of beauty and dress, how is it that she is here? She has come down from heaven! She is a spiritual being!' Lacharme takes 帝 in the sense of emperor:—Tu primo aspectu cœlos (pulchritudine) et imperatorem (majestate), adœquas! But 帝 was not in use at this time in the sense of emperor. The rulers of China were only kings. I take 胡 然,' 'how so,' as an expression of surprise and admiration. 天＝天 人, 'a heavenly person.' 帝＝'a goddess.' Elsewhere we have 帝 女 in this sense.

St. 3. 瑳 has the same meaning as 玼, in the last st. 展 (in the 3d tone) was the name of 'a robe worn at ceremonial interviews with the ruler, and in receiving guests.' K'ang-shing points out that the character should be 襢; which we have in the Le Ke. 蒙, 'covering,'

扬。扬且之颜也。展如之人兮。邦之媛也。

Clear are her eyes; fine is her forehead;
Full are her temples.
Ah! such a woman as this!
The beauty of the country!

IV. *Sang-chung.*

桑中
一章
爰采唐矣。沬之乡矣。云谁之思。美孟姜矣。期我乎
桑中。要我乎上宫。送我乎淇之上矣。

1   I am going to gather the dodder,
In the fields of Mei.
But of whom are my thoughts?
Of that beauty, the eldest of the Këang.
She made an appointment with me in Sang-chung;
She will meet me in Shang-kung;
She will accompany me to K'e-shang.

=‘worn over.’ 绤 is the name for crape, a crinkled fabric; but I do not understand how that could be made from the fibres of the dolichos. I therefore adopt the explanation of Ying-tah, that the term denotes here ‘the finest quality of fine dolichos cloth.’ 是绁袢也 is almost unintelligible. Choo takes 绁袢 in the sense of ‘to bind tightly,’ as if the robe were worn tightly over the muslin; but in doing this he, as if unconsciously, changes 袢 into 绊. 袢 has the sense of ‘hot with garments,’ ‘abundance of clothing’ (see Morrison, *in ver.*). Maou keeps the meaning of 袢, but does not explain 绁, for which Ying-tah gives 去, ‘to remove,’ thereby changing it into 渫. This view seems the better of the two, as the fine dolichos was worn in summer. Both Maou and Choo think they have sufficiently explained 清 by 视清 明, ‘seeing clearly.’ ‘We do so,’ says Ying-tah, ‘with the eyes. Hence 清 is used as a name for them.’ 颜, denotes ‘fulness about the temples.’ 展如 =‘really,’ and Yen-Ts‘an carries

on the line to the next as its subject,—‘ Really this woman is the beauty of the country.’ It seems better, however, to make the meaning of the line complete in itself,—as in the translation. A beautiful woman is called 媛.

The rhymes are—in st.1, 珈, 佗, 河, 宜 *, 何, cat.17; in 2 崔 (prop. cat.2), 髢 (should have 易 below)*, 揥 *, 晳, 帝 *, cat. 16, t. 3: in 3, 展, 袢, 颜, 媛, cat.14.

Ode 4. Narrative. A GENTLEMAN SINGS OF HIS INTIMACY AND INTRIGUES WITH VARIOUS NOBLE LADIES. The piece, acc. to the ‘Little Preface,’ was directed against the lewd customs of Wei. This Choo denies. It will be well to remit the question of the interpretation to a concluding note.

In all the stt., ll. 1, 2. 爰,—see on iii. VI. 3. The *t‘ang* is a parasite growing on plants and trees, and yielding a seed, ‘like the grub of the silk worm,’ which is used in medicine. Maou improperly calls it the *mung* (蒙) vegetable, and Medhurst says, perhaps after him, that it is ‘a culinary vegetable;’ but the plant is not eaten as food. It has many names in the Pun-ts‘aou, and I was disposed to call it by one of them,

二章

爱采麦矣。沫之北矣。云谁之思。美孟弋矣。期我乎

桑中。要我乎上宫。送我乎淇之上矣。

三章

爱采葑矣。沫之东矣。云谁之思。美孟庸矣。期我乎

2　I am going to gather the wheat,
　　In the north of Mei.
　　But of whom are my thoughts?
　　Of that beauty, the eldest of the Yih.
　　She made an appointment with me in Sang-chung;
　　She will meet me in Shang-kung;
　　She will accompany me to K'e-shang.

3　I am going to gather the mustard plant,
　　In the east of Mei.
　　But of whom are my thoughts?
　　Of that beauty, the eldest of the Yung.

一金线草, 'the gold thread.' The Japanese plates, however, leave no doubt as to the plant's being the dodder (*cuscuta*). 麦 is the general name for grain with an awn. 葑,—see iii. X. 1. 沫,—see on the Shoo, V. X. 1, the 妹 there and the 沫 in the text being different forms of the same name. The tract of Mei had belonged in the first place, after the extinction of the Shang dyn., to Yung, but it fell afterwards under the power of Wei; and both Maou and Choo say upon the text that 'Mei was a city or tract of Wei.' 乡 is here=所. It is better translated by 'parts' or 'fields,' than by 'villages.'

Ll. 3,4. The nature of the ode now begins to come out. The gentleman proposed to gather the wheat and other things, and would seem to be doing so, but it was not for them that he cared; his thoughts were differently occupied. Këang, Yih and Yung are all surnames of ladies,—ladies from other States who were married in distinguished families of Wei, and they are called 孟, as being 'the eldest' of their respective surnames.—'the beautiful eldest Këang,' &c. The Këang must have been a daughter of the ruling House of Ts'e; Yung is supposed by some to have been the surname of the original holders of Yung (鄘), some branches of whom would be remaining in the State; Yih takes the place of 姒, in Kung-yang and Kuh-lëang's text of the Ch'un Ts'ëw, so that the Yih here may, possibly, have been a lady of Ke (杞), the seat of the descendants of the House of Hea.

Ll. 5-7, Sang-chung, Shang-kung, and K'e-shang were all the names of small places in the district of Mei, the last name being prolonged by the insertion of 之 between 淇 and 上, unless we translate—'above the K'e.' 期 means 'a set time;' here, used as a verb='to set a time.' 要 has the force of 迎, 'to meet.' These lines are best connected together by 或, 'or.' So, Yen Ts'an.

The rhymes are—in st.1, 唐, 乡, 姜, cat.10; 中, 宫, cat 9: in 2, 麦, 北, 弋, cat.1, t.3; 中 宫: in 3, 葑, 东, 庸, 中, 宫, cat. 9: and the final 上 in all the stanzas.

NOTE ON THE INTERPRETATION. It has been stated above, that Maou considers the piece as satirical, directed against the lewd practices of the wealthy and official classes of Wei. But there is not a word in it to indicate directly a satirical purpose. The actor in it, or the author personating him, describes his various intrigues,

桑中。要我乎上宫。送我乎淇之上矣。

She made an appointment with me in Sang-chung;
She will meet me in Shang-kung;
She will accompany me to K'e-shang.

V. *Shun che pun-pun.*

鹑之奔奔

一章
鹑之奔奔。鹊之强强。人之无良。我以为兄。

二章
鹊之强强。鹑之奔奔。人之无良。我以为君。

1　Boldly faithful in their pairings are quails;
　　Vigorously so are magpies.
　　This man is all vicious,
　　And I consider him my brother!

2　Vigorously faithful in their pairings are magpies;
　　Boldly so are quails.
　　This woman is all vicious,
　　And I regard her as marchioness!

and so far Choo is correct, when he says 'it was made by the adulterer himself.' Yen Ts'an vainly endeavours to get over the 我, 'I,' by distinguishing between the writer and the individual concerned, so that the 'I' is really equivalent to 汝, 'you,' as if the meaning were,—'You say that you are going to gather the wheat; but you have quite another intention. I know what intrigues you have in hand.' Such an exegesis is grammatically inadmissible, and takes all the spirit out of the piece.

The questions then arise—How did Confucius give such a vile piece a place in the She? and how is its existence reconcileable with his statement that all the odes might be summed up in one sentence,—'Have not a single depraved thought?' It is replied that the sage introduced this ode, showing, without blaming, the evil of the time, just as he related the truth of things in the Ch'un Ts'ew, not afraid to leave his readers to form their own opinion about them.

After all, looking at the structure of this ode, I think we may believe that it was made with a satirical design. If the speaker in it had confined himself to one 'beauty,' or one locality, it would not have been possible to regard it as other than a base love song. Seeing that a new lady comes

up in every stanza, it is possible to conceive of the piece as having been thus constructed to deride the licentiousness which prevailed. This view occurred to me long ago, and I am glad to see something like an approximation to it in the remarks of Tang Yuen-seih (邓元锡; Ming dyn.), appended by the imperial editors to their collection of notes on the piece.

Ode. 5. Allusive. AGAINST SEUEN KEANG AND HWAN AS WORSE THAN BEASTS. So the 'little Preface' interprets the piece, and Choo accepts the interpretation.

Ll. 1. 2. In explaining these, Maou simply says that 'quails are *pun-pun*-like, and magpies are *k'eang-k'eang*-like,' without indicating the significance of the terms. Choo, after K'angshing, says that 奔奔 and 强强 denote 'the app. of the birds dwelling together, and flying together in pairs.' This idea of faithfulness between pairs of the quail and the magpie is imported into the words however, from the known or supposed habits of the birds. 奔奔 denotes the boisterous vehement manner in which the quail *rushes* to fight;—to maintain, it is believed, its exclusive title to its mate; and 强强 denotes

VI. *Ting che fang chung.*

定之方中

一章

定之方中。作于楚宫。揆之以日。作于楚室。树之榛

栗。椅桐梓漆。爰伐琴瑟。

二章

升彼虚矣。以望楚矣。望楚与堂。景山与京。降观于

1   When *Ting* culminated [at night-fall],
He began to build the palace at Ts'oo.
Determining its aspects by means of the sun,
He built the mansion at Ts'oo.
He planted about it hazel and chesnut trees,
The *e*, the *t'ung*, the *tsze*, and the varnish-tree,
Which, when cut down, might afford materials for lutes.

2   He ascended those old walls,
And thence surveyed [the site of] Ts'oo.

the strong vigour with which the magpie does the same. We may construe 之 as meaning 'of,' but here, as so often in other odes, it has perhaps only the force of a particle, giving a descriptive vividness to the line.

Ll. 3, 4. The 人 in the first stanza is referred to the prince Hwan, and that in the second to Seuen Këang. The one duke Seuen's son, and the other his wife, they were cohabiting together. The 我 is referred to duke Hwuy, or Soh, Seuen Këang's son. He was himself vile enough to consent to any wickedness about his palace; and we must suppose that the piece sends a shaft against him as well as his mother and brother. 君 is in the sense of 小君;—see Ana. XV. xiv.

Morrison translates the 1st stanza under the character 奔 :—

'The quails fly together,
The magpies sort in pairs.
When man is dissolute,
Shall I yet call him brother?'

The rhymes are—in st. 1, 强, 良, 兄 *, cat. 10: in 2 强良 ;奔, 君, cat. 13.

Ode 6. Narrative. THE PRAISE OF DUKE WAN:—HIS DILIGENCE, FORESIGHT, SYMPATHY WITH THE PEOPLE, AND PROSPERITY. The last ode, we have seen, makes reference to the marquis Soh, or duke Hwuy. He died in B. C. 668, and was succeeded by his son Ch'ih (赤), known as duke E (懿 公), who perished in fighting with the Teih in B. C. 659. Wei was

then reduced to extremity, and had nearly disappeared from among the States of China. The people destroyed all the family of Hwuy, and, what we cannot but be surprised at, called to their head Shin (申), a son of Seuen Këang and Ch'aou-pih Hwan, He was duke Tae (戴 公), and crossed the Ho with the shattered remnant of the people, with whom he camped in the neighbourhood of Ts'aou. Dying that same year, his brother Wei (毁), known as duke Wăn, was called to his place, and became a sort of second founder of the State. It is of him that this ode speaks.

St. 1. *Ting* is the name of a small space in the heavens, embracing ʊ Markab (室 宿) and another star of Pegasus. It culminated at this time of the Chow dyn. at night-fall, in the 10th Hea or the 12th Chow month, and was regarded as the signal that now the labours of husbandry were terminated for the year, and that building operations should be taken in hand. The urgency was great for the building of Ts'oo-k'ew, his new capital, but duke Wăn would not take it in hand, till the proper time for such a labour was arrived. 方 ='then.' 中, 'to be on the middle;' i. e., here, 'on the meridian.' We have to understand 昏 'at dusk or night-fall.' As K'ang-shing has it, 于 此 时, 定 星 昏 而 正 中. Maou takes 方 and 中, differently.

楚 宫 = 楚 邱 之 宫, 'the palace of Ts'oo-k'ew;'—see note on the title of Book 3d. It was to Ts'oo-k'ew that duke Wăn removed

桑。卜云其吉。终然允臧。

三章

灵雨既零。命彼倌人。星言夙驾。说于桑田。匪直也

He surveyed Ts'oo and T'ang,
With the high hills and lofty elevations about :
He descended and examined the mulberry trees ;
He then divined, and got a fortunate response ;
And thus the issue has been truly good.

3   When the good rains had fallen,
He would order his groom,

from Ts'aou, to rebuild from it, as a centre, the ruins of the broken State. He was assisted in doing so by the other States, under the presidency of duke Hwan of Ts'e; but the ode takes no notice of this. K'ang-shing understands by 宫, 'the ancestral temple,' and by 室 in l. 4, 'the residences.' Maou and Choo, however, do not distinguish between the two terms, and Choo says that 室 takes the place of 宫, merely for the sake of the rhythm with 日. 揆＝度, 'to measure,' or ＝考, 'to examine.' The meaning is that he determined the aspects, east and west, of the site which he had chosen, by means of the sun. How he did so, we need not inquire here. The trees mentioned in ll. 5, 6, would be planted about the moat and wall of the city principally. The selection of the different trees is understood to shew the duke's foresight of his future wants. 榛 and 栗,— see on iii. XIV. 4. The *t'ung* is said by Choo to be the woo-t'ung (梧桐), the *Eleococcus oleifera*, or the *Dryandra cordifolia* of Thunberg. This identification is generally regarded as incorrect, the *woo-t'ung* being of no use for the making of lutes. The tree here mentioned was probably what is called the 'white *tung* (白桐).' The Urh-ya makes the e and tsze to be the same tree, but the mention of both in the text seems to show that they were different, —varieties probably of the same tree, which is elsewhere called the *ts'ew* (楸);—with Medhurst, 'a kind of fir;' with Williams, 'like a yew or cypress.' They are both wrong, however. In the Japanese plates, in those of Seu, and in the 'Cyclopædia of Agriculture,' the *t'ung* is figured with large leaves. As it appears in the Japanese plates, the *t'ung* is the *bignonia*. The last line is too condensed to admit of a close translation. Choo says 爰＝于, but that will give no meaning. We must take it, with K'ang-shing as ＝曰, and call it a mere particle. K'ang-shing expands the whole line, 其长

大 可 伐 以 为 琴 瑟—as in the translation. This extends only to the trees in the last line. The best lutes are said to be those of which the upper part is made of *t'ung* wood, and the bottom of that of the *tsze*.

St. 2.   虚＝故 城, 'old walls,' 'the ruins of Ts'aou,' acc. to Maou. We read in iii. VI. 1, of the walling of this place, in B. C. 718. A hundred and fifty years had elapsed since that time, and now Ts'aou had become a ruin. For 虚, in the sense of the text, the same character with 土 at the side is now used. The Ts'oo is Ts'oo-k'ew, as in the last st. T'ang was the name of a town not far from Ts'oo-k'ew, which, we here see, could not be far from the old site of Ts'aou. Choo makes 景 a verb, meaning to determine the position of the hills by means of their shadows. It is simpler to take it with Maou as an adj., meaning 'great,' 'high.' Others take it as the name of a hill.   京 means 'a high mound,' whether natural or artificial. Here we must understand it of the natural elevations or heights in the neighbourhood. This survey would assist duke Wăn in fixing on the site of his new capital. He then descended and examined the mulberry trees, to see whether the ground was well adapted for their growth; and assured of this, he further consulted the tortoise shell (卜), to get the sanction of Spiritual Beings (稽 之 于 神), to this site.   卜 云 其 吉, 'he consulted the tortoise-shell; and it was fortunate.'   终 然＝既. 终然＝'having done thus.'   允＝'truly.'

The 3d st. celebrates Wăn's subsequent diligence in the duties of his position, after the new settlement was made.   灵＝善, 'good,' referring to the rains of spring. 零＝落, 'to fall.' 倌人 is explained by 主 驾 者, 'the

人。秉心塞渊。骡牝三千。

By starlight, in the morning, to yoke his carriage,
And would then stop among the mulberry trees and fields.
But not only thus did he show what he was ;—
Maintaining in his heart a profound devotion to his duties,
His tall horses and mares amounted to three thousand.

VII.　*Te tung.*

蝃蝀

一章

蝃蝀在东。莫之敢指。女子有行。远父母兄弟。

1　There is a rainbow in the east,
　　And no one dares to point to it.
　　When a girl goes away [from her home],
　　She separates from her parents and brothers.

superintendent of the carriage ;' but this meaning of the phrase is only known from the next line. 星＝见星, 'when he saw the stars.' 夙 = 'the early dawn.' 说,—as in ii. V. 3. All this was to stimulate and encourage the silk cultivators and husbandmen in their labours. The 5th line has vexed the critics. Maou explains 直 by 徒, which he takes as an adj.= 庸, 'ordinary,' and he refers the 人 to duke Wăn :—'no ordinary ruler was this.' Choo also refers the 人 to Wăn ; and taking 匪直 in the meaning of 'not only,' as Mencius in II. Pt. ii. VII. 2, he seems vaguely to bring out the meaning which I have given in the translation, and which Hwang Ch'un (黄樗 ; Sung dyn.) more clearly expresses :— 不直其为人也 如此. 秉 ＝ 操, 'to grasp, or hold fast.' 塞 ＝ 诚 or 实, 'sincere.' 渊 ＝ 深, 'deep.' The line might be rendered, 'In his steadfast heart he was sincere and profound.' The consequence of this was a great accession of general prosperity, one instance of which is given in the last line. Horses seven feet high and upwards are called *lae.* Maou says 骡马 与 牝马, showing that he considered the 牝 to be distinct from the *lae.* At the end of the 2d year of duke Min in the Ch'un Ts'ew, Tso-she praises very highly the merits of duke Wăn, and says that while his war chariots in the 1st year of his rule were only 30, they amounted in his last year to 300.

The rhymes are—in st.1, 中 宫, cat.9 ; 日, 室, 栗, 漆, 瑟, cat.12, t.3 : in 2, 虚, 楚, cat.5, t.2 ; 堂, 京 *, 桑, 藏, cat.10 : in 3, 雰 *, 人, 田, 渊, 千, cat.12, t.1.

Ode 7. Metaphorical and narrative. AGAINST LEWD CONNECTIONS. Maou thinks the piece celebrates the stopping of such connections by duke Wăn's good example and government. But there is nothing in it to indicate that it belonged to the time of Wăn, or had anything to do with him. It condemns an evil that is existing before the eyes of the writer, instead of expressing any joy that such an evil was a thing of the past.

Stt.1,2, ll.1.2. The Urh-ya has 螮蝀 instead of the name in the text. The characters denote a rainbow. Why the radical element in the name should be 虫, 'an insect,' I have been unable to discover. A rainbow is regarded as the result of an improper connection between the *yin* and the *yang,* the light and the dark, the masculine and feminine principles of nature ; and so it is an emblem of improper connections between men and women. Lacharme says that the superstition still prevails among the Chinese of holding it unlucky to point to a rainbow in the east :—an ulcer will forthwith be produced in the offending hand. The meaning then of these lines in the 1st st. is, that as the rainbow in the east was not fit to be pointed to, so the woman who formed an improper connection was not fit to be spoken about. In the 2d st., 隮 ＝ 升, 'to ascend,' but the subject is still a rainbow,

二章

朝隮于西。崇朝其雨。女子有行。远兄弟父母。

三章

乃如之人也。怀婚姻也。大无信也。不知命也。

2   In the morning [a rainbow] rises in the west,
    And [only] during the morning is there rain.
    When a girl goes away [from her home],
    She separates from her brothers and parents.

3   This person
    Has her heart only on being married.
    Greatly is she untrue to herself,
    And does not recognize [the law of] her lot.

VIII.   *Seang shoo.*

相鼠

一章

相鼠有皮。人而无仪。人而无仪。不死何为。

1   Look at a rat,—it has its skin ;
    But a man shall be without dignity of demeanour.
    If a man have no dignity of demeanour,
    What should he do but die ?

'suddenly appearing as if it had risen from beneath.' 崇朝 = 终朝, 'all the morning,' *i. e.*, the space between dawn and breakfast. The phrase seems here to be equivalent to 'for a short time,' or 'only for a short time,' like 终食之间, in Ana. IV. vii. 3. Choo Ile and others bring out the meaning by saying, 'In the course of (iu all) the morning, the rain will cease.' So fleeting were the pleasures of unlawful love. The old interpreters take a different view of these two lines, but I need not dwell on it. Even the imperial editors do not call attention to it.

Ll. 3, 4. Comp. iii. XIV. 2, ll. 3 4. Ying-tah brings out the meaning clearly enough :—'It is in the order of things for a young lady to go and be another's; she will as a matter of course leave her parents and brothers. But she ought to marry acc. to propriety. Why should she fear she will not get married, and be guilty of that licentious course?'

St. 3. Dropping all metaphor, the poet here proceeds to direct reproof. 乃如,—see on

iii. IV. 之人 = 是人 ,—as frequently. We must refer it to the lady in the connection which is the subject of the ode. 怀婚姻, 'cherishes marriage,' *i. e.* thinks of being married, and of that only. 大无信, 'is greatly without faith;' and for a girl to have faith, we are told, is 'not to lose herself (女子以不自失为信)。' I take 命 in the sense of 'lot,'—as in ii. X. Choo makes it = 正理 and 天理之正, 'the correctness of heavenly principle.' Maou and K'ang-shing take it as 'the orders of the parents.' The different views come to the same thing. Young people, and especially young ladies, have nothing to do with the business of being married. Their parents will see to it. They have merely to wait for their orders. If they do not do so, but rush to marriage on the impulse of their own desires and preferences, they transgress the rules of Heaven, and violate the law of their lot.

二章

相鼠有齒。人而无止。人而无止。不死何俟。

三章

相鼠有体。人而无礼。人而无礼。胡不遄死。

2   Look at a rat,—it has its teeth;
    But a man shall be without any right deportment.
    If a man have not right deportment,
    What should he wait for but death?

3   Look at a rat,—it has its limbs;
    But a man shall be without any rules of propriety.
    If a man observe no rules of propriety,
    Why does he not quickly die?

IX. *Kan maou.*

干旄

一章

孑孑干旄。在浚之郊。素丝纰之。良马四之。彼姝者

1   Conspicuously rise the staffs with their ox-tails,
    In the distant suburbs of Tseun,
    Ornamented with the white silk bands;
    There are four carriages with their good horses,
    That admirable gentleman,—
    What will he give them [for this]?

The rhymes are—in st. 1, 弟, 指, cat. 15, t. 2: in 2, 雨, 母, (prop. cat. 1), cat. 5, t. 2: in 3, 人, 姻, 信, 命, *, cat. 12, t. 1.

VIII. Allusive A MAN WITHOUT PROPRIETY IS NOT EQUAL TO A RAT. This piece is also referred to the time of duke Wǎn, through whose influence his people condemned not only licentiousness, as in the last ode, but also the want of propriety in the general carriage and demeanour.

In all the stanzas, l. 1. 相＝視, 'to see,' 'look at.' The Shwoh-wǎn explains it by 省視,＝'to mark.' A rat is a small and despicable creature, but it has its skin, its teeth, and its separate limbs (体＝支体),—all that it ought to have. So it is better than a man, who does not know to behave himself as *a man* ought to do.

L. 2. This line is generally explained as if it contained a question, 'Ought a man to be, or can he be a man who is, without propriety?' The rendering I have given brings the meaning out better. The next line proceeds on the supposition of such a case, and then it is added that such a man is not fit to live. 仪＝威仪, 'dignity of demeanour,' conduct which is becoming. 无止＝无所止息, 'nowhere to rest;' *i. e.,* all the movements are disordered and disjointed. See what Confucius is made to say on propriety in the Le Ke, XXVIII. 8. 礼 is the general term for propriety, expressing, as in the passage just referred to, 事之治, 'the good order or government of all one does.'

L. 4. The meaning is, as expressed by K'angshing,—不如其死, 'he had better die.' 遄＝速, 'quickly.'

The rhymes are—in st. 1, 皮 *, 仪 *, 仪 *, 为 *, cat. 17: in 2, 齒, 止, 止, 俟, cat. 1, t. 2: in 3, 体, 礼, 礼, 死, cat. 15, t. 2.

子，何以畀之。

二章

孑孑干旟。在浚之都。素絲組之。良馬五之。彼姝者

子。何以予之。

三章

孑孑干旌。在浚之城。素絲祝之。良馬六之。彼姝者

子。何以告之。

2 Conspicuously rise the staffs with their falcon-banners,
In the nearer suburbs of Tseun,
Ornamented with the white silk ribbons ;
There are five carriages with their good horses.
That admirable gentleman,—
What will he give them [for this]?

3 Conspicuously rise the staffs with their feathered streamers,
At the walls of Tseun,
Bound with the white silk cords.
There are six carriages with their good horses.
That admirable gentleman,—
What will he tell them [for this]?

Ode 9. Narrative. THE ZEAL OF THE OF-
FICERS OF WEI TO WELCOME MEN OF WORTH.
This piece, like the two preceding, is held to
show the good influence of duke Wăn. 'His
officers,' says the Little Preface, 'loved to learn
good principles and ways, and men of worth
rejoiced to instruct them.' Choo accepts this account of the ode, but he differs much from Maou
in the explanation of many parts of it. There
is, indeed, great difficulty with some of the lines.

Maou treats the whole as if proceeding from
some man of talents and virtue, expressing his
admiration of an officer of Wei, and wondering
what lessons of government he would be glad to
instruct him about. But this view only distresses
the student by the astonishing confusion and
absurdities in which it lands him. Even the
imperial editors take no notice of Maou's views
here, fond as they are of upholding them in
general; and I shall not further advert to them.

Acc. to Choo He, the first 4 lines describe an
officer or officers of Wei, meeting the man of
worth, a recluse, or a visitor from another State,
in the neighbourhood of Tseun. This man of
worth is then introduced in the 子 of the 4th
line. In this way some consistent explanation
can be given of the piece, though the language,
we shall find, is still attended with difficulties.

In all the stt.,ll.1,2. 孑孑 denotes 'the appearance of the flag or banner rising up on its staff.
干旄, denotes the staff and pennon of a great

officer, which was displayed from his chariot.
The top of the staff was adorned with feathers.
It was carved into the figure of some animal, or
had such a figure set upon it; and the pennon
hung down, consisting of ox-tails, dressed and
strung together. The yu was a flag with falcons
represented on it. It might be borne by great
officers of the highest rank, and ministers of the
States. The tsing was like the maou, but instead
of the ox-tails, the pennon was composed of
feathers of different colours, skilfully disposed
in spreading plumes. I have translated 干旄
and the other phrases in the plural, in consequence of the view which I take of the 4th line.
Tseun,—see on iii.VII.3. The flags appear
first in the suburbs, the open country, some
distance beyond the city, and finally by the
walls. This suggests to us the idea of a distinguished visitor from another State travelling to
the capital of Wei; and as he passes through
the district of Tseun, the officers of Wei pour
out from it to greet him. None of the explanations given of 都 in the dict. meet the exigency
of its occurrence here, nor does Maou or Choo
say anything about it to the point. Ho K'ëae
(何楷; Ming dyn.) observes that, on comparing
the 3 stanzas, we perceive that the too was ·inside
the suburbs and outside the walls.' I would venture, therefore, to identify it with the foo (郛)
of the Ch'un Ts'ew, and translate it accordingly.

X. *Tsae ch'e.*

载驰

一章

载驰载驱。归唁卫侯。驱马悠悠。言至于漕。大夫跋

涉。我心则忧。

1　I would have galloped my horses and whipt them,
　　Returning to condole with the marquis of Wei.
　　I would have urged them all the long way,
　　Till I arrived at Ts'aou.
　　A great officer has gone, over the hills and through the rivers;
　　But my heart is full of sorrow.

L. 3. This line is descriptive of certain cords or bands, woven of white silk thread, and used about the banners, tying the flag and pennons to the staff, or in some other conspicuous way. The dict. defines 纰 by 饰, 'to ornament;' but Choo calls it simply 织组, 'woven bands or ribbons.' Then 组 in the 2d st. is properly a noun, denoting the woven fabric. And in the same way we must take 祝＝属, as simply meaning 'bands.' The 之 gives the whole line a verbal force (if we are to seek any meaning in that term at all), and refers it to the 1st line, without indicating the use of the ribbons or bands.

L. 4 is perhaps still more troublesome and difficult. That in st. 1 is easy enough, as 4 horses were yoked in a chariot; but 5 horses, as in st. 2, and 6 as in the 3d, were not used. The numbers therefore cannot be applied to the horses; and to say that they are varied merely for the sake of the rhyme, as Choo He does in one place, is to set very little store by the sound sense of the writer. It remains, then, to take the horses, by synecdoche, for the horses and chariots together. The number of carriages meeting the visitor gets more numerous, the nearer he comes. As above, the 之 gives a verbal force to 四, 五, and 六. This is the view of Yen Ts'an.

Ll. 5, 6. The distinguished visitor at last appears in these lines, and the writer asks himself what he can give to the officers, or what he can teach them, for the enthusiastic welcome with which they have received him. 姝＝美, 'admirable.'

Yen Ts'an instances the cases of Ke-chah, a prince of Woo, who is mentioned in the Tso Chuen, as visiting many States, and imparting of his wisdom to their ministers; and of Tsze-ch'an of Ching, who is ever ready with his lessons at the court of Tsin. The arrival of some such visitor in Wei, he thinks, may be here celebrated.

The rhymes are—in st. 1, 旌, 郊, cat. 2; 纰, 四, 畀, cat. 15, t. 3: in 2, 旟, 都, cat. 5, t. 1; 组, 五, 予, ib. t. 2: in 3, 旌, 城, cat. 11; 祝, 六, 告, *, cat. 3, t. 3.

Ode 10. Narrative. THE BARONESS MUH OF HEU COMPLAINS OF NOT BEING ALLOWED TO GO TO WEI, TO CONDOLE WITH THE MARQUIS ON THE DESOLATION OF HIS STATE, AND APPEAL TO SOME GREAT POWERS ON ITS BEHALF. The wife of the baron of Heu was one of the daughters of Seuen Këang and Ch'aou-pih Hwan (see on iii.IX.), and a sister consequently of the dukes Tae and Wăn of Wei. Sorry for the ruin which the Teih had brought on Wei, she had wished, while the remnant of the people was collected about Ts'aou, to go and condole with her brother (probably duke Wăn), and consult with him as to what had best be done in his desperate case. It was contrary, however, to the rules of propriety for a lady in her position (see on iii.XIV.) to return to her native State, and she was not allowed to do so. In this piece we have, it is supposed, her complaint, and the vindication of her purpose.

St. 1. 载 can here, standing at the beginning of the ode, be taken simply as an initial particle. Its position renders the explanation of it by 则, which we find in K'ang-shing and Choo, inapplicable. 驰＝走马, 'to race the horses;' and 驱＝策马 'to whip them,' 'to urge them.' Choo would construe this line in the indicative mood, as if the lady had actually driven a long way on the road to Wei, until she was stopped by a great officer sent to recal her. It is better to construe it in the conditional mood,—with Ying-tah and Yen Ts'an. The baroness relates what she wished to do, and not what she did. 唁 is 'to condole with the living,' on occasion of their misfortunes; condoling on occasion of a death is expressed by 吊. 言

二章
既不我嘉。不能旋反。视尔不臧。我思不远。既不我

嘉。不能旋济。视尔不臧。我思不閟。

三章
陟彼阿丘。言采其蝱。女子善怀。亦各有行。许人尤

之。众稚且狂。

2 You disapproved of my [proposal],
    And I cannot return [to Wei];
    But I regard you as in the wrong,
    And cannot forget my purpose.
    You disapproved of my purpose,
    And I cannot return across the streams;
    But I regard you as in the wrong,
    And cannot shut out my thoughts.

3 I will ascend that mound with the steep side,
    And gather the mother-of-pearl lilies.
    I might, as a woman, have many thoughts,
    But every one of them was practicable.
    The people of Heu blame me,
    But they are all childish and hasty [in their conclusions].

in l. 4, is the particle. 跋 涉 denotes a toil-some journey, now over hills and across grassy plains (草 行 曰 跋), now through rivers (水 行 曰 涉). Who the great officer of this line was is much disputed. Ying-tah thinks he was the messenger from Wei who had brought the news of its desolation. Choo thinks he was an officer of Heu, who had pursued her to stop the return which the baroness was attempting. Yen Ts'an thinks he was the messenger who had been despatched to express the condolences of Heu in the circumstances of Wei. This last seems the preferable view. Such an officer had been sent, but the lady thinks it would have been better for her to go, and is sad.

St. 2. 嘉＝善, used as a verb, 'to approve of.' Choo takes the 3rd line as meaning—'Though I see that you do not approve of my movement (虽 视 尔 不 以 我 为 善).' I prefer the construction in the translation, which is, again, that of Ying-tah and Yen Ts'an. 尔 is to be referred to 许 人, 'the people, and more especially the ministers, of Heu.' 远 may be taken as equivalent to 忘, 'to forget.'

济 refers to some stream or streams in the route between Heu and Wei. 閟＝闭, 'to shut up;' also, 'to repress.'

St. 3. The Urh-ya defines 阿 丘 as 'a mound high on one side.' The difference between this and 旄 丘, in iii.XII., does not immediately appear. It must depend on the spectator's point of view 言 is the particle. 蝱, or 莔, is a lily, called the 'mother of pearl,' from the appearance of its shining bulbous roots, or as others say, from that of its flower. It is the *fritillaria Thunbergiæ;* and I should have called it the fritillary, if I had met anywhere with the term. Many medical qualities are ascribed to the root: among them that of dissipating melancholy;—for which the baroness proposes to use it. If we attempt, with the old interpreters, to treat these two lines allusively, we experience great difficulties. In l. 3, 善 is considered as equivalent to 多, 'many.' A woman is 'good at fancying things with an anxious mind.' The people of Heu, it would appear, had charged this on the baroness; and she vindicates herself. 行 is explained by 道.

四章

我行其野。芃芃其麦。控于大邦。谁因谁极。大夫君

子。无我有尤。百尔所思。不如我所之。

4　I would have gone through the country,
　　Amidst the wheat so luxuriant.
　　I would have carried the case before the great State.
　　On whom should I have relied? Who would come [to the help
　　　of Wei]?
　　Ye great officers and gentlemen,
　　Do not condemn me.
　　The hundred plans you think of
　　Are not equal to the course I was going to take.

'Every one of her ideas,' she says, 'had a principle of reason in it.' This does not seem to be necessary. 尤 has the sense of 訧, with which it is interchangeable,—'a fault,' and here, 'to count as a fault.' 狂,—as in Ana. V. xxi.

St. 4. The lady here speaks more fully of what her purpose had been, and again asserts its superiority to the course taken by the State. We must take the first four lines in the conditional mood as in st. 1. 芃芃 expresses the luxuriant appearance of the wheat in the fields. 野 is evidently 'the country' simply; not a wild, uncultivated tract. Maou explains 控 by 引, 'to lead,' which we find also in the Shwoh-wăn; but that meaning of the term is not applicable here. Han Ying made it 赴, 'to go to,' and we find 告 'to inform,' as one of the definitions of it in the dict. The meaning evidently is that in the translation. I translate 大邦 by 'the great State,' because the baroness could only have meant Ts'e, which at this time had the presidency of all the States of the kingdom. At a later time we find the same designation often applied in the Tso Chuen to Tsin, after it had taken the place of Ts'e. It may be worth while to give here an account of the lady, as related by Lëw Heang (列女传). He says: 'The wife of Muh of Heu was a daughter of duke E of Wei. [This is an error. Tso-she is a better authority in such a matter, and acc. to him she was a daughter of Ch'aou-pih Hwan and Seuen Këang,—as I have said. See Këang Ping-chang on this ode]. She was

sought in marriage both by Heu and Ts'e; and when her father was about to assent to the proposals of Heu, the young lady sent a message to him by her instructress in the harem, to the effect that Heu was a small and distant State, while Ts'e was large and near to Wei; and that, as there was trouble from the Jung on the borders of Wei, when he wanted to apply to "the great State (赴 告 大 邦)," it would be better for her to be married there. Duke E, however, did not act according to her suggestion.' 因,—as in Ana. I. xiii. 极＝至, 'to come to.' 谁 极 has been explained as meaning, 'Who would have been willing to come?' (So, Yen Ts'an); or, 'To whom should I have gone?' (So, Hwang Yih-ching, 黄 — 正 ; Ming dyn). 无 —毋, 'do not;' Imperative. Choo thinks the 大 夫 is the same as that in st. 1, and that 君 子 refers to 'all the people of the State of Heu.' I think he is wrong, and that the lady is here addressing generally the ministers and officers of the court of Heu. 百 ＝ the hundred things or plans. 之 ＝往 or 适 , so that the line might be translated—'Are not equal to my going,'—what my going would have accomplished.

In Maou, the ode is divided into 5 stanzas: the 1st of 6 lines; the 2d and 3d of 4 each; the 4th of 6; and 5th of 8. In the Tso-chuen, however, under the 13th year of duke Wăn, an officer is made to sing the 4th stanza of this ode, which it appears must then have contained the lines 控 于 大 邦, 谁 因 谁 极. This suggested to Soo Ch'eh (苏 辙) to combine Maou's

2d and 3d stanzas in one; and Choo He adopted his arrangement.

The rhymes are—in st. 1, 驱 *, 侯, cat. 4, t. 1; 悠, 漕*, 忧 , cat. 3, t. 1: in 2, 反, 远. cat. 14; 济, 閟 (prop. cat.12), cat. 15, t.2: in 3, 虻 *, 行 *, 狂, cat.10: in 4, 麦 *, 极, cat. 1, t. 3; 尤 *, 思, 之, *ib.*, t.1.

CONCLUDING NOTE. The best of the odes of Yung is the 6th, celebrating the praise of duke Wăn. A retributive providence is to be recognized in the overthrow of Wei by the Teih; the iniquity of the ruling House had become full. That its restoration should come from a son of Seuen Këang is surprising. That two of her sons by Ch'aou-pih Hwan should have been accepted by the people of Wei as their marquises, and that their two daughters should have become the wives of the princes of other States, would seem to indicate a very low state of public feeling.

And yet those children proved themselves not unworthy. The praise of duke Wăn is recorded; and we cannot but sympathize with the barceness of Heu in the last ode, in her sisterly affection, and her regard for her native State. Though she did feel the rules of female propriety more strict than she was willing to submit to, we cannot wonder at it. The lady of the 1st ode is a true Chinese heroine, rejoicing in her chains, and preferring to remain single in her widowhood, even against the wishes of her parents. Similar conduct continues to this day in the greatest estimation. We can understand a widow remaining single from devoted attachment to the memory of her husband. That a widow should be expected to do so from a feeling that she cannot serve two masters,—from a feeling of duty, into which the element of affection does not enter, seems to arise from the lower position assigned to woman, as compared with man, in the social scale.

BOOK V, THE ODES OF WEI.

I. *K'e yuh.*

卫一之五

淇奥

一章

瞻彼淇奥。绿竹猗猗。有匪君子。如切如磋。如琢如磨。瑟兮僩兮。赫兮咺兮。有匪君子。终不可谖兮。

1   Look at those recesses in the banks of the K'e,
With their green bamboos, so fresh and luxuriant!
There is our elegant and accomplished prince,—
As from the knife and the file,
As from the chisel and the polisher!
How grave is he and dignified!
How commanding and distinguished!
Our elegant and accomplished prince,—
Never can he be forgotten!

TITLE OF THE BOOK. 卫，之五. 'Wei; Book V. of Part I.' To what has been said on Wei on the title of the 3d Book, it may be added here, that the State had a longer history, under the descendants of K'ang-shuh, its first marquis, than any of the other States of the Chow dynasty. It outlasted that dynasty itself,—through a period of 905 years, when the last prince of Wei was reduced to the ranks of the people under the 2d of the emperors of Ts'in.

Ode 1. Allusive. THE PRAISE OF DUKE WOO, —HIS ASSIDUOUS CULTIVATION OF HIMSELF; HIS DIGNITY; HIS ACCOMPLISHMENTS. The critics all agree to accept duke Woo as the subject of this ode. He has been referred to already, in the note on the subject of the 1st ode in the last Book. What is said of him there is not to his credit; but his rule of Wei subsequently was of unusual length (B. C. 811—757) and unusual success. 'He cultivated the principles of govt.,' says Sze-ma Ts'ëen, 'of which K'ang-shuh had

given the example. The people increased in number, and others flocked to the State. In his 42d year (B. C. 770), when the "dog Jung" killed king Yew (幽 王), he led a body of soldiers to the assistance of Chow, and did great service against the Jung, so that king P'ing appointed him a duke of the court.' The 'Little Preface' says this ode was made when duke Woo entered the court of Chow, and was a minister there; but whether he had acted in this capacity before the time of king P'ing or not, we cannot determine.

Ll. 1, 2, in all the stanzas. 淇, — see on iii.

XIV. 奥 means a recess, or little bay, made in the bank by the stream. Maou explains it by 隈; but the Urh-ya distinguishes between the two terms, saying that the former denotes 'a recess in the banks,' and the latter 'an advance of them into the channel of the stream.'

二章

瞻彼淇奥。绿竹青青。有匪君子。充耳琇莹。会弁如

星。瑟兮僩兮。赫兮咺兮。有匪君子。终不可谖兮。

三章

瞻彼淇奥。绿竹如箦。有匪君子。如金如锡。如圭如

2   Look at those recesses in the banks of the K'e,
     With their green bamboos, so strong and luxuriant!
     There is our elegant and accomplished prince,—
     With his ear-stoppers of beautiful pebbles,
     And his cap, glittering as with stars between the seams!
     How grave is he and dignified!
     How commanding and distinguished!
     Our elegant and accomplished prince,—
     Never can he be forgotten!

3   Look at those recesses in the banks of the K'e,
     With their green bamboos, so dense together!
     There is our elegant and accomplished prince,—
     [Pure] as gold or as tin,

绿 ='green,' though Maou makes it the name of a plant called 'king grass (王刍).' 猗猗 denotes 'the fresh and luxuriant' appearance of the bamboos; 青青, their 'strong and luxuriant appearance;' and 如箦, 'their denseness.' Choo, indeed, takes this last phrase as=床栈, 'bed boarding,' but all poetic feeling revolts from such a view. Maou explains 箦 by 积, 'collected together,'—thick as the stalks of grain in a field. The K'e was famous in old times for the luxuriance and quality of its bamboos. The sight of them, so rich and beautiful, suggested to the poet the idea of king Woo, with his admirable and attractive qualities.

Ll. 3,—5, in all the stt. 匪=斐, which we find for it in the 'Great Learning,' Comm. III., 4, where all this st. is quoted.—meaning 'elegant and accomplished.' The 君子 is duke Woo. Ll. 4, 5, in st. 1, tell how he had cultivated himself, as men work on bone or horn with the knife and file (切磋), and on stones and jade, with the chisel and hammer, and

sand (琢磨). In st. 2, they set Woo before us as he appeared in court in full dress. 充耳, lit. 'filling the ears,'= the 瑱 of iv. III. 2. Wang T'aou asserts that notwithstanding the name of this article, it was worn more for ornament than use,—that in fact it was not employed to stuff the ears. The ear-plugs of the king were made of jade; those of the princes of stones, precious but not so valuable as jade. All that the dictionaries tell us about 琇 and 莹 is that they are 'stones like jade.' The 弁 was a cap of leather, made, according to the Chinese shape, of several separate pieces sown together; and 会 (kwae) was the name of those pieces, or the space between the seams; such is the account of it by K'ang-shing (弁中之缝). Maou, however, makes it a separate thing from the cap, a pin used in fastening up the hair. The cap, between the seams, was stuck over with gems, 'like stars,' or the cap and this pin, if so we are to take 会, were so. In st. 3, these lines bring the duke before us, pure like gold and tin that have come from

璧。宽兮绰兮。猗重较兮。善戏谑兮。不为虐兮。

[Soft and rich] as a sceptre of jade!
How magnanimous is he and gentle!
There he is in his chariot with its two high sides!
Skilful is he at quips and jokes,
But how does he keep from rudeness in them!

II.　*K'aou pwan.*

考槃

一章

考槃在涧。硕人之宽。独寐寤言。永矢弗谖。

二章

考槃在阿。硕人之薖。独寐寤歌。永矢弗过。

1　He has reared his hut by the stream in the valley,
　　—That large man, so much at his ease.
　　Alone he sleeps, and wakes, and talks.
　　He swears he will never forget [his true joy].

2　He has reared his hut in the bend of the mound,
　　—That large man, with such an air of indifference.

the furnace, soft and rich like the jade formed into the sceptre-tokens of rank (see on the Shoo II. i. 7).

Ll. 6-9 in all the stt. The writer seems here hardly to be able to find words to express his admiration of the appearance and character of duke Woo. 瑟 sets forth, his 'gravity;' 僩, his 'awful dignity;' 赫, his 'glowing ardour;' 咺, the 'proclamation,' as it were, of all those qualities. 谖=忘, 'to forget' or 'be forgotten.' Again, 宽 sets forth his 'magnanimity,' and 绰 his 'slow and leisurely manner.' 猗 is an exclamation. 重较 (now read *ch'ung keoh*) has reference to the form of the carriage used by high ministers of the royal court. As this is represented in the 三礼通释, the sides of the box were in this form ⌐, the raised portion bring called 较. 善, as in iv. X. 3. 戏谑,—see, on iii. V. 1. The meaning of 虐 here does not amount to more than 'rude,' 'rudeness.'

The rhymes are—in st. 1, 猗 *, 磋, 磨, cat. 17; 僩, 咺, 谖, cat. 14: in 2, 青, 莹, 星, cat. ₁1; 僩, 咺 · 谖 : in 3, 簀, 锡, 璧, cat. 16, t. 3; 绰 *, 较 *, 谑 *, 虐 *, cat. 2.

Ode 2. Narrative. A HAPPY RECLUSE. This is all which we can gather from the ode itself. Maou says that it was directed against duke Chwang, who did not walk in the footsteps of his father Woo, and by his neglect of his duties led men of worth to withdraw from public life into retirement. But this is mere speculation, and gives no assistance in the interpretation of the piece.

L. 1, in all the stt. There is much difficulty with the first two characters. 考 = 成, 'to complete.' This meaning is sufficiently supported, and we find it used of the completion of buildings; e. g., in the Ch'un Ts'ew, I. v. 4. 槃 is more perplexing. The meaning of it which I have given may be said to have been made for the ode: Hwang Yih-ching says, 槃者架木为屋. Choo endeavours to get this sense out of another which the term has,—that of stopping in a given space and not advancing, which brings

三章
考槃在陆。硕人之轴。独寐寤宿。永矢弗告。

Alone, he sleeps and wakes, and sings.
He swears he will never pass from this spot.

3　He has reared his hut on the level height,
　　—That large man, so self-collected.
　　Alone, he sleeps and wakes, and sleeps again.
　　He swears he will never tell [of his delight].

III.　*Shih jin.*

硕人
一章
硕人其颀。衣锦褧衣。齐侯之子。卫侯之妻。东宫之

1　Large was she and tall,
　　In her embroidered robe, with a [plain] single garment over it:—
　　The daughter of the marquis of Ts'e,
　　The wife of the marquis of Wei,

us to something like the idea of a hermitage. Maou makes it= 乐, as if it vere 盤; but 成 乐, 'he has completed his joy,' is an awkward phrase, and seems unnatural in this place. Choo mentions a view which takes 考 = 扣, and 槃 = 器, 'an article of furniture;' which brings the recluse before us enjoying himself in beating his table, or something else, as music to his singing! 涧 —as in ii. II. The Shwoh-wän defines 阿 by 曲 阜, 'a curved mound.' 陆 denotes 'what is high and level,' a table-ground.

L. 2.　硕 人, — as in iii. XIII. 2.　宽,— much as in the last st. of the prec. ode. 之, here, and in a multitude of similar construc- tions, is most simply treated as a particle. There, is however, an echo of its meaning 'of,' which adds to the descriptive force of the lines. Choo acknowledges that he does not know the meaning of 适. Chaou explains it by 宽 大 貌,—as in the translation. 轴 means 'the roller of a map,' or of anything else; here, the self-collectedness of the recluse, rolled up on himself.

L. 3.　We can conceive the recluse singing, as in st. 2; his 'talking' all 'alone,' as in st. 1, is more perplexing. The meaning of 'to sleep

again' in 宿 was devised by Choo for the pas- sage, which it suits well. None of the meanings of the term in the dict. is applicable here,—not even 安, 'to rest in.'

L. 1.　矢,—as in iv. I. 谖 = 'to forget,' as in the last ode ; but we want an object for the verb, and also for 过 and 告, which we must supply, as we think most suitable. K'ang-shing is blamed for finding in all the lines the resent- ment of the recluse against his ruler, whose wickedness he would never forget, whose court he would never again pass, to whom he would never more offer good counsel. A man of this character. it is said, could never have found a place in the She.

The rhymes are—in st.1, 涧, 宽, 言, 谖, cat.14: in 2, 阿, 过, 歌, 适, cat.17: in 3, 陆, 轴, 宿, 告, cat. 3, t.3.

Ode 3. Narrative. CHWANG KEANG AS SHE APPEARED ON HER ARRIVAL IN WEI. HER GREAT CONNECTIONS; HER BEAUTY; HER EQUIPAGE; THE RICHES OF TS'E. From the ode itself it is plain that the subject of it is Chwang Këang, the principal points in whose unhappy history have been noticed on the 2d and some other odes of Book 3d. A difficulty arises as to the tense in which the greater part of the piece should be

妹。邢侯之姨。谭公维私。

二章
手如柔荑。肤如凝脂。领如蝤蛴。齿如瓠犀。螓首蛾

眉。巧笑倩兮。美目盼兮。

The sister of the heir-son of Ts‘e,
The sister-in-law of the marquis of Hing,
The viscount of T‘an also her brother-in-law.

2　Her fingers were like the blades of the young white-grass;
Her skin was like congealed ointment;
Her neck was like the tree-grub;
Her teeth were like melon seeds;
Her forehead cicada-like; her eyebrows like [the antennæ of]
　　the silkworm moth;
What dimples, as she artfully smiled!
How lovely her eyes, with the black and white so well defined!

translated;—in the present? or in the past? The 'Little Preface' says it was made 'in commiseration of the lady,' and this view is supported by an expression of Tso-she, in a narrative at the conclusion of the 3d year of duke Yin. There is little or nothing, indeed, in the ode to indicate this intention, though Yen Ts‘an, as we shall see, finds a hint of it in the last two lines of the 3d stanza; but I have deferred to the general opinion of the Chinese critics, and have employed the past tense. Lacharme uses the present, and calls the piece an ‘*Epithalamium*.'

St. 1. 硕人—as in III. XIII. 2. 颀 denotes 'the app. of being tall.' The 锦 was 'an embroidered robe,' worn by the princess in travelling from Ts‘e to Wei. Over it she wore a plain single garment (褧＝禅), made probably of linen. Tsze-sze quotes this line, in somewhat difft. words, in ‘The Doctrine of the Mean,' XXXIII. 1, and draws a moral from it, about the avoiding of all display. The remaining 4 lines exalt Chwang Këang on the ground of her birth and her connections. 东宫, ‘eastern palace,' is a designation of the eldest son, or heir-apparent of a State, from the part of the palace buildings which he occupied. Chwang Këang, it thus appears, was the daughter of the marquis of Ts‘e by his wife proper, and not by any lady of inferior rank. *Hing* was a marquisate, held by descendants of the duke of Chow, of which we read in the Ch'un Ts‘ew, till it was absorbed by Wei in B.C. 634. *T‘an* was a small State, whose lords were viscounts (子), adjacent

to Ts‘e. Why the viscount of T‘an should here be called duke (公), we cannot well tell, as it is not likely that he was dead at this time. 公 must be taken generally as＝the ruler of a State. A husband calls his wife's sisters 姨, and a lady calls her sisters' husbands 私.

St. 2 is occupied with the personal beauty of Chwang Këang. 手 is here not the ‘hand,' but ‘the fingers,'—soft, delicate, and white. 荑, —as in iii. XVII. 3. L. 2 describes the whiteness of her skin, and l. 3 that of her neck. 蝤蛴 is the name for the larvæ of a beetle which bores into wood, and deposits its eggs in trees. The larvæ are remarkable for their whiteness and length, and hence poets turn them to account as here! 瓠犀 is ‘the section of a melon,' (Williams strangely calls it ‘the carpel '), showing the seeds regular and white; such were the lady's teeth. 螓 is the name of one of the cicadæ, rather small, but remarkable for the broad and square formation of its head; such was Chwang Këang's forehead, like Seuen Këang's in iv. III.,—扬且之晳, 扬且之颜. 蛾 is here the moth of the silkworm, whose small curved antennæ are a favourite figure for the eyebrows of ladies. 倩 denotes ‘the app. of the dimple in smiling.' This exact significance of the term has been missed in all

三章
硕人敖敖。说于农郊。四牡有骄。朱幩镳镳。翟茀以

朝。大夫夙退。无使君劳。

四章
河水洋洋。北流活活。施罛濊濊。鳣鲔发发。葭菼揭

3   Large was she and tall,
     When she halted in the cultivated suburbs.
     Strong looked her four horses,
     With the red ornaments so rich about their bits.
     Thus in her carriage, with its screens of pheasant feathers,
          she proceeded to our court.
     Early retire, ye great officers,
     And do not make the marquis fatigued!

4   The waters of the Ho, wide and deep,
     Flow northwards in majestic course.
     The nets are dropt into them with a plashing sound,

our Chinese-and-English dictionaries. 盼 denotes the black and white of the eyes clearly defined.

St. 3 describes the appearance and equipage of Chwang Këang as she drew near to the capital of Wei. 敖敖 has the same meaning as 其颀 in st. 1. 说,—as in ii. V. 3. 农郊 are the suburbs, not far distant from the capital, which husbandmen had brought under cultivation. 四牡 are the four horses or stallions of the carriage; 有骄 expresses their 'appearance as strong.' Maou explains 幩 simply by 饰, 'to ornament,' or 'an ornament;' Choo, more fully, by 镳饰, 'the ornament of a bridle,' meaning more particularly the iron parts outside the bit in the mouth. In princely equipages these were twisted round with red cloth, both for ornament and a protection from the foam. Yen Ts'an takes 镳镳 as denoting 'all the bits;' Maou and Choo, better, as a descriptive adj., expressing the rich appearance of the ornamented instruments. 茀=蔽, 'a screen.' The front and rear of ladies' carriages were furnished with screens, made, in the case of princesses, with pheasants' feathers. The ruler of a State gave audience, with the dawn, to his ministers, and then withdrew to 'the small chamber,' and changed his robes. The last two lines are understood as the expression of the people's feelings, when they saw the beauty and splendour of Chwang Këang.--Such a wife was to be cherished by the marquis. Let not the ministers fatigue him with business, so

as to unfit him for showing due attention to her. The poet, it is supposed, repeats the words here, to insinuate his regret for the neglect with which the lady had come to be treated.

St. 4 is understood to indicate the rich resources and strength of Ts'e in the Ho, which then flowed northwards along the west of the State. 洋洋 describe the vastness of the stream, and 活活 'the appearance of its current.' 罛=鱼罟, 'a fish net.' 濊濊 express the sound of the nets entering the water. 鳣 is, no doubt the sturgeon. It is described as having a short snout, with the mouth under the chin, covered with bony plates, instead of scales. The flesh is yellow, in consequence of which one name of it is the 'yellow fish.' It is found sometimes of an immense size, and weighs 1,000 pounds. Of the 鲔 I was not so sure. It is described as like a sturgeon, but much smaller, the snout longer and more pointed, with the flesh white. Williams erroneously calls it 'a kind of eel or water snake, found in the Yang-tsze Këang.' The fish is common enough at Han-k'ow, Kew-këang, and other places on that river. We should no doubt find it also in the Ho. It is described in Blakiston's 'Five months on the Yang-tsze,' p.77. Figures of it are given on p.83 to help naturalists to identify the species. He says 'it had somewhat the appearance of a dogfish or shark;' but I believe the Chinese are correct in saying that it

揭。庶姜孽孽。庶士有朅。

Among shoals of sturgeon, large and small,
While the rushes and sedges are rank about.
Splendidly adorned were her sister ladies;
Martial looked the attendant officers.

IV. *Măng.*

氓

一章

氓之蚩蚩。抱布貿絲。匪來貿絲。來即我謀。送子涉

淇。至于頓丘。匪我愆期。子無良媒。將子無怒。秋

1　A simple-looking lad you were,
　Carrying cloth to exchange it for silk.
　[But] you came not so to purchase silk;—
　You came to make proposals to me.
　I convoyed you through the K'e,
　As far as Tun-k'ew.
　'It is not I,' [I said], 'who would protract the time;
　But you have had no good go-between.
　I pray you be not angry,
　And let autumn be the time.'

is a kind of sturgeon. The line might be translated, 'Amid shoals of sturgeon, the large and the snouted.' 發 發 may describe the abundance of the fishes, or their struggles in the nets. 葭,—as in ii. XIV. 1. 葵 is a kindred plant; other names for it are 薍 and 荻. 揭 揭 express the rank high growth of the rushes. The marchioness of Wei was a Kĕang (姜); by 庶姜 must be intended her cousins, attending her from Ts'e to her harem, —'the virgins, her companions;' 孽 孽 expresses the richness of their array. 庶士 are the officers escorting Chwang Kĕang and her companions from Ts'e; 有朅 expresses their martial appearance.

The rhymes are—in st. 1, 頎 (prop. cat. 15), 衣, 妻, 姨, 私, cat. 1 t. 1: in 2, 荑, 脂,

蝤, 犀, 眉, *ib.*; 倩, 盼, *,*, cat. 13 . in 3, 敖, 郊, 驕, 鑣, 朝, 勞, cat. 2; in 4, 活, 濊, 發, 揭, 孽, 朅, cat. 15, t. 3:

Ode 4. Narrative, with metaphorical and allusive portions interspersed. A WOMAN, WHO HAD BEEN SEDUCED INTO AN IMPROPER CONNECTION, NOW CAST OFF, RELATES AND BEMOANS HER SAD CASE. Maou refers the piece to the time of duke Seuen, of whose dissolute character notice has already been taken. He thinks, accordingly, that the piece was directed against the times, and holds up to approval the woman who relates her case in it, as a reformed character. The ode, however, gives no note of the time when it was composed, nor does anything more appear in it beyond what I have expressed in the above summary.

St. 1. Ll. 1—4 describe the way in which the seduction was accomplished. The 子 in l. 5 shows that we should translate them in the 2d

以为期。

二章

乘彼垝垣。以望复关。不见复关。泣涕涟涟。既见复

关。载笑载言。尔卜尔筮。体无咎言。以尔车来。以

我贿迁。

2   I ascended that ruinous wall,
To look towards Fuh-kwan;
And when I saw [you] not [coming from] it;'
My tears flowed in streams.
When I did see [you coming from] Fuh-kwan,
I laughed and I spoke.
You had consulted, [you said], the tortoise-shell and the reeds,
And there was nothing unfavourable in their response.
'Then come,' [I said],' with your carriage,
And I will remove with my goods.'

person. The whole piece, indeed, is addressed to the man, who had first led astray, and then cast off. 氓 = 民, 'one of the people.' The woman intimates by the term 'that at first she, did not know the man nor anything about him.' 蚩蚩 describes his 'ignorant look;' Maou says his 'honest looks.' 'Simple-looking' gives the meaning. 布 = 'cloth,' without saying of what material. The critics define it here by 币, 'pieces of woven silk.' 丝 is the raw silk. 贸, = 'to barter,' 'to exchange.' 即 = 就, 'to come to.'—'You came to me to consult,' i. e. to propose that I should at once elope with you. The other lines show how far the woman was wrought upon, and how, though yielding to some extent, she tried to bring about a regular marriage. Tun-k'ew was a place in Wei, but it cannot be identified. The last 4 lines are the substance of the woman's parting words. 愆 = 过, 'to go beyond;' here, = 'to protract.' 将 = 请, 'to beg,' 'to ask.' The man must have made his first approach in the beginning of summer, when the silk from the cocoons was ready for sale.

St. 2 describes the elopement, how anxious the woman was, when the time came, to see her lover, and how she sought, notwithstanding, to get some justification of her deed. 垝 = 毁, 'broken down,' 'dilapidated.' 垣 = 墙, 'a

wall.' Choo says that Fuh-kwan was 'the place where the man lived;' Maou, 'a place near which he lived.' The characters would appear to be the name of a barrier-gate, through which the visitor must come. Through modesty, she mentions the place, and not the person. The Urh-ya defines 涟涟, as 'the appearance of weeping;' but we must not lose the significance of 连连, denoting continuity. Choo supposes the last 4 lines to have been spoken by the woman, questioning the visitor. K'ang-shing, better, it appears to me, refers the first two to the man, and the others to the woman. 卜 is used of divination by the tortoise-shell, and 筮 of divination by the reeds or milfoil. 体,—see on the Shoo, V.vi.9,10. It properly belongs to the form on the burnt shell, but is here applied also to the diagrams indicated by the reeds. 贿 = 财, 'wealth, substance.' It does not appear in what the woman's wealth consisted. There was probably little of it, notwithstanding her use of the term. 'The man,' says Ying-tah, 'had never divined about the matter, and he only said so to complete the process of seduction. The critics dwell on the inconsistency of the parties' having recourse to divination in their case. 'Divination is good only if used in reference to what is right and moral.'

三章

桑之未落。其叶沃若。于嗟鸠兮。无食桑葚。于嗟女

兮。无与士耽。士之耽兮。犹可说也。女之耽兮。不

可说也。

四章

桑之落矣。其黄而陨。自我徂尔。三岁食贫。淇水汤

汤。渐车帷裳。女也不爽。士贰其行。士也罔极。二

3　Before the mulberry tree has shed its leaves,
How rich and glossy are they!
Ah! thou dove,
Eat not its fruit [to excess].
Ah! thou young lady,
Seek no licentious pleasure with a gentleman.
When a gentleman indulges in such pleasure,
Something may still be said for him;
When a lady does so,
Nothing can be said for her.

4　When the mulberry tree sheds its leaves,
They fall yellow on the ground.
Since I went with you,
Three years have I eaten of your poverty;
And [now] the full waters of the K'e
Wet the curtains of my carriage.
There has been no difference in me,

In st. 3, the woman is conscious of the folly she had committed. 沃若, = 沃然, 'glossy-like.' The dove here is not the turtle-dove of ii. I. but another species, called the *kwuh këw* (鹘 鸠), 'rather smaller than a pigeon, marked with greenish black spots, having a short tail, and noisy, from which it is named the chattering dove (鸣 鸠). It appears in the spring, and goes away in the winter.' 葚 denotes the berries of the mulberry tree. This dove is very fond of them, and they are supposed to intoxicate it. Here the allusive and metaphorical element comes in. The dove, drunk with the berries, represents the young lady who has been indiscreet. 耽 = 乐, 'to take pleasure,' or, as Yen Ts'an has it, 溺好,

'to be sunk—over head and ears—in love.' 说 is explained by 解, 'to explain,' found where we might render it by—'to give satisfaction for.' A man's sphere, it is said, is wide, and by good services and deeds he may expiate his indiscretion; but in a woman's limited sphere, if she lose her virtue, she loses all. The speaker in the ode finds this out—too late.

In st. 4 the woman appears cast off, and returning to her original home. In l. 2, 而 = 且, 'and.'—'The leaves become yellow and fall.' So was it now with her a faded beauty. In l. 3, 尔 is best taken as a particle, = 矣. 徂 = 往, 'to go away.' 汤 (*shang*) 汤 is descriptive of the full waters of the stream. 渐 = 渍, 'to wet.' A woman's carriage was curtained

三其德。

五章
三岁为妇。靡室劳矣。夙兴夜寐。靡有朝矣。言既遂

矣。至于暴矣。兄弟不知。咥其笑矣。静言思之。躬

自悼矣。

六章
及尔偕老。老使我怨。淇则有岸。隰则有泮。总角之

But you have been double in your ways.
It is you, Sir, who transgress the right,
Thus changeable in your conduct.

5 For three years I was your wife,
And thought nothing of my toil in your house.
I rose early and went to sleep late,
Not intermitting my labours for a morning.
Thus [on my part] our contract was fulfilled,
But you have behaved thus cruelly.
My brothers will not know [all this],
And will only laugh at me.
Silently I think of it,
And bemoan myself.

6 I was to grow old with you;—
Old, you give me cause for sad repining.
The K'e has its banks,
And the marsh has its shores.

at the sides. The curtains were to the car-riage what the lower garment (裳) was to the body, and hence they were called 帷裳. 女, of course, is the woman herself, and 士 the gentleman. We might translate in the 3d person:—'It was not the woman, who,' &c. 爽 =差, 'different.' Maou explains 极 by 中 =中正,='the path of the correct mean;' Choo, by 至, meaning the 'perfect' rule of conduct. 二三 have a verbal force, 'now two, now three,' i. e. varying.

St. 5. 靡室劳=不以室家之 务为劳,—as in the translation. L. 4, lit.,=

'did not have a morning.' 夙 and 夜, sepa-rated. as in l. 3, are difft. from the phrase 夙夜 in ii. II. 3, et al. In l. 5, K'ang-shing makes 言=我, 'I' and 遂=久, 'long.'—'I have thus been long with you.' But we cannot so explain the terms. 言=相约之言 'the words of their covenant,' and 遂=成, 'to complete,' 'to be complete.' Driven away, as she was, her brothers ignorant of all the cir-cumstances, would not acknowledge her. It is to be supposed her parents were dead. 咥 (he) is intended to express a sneering laugh. In l. 9, 言 is the particle.

St. 6. 老 in l. 2 is a stumbling block to the critics, as the woman had been the man's no-

宴。言笑晏晏。信誓旦旦。不思其反。反是不思。亦
已焉哉。

In the pleasant time of my girlhood, with my hair simply
　　gathered in a knot,
Harmoniously we talked and laughed.
Clearly were we sworn to good faith,
And I did not think the engagement would be broken.
That it would be broken I did not think,
And now it must be all over!

V.　*Chuh kan.*

竹竿

一章

籊籊竹竿。以钓于淇。岂不尔思。远莫致之。

1　With your long and tapering bamboo rods,
　　You angle in the K'e.
　　Do I not think of you?
　　But I am far away, and cannot get to you.

minal wife for only 3 years. I conceive, however, we are not to press a term in such a piece.
泮＝涯, 'a bank or shore.' The K'e had its
banks, and the marsh its shores; people knew
where to find them. But it was not so with the
man who acknowledged no rules nor bounds in
his conduct. 总角 describes the hair gathered, without any pins, into two horn-like
knots. Lads wore their hair so, till they were
capped, and girls, till they were married.
晏晏＝和柔, 'harmonious and soft.' 旦
旦＝明, 'clearly.'—'Our faithful oaths (pled-
ges) were distinct.' 不思其反, 'I did not
think of the going contrary,' *i. e.*, of the possi-
bility of the engagement's being broken.' Choo
expands the last line, 则亦如之何哉,
亦已而已矣. 'What then can be done?
It is all over; yes, all over.'

The rhymes are—in st. 1, 蚩, 丝, 丝, 谋 *,
淇丘 *, 媒 *, 期, cat. 1, t. 1: in 2, 垣, 关,
关, 涟, 关, 言, 言, 迁, cat. 14: in 3, 落,
若 *, cat. 5, t. 3: 葚 耽 (prop. cat. 8), cat. 7,
t. 1; 说, 说, cat. 15, t. 3: in 4, 陨, 贫 *, cat.

13; 汤, 裳, 爽, 行 *, cat. 10; 极, 德, cat. 1,
t. 3: in 5, 劳, 朝, 暴 *, 笑, 悼, cat. 2;? 瘵,
遂, cat. 15, t. 3: in 6, 怨, 岸, 泮, 宴 * 晏
旦, 反, cat. 14,; 思, 哉, cat. 1, t. 1.

Ode 5. Narrative. A DAUGHTER OF THE
HOUSE OF WEI, MARRIED IN ANOTHER STATE,
EXPRESSES HER LONGING TO REVISIT WEI. The
argument of this ode is thus the same with that
of i.i. XIV. This, however, is shorter and simpler. The 'Little Preface' says, indeed, that
the lady here was unhappy in her marriage, and
that she was able by a sense of propriety to
repress her longing. But neither of these things
appears in the piece. She thinks of the scenes
of her youth, and longs that she were back
among them. That cannot be, she is now so
far removed from them; and with an expression
of regret she submits to her lot. This is the
substance of the poem.

St. 1. 籊 籊 ＝ 'long and tapering.' I translate the first 2 lines in the 2d person, because of
the 尔 in the 3d line. When young, the

二章
泉源在左。淇水在右。女子有行。远兄弟父母。
三章
淇水在右。泉源在左。巧笑之瑳。佩玉之傩。
四章
淇水滺滺。桧楫松舟。驾言出游。以写我忧。

2   The Ts'euen-yuen is on the left,
       And the waters of the K'e are on the right.
       But when a young lady goes away, [and is married],
       She leaves her brothers and parents.

3   The waters of the K'e are on the right,
       And the Ts'euen-yuen is on the left.
       How shine the white teeth through the artful smiles!
       How the girdle gems move to the measured steps!

4   The waters of the K'e flow smoothly;
       There are the oars of cedar and the boats of pine.
       Might I but go there in my carriage and ramble,
       To dissipate my sorrow!

speaker had been pleased to look at the fishers, and she would be glad to be able to do so again. 远 莫 致 之, 'from the distance, there is no bringing it about,' *i. e.*, there is no getting a sight of the Wei anglers. As Gow-yang Sëw expands it, 远 适 异 国，不 得 见 焉.

Stt. 2, 3. The Ts'euen-yuen is 'The Hundred Springs,' referred to on iii. XIV. 1. It flowed 1st on the northwest of the capital of Wei, and then, after a southeast course, joined the K'e, which came from the southwest. The north was held to be 'on the left,' and the south 'on the right.' Hence the rivers are spoken of thus relatively. The lady remembers the pleasures she had experienced between those streams, and mourns that she no longer resided in Wei. If we seek for any allusive element in the two rivers, as the old interpreters do, we only fall into absurdities. 女 子，云 云,—see on ii. XIV. 2. The last two lines of st. 3 indicate more particularly what the lady's pleasures had been,—rambling with her companions, in happy converse and elegant dress. 瑳 is here explain-

ed by Maou, as 'the appearance of an artful smile;' but the word properly denotes 'the brilliant, white appearance of a gem.' Here it signifies the ivory of the teeth displayed in smiling. 佩 玉 = 'the gems attached to a girdle.' An ornament of various gems, variously strung together, was worn anciently by ladies at the girdle. We shall have occasion to speak of it again. The gems struck against each other, and made a noise in walking. 傩 means 'to walk with measured steps (行 有 节).'

St.4. 滺滺 denotes the 'app. of the flowing current.' 桧, called also 栝, is probably a cedar, 'having the leaf of the cypress, and the trunk of a pine.' 松 is the pine. 驾言, 云 云,—as in ii. XIV. 4.

The rhymes are—in st. 1, 淇, 思, 之, cat. 1, t. 1: in 2, 右 *, 母 *, *ib.*, t. 2: in 3, 左, 瑳, 傩 (prop. cat. 14), cat. 17: in 4, 滺, 舟, 游, 忧, cat. 3, t. 1.

VI. *Hwan-lan.*

芄兰

一章

芄兰之支。童子佩觿。虽则佩觿。能不我知。容兮遂

兮。垂带悸兮。

二章

芄兰之叶。童子佩韘。虽则佩韘。能不我甲。容兮遂

兮。垂带悸兮。

1   There are the branches of the sparrow-gourd;—
     There is that lad, with the spike at his girdle.
     Though he carries a spike at his girdle,
     He does not know us.
     How easy and conceited is his manner,
     With the ends of his girdle hanging down as they do!

2   There are the leaves of the sparrow-gourd;—
     There is that lad with the archer's thimble at his girdle.
     Though he carries an archer's thimble at his girdle,
     He is not superior to us.
     How easy and conceited is his manner,
     With the ends of his girdle hanging down as they do!

Ode 6. Allusive. PICTURE OF A CONCEITED YOUNG MAN OF RANK. Acc. to the 'Little Preface,' the subject of this piece is duke Hwuy of Wei,—Soh, the son of Seuen and Seuen Këang, who succeeded to the State after the murder of his brothers, Keih-tsze and Show;—see on iii.XIX. He was then 'young,' acc. to the Tso-chuen;—Too-yu says 15 or 16. Choo says he cannot tell who is the subject, and does not think it worth his while to attempt an application of it to any one in particular. Nothing more than what I have stated can be deduced from the language of the two stanzas.

L.1 in both stanzas. The *hwan lan* is a creeping plant, the stalk of which, when broken, exudes a white juice. Its leaves may be eaten, both raw and cooked. It has the names also of 藋, 萝藦, and 雀瓢; by the last of which I have translated it. From the Japanese plates, we might conclude that it was a *tylophora*. Some explain 支 by 荚, 'pods,' those of the plant, several inches long, hanging down from among the leaves, 'like an awl.' The *weakness* of the plant, unable to rise from the ground without support, is supposed to be the reason why it is introduced here, with an allusion to the weak character of the youth who is spoken of.

L.2. 童子 may be used of any one under 19. The *hwuy* was an ivory spike, worn at the girdle for the purpose of loosening knots. It belonged to the equipment of grown up men, and was supposed to indicate their competency for the management of business, however intricate. The youth in the ode had assumed it from vanity. The *sheh* was an instrument, also of ivory, worn by archers on the thumb of the right hand, to assist them in drawing the string of their bow. A ring of jade is now used for this purpose. K'ang-shing makes the *sheh* to have been a sort of glove, made of leather, and worn with the same object on 3 fingers of the right hand.

L.4. I agree with Wang Yin-che in taking 能 here as = 而, 'and yet,' responding to 虽 in

VII.　*Ho kwang.*

河广
一章
谁谓河广。一苇杭之。谁谓宋远。跂予望之。
二章
谁谓河广。曾不容刀。谁谓宋远。曾不崇朝。

1　Who says that the Ho is wide?
　　With [a bundle of] reeds I can cross it.
　　Who says that Sung is distant?
　　On tiptoe I can see it.

2　Who says that the Ho is wide?
　　It will not admit a little boat.
　　Who says that Sung is distant?
　　It would not take a whole morning to reach it.

1.3. The line is condemnatory of the youth, pretending to be a man, but without a man's knowledge or ability; but I cannot get Maou's idea out of it in st.1.—'He does not say (=think) that he has no knowledge, but is proud and insolent to others (不自谓无知，以骄慢人);' nor follow him in taking 甲 in st.2 as = 狎. The lines are at least translateable, as they are, and 甲 = 长, 'to be superior to,' 'to rule over.'

Ll. 5,6. 容 is 'the manner,' or 'air,' of the youth; and 遂, the appearance of it, as in the translation. 悸 expresses the appearance of his girdle hanging down,—'in a jaunty manner.'

The rhymes are—in st.1, 支, 觿 *, 觿 *, 知, cat.16, t.1; 遂, 悸, (and in st. 2), cat. 15, t.3: in 2, 叶 *, 㯰 *, 㯰 *, 甲, cat.8, t.3.

Ode 7. Narrative. OTHER THINGS, MORE DIFFICULT TO OVERCOME THAN DISTANCE, MAY KEEP ONE FROM A PLACE. Both Maou and Choo refer this short piece to a daughter of Seuen Këang, who was married to duke Hwan of Sung;—see on iii.IX. After giving birth to a son, who became duke Sëang, she was divorced, and returned to Wei. When that son succeeded to Sung, she wished to return to that State; but the rules of propriety forbade her, as having been divorced, to do so; and she is supposed to have made

these verses to reconcile herself to her circumstances. They are supposed, therefore to be much to her honour, as showing how she could subordinate her maternal longings to her sense of what was proper! Yen Ts'an started a difficulty about the time when the lines were written, making them earlier than the accession of duke Sëang, and this would affect the general interpretation. It is hardly worth while, however, to discuss this point.

Ll. 1, 2, in both stt. 苇,—'a reed or rush.' 杭=渡, 'to cross over.' I agree with Ying-tah in taking 一 苇 as meaning, not 'a single reed,' but 'a bundle of reeds.' 曾 = 则. We can hardly translate it. If we try to do so, *but* would come nearest to its meaning:—'It is not wide, but,' &c. 刀 means a small boat. A more modern form of the character has 舟 at the side. It is not true that the Ho is so narrow, or that we could cross it with the help of a bundle of reeds; but the speaker thus intimates that if nothing but the stream of the Ho stood in her way, she could easily get across it. So, in the other lines.

Ll. 3, 4. 跂 (*k'e*, 2d tone) = 举 踵, 'to raise the heel,' *i. e.* to stand on tiptoe. 崇朝, —see on iv. VII. 2.

The rhymes are—in st. 1, 杭、望, cat. 10; in 2, 刀、朝, cat. 2.

VIII. *Pih he.*

伯兮

一章

伯兮朅兮。邦之桀兮。伯也执殳。为王前驱。

二章

自伯之东。首如飞蓬。岂无膏沐。谁适为容。

三章

其雨其雨。杲杲出日。愿言思伯。甘心首疾。

1   My noble husband is how martial-like!
     The hero of the country!
     My husband, grasping his halberd,
     Is in the leading chariot of the king's [host].

2   Since my husband went to the east,
     My head has been like the flying [pappus of the] **artemisia**.
     It is not that I could not anoint and wash it;
     But for whom should I adorn myself?

3   O for rain! O for rain!
     But brightly the sun comes forth.
     Longingly I think of my husband,
     Till my heart is weary, and my head aches.

Ode 8. Narrative and metaphorical. A WIFE MOURNS OVER THE PROTRACTED ABSENCE OF HER HUSBAND ON THE KING'S SERVICE. Maou thinks that this piece was directed against the warlike character of the times, when officers were long kept on service away from their families. K'ang-shing, more particularly, and I believe correctly, referred it to the year B. C. 706, when, as we learn from the Ch'un Ts'ew (II. v. 6), Wei and some other States did service with the king against the State of Ch'ing. That was in the time of duke Seuen of Wei.

St. 1. Choo takes 伯 as a designation of her husband by the lady. This is much better than to take it, with Maou, as a designation of him by his office, which he supposes to have been the presidency or charge of a district (州伯).

朅＝武貌, 'martial-like.' 桀,—'one of a myriad,'＝ a hero. The *shoo* was a club or halberd, 10 or more cubits long, made of wood, thick and heavy towards the point, but without a sharp edge. It was used to strike down, not to pierce. The lady sees her husband in his chariot. and in the front of the king's host,—the post of daring and danger.

St. 2. Ch'ing lay to the south-west of Wei The troops of Wei and the other States must first have marched west to the capital, to join the royal army, and then gone east to attack Ch'ing. 蓬,—see on ii. XIV. 2. It is here called 'the flying *fung*,' with reference to its bristly or feathery *pappus*, through which its seeds are dispersed by the wind. Such had the lady's hair become. 膏沐 are both nouns;— 'Have I no ointment and wash?' The wash for the head was congee water. Both Maou and Choo explain 适 (*teih*) by 主, 'to pay chief attention to,' 'to set the mind on,'—as in Ana. IV. x. 为 is in the 3d tone,—'for.' 容＝ 妆饰 容貌 'to adorn the person.' The 'Complete Digest' expands the line.— 今君子在外,我固无所主矣, 则谁所主而为之容耶. ……

St. 3. 其雨,—其 has here the optative or imperative force, which is so common in the Shoo. Wang Yin-che explains it, in this signifi-

一章

焉得谖草。言树之背。愿言思伯。使我心痗。

4　How shall I get the plant of forgetfulness?
　　I would plant it on the north of my house.
　　Longingly I think of my husband,
　　And my heart is made to ache.

IX.　*Yëw hoo.*

有狐

一章

有狐绥绥。在彼淇梁。心之忧矣。之子无裳。

二章

有狐绥绥。在彼淇厉。心之忧矣。之子无带。

1　There is a fox, solitary and suspicious,
　　At that dam over the K'e.
　　My heart is sad;—
　　That man has no lower garment.

2　There is a fox, solitary and suspicious,
　　At that deep ford of the K'e.

cance, by 尚, and 庶几· 杲杲＝日色明, 'the sun looking bright.' These two lines are metaphorical.—As, when one longs for rain, and day after day is disappointed by a brilliant sun, so was it with the lady longing for the return of her husband, while yet that return was continually delayed. 甘心 generally means—'with a pleased or contented mind;' but that signification cannot well be applied here. Maou explains 甘 by 厌, 'to be satiated, or surfeited,' and Wang T'aou observes that 'satisfaction of mind is expressed by 甘心, and so is also is a fulness of anxious thoughts (快意谓之甘心,忧念之思满足于心,亦谓之甘心).' 愿言, —see on iii. XIX. 1.

St. 4. 谖,—as in I. 1, 'to forget.' There is a plant which is fancied to have the quality of making people forget their sorrows, for which purpose the flowers and leaves are cooked together. It is called 萱草 and 谖草, and also 鹿葱, 'stag's onions.' In the Japanese plates it is the *hemerocalta Japonica*, or Day lily. 背, 'the back,' is considered to be 'the north

of the body.' Here the term denotes 'the part of a house behind the apartments and chambers,' which was called 北堂, 'the north hall.' Outside and below this was a small piece of ground, where a few flowers and shrubs could be planted; and here the lady says she would plant 'the grass of forgetfulness.' 痗＝病, 'to be sick,' 'to ache.'

The rhymes are—in st. 1, 揭, 桀, cat. 15, t. 3; 叟 *, 驱, cat. 4, t. 1: in 2, 东, 蓬, 容, cat. 9: in 3, 日, 疾, cat. 12, t. 3: in 4, 背*, 痗*, cat. 1, t. 2.

Ode 9. Metaphorical. A WOMAN EXPRESSES HER DESIRE FOR A HUSBAND. She does so certainly in a singular way, and there is considerable difficulty in explaining satisfactorily these few lines. The 'Little Preface' says the piece is directed against the times.—Through the misery and desolation of Wei, many, both men and women, were left unmarried, or had lost their partners; and in such circumstances, acc. to ancient practice, the marriage rules might have been relaxed, and made more simple and easy, to encourage unions and the increase of the people. Because the government took no action in this direction, this piece was written to censure it.

三章
有狐绥绥。在彼淇侧。心之忧矣。之子无服。

My heart is sad ;—
That man has no girdle.

3　There is a fox, solitary and suspicious,
　　By the side there of the K'e.
　　My heart is sad ;—
　　That man has no clothes.

X. *Muh kwa.*

木瓜
一章
投我以木瓜。报之以琼琚。匪报也。永以为好也。

1　There was presented to me a papaya,
　　And I returned for it a beautiful *keu*-gem;
　　Not as a return for it,
　　But that our friendship might be lasting.

But, as Choo observes, there is nothing in the language of the ode to suggest to us that such was its design. The language, indeed, must be strained to reconcile it with this interpretation. Ll.1,2. in all the stt. 绥 is read *shwuy*, and the dict. Yuh-p'ëen (玉篇 ; A. D. 523) quotes l.2 of viii.VI., with 久久, instead of 绥绥. The K'ang-he dict. refers to the line under this sound of the character, and would fain deduce the meaning of the phrase from that of 毿毿 ' having long hair,' or 'fox-like.' It concludes however, with giving the explanation of it by Maou,—匹行貌, 'the app. of walking in pairs.' The 1st line then, is with Maou= 'There is a pair of foxes;' and the piece becomes allusive. It is all as it should be with the foxes. Those unmarried multitudes are worse off. Choo on the other hand makes 绥绥 to mean 'the app. of walking solitary, seeking a mate (独行求匹之貌);' so that the piece becomes metaphorical,—' As is the fox, so is the individual, who is in the speaker's eye.' The ' seeking a mate ' is imported into the phrase. Yen Ts'an seems to give the best account of it.—'The fox is by nature suspicious. 绥绥 describes one walking soli-

tary, slowly and suspiciously.' 梁,—as in iii.X.3. 厉, — see on iii.IX.1, where the character is used as a verb, meaning 'to go through deep water with the clothes on.' Here it is a noun, meaning a deep ford, which must be crossed in such a way. Two other significations of the term are given in the dict., to which some critics hold here. One is ' stepping stones ;' the other, 'a high and dangerous bank.'

Ll.3,4. 心之忧矣 must be understood of the speaker, or of the writer. 之子 = 是人, as in i.VI., *et al.* It is most naturally taken as masculine. Maou's interpretation of the ode requires the phrase to be taken in the plural ;—'those parties,' the men and women, who were left, through the unhappiness of the times, without partners. 无裳, 无带, and 无服 describe the desolate appearance of the wifeless man, and intimate that the speaker would be glad to supply his wants,— make him lower garments, a girdle, and clothes in general ; *i. e.*, would be glad to become his wife. It is a strange way of intimating her wish. 裳 it is supposed, is used in the 1st, st., because a man walks along the top of a dam with his lower garment on ; and 带 in the 2d.,

二章
投我以木桃。报之以琼瑶。匪报也。永以为好也。
三章
投我以木李。报之以琼玖。匪报也。永以为好也。

2　There was presented to me a peach,
　　And I returned for it a beautiful *yaou*-gem ;
　　Not as a return for it,
　　But that our friendship might be lasting.

3　There was presented to me a plum,
　　And I returned for it a beautiful *këw*-stone ;
　　Not as a return for it,
　　But that our friendship might be lasting.

because he would have taken off his girdle in crossing the ford.

The rhymes are—in st.1, 梁, 裳, cat. 10: in 2, 厉, 带, cat. 15, t. 3: in 3, 侧, 服 *, cat. 1, t. 3.

Ode 10. Metaphorical. SMALL GIFTS OF KINDNESS SHOULD BE RESPONDED TO WITH GREATER; BUT FRIENDSHIP IS MORE THAN ANY GIFT. When Wei was nearly extinguished by the Teih, duke Hwan of Ts'e, as the leading prince among the States, came grandly and munificently to its help; and Maou finds in this ode the grateful sentiments of the people of Wei towards him. We can hardly conceive that this is the correct historical interpretation of the piece. If it be so, Hwan's all but royal munificence and favour is strangely represented by the insignificant present of fruit. Choo compares the piece with ii. XVII., and thinks it may refer to an interchange of courtesies between a lover and his mistress. We need not seek any particular interpretation of it. What is metaphorically set forth may have a general application.

Ll. 1, 2 in all the stt. 投 means, properly, 'to throw at or to;' but here='to present.' 木瓜 is the well-known *carica papaya;* called a 瓜, we presume, from its gourd-like fruit. We must understand the terms here of the fruit, and not of the tree. But what are we to make of the 木桃 and 木李 in the other stanzas? Neither Maou nor Choo says anything in explanation of the 木, nor does the Urh-ya mention such trees. The probability is, therefore, that we are to understand by the phrases simply the peach proper and the plum proper. The *Pun-ts'aou,* indeed, gives the name of 木桃 to the *cha-tsze* (楂 子), 'a kind of bad

pear,' and of 木李 to the *ming cha* (榠 樝) which is described as an inferior variety of the *muh kwa.* But these identifications have been made for the sake of the texts before us. Maou quotes a saying of Confucius, that in this ode he saw 'the ceremony of sending presents in bundles made of rushes (苞苴之礼行),' which might lead us to translate 'a bundle of the papaya,' &c.; but where Maou found the saying, we do not know. It appears, indeed, in the fabrication by Wang Suh, attributed to K'ung Ts'ung (孔从子); but it was stolen, probably, by Suh from Maou. The Shwoh-wǎn defines 琼 as 'a gem of a carnation colour;' but in this ode the term is used as an adj.,= 'beautiful (玉之美名).' 琚 is the name of a gem. Two square *këus* formed part of the furniture of the girdle appendages;—see on V. 3. The *yaou* was another prized gem, or stone, acc. to the Shwoh-wǎn; and the *këw* was a stone, ranking in value immediately after the gems.

Ll. 3, 4. As expanded by Yen Ts'an, these two lines are— 此 非 足 为 报，欲 以 结 好 于 永 久。'This is not sufficient to be a return, but I wish by means of it to tie the bonds of friendship for ever.'

The rhymes are—in st. 1, 瓜 *, 琚, cat. 5, t. 1; (and in 2, 3), 报 *, 好 *, cat. 3, t. 2: in 2, 桃, 瑶, cat. 2: in 3, 李, 玖 *, cat. 1, t. 2.

CONCLUDING NOTE. We have thus arrived at the end of the odes of Wei. Those in this 3d Book of them do not differ much in character from those in the others, though there is less in them of the licentiousness which often disgraced the court, and of the oppression of the government. The 3d and 4th pieces are the most interesting and ambitious. Chang Tsae, a friend of Choo He's, says, 'The State of Wei lay along the banks of the Ho. The soil was not deep, and the disposition of the people was volatile; the country was level and low, and so the people were soft and weak; it was fertile, and did not require much agricultural toil, so that the people were indolent. Such was the character of the inhabitants, and their songs and music were licentious and bad. To listen to them would induce idleness, insolence, and depravity. So is it also with the odes of Ch'ing.'

More favourably, Choo Kung-ts'een says, Wei had many superior men. In the odes there appear duke Woo (v.I.) a ruler whose equal is hardly to be found in other States; and duke Wăn (iv. VI.), the restorer of the State. Besides these, we have the filial sons of iii. VII., the faithful minister of iii. XV., the wise man of iii. XVI., the worthy great officers of iv. IX., the worthy musician of iii. XIII., and the recluse of v. II. All these stand eminently out in a time of degeneracy. Next to them are to be ranked the two princes of iii. XIX., striving to die for each other. Then there are the six worthy princesses:—Chwang Kĕang, Kung Kĕang, the wives of Muh of Heu and Hwan of Sung, and the two heroines of iii. XIV., and v. V. There are, moreover, in addition to these, Tae Kwei of iii. III, virtuously careful of her person; the lady of v. VIII., so devoted to her husband; she of iii. VIII., so well acquainted with what constituted virtuous conduct; and she of iii. X., cast off, and yet maintaining her good name. Wei had thus not only many superior men, but many wives of ability and virtue.'

BOOK VI. THE ODES OF THE ROYAL DOMAIN.

I. *Shoo li*

王一之六

黍离

一章

彼黍离离。彼稷之苗。行迈靡靡。中心摇摇。知我者。谓我心忧。不知我者。谓我何求。悠悠苍天。此何人哉。

1 There was the millet with its drooping heads;
There was the sacrificial millet coming into blade.
Slowly I moved about,
In my heart all-agitated.
Those who knew me
Said I was sad at heart.
Those who did not know me
Said I was seeking for something.
O distant and azure Heaven!
By what man was this [brought about]?

TITLE OF THE BOOK.— 王 一 之 六, 'Wang; Book VI. of Part I.' By *Wang* (King or King's) we are to understand the territory which constituted the royal domain or State, attached to Loh, or the eastern capital of Chow. At the beginning of that dynasty, king Wăn occupied the city of Fung, from which his son moved the seat of govt. to Haou (see the Shoo on V. iii. 6). In the time of king Ching, a city was built by the duke of Chow, near the pres. Loh-yang, and called 'the eastern capital.' Meetings of the princes of the States assembled there, but the court continued to be held at Haou, till the accession of king P'ing, who removed to the east in B.C. 769. From this time the kings of Chow sank nearly to the level of the princes of the States; and the poems collected in their domain were classed among the 'Lessons of Manners,' though still distinguished by the epithet of 'Royal,' prefixed to them.

Ode 1. Narrative. AN OFFICER DESCRIBES HIS MELANCHOLY AND REFLECTIONS ON SEEING THE DESOLATION OF THE OLD CAPITAL OF CHOW. There is nothing in the piece about the old capital of Chow, but the schools both of Maou and Choo are agreed in this interpretation of it. In Han Ying and Lëw Hëang we find it differently attributed, and with more than one meaning; but we need not enter on their views, which are valuable only as showing that the historical interpretation of the odes was made, in the end of the Chow and the beginning of the Han dyn., by different critics, according to their own ability and presumptions. The place of the piece, at the commencement of this Book, should be decisive in favour of the common view.

Ll. 1—4, in all the stt. describe what the writer saw, and how he felt. Maou makes 彼, ='there,' the site of the ancestral temple and the buildings of the old palace, from which they had disappeared. We must construe it,

二章

彼黍离离。彼稷之穗。行迈靡靡。中心如醉。知我

者。谓我心忧。不知我者。谓我何求。悠悠苍天。此

何人哉。

三章

彼黍离离。彼稷之实。行迈靡靡。中心如噎。知我

者。谓我心忧。不知我者。谓我何求。悠悠苍天。此

何人哉。

2　There was the millet with its drooping heads;
　There was the sacrificial millet in the ear.
　Slowly I moved about,
　My heart intoxicated, as it were, [with grief].
　Those who knew me
　Said I was sad at heart.
　Those who did not know me
　Said I was seeking for something.
　O thou distant and azure Heaven!
　By what man was this [brought about]?

3　There was the millet with its drooping heads;
　There was the sacrificial millet in grain.
　Slowly I moved about,
　As if there were a stoppage at my heart.
　Those who knew me
　Said I was sad at heart.
　Those who did not know me
　Said I was seeking for something.
　O thou distant and azure Heaven!
　By what man was this [brought about]?

however, with 黍 and 稷,—'that millet,' &c., meaning, no doubt that which the writer had seen where the seat of the kings formerly was. *Shü* and *tseih* are both varieties of the millet, 黍, acc. to Williams, being *milium nigricans*, and 稷 simply *milium*. The *Pun-ts'aou* makes the essential difference between them to be that 'the grains of the *shü* are glutinous, and those of the *tseih* not.' A spirit is distilled from the former; the latter are more used for food. The 稷 is also called 明 粢, and 穄, and was used much as a sacrificial offering. Until the plants are authoritatively identified, I call 黍 'millet' simply, and 稷, 'sacrificial millet.' 离 离 is descriptive of 'the drooping appearance'(垂 貌)' of the heads of the *shü*, which is very characteristic in the best pictures of the plant. 苗 is the plant shooting up in the blade;

II. *Keun-tsze yu yih.*

君子于役

一章

君子于役。不知其期。曷至哉。鸡栖于塒。日之夕

矣。牛羊下来。君子于役。如之何勿思。

二章

君子于役。不日不月。曷其有佸。鸡栖于桀。日之夕

1   My husband is away on service,
    And I know not when he will return.
    Where is he now?
    The fowls roost in their holes in the walls;
    And in the evening of the day,
    The goats and cows come down [from the hill];
    But my husband is away on service.
    How can I but keep thinking of him?

2   My husband is away on service,
    Not for days [merely] or for months.
    When will he come back to me?

穗, the inflorescence, or the plant in the ear; and 实, the plant when the grain is fully formed. The *shŭ* ripens much earlier than the *tseih*, and there is supposed to be a reference to this in st. 1; but the other stt. seem to make this point doubtful. 迈,—as in iii. XIV. 3. 靡靡 = 迟迟, 'slowly.' 摇摇,—'tossed about,' 'agitated.' 醉,—'intoxicated;' 'intoxicated with sorrow,' Maou says. 'The officer,' says Le Kung-k‘ae, 'lost in his sorrow all consciousness, as if he had been intoxicated with spirits.' 噎,—'an interruption of breathing,' as in sobbing from grief. Morrison says, 'The line here denotes deep sorrow, or, as we express it, A load or weight upon the mind.'—Choo He finds an allusive element between the 1st and 2d lines and the 3d and 4th. This does not seem to be necessary.

Ll. 5—8 describe the different judgments suggested by the movements and appearance of the writer to those who saw him, according as they sympathized with his feelings or not.

Ll. 9, 10 contain the writer's appeal to Heaven on the desolation before him. 悠悠 = 远貌, 'the app. of distance.' 苍 is the azure of the lofty, distant sky. 苍天 is used by metony-my for providence, the Power supposed to dwell above the sky.

The rhymes are—in st. 1. (and in 2, 3), 离 *, 靡 *, cat. 17; 苗, 摇, cat. 2; (and in 2, 3), 忧, 求, cat. 3, t. 1; (and in 2, 3), 天, 人, cat. 12, t. 1: in 2, 穗, 醉, cat. 3, t. 1: in 3, 实, 噎, cat. 12, t. 3.

Ode 2. Narrative. THE FEELINGS OF A WIFE ON THE PROLONGED ABSENCE OF HER HUSBAND ON SERVICE, AND HER LONGING FOR HIS RETURN. This is the interpretation of the piece given by Choo, and even the imperial editors approve of it, as more natural than that of Maou, who attributes the ode to the great officers who remained at court, and, indignant at the protracted service on which their companion was employed, thus expressed their disapprobation of king P‘ing.

Ll. 1—3 in both stt. 君子,—as in i. X., ii. III, *et al.* 于役 might be construed, taking 于 in the meaning of 往, 'to go away,' which K‘ang-shing always gives it; but it is better to consider 于 as the mere particle, as in 于飞 in i. II., *et al.* 其期 = 其反还之

矣。牛羊下括。君子于役。苟无饥渴。

The fowls roost on their perches;
And in the evening of the day,
The goats and cows come down and home;
But my husband is away on service.
Oh if he be but kept from hunger and thirst!

III.   *Keun-tsze yang-yang.*

君子阳阳

一章
君子阳阳。左执簧。右招我由房。其乐只且。

二章
君子陶陶。左执翿。右招我由敖。其乐只且。

1   My husband looks full of satisfaction.
    In his left hand he holds his reed-organ,
    And with his right he calls me to the room.
    Oh the joy!

2   My husband looks delighted.
    In his left hand he holds his screen of feathers,
    And with his right hand he calls me to the stage.
    Oh the joy!

期, 'the time of his return.' 不日不月,—as in the translation. Choo says, 'The length of his service is not to be calculated by days and months (不可计以日月). 曷至哉 is taken by Choo of the place where the officer was at the time. As the 'Complete Digest' expands it, 且今何所至哉, 其所至之地, 吾亦不得而知之也. K'ang-shing connects the line closely with the preceding:—'I do not know the set time of his return,—the time when he ought to come.' That is the meaning of the 3d line in st. 2, where 佸=会, 'to assemble,' 'to meet.' In st. 1, 曷='where;' in 2,='when.'

Ll. 4,6. The creatures around her had their nightly resting places, while her husband had none. 塒 is the name for holes made in the walls for fowls,—'chiselled out,' as Maou says, from the walls of earth and lime, of which the houses were built. 桀=杙, 'a post;' but we must think rather of 'a perch.' K'ang-shing, unnaturally, explains 下来 by 从下牧地而来, 'come from their low pasture-grounds.' 括=至, 'to come,' 'to arrive.'

Ll. 7,8. 苟, 'if,' must be taken as expressing a wish or prayer. As Le Kung-k'ae puts it, 既不得归, 则庶几其在道路之间, 且无饥渴之患, 亦可矣, 'Since he cannot come immediately, if peradventure in his travelling he escape the suffering of hunger and thirst, so far well.'

IV. *Yang che shwuy.*

扬之水
一章
扬之水。不流束薪。彼其之子。不与我戍申。怀哉怀
哉。曷月予还归哉。

1   The fretted waters
 Do not carry on their current a bundle of firewood!
 Those, the members of our families,
 Are not with us here guarding Shin.
 How we think of them! How we think of them!
 What month shall we return home?

The rhymes are—in st. 1, 期, 哉, 堋, 来, 思, cat. 1, t. 1: in 2, 月, 佸, 桀, 括, 渴, cat. 15, t. 3.

Ode 3. Narrative. THE HUSBAND'S SATIS-FACTION, AND THE WIFE'S JOY, ON HIS RETURN. This again is the view of Choo He, who regards this ode as a sequel of the preceding one; and I do not think anything better can be made of it. Still it does not carry with itself the witness of its own correctness, so much as the interpretation of ode 2. Choo refers, as if with some doubt of his own view, to that of the old school, that the piece is expressive of commiseration for the disordered and fallen condition of Chow, and that it shows us, more especially, the officers encouraging one another to take office, for the sake of preserving their lives. To my mind the piece, as a whole and in its details, is accompanied with greater difficulties on this interpretation than on the other.

Both stanzas. 阳 阳 = 得 志 之 貌, 'the appearance of satisfaction, having got one's will.' So, Choo. Maou's explanation is nearly the same,—'not exercising the mind on anything.' 陶 陶 indicates 'the app. of harmony and joy.' 簧 is used for 笙, an instrument in which the ancient Chinese had the rudiments of the organ. It consisted of 13 or of 19 tubes, set up in the shell of a gourd, each with an orifice near the bottom, to which a moveable tongue of metal called 簧 was fitted. The whole was blown by the mouth. 翿 was a sort of flag or screen carried by dancers, with which they could screen themselves at parts of their performance. The 3d lines are the most difficult, and none of the critics throw much light upon them. Acc. to Maou, by 房 we are to understand 'the music in the apartment,' and 由 = 用, 'to use.' The king, it is said, had the pieces of the *Chow Nan* sung to him with music in an inner apartment of the palace, and the officer of the ode is made to appear beckoning to his friends to follow him, and take part in the performance, all unworthy, as it was, of his and their position and abilities. In the 2d stanza, he beckons to them, in the same way, to follow him to the place where the dancers or pantomimes performed their part ;— 放 = 舞 位, 'the places for the dancers.' All this is very harsh and forced ; and could hardly be followed by the expression of delight in the last line. Choo contents himself with simply explaining the terms, and that obscurely. He defines 由 by 从, which we must take as meaning 'to follow to,' in order to construe it similarly in both stanzas. The general meaning is plain enough. The husband, returned from his long service, forgets all his toils, and is ready to express his pleasure by music and dancing ; and his wife shares in his joy. 只 且 —as in iii. XVI.

The rhymes are—in st. 1, 阳, 簧, 房, st. 10: in 2, 陶 ₊, 翿 ₊, 放 (prop. cat. 2), cat. 3, t. 2: in the two stanzas, 乐, 乐, cat. 2.

Ode. 4. Allusive. THE TROOPS OF CHOW, KEPT ON DUTY IN SHIN, MURMUR AT THEIR SEPARATION FROM THEIR FAMILIES. The mother of king P'ing was a Këang, a daughter of the House of Shin. That State had suffered repeatedly from the attacks of Ts'oo, and the king, after removing to the eastern capital, sent his own people to occupy and defend it, and kept them long absent from their homes on the service. The piece contains their murmurings at their separation from their families. This is the interpretation given by Maou, and adopted by Choo,—with differences in the details. Gow-yang Sëw had proposed, before Choo's time, a somewhat different view, which has had many followers. L. 3 is to be taken, they think, not of the families of the troops employed in Shin, nor of other troops of Chow which were left at home, but of the troops of other States, which should have been called forth by the king for the duty. This modification of the interpretation shows us better the nature of the allusion in the 1st two lines, but does not agree so well with the last

二章
扬之水。不流束楚。彼其之子。不与我戍甫。怀哉怀
哉。曷月予还归哉。

三章
扬之水。不流束蒲。彼其之子。不与我戍许。怀哉怀
哉。曷月予还归哉。

2　The fretted waters
　　Do not carry on their current a bundle of thorns!
　　Those, the members of our families,
　　Are not with us here guarding P‘oo.
　　How we think of them! How we think of them!
　　What month shall we return?

3　The fretted waters
　　Do not carry on their current a bundle of osiers!
　　Those, the members of our families,
　　Are not with us here guarding Heu.
　　How we think of them! How we think of them!
　　What month shall we return?

two. I feel unable myself to express any decisive opinion in the case.

Ll. 1,2. in all the stt. 扬 is explained by Maou by 激扬, 'to impede and excite,'—as rocks do the waters of a stream; but he does not explain the nature of the allusion which underlies the statement that a stream thus fretted is yet not able to carry away so slight a thing as a bundle of firewood. Acc. to K‘angshing, it is that, though the king's commands were so urgent and exacting, no kindness flowed from him to the people. This is unsatisfactory; and Ying-tah and Wang Taou insist that the lines should be taken interrogatively, or that ll. 2 and 4 should be understood as strong assertions, and not negations. Carrying out this view, Wang would farther refer the 之子 in l.3 to king P‘ing, and take 与 in l.4 as 用, 'to employ.' This would meet the difficulty about the allusion; but the murmuring of the troops becomes thus very violent. It is inconsistent with the spirit of the odes to express disapprobation of the king so directly; and the last two lines seem to require us to interpret l.3 of the families of the soldiers.

Choo adopts a different exegesis of l.1. Referring to a phrase, 悠扬, meaning the 'long and rippling' course of a stream, he explains 扬之水 as 'the appearance of water flowing gently;'—so gently and feebly in this case, that the current would not bear away a small bundle of anything. How the lines thus understood bear allusively on the rest of the stanza, he does not at all make clear, saying that it is to be found in the two 不,—in lines 2 and 4. Gow-yang and those who follow him, taking *yang* in the same way, make out the allusion to be to the feebleness of king P‘ing, who could not command the services of the States to guard Shin, but was obliged to lay the duty on his own people.—This meaning of 扬 is not given in K‘ang-he's dict., and I feel constrained to keep to Maou's account of the term with all its difficulties. 薪 and 楚,—see on i. IX. 2. Maou takes 蒲 in the sense of 'rushes;' but it also means 'osiers,' from which arrow-shafts could be made, which seems more suitable here.

Ll. 3, 4. The 其 is read *ke*, and is treated as a mere particle. Wang Yin-che gives 记, 忌, 已 and 迤, as synonyms of it, which are found used (and are interchanged) in the same way. 之子＝是子, 'those parties,'—'the fami-

V. *Chung kuh.*

中谷有蓷

一章

中谷有蓷。暵其干矣。有女仳离。嘅其叹矣。嘅其叹

矣。遇人之艰难矣。

二章

中谷有蓷。暵其修矣。有女仳离。条其歗矣。条其歗

1 In the valleys grows the mother-wort,
But scorched is it in the drier places.
There is a woman forced to leave her husband;
Sadly she sighs!
Sadly she sighs!
She suffers from his hard lot.

2 In the valleys grows the mother-wort,
But scorched is it where it had become long.

lies of the absent soldiers, 'their parents, wives, and children,' acc. to K'ang-shing. It has been mentioned that king P'ing's mother belonged to Shin,—a marquisate held by Këangs, the capital of which was near the site of the pres. dep. city of Nan-yang, Ho-nan. P'oo is identified by Ying-tah and Choo with Leu (see note on the name of the 22d Bk. of the Shoo, Pt. V.) It was also a marquisate held by Këangs, and adjoined Shin. Heu was another Këang State, in the pres. Heu Chow, Ho-nan. Shin and P'oo were contiguous, but Heu was at some considerable distance from them. Heu K'ëen (许谦; Yuen dyn.) thinks that the troops of Chow were not really guarding the territories of P'oo and Heu; but that the poet, to vary his rhymes, introduces the names of those other States, as belonging to Këangs. We may rather suppose, however, that through the consanguinity of their chiefs, the three States were confederate, all threatened by Ts'oo, and all hence requiring aid. 戍＝屯兵以守, 'to station troops throughout a country to maintain it.'

Ll. 5, 6. The object of 怀 is to be sought in the parties intended by 之子, and this term, as well as the line that follows, are in favour of the interpretation of the piece adopted by Maou and Choo. The soldiers did not wish their families to be with them, keeping guard in Shin,—such a thing would have been contrary to all rules of propriety; but they grudged their prolonged absence from them, and wished that they might soon return to Chow.

The rhymes are—in st. 1, (and in 2, 3), 水, 子 (prop. cat. 1), cat. 15, t. 2; 薪, 申, cat 12, t. 1; (and in 2, 3), 怀, 归, cat. 15, t. 1 : in 2, 楚, 甫, cat. 5, t. 2 : in 3, 蒲, 许, *ib.*, t. 1.

Ode 5. Allusive. THE SAD CASE OF A WOMAN FORCED TO SEPARATE FROM HER HUSBAND THROUGH PRESSURE OF FAMINE. Maou says the piece is expressive of pity for the suffering condition of Chow. Many later critics seek to find in it a condemnation of the govt. of king P'ing, and of the morals of the people; but this has to be argued out of the language, and is not implied in it. Choo attributes the composition to the suffering wife herself; but I agree with Heu K'ëen in attributing it to another, who has her case—one of many—vividly before him (详味其辞, 人在言外, 盖当时君子之言, 非妇人所自作也).

Ll. 1, 2 in all the stt. The 蓷 has many names, of which the most common are 茺蔚, and 益母草. Medhurst calls it the 'bugloss;' but I should have preferred to call it by its popular name of 'mother's help,' if it did not clearly appear in the Japanese plates as the *leonurus sibiricus*, or mother-wort. It is described as having a square stem, and white flowers which grow between the sections of the stem. The seeds, stalk, flowers, and leaves are all believed to have medical virtues, and to be specific in

矣。遇人之不淑矣。

三章

中谷有蓷。暵其湿矣。有女仳离。啜其泣矣。啜其泣

矣。何嗟及矣。

> There is a woman forced to leave her husband,
> Long-drawn are her groanings!
> Long-drawn are her groanings!
> She suffers from his misfortune.

3   In the valleys grows the mother-wort,
But scorched is it even in the moist places.
There is a woman forced to leave her husband;
Ever flow her tears!
Ever flow her tears!
But of what avail is her lament?

VI. T'oo yuen.

兔爰

一章

有兔爰爰。雉离于罗。我生之初。尚无为。我生之

1   The hare is slow and cautious;
The pheasant plumps into the net.
In the early part of my life,
Time still passed without commotion.
In the subsequent part of it,

many troubles of women, before and after child-birth; hence, its common name. The plant grows best in moist situations, and Maou erred greatly in supposing that a high situation and dry soil suited it best, so that the decay of it, spoken of here, was owing to its situation in a valley. That decay is evidently ascribed to the prevailing drought, killing it first in the drier grounds; next, where it had attained a good height and was vigorous; and finally, even in damp places, best adapted for it. Such a plant drooping and dying in the valleys, we may conceive how all other vegetation was scorched up, and famine, with its miseries, desolated the country. 暵 = 燥, 'to dry up,' 'to be dried up or scorched.' 其干 = 生于干者,—as in the translation. 修 = 长, 'long.'

Ll. 3—6. 仳 = 别, 'to be separated.' 仳离 does not mean that the woman had been cast off by her husband, but that they had been obliged to separate from each other, and try if they could manage to subsist apart. 嘅 is designed to give 'the sound of her sighing.' 歗 is synonymous with 啸 in ii.XI. 3; not, however, meaning, here, 'to whistle,' but an audible sound emitted from the mouth, and long-protracted. This idea of 'long-drawn' is conveyed by 条 = 长. 啜 denotes 'the appearance of weeping.' In l. 4 we must understand 人 of the husband of the woman. K'ang-shing explains it by 君子, which we have often met with in

后。逢此百罹。尚寐无吡。

二章

有兔爰爰。雉离于罦。我生之初。尚无造。我生之

后。逢此百忧。尚寐无觉。

三章

有兔爰爰。雉离于罿。我生之初。尚无庸。我生之

后。逢此百凶。尚寐无聪。

We are meeting with all these evils.
I wish I might sleep and never move more.

2　The hare is slow and cautious;
The pheasant plumps into the snare.
In the early part of my life,
Time still passed without anything stirring.
In the subsequent part of it,
We are meeting with all these sorrows.
I wish I might sleep, and never wake more.

3　The hare is slow and cautious;
The pheasant plumps into the trap.
In the early part of my life,
Time still passed without any call for our services.
In the subsequent part of it
We are meeting with all these miseries.
I would that I might sleep, and hear of nothing more.

---

the sense of husband. It might also be taken generally:—'she has met with—fallen on—a time when people are in distress.' 不淑 is the 'evil' lot, not evil conduct.

The rhymes are—in st. 1, 干, 叹, 叹, 难, cat, 14: 修, 歝 *, 歝 *, 淑, cat. 3, t. 1: 湿, 泣, 泣, 及, cat. 7, t. 3.

Ode 6. Metaphorical. AN OFFICER OF CHOW DECLARES HIS WEARINESS OF LIFE BECAUSE OF THE GROWING MISERIES OF THE STATE. The 'Little Preface' refers this piece to the time of king Hwan, the grandson of king P'ing (B.C.718—696), who became involved in hostilities with the State of Ch'ing in B. C. 706, and received a severe defeat from his feudatory; but there is nothing in it to indicate such a reference. The growing misery of the country, and the writer's weariness of his life, are all that is before us.

Ll.1,2. in all the stt. 爰爰 conveys the meaning of being 'slow and cautious.' The rabbit or hare is said to be of a secret and crafty nature, while the pheasant is bold and determined. The former, consequently, is snared with difficulty, while the latter is easily taken. 罗 = 纲, the general name for a net. 罦 and 罿 are terms for nets with some peculiarity in their construction, but they are used, not because of that, but to vary the rhythm. Indeed, the Urh-ya gives 罬, 罿, 罩, and 罦, all as names of the same thing, which is also called 覆车, 'an inverted carriage.' It seems to have been a net extended between, or a noose suspended from, two poles, which were made to close by a spring when the rabbit or bird entered. 离,—as in iii. XVIII. 3. In the crafty hare, acc. to Choo, we have the mean men, who stirred up disorder,

VII. *Koh-luy.*

葛藟
一章
绵绵葛藟。在河之浒。终远兄弟。谓他人父。谓他人

父。亦莫我顾。
二章
绵绵葛藟。在河之涘。终远兄弟。谓他人母。谓他人

母。亦莫我有。

1   Thickly they spread about, the dolichos creepers,
     On the borders of the Ho.
     For ever separated from my brothers,
     I call a stranger father.
     I call a stranger father,
     But he will not look at me.

2   Thickly they spread about, the dolichos creepers,
     On the banks of the Ho.
     For ever separated from my brothers,
     I call a stranger mother.
     I call a stranger mother,
     But she will not recognize me.

and then contrived to escape from its consequences; in the bold and impetuous pheasant, the superior men, who would do their duty in the disorder,—and suffered. Maou and others make these two lines allusive.

Ll. 3—6. 尚 = 犹, 'still.' The speaker, it would appear, had seen the time when the royal House was strong, and able to control the various States. 无为 = 无事. 'there was nothing doing,' 'there was no trouble;' 无造, the same; 无庸 = 无用, 'no service.' 罹 is synonymous with 忧, 'sorrows,'—things falling out untowardly.

L. 7. 尚 here is different from that in l.3, and has the same force as 其, used optatively,—庶几, or 宁可. 呬 = 动,—' to move;' 觉 = 寤, to 'awake;' 聪 = 闻, 'to hear.' The line, in its various forms, expresses the idea that the speaker had no enjoyment of his life, and would prefer to die.

The rhymes are—in st. 1, 罗, 为 *, 罹 *, 吡, cat. 17: 罩 *, 造 *, 忧, 觉 *, cat. 3, t. 2: in 3, 罝, 庸, 凶, 聪, cat. 9.

Ode 7. Allusive. A WANDERER FROM CHOW, SEPARATED FROM HIS KIN, MOURNS OVER HIS LOT. The 'Little Preface' says the piece was directed against king P'ing, who had thrown aside all care for the nine classes of his kindred (see on the Shoo, I.2). Nothing more, however, than what I have stated can be concluded from the piece itself.

Ll.1,2. 葛藟,—as in i.IV. 绵绵 is descriptive of the dolichos, spreading and intertwining its branches, all connected together. There is little difference between 浒, 涘, and 漘. It is said, 'The space above, on the banks,' is called 浒; and 'where the banks are level, but underneath the earth caves in, and the banks hang over like lips,' is called 漘. The thick, continuous growth of the creepers, on the soil proper to them, is presented by the speaker in contrast to his own position, torn from his family and proper soil.

三章

绵绵葛藟。在河之漘。终远兄弟。谓他人昆。谓他人

昆。亦莫我闻。

3   Thickly they spread about, the dolichos creepers,
     On the lips of the Ho.
     For ever separated from my brothers,
     I call a stranger elder-brother;
     I call a stranger elder-brother,
     But he will not listen to me.

VIII.   *Ts'ae koh.*

采葛

一章

彼采葛兮。一日不见。如三月兮。

二章

彼采萧兮。一日不见。如三秋兮。

三章

彼采艾兮。一日不见。如三岁兮。

1   There he is gathering the dolichos!
     A day without seeing him
     Is like three months!

2   There he is gathering the oxtail-southernwood!
     A day without seeing him
     Is like three seasons!

3   There he is gathering the mugwort!
     A day without seeing him
     Is like three years!

Ll. 3—6. Following out the view of the Preface, K'ang-shing takes 远 actively, with 王 or 'the king,' as its subject; but the view in the translation is more simple and natural, and agrees better with the usage of 远,—as in iii.XIV., iv.VII., *et al.* 他人, 'another man,' = 'a stranger.' 昆 = 兄, 'an elder brother.' 莫我有,—'does not have me.' K'ang-shing and Choo explain 有 by 识 有, 'to remember that there is such a person.'

The rhymes are—in st. 1, 藟, 弟 (and in 2, 3), cat. 15, t. 2; 浒, 父, 父, 顾, cat. 5, t. 2: in 2, 涘, 母*, 母*, 有*, cat. 1, t. 2: in 3, 漘, 昆, 昆, 闻, cat. 13.

Ode 8. Narrative. A LADY LONGS FOR THE SOCIETY OF THE OBJECT OF HER AFFECTION. So Choo interprets this little piece; and his view of it is more natural than that of the old interpreters, who held that it indicates the fear of slanderers, entertained by the officers of Chow. So bad, they say, was the govt. of king Hwan, that if any of the ministers, great or small, was sent away on duty for however short a time, a crowd of slanderous parasites was sure to supplant him, or injure him in some way. The 1st line, on this view, is allusive of the services on which a minister might be commissioned; and it is the king that is spoken of in the other lines. This interpretation is, surely, imported very violently into the simple verses. Choo's is more natural. A short absence from the loved object seems to be long, and longer the more it is dwelt upon. The lady fancies her lover engaged as the first lines describe, and would fain go and join him in his occupations.

IX. *Ta keu.*

大车
一章
大车槛槛。毳衣如菼。岂不尔思。畏子不敢。
二章
大车啍啍。毳衣如璊。岂不尔思。畏子不奔。
三章
谷则异室。死则同穴。谓予不信。有如皦日。

1　His great carriage rumbles along,
　　And his robes of rank glitter like the young sedge.
　　Do I not think of you?
　　But I am afraid of this officer, and dare not.

2　His great carriage moves heavily and slowly,
　　And his robes of rank glitter like a carnation-gem.
　　Do I not think of you?
　　But I am afraid of this officer, and do not rush to you.

3　While living, we may have to occupy different apartments;
　　But when dead, we shall share the same grave.
　　If you say that I am not sincere,
　　By the bright sun I swear that I am.

彼 is best taken as demonstrative of the individual thought of,—with K'ang-shing; though we may also understand it, with Yen Ts'an, as ='there.' 萧 = 荻, which Medhurst calls 'southernwood.' It is understood to be here what is called the 牛,尾蒿,—as in the translation; 'with whitish leaves, the stalk brittle, bushy and fragrant.' 艾 is the mugwort, the down of which yields the moxa, which is burnt upon the skin to produce counter-irritation. 三秋, 'three autumns'= 三时, 'three seasons.' Ying-tah points out that 三春 and 三夏 are employed in the same way.

The rhymes are—in st. 1, 葛, 月, cat. 15, t. 3: in 2, 萧*, 秋, cat. 3, t. 1: in 3, 艾, 岁, cat. 15, t. 2.

Ode 9. Narrative. THE INFLUENCE OF A SEVERE AND VIRTUOUS MAGISTRATE IN REPRESSING LICENTIOUSNESS. According to the old school, this piece should be translated in the past tense, as setting forth the manners of a former time, when licentiousness was repressed by virtuous magistrates, and did not dare to show itself; and this, it is supposed, is done, as a lamentation over the different state of things under the eastern Chow. Nothing is gained by thus dragging antiquity into the ode, and the explanation of it is only thereby made difficult and unnatural. The whole is simple, if we take it, with Choo, as spoken by some lady of the eastern Chow, that would fain have gone with her lover, but was restrained by her fear of some great officer, who, amid the degeneracy of the times, retained his purity and integrity. Both interpretations, however, admit the licentiousness of the age; and the character of this piece supplies an argument for the correctness of the view which we took of the preceding.

Ll. 1, 2 in stt. 1, 2. 槛 槛 (*hëen*) denotes the noise made by the carriage of the officer, the 子 of the 4th line. It is called 'a great carriage,' because great officers of the court, when travelling in the discharge of their duties, were privileged to ride in a carriage of the same materials and structure as that of a prince of a State. They wore also the robes of a viscount or baron, which are here called 毳衣. These

X. *K'ew chung yëw me.*

丘中有麻

一章

丘中有麻。彼留子嗟。彼留子嗟。将其来施施。

二章

丘中有麦。彼留子国。彼留子国。将其来食。

I On the mound where is the hemp,
Some one is detaining Tsze-tsëay.
Some one is there detaining Tsze-tsëay ;—
Would that he would come jauntily [to me] !

2 On the mound where is the wheat,
Some one is detaining Tsze-kwoh.
Some one is there detaining Tsze-kwoh ;—
Would that he would come and eat with me !

had five of the emblematic figures mentioned in the Shoo, II. iv. 4 upon them :—the temple-cup, the aquatic grass, and the grains of rice, painted on the upper robe; and the hatchet, and the symbol of distinction, embroidered on the lower. 黹 means the down of birds, or the fine undergrowth of hair on animals, and those robes were so denominated, probably, from the materials of which they were made, but we lack information on this point ;—see the Chow Le, XXI. 8 and 17. The painting and embroidery were in all the five colours; hence the green is described as being equal to that of a young sedge (see v. III. 4), and the red to that of a *mwan*, a gem of a carnation colour. 嘽嘽 is descriptive of the 'slow and heavy motion' of the carriage.

Ll. 3, 4. 尔思 , 'think of you,'='wish to be with you,' or, 'to follow you.'

St. 3. The lovers might be kept apart all their lives, but they would be united in death, and lie in the same grave. So the lady gives expression to her attachment. 谷＝生 , 'to be living.' 穴 , 'a cave;' here,='the grave.' 有 如 in l. 4 is the common form of an oath among the Chinese. 'The Complete Digest' thus expands it,—此予由衷之言也，若以予言为不信，则有如皦日在上以鉴我矣。予言岂不信者哉, 'These are words from my heart. If you think that my words are not sincere, there is *a Power* above like the bright sun observing me. How should my words not be sincere ?' Acc. to the old interpreters, this stanza is addressed to the magistrates of Chow. 'In the old days,' it is said, 'husbands and wives kept to their separate

apartments, and only in death were they long together.' It was difficult for an officer in the degenerate times of Chow to believe that there had ever been such purity of manners : but verily there had been !

The rhymes are—in st. 1, 檻, 葵, 敢, cat. 8, t. 1 : in 2, 嘽, 瑲, 奔, cat. 13 : in 3, 室, 穴, 日, cat. 12, t. 3.

Ode 10. Narrative. A WOMAN LONGS FOR THE PRESENCE OF HER LOVERS, WHO, SHE THINKS, ARE DETAINED FROM HER BY ANOTHER WOMAN. This interpretation of the ode lies upon the surface of it, and is that given by Choo He. We might have expected a different view from the old interpreters, and we have one. They refer the piece to the time of king Chwang (B. C. 695—679), who drove away from their employments officers of worth through his want of intelligence. The people, they say, mourned the loss of such men, and expressed their desire for their return in these verses. The imperial editors indicate their approval of this view, and say that many scholars have doubted the correctness of Choo's interpretation, on the ground that Confucius would not have admitted so licentious a piece into his collection of ancient poems. If the books to which Maou had access had been preserved, they think, there would have been sufficient evidence of the correctness of his view. But the difficulty here, and in other odes, lies in reconciling the words before us with the interpretation put upon them. The writers, to convey the ideas in their minds, must have used language the most remote from that calculated to do so. As to the unlikelihood of Confucius giving a place to a licentious piece like this in the *She*, if he admitted the ode that precedes, even taking Maou's interpretation of it, I do not see that he need have been squeamish about this.

三章
丘中有李。彼留之子。彼留之子。贻我佩玖。

3　On the mound where are the plum trees,
　　Some one is detaining those youths.
　　Some one is there detaining those youths;—
　　They will give me *kĕw*-stones for my girdle.

Ll. 1,2 in all the stt. No special meaning is to be sought in the mention of the mound, and the things growing on it. The lady misses her friend, and she supposes he may be detained on such a place in a way she does not approve of. 彼 = 'there.' 留 = 有留者, 'there is some one detaining.' 子嗟 is the designation of the friend who does not make his appearance. 子国 is the designation of another similar friend. With this we may compare the variation of the surnames in the different stanzas of iv.IV.

Acc. to Maou, 留 is the clan-name of the officers introduced, and Tsze-kwoh is the father of Tsze-tsëay. A mound is a stony, barren spot, where we do not look for hemp or wheat or plum-trees. Yet these Lëws, banished from the court, had laboured on such a spot, and made it fruitful, in consequence of which the people longed the more to see them back in office!

In st.3, 之子, = 是子, 'those gentlemen,' —referring to Tsze-tsëay and Tsze-kwoh. L.4. 将, —as in v.IV.1. 施施, —as in Mencius, IV. Pt.ii.XXXIII.1. The line in st.3 is also to be taken as a wish; Choo says, 冀其有以赠已, 'she hopes that they will have gifts for her.' 玖, —as in v.X.3:

Maou says nothing on the 将, but seems to take it as the sign of the future. 施施, he says, means 'the difficulty of advancing,' of which it is difficult to see the significancy in the case. On 将其来食 he says, 'when Tsze-kwoh comes again, we shall get food!' His misapprehension of the nature of the ode makes it impossible for him to explain its parts satisfactorily.

The rhymes are—in st. 1, 麻, 嗟, 嗟, 施 *, 17: in 2, 麦 *, 国 国, 食, cat. 1, t. 3: in 3, 李, 子, 子, 玖 *, *ib.,* t. 2.

CONCLUDING NOTE. The odes of the Royal domain afford sufficient evidence of the decay of the House of Chow. They commence with a lamentation over the desolation of the ancient capitals of Wǎn and Woo, and, within the territory attached to the eastern capital, we find the people mourning over the toils of war and the miseries of famine. The bonds of society appear relaxed, and licentiousness characterizes the intercourse of the sexes. There are some odes, however which relieve the picture. The 2d and 3d show us the affection between husband and wife, and the pleasantness of their domestic society, while the 9th tells us that amid abounding licentiousness there were officers who helped to keep it in check.

BOOK VII. THE ODES OF CH'ING

I. *Tsze e.*

郑一之七

缁衣

一章

缁衣之宜兮。敝予又改为兮。适子之馆兮。还予授子
之粲兮。

二章

缁衣之好兮。敝予又改造兮。适子之馆兮。还予授子

1   How well do the black robes befit you!
     When worn out, we will make others for you.
     We will go to your court,
     And when we return [from it], we will send you a feast!

2   How good on you are the black robes!
     When worn out, we will make others for you.

TITLE OF THE BOOK. 郑, 一 之 七,
'Ch'ing; Bk. VII. of Pt. I.' The State of
Ch'ing was not one of the oldest fiefs of the
Chow dyn. King Seuen (B. C. 826—781) conferred on his brother Yëw (友), in B. C. 805,
the appanage of Ch'ing, a city and district adjoining,—in the pres. Hwa Chow (华州), dep.
T'ung-chow (同州), Shen-se. This Yew, who
is called duke Hwan in the list of the lords of
Ch'ing (桓公), acted as minister of Instruction at the royal court, and was killed, in B. C.
773, not long before the Jung hordes took the capital, and put to death king Yëw (幽王). His son
Keuh-t'uh (掘突) was of great service to
king P'ing when he moved the capital to the east,
succeeded to his father's office, and becoming
possessed of the lands of Kih and K'wei (虢
桧之地), 'south of the Ho, north of the
Ying, east of the Loh, and west of the Tse,' he
removed there, and called his State 'New Ch'ing,'
which is still the name of one of the districts in
the dep. of K'ae-fung, Ho-nan. He is duke Woo
(武公) of Ch'ing. For further information
about Ch'ing see on the title of Bk. XIII.

Ode 1. Narrative. THE PEOPLE OF CHOW
EXPRESS THEIR ADMIRATION OF AND REGARD
FOR DUKE WOO OF CH'ING. We have the authority of Confucius for understanding this piece
as expressive of the regard that is due to virtue
and ability;—see the Le Ke, Bk. XXXIII. 2.
The critics agree that it is to be interpreted of
the admiration and affection which the people
of Chow had for duke Woo, son of the founder
of the House of Ch'ing. He had so won upon
them in the discharge of his duties as a minister, that they ever welcomed his presence, and
would gladly have retained him at the court.
The structure of the piece is exceedingly simple.
The stanzas are varied merely by the change of
two characters in each, without giving any new
meaning,—to produce a variety of rhymes. The
'Little Preface' is wrong in attributing the ode
to the people of Ch'ing.

Ll. 1, 2, in all the stt. 缁 denotes the deep-
est black,—that which has been subjected to the
dye seven times. Ministers of the court wore robes
of this colour,—not in the king's court, when
having audience of him; but in their own courts
or offices, to which they proceeded after the
morning audience, and discharged their several
duties. 宜 = 称, 'to be fit,' 'to correspond
to.' As Yen Ts'an expands the line, 'That duke
Woo should be a minister of the king and wear

之粲兮。

三章

缁衣之席兮。敝予又改作兮。适子之馆兮。还予授子

之粲兮。

We will go to your court,
And when we return [from it], we will send you a feast!

3 How easy sit the black robes on you!
  When worn out, we will make others for you.
  We will go to your court.
  And when we return [from it], we will send you a feast!

II.   *Tsëang Chung-tsze.*

将仲子

一章

将仲子兮。无逾我里。无折我树杞。岂敢爱之。畏我

父母。仲可怀也。父母之言。亦可畏也。

1 I pray you, Mr. Chung,
  Do not come leaping into my hamlet;
  Do not break my willow trees.
  Do I care for them?
  But I fear my parents.
  You, O Chung, are to be loved,

these black robes is most proper; his virtue corresponds to his robes (甚宜，德称其服).' We may construe 之 as the sign of the genitive;—'O the befittingness of the black robes!' But it is better to take it as a particle, —'How befitting are they!' 好 and 席 in the other stanzas must convey a similar meaning to 宜. There is no difficulty with the former, but Maou and Choo both explain the latter by 大, 'great,' which Ying-tah expands by 服缁衣，大得其宜. 'In him to wear the black robes is *greatly* befitting.' I prefer the meaning of 安舒, 'easy and natural,' given by one of the Ch'ings. In the 2d line the people express their affection for duke Woo by saying they would make new robes for him, when those were worn out. 改＝更, 'a change,'＝others. 为, 造, and 作 all mean 'to make.'

Ll. 3, 4, 适＝之, 'to go to.' 馆＝舍, 'a lodging house;' but the idea is more that of a hotel in the sense which that term has in France. It was the residence assigned to the minister during his residence at the capital, where he lived with his retinue and had his own office or court. The 子 leads us to translate the whole piece in the 2d person, as if it were addressed to duke Woo,—the welcome of the people of Chow to him. The people would go to his court, to see that he was lodged there comfortably on his arrival from Ch'ing. We learn from narratives of Tso-she on the Ch'un Ts'ëw, that the govt. of the capital was sometimes remiss in keeping these public buildings in proper repair. The people go on to say, that when they were satisfied the building was all in good order, they would send him viands. To the present day, the good will of the people of China, of all

二章

将仲子兮。无逾我墙。无折我树桑。岂敢爱之。畏我

诸兄。仲可怀也。诸兄之言。亦可畏也。

But the words of my parents
Are also to be feared.

2   I pray you, Mr. Chung,
Do not come leaping over my wall;
Do not break my mulberry trees.
Do I care for them?
But I fear the words of my brothers.
You, O Chung, are to be loved,
But the words of my brothers
Are also to be feared.

ranks, expresses itself in this form. Fowls, ducks, geese, flesh, cakes, and fruits, figure largely in complimentary offerings.

The rhymes are—in st. 1, 宜 *, 为 *, cat. 17; 馆, 粲 (and in 2, 3), cat. 14: in 2, 好 *, 造 *, cat. 3, t. 2: in 3, 席 *, 作 *, cat. 5, t. 3.

Ode 2. Narrative. A LADY BEGS HER LOVER TO LET HER ALONE, AND NOT EXCITE THE SUSPICIONS AND REMARKS OF HER PARENTS AND OTHERS. Such is the interpretation of this piece, given by Choo, after Ch'ing Ts'ëaou (郑樵), an earlier critic of the Sung dynasty; and no one, who draws his conclusion simply from the stanzas themselves, can put any other upon it. The 'Little Preface,' however, gives an historical interpretation of it, which is altogether different, and for which something like an argument has been constructed. To understand it, some details must be given.—Duke Woo of Ch'ing, the subject of the last ode, was succeeded, in B.C. 742, by his son Woo-shang, known as duke Chwang, to whom his mother had a great dislike, while a brother, named Twan (段), was her favourite. At the mother's solicitation, Twan was invested with a large city; and he proceeded, in concert with her, to form a scheme for wresting the earldom from duke Chwang. The issue was the ruin of Twan; but his brother was dilatory, as it appeared to his ministers, in taking measures against him, and Maou understands the piece as the duke's reply to Chung of Chae (祭仲), one of his ministers, whose advice that he should take swift and summary

measures with Twan he declined to follow. At the same time, he had no more liking for Twan than his minister had. Acc., then, to this view, the Chung of the ode is Chung of Chae, the minister; the 2d and 3d lines are metaphorical ways of telling him not to incite the duke to injure his brother; the 4th line tells the duke's own disregard for and dislike of his brother; and the 6th line, ' You, O Chung, are to be cherished,' is taken of 'the words of the minister,' which the duke would keep in mind. The lesson of the whole, acc. to the 'Little Preface,' is that duke Chwang, not venturing to follow the advice given him, which would have needed but little exertion of power, had afterwards to deal with Twan by calling into requisition all the resources of the State. It must be said, without hesitation, that if this be the correct interpretation of it, then the piece is a riddle, which only appears the more absurd, when the answer to it is told.

The imperial editors are willing to admit that Choo's interpretation is the more natural, but they find strong confirmation of the older view, in a passage of Tso-she's commentary on the Ch'un Ts'ew IX.xxvi. 5.—In B.C. 548, the marquis of Wei was kept a prisoner in Tsin, and the lords of Ts'e and Ch'ing went to the court of that State to intercede for him; and in their negotiations for that purpose, the minister, who was in attendance on the earl of Ch'ing, sang this piece, as suggesting a reason why the prisoner should be let go. But the only sentiment in the ode applicable to that occasion, as Too Yu points out, is that the general feeling and remarks of men are not to be disregarded. So far, the use of it was appropriate in the circumstances, whichever interpretation we adopt. Even Yen Ts'an, who follows Maou's view, thinks

三章

将仲子兮。无逾我园。无折我树檀。岂敢爱之。畏人

之多言。仲可怀也。人之多言。亦可畏也。

3　I pray you, Mr. Chung,
　　Do not come leaping into my garden;
　　Do not break my sandal trees.
　　Do I care for them?
　　But I dread the talk of people.
　　You, O Chung, are to be loved,
　　But the talk of people
　　Is also to be feared.

III.　*Shuh-yu-t‘ëen.*

叔于田

一章

叔于田。巷无居人。岂无居人。不如叔也。洵美且仁。

1　Shuh has gone hunting;
　　And in the streets there are no inhabitants.
　　Are there indeed no inhabitants?
　　[But] they are not like Shuh,
　　Who is truly admirable and kind.

that the lesson of the piece mentioned in the ‘Little Preface’ is wide of the mark. I do not see why the use of the piece, as preserved by Tso-she, nearly 200 years after it was written, should make us reject the only view on which it can be naturally and simply explained.

Ll.1—3 in all the stt. 将,—as in vi.X., *et al.* 仲子,—仲 is the designation of the person addressed,—indicating his place among his brothers. The 子 is equivalent to our ‘Mr.’ 里 may be translated ‘hamlet.’ Anciently, ‘5 families constituted *a neighbourhood* (邻), and 5 neighbourhoods constituted a *le*, or hamlet.’ The 杞 was a species of willow, ‘growing by the water-side, the leaves whitish, with the lines in them slightly red.’ The wood of it was valuable for bowls and other articles of use. ‘These willows,’ says Choo, ‘would be those planted about the ditch that surrounded the

hamlet.’ 树 =‘planted.’ Ying-tah says 无损折我所树之杞木, ‘Do not injure or break the willows which I planted.’ I have translated 檀 by ‘sandal trees’ not meaning the sandal-wood tree of commerce, which is called *t‘an-heang* (檀香). The *Pun-ts‘aou* says on the *t‘an*, that it is found on the hills about the Këang, the H‘wae, and the Ho, and is of the class of the *t‘an-heang*, but without its fragrance.

L.4. ‘How dare I love them?’ but 爱 is to be taken in the sense of ‘to grudge,’ which it often has. Of course, on the old and orthodox view, the 之 must be referred to duke Chwang’s brother, and there is no antecedent to it in the ode.

Ll.5—9. There is a difficulty with 父 on the old view, because duke Chwang’s father was dead, and with 兄, because his cousins—his

二章
叔于狩。巷无饮酒。岂无饮酒。不如叔也。洵美且好。

三章
叔适野。巷无服马。岂无服马。不如叔也。洵美且武。

2. Shuh has gone to the grand chase;
And in the streets there are none feasting.
Are there indeed none feasting?
[But] they are not like Shuh,
Who is truly admirable and good.

3 Shuh has gone into the country;
And in the streets there are none driving about.
Are there indeed none driving about?
[But] they are not like Shuh,
Who is truly admirable and martial.

ministers who were his kin—were all urging him to take summary measures with Twan. 人之 多言,—'men's many words,'—'people's talk.'

The rhymes are—in st.1, 子, 里, 杞, 母,, cat.1, t.2; 怀, 畏 (and in 2,3), cat.15 t.1: in 2, 墙, 桑, 兄,, cat.10: in 3, 园, 檀, 言, cat.14.

Ode 3. Narrative. THE ADMIRATION WITH WHICH SHUH-TWAN WAS REGARDED. The Shuh of this ode is the Twan, the brother of duke Chwang, of whom I have spoken on the interpretation of the last piece. His character was the reverse of being worthy of admiration; and we must suppose that this ode and the next express merely the sentiments of his parasites and special followers. His brother conferred upon him the city of King, where he lived in great state, collecting weapons, and training the people to the use of them, with the ulterior design of wresting the State from his brother. The Preface says that the piece was directed against duke Chwang, but there is not a word in it, which should make us think so. Choo has animadverted on this, but he agrees with the Preface in referring the ode to the people of Ch'ing generally, as being smitten with the dash and bravado of Twan, and inclining to support him. On this point, the view of Yen Ts'an is more likely,—that the piece does not express the sentiments of the people generally, but of the people of King, and only of those among them who were Twan's partizans and flatterers. The mass fell off from him, when the duke took active measures against him.

L.1, in all the stt. 叔 is the designation of Twan as being younger than duke Chwang. The eldest of 4 brothers is called pih (伯); the 2d, chung (仲); the 3d, shuh (叔); the 4th, ke (季). Frequently, however, we find the younger brothers called shuh indiscriminately. 于 is the particle. 田,—'to hunt.' Maou explains it here by 取禽, 'to take birds;' but it is best regarded as a general name for hunting. 狩 was the term appropriate to the winter hunt; but the idea of winter need not be expressed in a translation. Too Yu finds in the character the idea which I have indicated. 野 is the country beyond the suburbs, where the hunting was carried on.

Ll. 2—5. 巷 is defined as 里涂, 'the way or road of the le. The le, we saw on the last ode, was a hamlet of 25 families, which would have, probably, their houses on either side of a street running through them, and we must understand here, I think, that the speakers have in view the quarter of King, or perhaps a hamlet outside it, where Twan had his residence. He had gone into the country hunting; and the street seemed quite empty. The life and glory of it had departed. Those who remained were not worthy of being taken notice of. 无饮 酒,—'no drinking of spirits,'= no feasting. 无服马 = 'no subjugating of horses,'= 无 乘马, 'no riding with horses.' We must not understand the phrase of riding on horseback, —a thing which was all but unknown in those early times, but of driving in chariots. 仁 can here only have the modified signification of 'kind.' Choo explains it by 爱人, 'loving people.'

IV. *Shuh yu t'een.*

大叔于田

一章

叔于田。乘乘马。执辔如组。两骖如舞。叔在薮。火
烈具举。襢裼暴虎。献于公所。将叔无狃。戒其伤
女。

1 Shuh has gone hunting,
Mounted in his chariot and four.
The reins are in his grasp like ribbons,
While the two outside horses move [with regular steps], as dancers do.
Shuh is at the marshy ground;—
The fire flames out all at once,
And with bared arms he seizes a tiger,
And presents it before the duke.
O Shuh, try not [such sport] again;
Beware of getting hurt.

The rhymes are—in st. 1, 田, 人, 人, 仁, cat. 12, t. 1: in 2, 狩, 酒, 酒, 好 *, cat. 3, t. 2: in 3, 野 *, 马 *, 马 *, 武, cat. 5, t. 2.

Ode 4. Narrative. CELEBRATING THE CHA-RIOTEERING AND ARCHERY OF SHUH-TWAN. Twan, the brother of duke Chwang, is the subject of this piece as of the last; and the two are much of the same character. The 'Little Preface' says this also was directed against duke Chwang,—with as little foundation. To the title of it the Preface prefixes the character 大, or 'great,' to distinguish it from ode 3; and in many editions this is admitted, by mistake, into the 1st line of st. 1.

Ll. 1—4, in all the stt. 叔于田,—see on last ode. The hunting there, however, was presided over by Twan himself, followed by his own people from his city of King. Here, it appears from l. 8, st. 1, the hunting is presided over by the duke, and Twan is in his train. 乘乘马,—the 1st 乘 is a verb,—'to mount,' 'to ride in,' 'to drive;' the 2nd (3d tone), is a noun,—'a team of 4 horses.' 执辔如组,—see on iii. XIII. 2. The 4 horses were driven all abreast; the two inside ones, which were called 服, being kept a little ahead of the others,

which were called ts'an (骖). In st. 1 the two outsides are driven so skilfully, that they move like dancers,—i. e., with regular and harmonious step. In st. 2, they move 'in goose column,' i. e. keeping behind the leaders, acc. to the order observed in a flock of wild geese in the sky; and in st. 3, they are behind them, as the arms may be said to be behind the head. The 'yellow' colour of the horses in st. 2 is a light bay, said to be the best colour for horses. 上襄 may be translated—'of a superior yoke;' for 襄 = 驾, 'to put to a carriage.' K'ang-shing says, 'The phrase means the very best horses.' In st. 3 鸹 is a kind of wild goose, of a grey colour; and the term is used here to describe the colour of the horses, 'black and white mixed together,'=grey. The characters are varied; now ='yellow,' now='grey,' for the rhythm,—which is so common a characteristic of these odes.

Ll. 5, 6. 薮 is defined by 泽, 'a marsh;' but that does not give us a correct idea of what the term conveys. Williams calls it 'a marshy preserve in which game is kept and fish reared.' In hunting during the winter, fire was set to the grass, which drove the birds and beasts from their coverts, and gave the hunters an opportunity of discharging their arrows at them. 烈 is best taken with Choo as 炽盛貌,

二章

叔于田。乘乘黄。两服上襄。两骖雁行。叔在薮。火

烈具扬。叔善射忌。又良御忌。抑磬控忌。抑纵送

忌。

三章

叔于田。乘乘鸨。两服齐首。两骖如手。叔在薮。火

烈具阜。叔马慢忌。叔发罕忌。抑释掤忌。抑鬯弓

忌。

2 Shuh has gone hunting,
   Mounted in his chariot with four bay horses.
   The two insides are the finest possible animals,
   And the two outsides follow them regularly as in a flying
      flock of wild geese.
   Shuh is at the marshy ground;—
   The fire blazes up all at once.
   A skilful archer is Shuh!
   A good charioteer also!
   Now he gives his horses the reins; now he brings them up;
   Now he discharges his arrow; now he follows it.

3 Shuh has gone hunting,
   Mounted in his chariot with four grey horses.
   His two insides have their heads in a line,
   And the two outsides come after like arms.
   Shuh is at the marsh;—
   The fire spreads grandly all together.

'the appearance of the spreading flames.' Maou explains it by 列, 'rows,' and K'ang-shing says that 'men were arranged in order carrying fire;' but why should we depart from the proper meaning of the term, which is quite applicable in the case? 具 = 俱, 'all at once,' 'all to-gether.' 阜 = 盛, 'abundantly,' 'grandly.'

Ll. 7—10. In st.1, 檀裼 means to strip off the clothes, so as to leave the upper part of the body bare. 暴 = 空手博兽, 'with unarmed hands to attack and seize a wild beast.' Comp. Mencius, VII. Pt.ii. XXIII. 2. Ll. 9,10 are to be taken as spoken by the people, affectionately cautioning Twan against such perilous displays of his courage and strength.

狃 = 习, 'to practise,' or, as the Urh-ya de-fines it, = 复, 'to repeat.'

In stt 2, 3, 抑 and 忌 are to be taken as two particles, which cannot be translated:—the former initial; the other final. In st. 2, these lines describe Twan's action, when the chase was at its height; in st. 3, when it was drawing to a close. 磬 = 骋马, 'to gallop his horses,' making them in their action resemble a k'ing. 控 = 止马, 'to stop, or check, his horses.' 纵 is 'the discharge of the arrow;' the meaning of 送 in this connection is not so clear. Maou understands it in the sense of 'following the arrow to make sure of the game;' but it is evidently, like 纵, descriptive simply of Twan's

His horses move slowly;
He shoots but seldom;
Now he lays aside his quiver;
Now he returns his bow to the case.

V.   *Ts'ing jin.*

清人

一章
清人在彭。駟介旁旁。二矛重英。河上乎翱翔。
二章
清人在消。駟介麃麃。二矛重喬。河上乎逍遥。

1   The men of Ts'ing are in P'ang;
The chariot with its team in mail ever moves about;
The two spears in it, with their ornaments, rising, one above
    the other.
So do they roam about the Ho.

2   The men of Ts'ing are in Seaou;
The chariot with its team in mail looks martial,
And the two spears in it, with their hooks, rise one above the
    other.
So do they saunter about by the Ho.

shooting, and indicates something done with the left hand, which held the bow, that was called 'escorting the arrow.' 釋　掤—the critics all take *ping* as 'the cover of the quiver.' We must suppose that this was tied up somehow during the chase, that the arrows might be readily taken out; when they were no more wanted, the fastening was 'loosed,' and the quiver closed. We find in the Tso Chuen 冰 instead of the character in the text. 圀 ＝鞬, 'a bow-case.' It is here used as a verb;—'He cases his bow.'

The rhymes are—in st. 1, 馬 *, 組, 舞, 舉, 虎, 所, 女, cat. 5, t. 2: in 2, 黃, 襄, 行 *, 揚, cat. 10; 射, 御, cat. 5, t. 2; 控, 送, cat. 9; in 3, 鴇, 首, 手, 阜, cat. 3, t. 2; 慢, 罕, cat. 14; 掤, 弓, cat. 6.

Ode 5. Narrative. THE USELESS MANŒUV-
RING OF AN ARMY OF CH'ING ON THE FRONTIERS.

The Tso-chuen, on the 2d year of duke Min, pp. 7, 8, that 'the Teih entered Wei,' and 'Ch'ing threw away its army,' says that 'the earl of Ch'ing hated Kaou K'ih, and sent him with an army to the Ho,' (to resist the Teih), 'where he was stationed for a long time, without being recalled. The troops dispersed and returned to their homes. Kaou K'ih himself fled to Ch'in; and the people of Ch'ing, with reference to the affair, made the *Ts'ing-jin.*' This account of the piece is adopted substantially in the 'Little Preface,' which adds, what does not appear from the piece itself, that it was directed against duke Wăn, who took this method of getting rid of Kaou K'ih, a minister who was distasteful to him.—Duke Wăn ruled in Ch'ing, B.C. 662—627). The attack of Wei by the Teih was often referred to in Bkk. IV.—VI. It took place in B.C. 659.

L 1, in all the stt. Ts'ing was a city of Ch'ing, —that belonging, it is supposed, to Kaou K'ih, the people of which he had been ordered to lead to defend the frontiers of the State against the Teih. P'ang, Seaou, and Chow, were all cities near the Ho, which flowed through both the

三章
清人在軸。駟介陶陶。左旋右抽。中軍作好。

3 The men of Ts'ing are in Chow;
   The mailed team of the chariot prance proudly.
   [The driver] on the left wheels it about, and [the spearman]
      on the right brandishes his weapon,
While the general in the middle looks pleased.

VI. *Kaou k'ew.*

羔裘
一章
羔裘如濡。洵直且侯。彼其之子。舍命不渝。

1 His lamb's fur is glossy,
   Truly smooth and beautiful.
   That officer
   Rests in his lot and will not change.

States of Ch'ing and Wei. Maou seems to say that P'ang was in Wei, as if the troops of Ch'ing had passed into that State, to intercept any movement of the Teih to the south.

Ll. 2, 8. 駟, as the composition of the character intimates, denotes 'four horses,'—the number driven in one chariot. 介＝甲, 'mail,' and here＝被甲, 'clothed with mail,'—referring to a defensive armour against the spears and arrows of the enemy, with which war-horses were covered. We are to understand by this mailed team that of the chariot of Kaou K'ih, who commanded the troops of Ch'ing. I may say that we must do so in the 3d st., and the conclusion there must be extended to the other stanzas. Of course, where the chariot of the leader was, there also would the rest of his force be. 旁旁 is explained as 'the appearance of racing about without ceasing;' 麃麃 as 'martial-looking;' and 陶陶 as 'the appearance of being pleased and satisfied.' The 'two spears' were set up in the chariot. Maou says nothing about them, but Choo follows K'ang-shing in saying they were the ts'ew (酋) spear, and the e (夷),—the former 20 cubits long, and the latter 24. Hwang Yih-ching says that the maou was pointed, and had also a hook, near the point, so that it could be used both for thrusting and piercing, and for laying hold. From this hook there was hung an ornament of feathers dyed red, which was called 英. Owing to the difft. length of the spears, these ornaments fluttered 'one above the other (重叠

而见).' In the 2d st., only the 'hooks of the spears (乔)' are seen, the ornaments having disappeared in consequence of the length of time that the troops were kept on service. Maou took the 3d line in st. 3 as describing the movements of the whole army; but K'ang-shing, more correctly, understood the 左 of the driver of the chariot, who sat on the left of the general, and the 右 of the spearman, who sat on his right. In this way the chariot of Kaou K'ih is represented as moving about with a vain display. 旋＝还车, 'turns the chariot;' 抽＝拔刃, 'draws and brandishes his weapon.'

L. 4. 翱翔 and 逍遥 are of cognate signification, the former representing the wheeling about of a bird in the air, and the latter the aimless sauntering of a man. In st. 3, 中军 points out K'aou K'ih, occupying the central place in his chariot, and supposed to be the centre of his army. He made it his business simply 'to act the pleased.'—Nothing could be expected from an army thus commanded.

The rhymes are—in st. 1, 彭*, 旁*, 英*, 翔, cat. 10: in 2, 消, 麃, 乔, 遥, cat. 2: in 8, 轴, 陶*, 抽, 好*, cat. 3, t. 2.

Ode 6. Narrative. CELEBRATING SOME OFFICER OF CH'ING. No conjecture even can be hazarded as to the officer whom the writer of this piece had in mind, but that can be no reason for adopting any other interpetation of it than

二章
羔裘豹飾。孔武有力。彼其之子。邦之司直。

三章
羔裘晏兮。三英粲兮。彼其之子。邦之彦兮。

2　His lamb's fur, with its cuffs of leopard-skin.
Looks grandly martial and strong.
That officer
In the country will ever hold to the right.

3　How splendid is his lamb's fur!
How bright are its three ornaments!
That officer
Is the ornament of the country.

VII.　*Tsun-ta loo.*

遵大路

一章
遵大路兮。摻執子之袪兮。无我惡兮。不寁故也。

1　Along the highway,
I hold you by the cuff.
Do not hate me;—
Old intercourse should not be suddenly broken off.

what I have given. The 'Little Preface' makes the same mistake here as in its account of the 9th ode of last Book, and refers the subject to some officer of a former time, who is here praised, to brand more deeply the court of Ch'ing, which had come to be without such men. —There are two other odes having the same title as this, x. VII., and xiii. I. They are distinguished by prefixing to the title the name of the Book to which they belong. This is *Ch'ing Kaou-k'ew*.

Ll.1,2, in all the stt. 裘 signifies 'fur garments, furs after they are made up.' Here it is used for the upper garment or jacket, worn at audiences. both by the princes of States and their officers, and made of lamb's fur. The jackets of the officers, however, were distinguished by cuffs—in st.2, called 'ornaments'—of leopard-skin. 如濡 'glossy,'—as if wet and shining with ointment. 晏 in st.3 is defined by Maou and Choo as meaning 'fresh and rich-looking.' The 2d line is best treated as descriptive of the lamb's fur. Maou explains it of the character of the officer; but st.3 would seem to be decisive in favour of Choo's view, which I have followed. Moreover, the officer comes in directly in l.3. 直＝順, 'straight,' 'all in order.' 侯 ＝美, 'admirable.' This explanation of 侯 appears in Han Ying. 三英 is descriptive of ornaments sewn upon the jacket, but we have not the means of describing them. Comp. 素絲五紽, &c., in ii.VII. This meaning of 英 would come under the definition of that term by 美 in the dict.

Ll.3,4. 彼其之子,—see on vi.IV. 舍命,—命 here ＝ 'the lot,' and all the duties belonging to it; 舍, in the 3d tone,＝ 處, 'to occupy,' 'to rest in.' 渝＝變, 'to change.' *i. e.*, in this case, to deviate from his principles. 邦之司直 ＝ 'the country's master of the right,'—one who makes the right his constant aim, as if for 司 we had 主. 彦,—as in the Shoo, IV.v. Pt.i.5, *et al.*

二章

遵大路兮。掺执子之手兮。无我魗兮。不寁好也。

2 Along the high way,
I hold you by the hand.
Do not think me vile;—
Old friendship should not hastily be broken off.

VIII. *Neu yueh ke ming.*

女曰鸡鸣

一章

女曰鸡鸣。士曰昧旦。子兴视夜。明星有烂。将翱将

1 Says the wife, 'It is cock-crow;'
Says the husband, 'It is grey dawn.'
'Rise, Sir, and look at the night,—
If the morning star be not shining.

The rhymec are—in st.1, 濡 *, 侯, 渝 *, cat. 4, t. 1: in 2, 饰, 力, 直, cat. 1, t. 3: in 3, 晏 粲, 彦, cat. 16.

Ode 7. Narrative. OLD FRIENDSHIP SHOULD NOT BE HASTILY BROKEN OFF. I will not venture any interpretation of this brief and trivial ode. Choo hears in it the words of a woman entreating her lover not to cast her off. Maou understands it of the people of Ch'ing wishing to retain the good men who were dissatisfied with duke Chwang, and leaving the public service. So far as the language of the ode is concerned, we must pronounce in favour of Choo; but the 'highway' is a strange place for a woman to be detaining her lover in, and pleading with him. He, however, fortifies his view by the opinion of Sung-yuh (宋 玉), a poet of the end of the Chow dyn.;—see the 登 徒 子 好 色 赋, in the 19th Book of Seaou T'ung's 'Literary Selections.' The imperial editors evidently incline to the old view. Choo He, they say, at one time held it himself; and few of the scholars of the Sung, Yuen, and Ming dynasties adopted his interpretation.

Ll.1,2 in both stt. 遵,—as in i.X. 大 路, 'the grand road,' == the high or public way. 掺 = 揽, 'to hold,' 'to grasp.'

Ll.3,4. 无 = 毋, 'do not.' 魗 is another form of 丑, 'ugly,' and this would seem to be decisive in favour of Choo's interpretation:— 'Do not look on me as ugly.' Still, I have not pressed this. The Shwoh-wǎn quotes the line with another variation of the character, and

explains the term by 弃, 'to reject.' The 4th line is not a little difficult. 不 is for the most part our negative 'not,' and is not to be taken imperatively. So Maou appears to take it here,—as indicative. 寁 = 速, 'hurriedly,' or 'to do anything hurriedly.' K'ang-shing explains the lines in the 1st st. thus:—'Do not hate me for trying thus to detain you; it is because duke Chwang is not swift to pursue the way of our former ruler that I do so.' Similarly he deals with them in the next stanza, taking 好 in the 2nd tone,='good ways.' Even the scholars who reject Choo's view shrink from thus explaining 寁. They take 不 imperatively; which is allowable:—see Wang Yin-che on the term. Then 故 = 旧, 'old intercourse,' and 好='friendship;'—in 3d tone:— 'Do not deal thus hastily with old intercourse.'

The rhymes are—in st.1, 路, 袪, 故, cat. 5, st.1: in 2, 手, 魗, 好 *, cat.3, t.2.

Ode 8. Narrative. A PLEASANT PICTURE OF DOMESTIC LIFE. A WIFE SENDS HER HUSBAND FROM HER SIDE TO HIS HUNTING, EXPRESSES HER AFFECTION, AND ENCOURAGES HIM TO CULTIVATE VIRTUOUS FRIENDSHIPS. The 'Little Preface' falls into the same absurdity here, as in the interpretation of ode 6, and says we have in the piece a description of the better morals of a past age, by way of contrast to the lascivious indulgences which characterized the domestic life of Ch'ing when it was written. The first ode of next book is something akin to this; but the parties there are a marquis and marchioness of Ts'e, while here we have simply an officer (not

翔。弋凫与雁。

二章

弋言加之。与子宜之。宜言饮酒。与子偕老。琴瑟在

御。莫不静好。

三章

知子之来之。杂佩以赠之。知子之顺之。杂佩以问

Bestir yourself, and move about,
To shoot the wild ducks and geese.

2 'When your arrows and line have found them,
I will dress them fitly for you.
When they are dressed, we will drink [together over them],
And I will hope to grow old with you.
Your lute in your hands
Will emit its quiet pleasant tones.

3 'When I know those whose acquaintance you wish,
I will give them of the ornaments of my girdle.
When I know those with whom you are cordial,

of high rank) of Ch'ing and his wife; and to suppose, with Maou, that the wife rouses her husband that he may go to court destroys the life and spirit of the ode.

St. 1. The 日 in ll, 1, 2, is evidently the verb, and not the particle. It = 'says.' 昧旦, 'dark and bright,' denotes the early dawn, when the first beams of light are making the darkness visible. The dawn is subsequent to the time of cock-crowing. The husband does not here, as in viii.I., show any unwillingness to get up. We must take 1.3 and all the rest of the piece, as spoken by the wife who occupies the prominent place. 明星有烂—'the bright star is shining.' By 'the bright star' we are to understand the morning star. Maou does not say so expressly, but his words, that 'the small stars had now disappeared,' are not inconsistent with the view. 翱翔,—as in v. I. 2. The terms are appropriate to describe the motions of a hunter, moving from place to place in quest of his game. 将 has a little of the imperative force, and of its meaning of the future. The 'Complete Digest' gives for the 5th line,— 于斯时当翱翔而往, 'At this time you ought to be moving about and going.' 弋.—as in Ana. VII.xxvi.

St. 2. The 言, in ll. 1, 3, is the particle; the 子 in ll. 2, 4, must refer to the husband, the

子 of st. 1; the 之, to the wild ducks and geese. K'ang-shing takes it of the husband's guests, and makes the whole st. to be spoken by him, having no perception of the unity of the piece. The wife supposes that the husband's shooting is sure to be successful. The string attached to his arrows is securely fixed on his game (加诸凫雁之上), which is brought home: and then her task with it commences. 宜之,—'will deal fitly with it;' i. e., will cook it, and serve it up with its proper accompaniments. The 3d and 4th lines express the happiness of the couple, and the affection especially of the wife; the 5th and 6th indicate more particularly the enjoyment of the husband. 琴 瑟 is not to be taken as plural, or denoting both instruments so called; but either the one or the other. The phrase 在 御 is difficult to construe, though the meaning is obvious enough. We may refer 御 to the definition of it in the dict. by 进, 'put forward,' = 'to use.' The superior man. acc. to the rules of antiquity, was never, without some urgent reasons, to be without his lute by his side, so that it might always be at hand for his use. The quiet harmony of the lute was a common image for conjugal affection.

St.3. While the wife was so fond of her husband, she did not wish to monopolize him; and she here indicates her sympathy with him in cultivating

之。知子之好之。杂佩以报之。

I will send to them of the ornaments of my girdle.
When I know those whom you love,
I will repay their friendship from the ornaments of my girdle.'

IX.　　*Yew neu t'ung keu.*

有女同车

一章

有女同车。颜如舜华。将翱将翔。佩玉琼琚。彼美孟

1　There is the lady in the carriage [with him]
With a countenance like the flower of the ephemeral hedge-tree.
As they move about,
The beautiful *keu*-gems of her girdle-pendant appear.

the friendship—we must suppose of men of worth like himself, his friends. She would despoil herself of her feminine ornaments to testify her regard for them. The 之 at the end of the lines, is to be taken of the friends, whose acquaintance the husband enjoyed or wished to cultivate. 来 is to be taken with a *hiphil* force,='to make to come,' 'to draw to one's-self.' 顺, 'to accord with,'=here, 'to find one's-self in cordial sympathy with.' 问, 'to ask,' was used also of the offerings which were sent, by way of compliment, along with the inquiries or messages which were sent to individuals. 杂佩 means the various appendages which were worn at the girdle. Maou and Choo understand the phrase here of the gems and pearls, worn by ladies of rank and wealth, and called 佩玉, see on v. V. 2, VI. 1, 2, *et al.* These are all represented in the annexed figure, in which the strings connecting the different gems are all strung with pearls.

Others, arguing from the supposed position of the husband in this piece, hold that we are not to think of anything so valuable as these ap-

pendages; and I incline to their view.—See the translation of the ode, and the remarks on it in the introduction to Le Marquis D'Hervey-Saint-Denys' 'Poésies de l'epoque des Thang;' where the author has been misled by the version of P. Lacharme.

The rhymes are—in st. 1, 且, 烂, 雁, cat. 14: in 2, 加, 宜 *, cat. 17; 酒, 老, 好 *, cat. 3, t. 2: in 3, 来 (prop. cat. 1), 赠, cat. 6; 顺, 问, cat. 13; 好 *, 报 *, cat. 3, t. 2.

Ode 9. Narrative. THE PRAISE OF SOME LADY. I cannot make any more out of the piece than this. The old school, of course, find a historical basis for it. Hwuh, the eldest son of duke Chwang, twice refused an alliance which was proffered to him by the marquis of Ts'e, and wedded finally a lady from a smaller and less powerful State. His counsellors all wished him to accept the overtures of Ts'e, which would have supported him on his succession to the marquisate. As it turned out, he became marquis of Ch'ing in B. C. 700; was driven out by a brother the year after; was restored in 696; and murdered in 694. He is known as duke Ch'aou (昭). The Preface says that in this piece the people of Ch'ing satirize Hwuh for his folly in not marrying a daughter of Ts'e. But there is no indication of satire in the ode; and neither by ingenuity nor violence can an explanation of the lines be given, which will reasonably harmonize with this interpretation. I will not waste time or space by discussing the different exegeses, on this view, of Ying-tah and Yen Ts'an. Dissatisfied with the old interpretation, Choo had recourse to his usual solvent, and makes the ode to be spoken by a lover about his mistress. But the language is that of respect more than of love,

姜。洵美且都。

二章

有女同行。颜如舜英。将翱将翔。佩玉将将。彼美孟

姜。德音不忘。

> That beautiful eldest Këang
> Is truly admirable and elegant.

2　There is the young lady walking [with him],
　　With a countenance like the ephemeral blossoms of the hedge-
　　As they move about,　　　　　　　　　　　　　　　　[tree.
　　The gems of her girdle-pendant tinkle.
　　Of that beautiful eldest Këang
　　The virtuous fame is not to be forgotten.

X.　*Shan yew foo-soo.*

山有扶苏

一章

山有扶苏。隰有荷华。不见子都。乃见狂且。

1　On the mountains is the mulberry tree ;
　　In the marshes is the lotus flower.
　　I do not see Tsze-too,
　　But I see this mad fellow.

We must take the piece as it is, and be content to acknowledge our ignorance of the special object of the author in it.

Ll. 1, 2, In both stt. 同行 must be taken as in the translation, because of the 4th line. The lady is seen first sitting in a carriage, and then walking along the road. The *shun*, generally and more correctly written with 艹 at the top, is, no doubt, one of the *malvaceæ*, noted for the beauty of its fugitive flowers. It has many names;—木, 槿, 橓, 椵, and 王蒸. It is also called 日及, 'the ephemeral,' with reference to the fall of its five-petalled flowers in the evening of the day when they open, and 藩篱草, 'fence' or 'hedge-plant,' from its being much used for hedges, especially in Hoo-nan and Hoo-pih. I have combined these two namesi n the translation. 英＝华, 'flower,' or 'blossoms.'

Ll. 3, 4. L. 3, as in st. 1 of last ode. The 将 approaches our 'whenever.' 佩玉,—as in v.

V. 3. 琼琚,—see on v. X. 1. 将将 is intended to denote the tinkling of the gems.

Ll. 5, 6. The surname *Këang* indicates that the lady was of Ts'e; and 孟, that she was the eldest daughter of the family. I must understand, contrary to the opinion of Yen Ts'an, that this Këang is the same with the lady in the previous lines. 都 means 'of an elegant carriage (闲雅).' 德音,—as in iii X. 1.

The rhymes are—in st. 1. 车*, 华*, 琚, 都, cat. 5, t. 1 ; 翔, 姜, cat. 10: in 2, 行*, 英*, 翔, 将, 姜, 忘, *ib.*

Ode 10. Allusive. **A LADY MOCKING HER LOVER.** This is Choo's interpretation of the piece, but it is much demurred to. The Preface says the piece is directed aginst the marquis Hwuh,—duke Ch'aou, who gave his confidence to men unworthy of it. The same difficulty attaches to this as to so many other of the old interpretations, that make the odes into riddles, which we are obliged, when the answer

二章

山有桥松。隰有游龙。不见子充。乃见狡童。

2   On the mountains is the lofty pine;
    In the marshes is the spreading water-polygonum.
    I do not see Tsze-ch'ung,
    But I see this artful boy.

XI.   *T'oh he.*

择兮

一章

择兮择兮。风其吹女。叔兮伯兮。倡予和女。

二章

择兮择兮。风其漂女。叔兮伯兮。倡予要女。

1   Ye withered leaves! Ye withered leaves!
    How the wind is blowing you away!
    O ye uncles,
    Give us the first note, and we will join in with you.

2   Ye withered leaves! Ye withered leaves!
    How the wind is carrying you away!
    O ye uncles,
    Give us the first note, and we will complete [the song].

has been told us, to pronounce to be very badly constructed ones.

Ll.1,2, in both stt. 扶苏 is evidently the name of a tree; but of what tree is not well ascertained. Choo, following Maou, says it is the 扶胥, 'a small tree;' but the best editions of Maou throw the 'small' out of his text, —and with reason. Kwei Wăn-ts'an (桂文 灿 ; pres. dyn) has a long criticism which it is not worth while to repeat here, arguing that the mulberry tree is meant. 荷 is the nelumbium, or lotus. 华 indicates that it is spoken of as in flower. 乔,—as in i.IX.1. 龙 is one of the *polygonaceœ*,—the *polygonum aqualicum*, called 'wandering,' from the way in which its branches and leaves spread themselves out. It has many names, particularly 红花 and 水 红, from the reddish colour of the leaves.—The mountains and the marshes were all furnished with what was most natural and proper to them. It was not so with the speaker and her friends.

Ll.3,4. Tsze-too is understood, in both interpretations, to be a designation expressive of the beauty of the individual to whom it is applied, derived from the Tsze-too referred to in Mencius, VI. Pt.i. VII. 7, so that we might translate—'I do not see a Tsze-too.' Consistently enough with the character of the original, Choo understands that it was merely the beauty of the outward form which the speaker had in view. Most inconsistently with that character, the other interpretation renders it necessary to suppose the idea is of moral beauty or goodness. But if Tsze-too is thus to be taken as a metaphorical designation, so must Tsze-ch'ung in st.2 be taken; and existing records do not supply us with any individual so styled, before the date of the ode. Why should we think that the two are more than the current designations of two gentlemen, known to the lady and her lover, whom she calls, mockingly, 'foolish,' and 'an artful boy?' Maou takes the artful boy intended to be duke Ch'aou; but even those who adopt his general view of the piece see the inapplicability of such a reference.

The rhymes are—in st.1, 苏, 华 *, 都, 且 *, cat.5, t.1: in 2. 松, 龙, 充, 童, cat.9,

XII.   *Këaou t'ung.*

狡童

一章

彼狡童兮。不与我言兮。维子之故。使我不能餐兮。

二章

彼狡童兮。不与我食兮。维子之故。使我不能息兮。

1   That artful boy!
    He will not speak with me!
    But for the sake of you, Sir,
    Shall I make myself unable to eat?

2   That artful boy!
    He will not eat with me!
    But for the sake of you, Sir,
    Shall I make myself unable to rest?

Ode 11. Metaphorical. AN APPEAL FROM THE INFERIOR OFFICERS OF CH'ING TO THEIR SUPERIORS ON THE SAD CONDITION OF THE STATE. This interpretation is a modification of that given in the 'Little Preface,'—elaborated mainly by Yen Ts'an. Maou treats the ode as allusive, the first two lines introducing the exposition of the abnormal relations between the marquis Hwuh and his ministers, as indicated in the last two. This view cannot be sustained, and Yen himself is wrong in continuing to say that the piece is allusive. Choo hears in it the words of a bad woman soliciting the advances of her lovers, and offering to respond to them. This does not appear, however, on the surface of the words. We have already in iii. XII. met with 叔兮 伯兮 in the sense which the characters have on Yen's view, while on Choo's we should have to translate the 3d line—'O Sir! O Sir!' It is not *necessary here* to follow Choo in the peculiar interpretation which he adopts of many of these odes of Ch'ing; where there is not more difficulty in following a more honourable one, it should be done.

Ll. 1, 2, in both stt. 萚 is used of a tree whose leaves are withered and ready to fall. Elsewhere, it is explained by 落, 'to fall.' 漂 is cognate with 摽, in ii. IX. Maou says it is synonymous with 吹 in st. 1, and Choo takes it as equivalent to 飘, 'blown about.' These two lines are metaphorical of the state of things in Ch'ing, all in disorder and verging to decay.

Ll. 3, 4. 叔兮 伯兮,—as in iii. XII. The high officers of Ch'ing, we are to suppose, are thus addressed by those below them, who go on to exhort them to take the initiative in encountering the prevailing misgovernment, and promise to second their efforts. 倡 is 'to lead in singing,' and to take the lead generally. 要 = 成, 'to complete,' 'to carry out.' 和, in 3d tone,—'to join in with,' 'to second.'

The rhymes are—in st. 1, 萚, 伯*, (and in 2), cat. 5, t. 3; 吹*, 和, cat. 17: in 2, 漂, 要, cat. 2.

Ode 12. Narrative. A WOMAN SCORNING HER SCORNER. Here again I follow the interpretation of Choo. As between it and the interpretation of the Preface, according to the exposition of Maou, we cannot hesitate; but Yen Ts'an has here again modified the old view so as to give a not unreasonable exegesis of the ode. The Preface says it was directed against Hwuh, who would not consult with men of worth about the affairs of the State, but allowed the young and arrogant minions about him to take their own way. Those men of worth consequently gave expression to their sorrow and apprehension in these lines. Adopting this explanation, Maou makes both 'the artful boy,' and the 'you, Sir,' to refer to Hwuh, as if any officer of worth would have permitted himself to apply such a term as 狡童 to his ruler! The K'ang-he editors allow that this is inadmissible. To obviate this difficulty, Yen Ts'an pro-

XIII.　*K'ëen chang.*

褰裳

一章

子惠思我。褰裳涉溱。子不我思。豈无他人。狂童之

狂也且。

二章

子惠思我。褰裳涉洧。子不我思。豈无他士。狂童之

狂也且。

1　If you, Sir, think kindly of me,
　I will hold up my lower garments, and cross the Tsin.
　If you do not think of me,
　Is there no other person[to do so]?
　You, foolish, foolish fellow!

2　If you, Sir, think kindly of me,
　I will hold up my lower garments, and cross the Wei.
　If you do not think of me,
　Is there no other gentleman [to do so]?
　You, foolish, foolish fellow!

posed to take 狡 童 in the plural,—of 'the crafty youths,' the unworthy ministers who ruled in Hwuh's court, and the 子 in l. 3 of Hwuh himself, still dear to those who cared for the welfare of the State, so that in their anxiety for him they were hardly able to take their food or to rest. The editors think this gives a sufficient explanation of the piece. To my mind, the referring 狡 童 in l. 1, and 子 in l. 3 to different subjects is unnatural and forced,—to get over a difficulty. At the same time Choo's exegesis of ll. 3, 4, which I have indicated by translating them interrogatively, goes on a foregone conclusion as to the meaning of the whole.

The rhymes—are in st. 1, 言, 餐, cat. 14: 食, 息, cat. 1, t. 3.

Ode 13. Narrative. A LADY'S DEFIANT DE-CLARATION OF HER ATTACHMENT TO HER LOVER. Here, as in most of the odes hereabouts, Choo and the critics of the old school widely differ. The Preface understands the piece as the expression of the wish of the people of Ch'ing that some great State would interfere, to settle the struggle between the marquis Hwuh and his brother Tuh. Hwuh succeeded to his father in B. C. 700; and that same year he was driven from the State by his brother Tuh. In 696, Tuh had to flee, and Hwuh recovered the earldom, but before the end of the year Tuh was again master of a strong city in Ch'ing, which he held till Hwuh was murdered in 694. The old school holds that Tuh is 'the madman of all mad youths' in the 5th lines; but how an interpretation of the other four lines, acc. to the view of the Preface, was ever thought of as the *primary* idea intended in them, I cannot well conceive. The K'ang-he editors appeal to the use which is made of the ode in a narrative introduced into the Tso Chuen under X.xvi. 2, as a proof that, in the time of Confucius, it was not considered a love song. A minister of Ch'ing there repeats it to an envoy of Tsin, to sound him whether that State would stand by Ch'ing. Why might he not turn the piece in which a lady is sounding her lover to that application? It seems to me very natural that he should do so. 子 is the party whom the speaker addresses;—acc. to the old school, the chief minister of some other State; but this is quite inconsistent with the 人 and 士 in the 4th lines. Tsin and Wei were two rivers in Ch'ing. See them mentioned in Mencius, IV. Pt. ii. II. 1, in connection with fords over their separate streams, or a ford over their united waters after their junction. 且 at the end is the particle.

The rhymes are—in st. 1, 溱, 人, cat. 12, t. 1: in 2, 洧*, 士, cat. 1, t. 2: in both stt., 狂, 狂, cat. 10.

XIV. *Fung.*

丰

一章
子之丰兮。俟我乎巷兮。悔予不送兮。

二章
子之昌兮。俟我乎堂兮。悔予不将兮。

三章
衣锦褧衣。裳锦褧裳。叔兮伯兮。驾予与行。

四章
裳锦褧裳。衣锦褧衣。叔兮伯兮。驾予与归。

1　Full and good looking was the gentleman,
　　Who waited for me in the lane!
　　I repent that I did not go with him.

2　A splendid gentleman was he,
　　Who waited for me in the hall!
　　I regret that I did not accompany him.

3　Over my embroidered upper robe, I have put on a [plain]
　　　　single garment;
　　Over my embroidered lower robe, I have done the same.
　　O Sir, O Sir,
　　Have your carriage ready for me to go with you.

4　Over my embroidered lower robe, I have put on a [plain]
　　　　single garment;
　　Over my embroidered upper robe, I have done the same.
　　O Sir, O Sir,
　　Have your carriage ready to take me home with you.

Ode 14. Narrative. A WOMAN REGRETS LOST OPPORTUNITIES, AND WOULD WELCOME A FRESH SUITOR. In the interpretation of this piece the old and new schools approach each other. The former finds in it a lady regretting that she had not fulfilled a contract of marriage; the latter, a lady regretting that she had not met the advances of one who sought her love. But there is nothing in the stanzas to indicate that there had been a previous contract of marriage between the lady and the gentleman who waited for her. Had there been so, the matter would have been out of her hands, and she could not have refused to go with him when he came in person for her. Choo's interpretation is the preferable. The imperial editors speak of the piece as, on either view, an illustration of the light and loose manners of Ch'ing. With this ode before us, we need not to be stumbled at the view which Choo gives of several others in the Book.

XV. *Tung mun che shen.*

东门之埠

一章
东门之埠。茹藘在阪。其室则迩。其人甚远。

二章
东门之栗。有践家室。岂不尔思。子不我即。

1 Near the level ground at the east gate,
Is the madder plant on the bank.
The house is near there,
But the man is very far away.

2 By the chestnut trees at the east gate,
Is a row of houses.
Do I not think of you?
But you do not come to me.

Stt.1,2. 丰 describes the plumpness and good looks of the gentleman; 昌, the richness and splendour of his appearance. 之 is the particle, giving a vividness to the description. 巷 is the lane, or street, outside the house where the lady lived; 堂, the hall, or raised floor, to which visitors ascended as the reception-room. 送 and 将 are synonyms,—as in ii.I.

Stt.3, 4. 衣锦裳衣, see on v. III. 1. The 裳, or lower garment is here introduced also, to vary the rhythm in the two stt. Comparing this ode and v.III., we understand that it was the fashion of ladies, when travelling, to dress in the style described. 叔兮伯兮 is here evidently equivalent to our ‘O Sir, O Sir,’ or ‘any Sir.’ The same mode of mentioning gentlemen, or speaking to them, is still common. Maou thinks the gentleman, who had previously come to meet her, in a lawful way, is intended; but the indefiniteness of the 3d line is against this, and moreover, it requires us to construe 驾 in the imperative mood. Maou’s construction makes the piece more licentious than Choo’s. Le Hoo (李樗; Sung dyn.) says: ‘The woman, having refused to go with her bridegroom, and yielded herself to another man, now wishes him to come for her again. This is a specimen of the manners of Ch‘ing.’

The rhymes are—in st. 1, 丰, 巷, 送, cat. 9: in 2 昌, 堂, 将, cat. 10: t: in 3, 裳, 行*, ib.: in 4, 衣, 归, cat. 15, t. 1.

Ode 15. Narrative. A WOMAN THINKS OF HER LOVER’S RESIDENCE, AND COMPLAINS THAT HE DOES NOT COME TO HER. In the interpretation of this, even more than of the last piece, there is an agreement.

Ll. 1, 2, in both stt. The east gate is that of the capital of Ch‘ing,—the principal gate of the city. From the Tso Chuen, on the 4th year of duke Yin, we know that there was an open space about it, sufficient to receive a numerous enemy, which may explain the reference to ‘the level ground.’ 埠 is explained as ‘the levelling of the ground, and removing the grass.’ Sometimes it is used of ‘the level ground at the foot of an altar;’ but we must think here of a larger space. Near this was a bank (陂者曰阪), where the madder plant was cultivated. The 茹藘 has other names,—茅蒐, 蒨草, 茜, &c. On the space also was a road, along which chestnut trees were planted, and by one or more of them was a row of houses. 践 = 行列貌, ‘the appearance of things in a row.’ In this row lived the object of the lady’s affection.

Ll. 3, 4. The house was near, but the man was distant;—not really so, but as she did not see him, it was the same to her, as if he were far away. 即,—as in v. IV. 1.

The rhymes are—in st. 1, 埠, 阪, 远, cat. 14: in 2, 栗, 室, 即*, cat. 12, t. 3.

XVI. *Fung yu.*

风雨
一章
风雨凄凄。鸡鸣喈喈。既见君子。云胡不夷。

二章
风雨潇潇。鸡鸣胶胶。既见君子。云胡不瘳。

三章
风雨如晦。鸡鸣不已。既见君子。云胡不喜。

1   Cold are the wind and the rain,
And shrilly crows the cock.
But I have seen my husband,
And should I but feel at rest?

2   The wind whistles and the rain patters,
While loudly crows the cock.
But I have seen my husband,
And could my ailment but be cured?

3   Through the wind and rain all looks dark,
And the cock crows without ceasing.
But I have seen my husband,
And how should I not rejoice?

Ode 16. Narrative. A ᴡɪꜰᴇ ɪѕ ᴄᴏɴѕᴏʟᴇᴅ, ᴜɴ-ᴅᴇʀ ᴄɪʀᴄᴜᴍѕᴛᴀɴᴄᴇѕ ᴏꜰ ɢʟᴏᴏᴍ, ʙʏ ᴛʜᴇ ᴀʀʀɪᴠᴀʟ ᴏꜰ ʜᴇʀ ʜᴜѕʙᴀɴᴅ. I venture, in the interpretation of this ode, to depart both from the old school and from Choo. On the view of the former, the speaker is longing for 'superior men (君子)' to arise and settle the disturbed state of Ch'ing, men who should do their duty as the cocks in the darkest and stormiest night;—so that the piece is allusive. Choo thinks the speaker tells in it of the times of her meeting with her lover, and of the happiness their interviews gave her. It has been urged that on this view the appellation of 君子 is inappropriate, such a name being inapplicable to one indulging in an illicit connexion. I have been led to the view which I have proposed, mainly by a comparison of the piece with ii. III. 君子 is there used of a husband, and the structure and sentiment of the two are very much akin.

Ll. 1, 2, in all the stt. 凄凄,—see on iii. II. 4. The reduplication of the term describes, as it were, the feeling of the cold. 潇 (should, probably, be without the 艹 at the top) 潇 gives the sound of the wind and rain; and 胶 (elsewhere, and better, with 口 at the side) 胶, that of the cock's crowing.

Ll. 3, 4. 君子 is used for 'husband,' as in ii. III, *et al.* 云 is the particle. Maou explains 夷 by 悦, 'to be pleased;' but its common meaning of 平, 'to be pacified,' 'made quiet,' answers sufficiently well. 瘳,—'to be cured.' Her anxieties had been as troublesome to her as if she had been labouring under disease.

The rhymes are—in st. 1, 凄, 喈, 夷, cat. 15, t. 1: in 2, 潇 *, 胶*, 瘳, cat. 3, t. 1: in 3. 晦 *, 已, 子, 喜, cat. t. 2.

XXVII. *Tsz' K'en.*

子衿

一章
青青子衿。悠悠我心。纵我不往。子宁不嗣音。

二章
青青子佩。悠悠我思。纵我不往。子宁不来。

三章
挑兮达兮。在城阙兮。一日不见。如三月兮。

1 O you, with the blue collar,
  Prolonged is the anxiety of my heart.
  Although I do not go [to you],
  Why do you not continue your messages [to me]?

2 O you with the blue [strings to your] girdle-gems,
  Long, long do I think of you.
  Although I do not go [to you],
  Why do you not come [to me]?

3 How volatile are you and dissipated,
  By the look-out tower on the wall!
  One day without the sight of you
  Is like three months.

Ode 17. Narrative. A LADY MOURNS THE INDIFFERENCE AND ABSENCE OF HER LOVER. I cannot adopt any other interpretation of this piece than the above, which is given by Choo. The old interpreters find in it a condemnation of the neglect and disorder into which the schools of Ch'ing had fallen. The attendance at them was become irregular. Some young men pursued their studies, and others played truant; and one of the former class is supposed to be here upbraiding a friend in the second. The imperial editors approve of this view, and say that Choo himself once held it; but the language of the ode is absurd upon it.

Ll. 1, 2, in all the stt. 衿, *i. q.* 襟, is the collar of the jacket or upper garment. 青 denotes a light green, or blue inclining to green, like the azure of the sky. The repetition of the term does not here, as often, give intensity to the meaning;—see Ying-tah *in loc.* Up to the time of the present dyn., students wore a blue collar, and the phrase 青衿 is a designation for a graduate of the 1st degree. The gentleman spoken of in the piece was probably a student. By 佩 is understood 佩玉, 'the gems worn at the girdle;' and 青青 is taken as descriptive of the colour of the strings on which they were worn (士佩瑞珉而青组绶也, 故云青青, 谓组绶也). 悠悠,—as in i. I. 2, 挑 expresses the idea of 'lightness in leaping about;' 达 that of 'dissipation (放恣).' Maou explains them both together as denoting 'the app. of coming and going.' 阙 was a tower or look-out on the top of the city-wall,—a place where idle people were likely to collect.

Ll. 2, 3. 宁 = 何, 'why.' 嗣音 = 继续其声问, 'to continue communication and inquiries.' Maou explains 嗣 by 习, 'to practise,' and understands 音 of the lessons of music which the truant had learned at school! Even Yen Ts'an, however, who adheres to the old interpretation, understands this phrase as Choo does:—汝宁不继声以问我乎.

XVIII.　*Yang che shwuy.*

扬之水

一章

扬之水。不流束楚。终鲜兄弟。维予与女。无信人之
言。人实迁女。

二章

扬之水。不流束薪。终鲜兄弟。维予二人。无信人之
言。人实不信。

1　The fretted waters
　　Do not carry on their current a bundle of thorns.
　　Few are our brethren;
　　There are only I and you.
　　Do not believe what people say;
　　They are deceiving you.

2　The fretted waters
　　Do not carry on their current a bundle of firewood.
　　Few are our brethren;
　　There are only we two.
　　Do not believe what people say;
　　They are not to be trusted.

The rhymes are—in st. 1, 衿, 心, 音, cat. 7, t. 1: in 2, 佩., 思, 来, cat. 1, t. 1: in 3, 达, 阙, 月, cat. 15, t. 3.

Ode 18. Allusive. ONE PARTY ASSERTS GOOD FAITH TO ANOTHER, AND PROTESTS AGAINST PEOPLE WHO WOULD MAKE THEM DOUBT EACH OTHER. Who the parties are we really cannot tell. Choo thinks, in his commentary on the *She* (he has elsewhere expressed a different view), that they are two lovers, warning each other against some who were attempting to sow doubt and jealousy between them. Maou and his school say the piece was directed against the weakness of the marquis Hwuh, and the faithlessness of his officers and counsellors. Both interpretations have difficulties, and it is better not to insist on either, but to leave the question as to the aim of the writer undetermined.

Ll. 1, 2, in both stt. See on vi. IV.

Ll. 3, 4. 终＝既, as when it is followed by 且. We can hardly translate it. 鲜, in the 2d tone,＝'few.' 兄弟 would be very perplexing on Choo's view. He takes the phrase as meaning *relatives*, and refers to a passage in the Le Ke, VII. Pt. i. 17, where 兄弟 is used for husband and wife, or the affinities formed by a marriage. 人＝他人, 'other men,' 'people.' 迁＝诳, 'to deceive.'

The rhymes are—in st 1 (and in 2), 水, 弟, cat. 15, t. 2; 楚, 女, 女, cat. 5, t. 2: in 2, 薪, 人, 信, cat. 12, t. 1.

XIX. *Ch'uh k'e tung mun.*

出其东门

一章

出其东门。有女如云。虽则如云。匪我思存。缟衣綦

巾。聊乐我员。

二章

出其闉阇。有女如荼。虽则如荼。匪我思且。缟衣

茹蔍。聊可与娱。

1　I went out at the east gate,
　　Where the girls were in clouds.
　　Although they are like clouds,
　　It is not on them that my thoughts rest.
　　She in the thin white silk, and the grey coiffure,—
　　She is my joy!

2　I went out by the tower on the covering wall,
　　Where the girls were like flowering rushes.
　　Although they are like flowering rushes,
　　It is not of them that I think.
　　She in the thin white silk, and the madder-[dyed coiffure],—
　　It is she that makes me happy!

Ode 19. Narrative. A MAN'S PRAISE OF HIS OWN POOR WIFE, CONTRASTED WITH FLAUNTING BEAUTIES. The 'Little Preface' says this piece was directed against the prevailing disorders, in consequence of which families were divided and scattered, and the people kept anxiously thinking how they could preserve their wives. The K'ang-he editors rightly condemn this interpretation, and approve of that of Choo, saying that the language of the ode is the reverse of what we should expect, if it had reference to contentions and abounding misery.

Ll. 1, 2, in both stt. 闉 was an outer wall built in a curve from the principal one, in front of the gates, to which it served as a curtain or defence; 阇 was a tower on this wall over against the gate. We are to understand that these terms belong to the east gate of st. 1. Choo takes the 'like clouds' as descriptive of the 'beauty,' as well as of the 'number,' of the ladies about the gate. 荼 is 'a kind of flowering rush (野菅白华),' and not the sow-thistle of iii. X. 2. Choo seems to go too far in setting down all these ladies as of loose character (淫奔之女); it is enough to say their manners were free.

Ll. 3—6. 匪我思存一非我思之所存, 'She of whom I think is not among them,' or 'they are not those on whom my thoughts rest.' I prefer the former construction. In st. 2, 且 is the particle. The 5th line is descriptive of the speaker's wife in poor, unassuming dress. 缟 is a fabric of thin silk, in its natural colour, undyed. 衣 is the upper garment. 巾 is a napkin or kerchief, frequently denoting a handkerchief or towel; here it seems to be used of a head-dress, the kerchief being employed for that purpose. The dict. gives this meaning of the character;—but without reference to this passage. 綦 denotes the colour of the kerchief, 'light blue, with a whitish tint, like the colour of mugwort.' 茹蔍,—as in XV. 1. We must bring on the 巾 of st. 1, —here dyed with madder. 聊,—as in iii. XIV. 1. 员一云, and so read, is the particle. 娱一乐, 'to rejoice,' 'have pleasure.'

XX.   *Yay yew man ts'aou.*

野有蔓草

一章

野有蔓草。零露溥兮。有美一人。清扬婉兮。邂逅相

遇。适我愿兮。

二章

野有蔓草。零露瀼瀼。有美一人。婉如清扬。邂逅相

遇。与子偕臧。

1   On the moor is the creeping grass,
    And how heavily is it loaded with dew!
    There was a beautiful man,
    Lovely, with clear eyes and fine forehead!
    We met together accidentally,
    And so my desire was satisfied.

2   On the moor is the creeping grass,
    Heavily covered with dew.
    There was a beautiful man,
    Lovely, with clear eyes and fine forehead!
    We met together accidentally,
    And he and I were happy together.

The rhymes are—门, 云, 云, 存, 巾, 员 *, cat. 13: in 2, 阁, 茶, 茶, 且 *, 蕙, 娱, cat.5, t. 1.

Ode 20. Narrative and allusive. A LADY REJOICES IN AN UNLAWFUL CONNECTION WHICH SHE HAD FORMED. This is the view, substantially, which Choo takes of this piece; and the K'ang-he editors allow that the language in itself bears it out. Twice, however, the ode is introduced by Tso K'ew-ming,—under the 4th year of duke Chwang, and the 27th year of duke Sëang, where the application of such a piece seems out of place. Han Ying also puts it into the mouth of Confucius (外传, II. 14), to illustrate the accidental meeting of himself and another worthy. Even Maou's account of it is as hard to reconcile with those citations of it, as Choo's, for he thinks that it expresses the wish of the bachelors and spinsters of Ch'ing to get married in any way, the disorders of the state having made them pass the flower of their age unmarried. Yen Ts'an says that Maou mistook the meaning of the 1st sentence in the 'Little Preface' about it, and then of the ode itself; and then proceeds to explain it himself in harmony with the passages in the Tso Chuen; but it is not worth while trying to unravel all the perplexities of the interpretation.

Ll.1,2, in both stt. 零,—as in iv. VI. 3. 零露 = 'the fallen dew.' 溥 denotes 'the app. of much dew;' and so, 瀼瀼.

Ll.3,4. 清扬,—see on iv. III. 3. 婉 = 'beautiful;' 婉如, 'beautiful-like.' The analogy of iv. III. would make us understand 清扬 of a lady, and translate the 3d line— 'There was a beautiful lady.' So, Yen Ts'an. But the 子 in the last line of st.2 will not allow us to do so.

Ll.5,6. 邂逅 = 'accidentally,' or, as Choo and Maou say, 'a meeting not previously arranged for.' 适 = 'to accord with,' 'be according to.' 臧 = 善, 'good,' or 'to esteem good.'

The rhymes are—in st.1, 溥, 婉, 愿, cat. 14: in 2, 瀼, 扬, 臧, cat.10.

XXI. *Tsin Wei.*

溱洧

一章

溱与洧。方涣涣兮。士与女。方秉蕑兮。女曰观乎。

士曰既且。且往观乎。洧之外。洵訏且乐。维士与

女。伊其相谑。赠之以勺药。

1   The Tsin and the Wei
Now present their broad sheets of water.
Ladies and gentlemen
Are carrying flowers of valerian.
A lady says, 'Have you been to see?'
A gentleman replies, 'I have been.'
'But let us go again to see.
Beyond the Wei,
The ground is large and fit for pleasure.'
So the gentlemen and ladies.
Make sport together,
Presenting one another with small peonies.

Ode 21. Narrative. A FESTIVITY OF CH'ING, AND ADVANTAGE TAKEN OF IT FOR LICENTIOUS ASSIGNATIONS. The old and new schools are, happily, agreed in their interpretation of this piece. Choo says there is an allusive element in it, but I am unable to perceive it. The introduction of it would only lead to perplexity.

Ll. 1—4, in both stt. The Tsin and the Wei, —see on XIII. 1, 2. 方 = 'now;' an indication of time. 涣涣 (Han Ying gives 洹洹; and the Shwoh-wăn, 泛泛, where 泛 should, perhaps, be 汛) denotes 'the appearance of swollen waters.' The ode is understood to have reference to the 3d month of the year, when the streams were all swollen by the melting of the ice and snow. 浏 is defined as 'the appearance of depth.' 蕑, both by Maou and Choo, is defined by 兰, but we are not much helped thereby to an identification of the plant; for that term enters into the names of a multitude of flowers. Williams says that it is a general name for gynandrous flowers, and others with a single flower on a peduncle. The particular plant here intended is also called 'the fragrant grass (香 草),' but that name is also variously given. The stalk and leaf are like those of the 'marsh *lan* (泽 兰);' the joints are wide apart, and the stalk between them is red. The plant grows in marshy places, and near rivers, and rises to a height of 4 and 5 feet. The *Pun-ts'aou kang-muh* gives 3 different names for it, one of them being 孩儿菊, or 'child's chrysanthemum' which I should have adopted, but that in the Japanese plates the plant plainly appears to be valerian, *valeriana villosa*. It was a custom in Ch'ing for men and women, on the 1st *sze* (巳) day of the 3d month, to gather it, for the purpose of driving away pestilential influences, and of using it in baths; and the custom had become one of festivity and dissipation. 殷 = 众 'a multitude.' 盈 says that the banks of the streams were 'full,'— covered with the festive companies.

Ll. 5, 6. The 乎 is not so much interrogative, as an exclamation. Both Choo and Yen Ts'an explain 观 乎 by 盍 往观 乎, 'why not go and see?' The 且 in l. 6 is the particle.

二章
漤与洧。浏其清矣。士与女。殷其盈矣。女曰观乎。

士曰既且。且往观乎。洧之外。洵讦且乐。维士与

女。伊其将谑。赠之以勺药。

2　The Tsin and the Wei
　　Show their deep, clear streams.
　　Gentlemen and ladies
　　Appear in crowds.
　　A lady says, 'Have you been to see?'
　　A gentleman replies, 'I have been.'
　　'But let us go again to see.
　　Beyond the Wei,
　　The ground is large and fit for pleasure.'
　　So the gentlemen and ladies
　　Make sport together,
　　Presenting one another with small peonies.

Ll. 7—9. 且 (*ts'ëay*) in l.7 = 姑, having the force of 'but let us.' We are to understand that these lines were spoken by the lady, as if they were preceded by another 女曰. 讦 = 大, 'large.' 洵讦,—'truly large.' 且乐,—且 = 'and.'

Ll. 10—12. 维 is here = 于是 'on this.' I think we should take 士 and 女 in the plural, so that the conversation in 5—9, between one lady and one gentleman, is but a specimen of what was generally going on. 伊 is here simply an initial particle. 将 in st. 2 is probably a mistake for 相. 勺 (generally 芍) 药 is the small peony, *pœonia albiflora*. 赠之, 'gifting it,'= 'presenting it to one another.'

The rhymes are—in st. 1, 涣, 萳, 观, 观, 观, cat. 14; 乐 *, 谑 *, 药 * (and in 2), cat. 2: in 2, 清, 盈, cat. 11; 观, 观.

Cᴏɴᴄʟᴜᴅɪɴɢ ɴᴏᴛᴇ ᴏɴ ᴛʜᴇ Bᴏᴏᴋ. Choo He says, 'The music of Ch'ing and Wei was noted for its licentious character; and when we examine the odes of the two States, a fourth only of the 39 pieces of Wei are of a lewd nature, while more than five sevenths of the 20 pieces of Ch'ing are so. Moreover, in the odes of Wei, the language is that of the men expressing their feelings of delight in the women, and there is 'in many of them an element of satire and condemnation; whereas in those of Ch'ing we have mostly the women leading the men astray, and giving expression to their feelings, without any appearance of shame or regret. In this way the lewdness of the music of Ch'ing was greater than that of Wei, and hence, the Master, in speaking of how a State should be administered (Ana. XV.x.), warned against the music of Ch'ing only, without speaking of Wei, mentioning simply that in which what he condemned was most apparent.'

The language of Confucius, to which Choo He thus refers, is confirmatory of the view which he took of most of the odes of Ch'ing, in opposition to the interpretation of them in the 'Little Preface,' and by Maou and his school. Yen Ts'an endeavours to meet this by saying that though the odes of Ch'ing of a lewd character, which we have in the She, are more than those of Wei, Confucius is speaking of the multitude of others which he excluded from his collection; —which is very unlikely.

The 8th ode and the 19th, however, stand out conspicuously among the others.

BOOK VIII. THE ODES OF TS‘E.

I. *Ke ming.*

齐一之八

鸡鸣

一章
鸡既鸣矣。朝既盈矣。匪鸡则鸣。苍蝇之声。

二章
东方明矣。朝既昌矣。匪东方则明。月出之光。

1 'The cock has crowed;
  The court is full.'
  But it was not the cock that was crowing;—
  It was the sound of the blue flies.

2 'The east is bright;
  The court is crowded.'
  But it was not the east that was bright;—
  It was the light of the moon coming forth.

TITLE OF THE BOOK.— 齐, 一之八, '*The odes of* Ts‘e; Bk. VIII. of Pt. I.' Ts‘e was one of the great fiefs of the kingdom of Chow. King Woo, on his overthrow of the Shang dynasty, appointed Shang-foo (尚 父), one of his principal ministers, known also as 'Grand-father Hope (太公 望),' marquis of Ts‘e, his capital being at Ying-k‘ëw (營 邱),—in the pres. dis. of Lin-tsze, dep. Ts‘ing-chow, Shan-tung. The State greatly increased in population and territory, having the Ho on the west, the sea on the east, and Loo on the south. . Shang-foo claimed to be descended from Yaou's chief minister; hence the family surname was Këang (姜). Sometimes we find the surname of Leu (吕), from a State so called in the Shang dynasty, of which his ancestors had been chiefs. The Këangs ruled in Ts‘e for about six centuries and a half. Their last representative died in B. C. 378.

Ode 1. Narrative. A MODEL MARCHIONESS STIMULATING HER HUSBAND TO RISE EARLY, AND ATTEND TO HIS DUTIES. So far Choo and the early critics agree in their view of this piece. The Preface, however, refers it further to the time of duke Gae (B. C. 934—894), who, it says, was 'licentious and indolent,' so that this ode was made to admonish him by a description of the better manners of an earlier time. Yen Ts‘an agrees in this reference, for which there is no historical ground, but interprets differently the verses, as will be pointed out below.

Stt.1,2, ll.1,2. These lines are to be taken as the language of the good wife, thinking it was time for her husband to be stirring, and give audience in his court. Yen Ts‘an puts them into the mouth of the grand-master, whose duty it was to announce cock-crow to his ruler, and call him to the court. 昌 is explained by 盛, 'all-complete.' It is a stronger term than 盈 of st.1.

三章
虫飞薨薨。甘与子同梦。会且归矣。无庶予子憎。

3 'The insects are flying in buzzing crowds;
　It would be sweet to lie by you and dream,
　But the assembled officers will be going home.—
　'Let them not hate both me and you.'

II.　*Seuen.*

还
一章
子之还兮。遭我乎猫之间兮。并驱从两肩兮。揖我谓

我儇兮。
二章
子之茂兮。遭我乎猫之道兮。并驱从两牡兮。揖我谓

1　How agile you are!
　You met me in the neighbourhood of Naou,
　And we pursued together two boars of three years.
　You bowed to me, and said that I was active.

2　How admirable your skill!
　You met me in the way to Naou,

Ll. 3, 4. In the translation these lines are from the writer of the piece. The lady was wrong, and mistook the noise of flies for the crow of the cock, &c.; but that only showed her anxiety that the marquis should not lie in bed too long. Yen-she takes the lines as the reply of the marquis to the call to him to get up, indicative of his habits of luxurious self-indulgence and indolence. The 匪 .... 则 seems to suit better the former view, 则 = 'and so,' or 'so that.'

St. 3 is to be taken as, all, the language of the wife, *coaxing* the marquis to get up. Yen-she understands the lines as addressed by him to her. He is obliged unwillingly to rise, and thus excuses himself, so betraying his uxoriousness. This is unnatural, and should put his view of the latter part of the other stanzas out of court. 薨 薨,—see on i. V. 3.　甘 is used as a verb, = 乐, 'to rejoice,' 'to like.'　梦, 'to dream;' here, evidently,= ' to lie in bed.'　L. 3 speaks of the ministers or officers assembled in the court. If the marquis did not soon appear, they would return to their own houses or offices.　无 = 毋, 'do not.'　庶 is here adverbial, — 'thus

peradventure.' Most commentators give to the line this meaning—'Do not let them, on my account, make you also the object of their dislike.'

The rhymes are in st. 1, 鸣, 盈, 鸣, 声, cat. 11: in 2, 明*, 昌, 明*, 光, cat. 10: in 3, 薨, 梦*, 憎, cat. 6.

Ode 2. Narrative. FRIVOLOUS AND VAIN-GLORIOUS COMPLIMENTS INTERCHANGED BY THE HUNTERS OF TS'E. The piece is of little value. It is referred, in the Preface, to duke Gae, like the last, and is said to be directed against his inordinate love of hunting, which infected the manners of the officers and people. Chang Hwang (章 潢; Ming dyn.) says, 'In the 1st line of each stanza, the speaker praises another; in the last, that other praises him; in the 3d, he takes credit to himself and the other for ability. The poet simply relates his words, without any addition of his own;—a specimen of admirable satire, through which the boastful manners of the people of Ts'e are clearly exhibited.'

Ll. 1 and 4 in all the stt. 还 (*seuen*) is defined as 'the app. of being nimble,' and the meaning of 儇 is akin to it. There is the same

我好兮。

三章

子之昌兮。遭我乎猺之阳兮。并驱从两狼兮。揖我谓

我臧兮。

    And we drove together after two males.
    You bowed to me, and said that I was skilful.
3 How complete your art!
    You met me on the south of Naou,
    And we pursued together two wolves.
    You bowed to me, and said that I was dexterous.

III. *Choo.*

著

一章

俟我于著乎而。充耳以素乎而。尚之以琼华乎而。

1 He was waiting for me between the door and screen.
    The strings of his ear-stoppers were of white silk,
    And there were appended to them beautiful *hwa*-stones.

relation between 茂 and 好, and 昌 and 臧. The terms must all be taken of the skill and dexterity of the parties in driving their chariots and hunting.

Ll. 3, 4. Naou was a hill in Ts'e, not far from the capital. 间 must be translated—'neighbourhood,' some point *between* Naou and the city. 阳,—as in ii. VIII. 1. 驱 expresses their urging on of their horses; and 从＝逐, 'followed,' 'pursued.' 肩 is explained by 兽 三 岁, 'a beast of three years;' in this sense the term is interchanged with 豜, from which I render it by 'boars.' 牡,—'males,' without saying of what animal.

The rhymes are—in st. 1, 还, 间, 肩, 儇, cat. 14: in 2, 茂*, 道*, 牡*, 好*, cat. 3, t. 2: in 3, 昌, 阳, 狼, 臧, cat. 10.

Ode 3. Narrative. A BRIDE DESCRIBES HER FIRST MEETING WITH THE BRIDEGROOM. The critics, old and new, suppose that the piece was directed against the disuse of the practice which required the bridegroom, in person, to meet his bride at her parents' house, and conduct her to her future home. This does not appear, however, in the piece itself; and indeed, there is nothing in it about a bride and bridegroom, though it is not unnatural to suppose that the speaker in it is a bride. Some suppose that we have three brides and as many bridegrooms, the latter all of different rank; but I prefer to think that the places where they meet, and the colour of the stones of the ear-stoppers, are varied simply to prolong the piece, and give new rhymes. We have found this a characteristic of many previous odes.

L. 1, in all the stt. 著 (*al,* 箸) is defined as 'the space between the door and the screen (门屏之间),' called also 宁. Passing round the screen, one would advance on to the 庭, 'the open court' of the mansion, in front of the 堂, the raised 'hall,' or reception-room, from which the chambers led off. The 而 is used simply as a final particle (句绝之辞; Wang Yin-che); and 乎 is a particle of admiration.

二章
俟我于庭乎而。充耳以青乎而。尚之以琼莹乎而。

三章
俟我于堂乎而。充耳以黄乎而。尚之以琼英乎而。

2　He was waiting for me in the open court.
　　The strings of his ear-stoppers were of green silk,
　　And there were appended to them beautiful *yung*-stones.

3　He was waiting for me in the hall.
　　The strings of his ear-stoppers were of yellow silk,
　　And there were appended to them beautiful *ying*-gems.

IV.　*Tung fang che jih.*

东方之日

一章
东方之日兮。彼姝者子。在我室兮。在我室兮。履我
即兮。

1　The sun is in the east,
　　And that lovely girl
　　Is in my chamber.
　　She is in my chamber;
　　She treads in my footsteps, and comes to me.

L. 2. 充耳,—see on v. I. 2. We must understand the line of the strings or ribbons by which the ear-stoppers were suspended, which were called *tan* (紞);—in st. 1, of white silk, in 2, of green; in 3, of yellow.

L. 3 is most naturally taken of the stones which formed the ear-stoppers, the *teen* of iv. III. 2. 尚＝加, 'to add, or append to.' 琼,—as in v. X, an adjective. It is commonly construed with the terms following, as a compound name of the precious stones used for the ear-stoppers. Maou erroneously takes those stones as belonging to the girdle-pendant.

The rhymes are—in st. 1, 著, 素, 华 *, cat. 5, t. 1: in 2, 庭, 青, 莹, cat. 11: in 3, 堂, 黄, 英 *, cat. 10.

Ode 4. Narrative. Tʜᴇ ʟɪᴄᴇɴᴛɪᴏᴜs ɪɴᴛᴇʀ-ᴄᴏᴜʀsᴇ ᴏꜰ ᴛʜᴇ ᴘᴇᴏᴘʟᴇ ᴏꜰ Ts‘ᴇ. I do not see how this short piece is to be understood in any other way. Choo, indeed, agrees with the old interpreters, in taking the 1st line as allusive; but the question then occurs,—allusive of what? which has been very variously answered. At the same time there are difficulties about the view which I have followed. That the lady should seek her lover in the morning, and leave him at night, is not in accordance with the usual ways of such parties. Këang Ping-chang (姜 炳 璋 ; pres. dyn.) observes that the incongruousness of this should satisfy us that, under the figuration of these lovers, is intended a representation of Ts‘e, with bright or with gloomy relations between its ruler and officers. But when we depart from the more natural interpretation of the lines, we launch out on a sea of various fancies and uncertainties.

二章

东方之月兮。彼姝者子。在我闼兮。在我闼兮。履我

发兮。

2   The moon is in the east,
And that lovely girl
Is inside my door.
She is inside my door;
She treads in my footsteps, and hastens away.

V.   *Tung fung ming.*

东方未明

一章

东方未明。颠倒衣裳。颠之倒之。自公召之。

二章

东方未晞。颠倒裳衣。倒之颠之。自公令之。

1   Before the east was bright,
I was putting on my clothes upside down ;
I was putting them on upside down,
And there was one from the court calling me.

2   Before there was a streak of dawn in the east,
I was putting on my clothes upside down ;
I was putting them on upside down,
And there was one from the court with orders for me.

L. 1, in both stt. This has no difficulty in st. 1, as the sun always rises in the east; but why the action of the piece is fixed to the time when the moon rises there, is a question. Does it not indicate that the lines are narrative, and not allusive?

L. 2. This must be understood here of a lady; but in iv. IX., we were obliged to interpret the same terms of 'an admirable officer.'

L. 3. 室,—'a chamber,' a room for refreshment and repose. 闼 is explained by Luh Tih-ming in the same way as 著 in the last ode,—'the space between the door and the screen.' We must understand the *door* as that leading from the hall to the chambers.

Ll. 4, 5. These lines are enigmatical in their brevity. 履＝蹑, 'to tread on.' 我＝我之迹, 'my footsteps.' 即＝相就 'to come to.' 发＝行去, 'to go away.'

The rhymes are—in st. 1, 日,室,室,即 *, cat. 12, t. 3: in 2. 月,闼,闼,发, cat. 15, t. 3.

Ode 5. Narrative and metaphorical. **THE IRREGULARITY AND DISORDER OF THE COURT OF TS'E.** Maou thinks that in the 3d stanza especially there is reference to the officer of·the clepsydra, who did not keep the marquis of Ts'e sufficiently informed of the time; but this is by no means apparent. The piece is evidently directed against the irregularity of the marquis's relations with his officers.

Stt. 1,2. The officer, who, we must suppose, is the writer, was not inattentive to his duties; but was hurriedly making preparations to attend the morning audience, when a summons came to him,—all out of time. Ying-tah defines 晞 by 日 之 光 气, 'the rays of the sun,' the first streaks of dawn. 衣 裳, varied for the sake of the rhyme to 裳 衣, 'the upper garment and the lower,'='clothes.' The anxiety of the speaker to be in time for the audience is graphically set forth by the 颠 倒, 'to turn upside down.' 公 = 公 所, 'duke's place,' the court;—see ii.II. 3, *et al.* 召 之, 'sum-

三章
折柳樊圃。狂夫瞿瞿。不能辰夜。不夙则莫。

3   You fence your garden with branches of willow,
     And the reckless fellows stand in awe.
     He, [however], cannot fix the time of night;
     If he be not too early, he is sure to be late.

VI.   *Nan shan.*

南山
一章
南山崔崔。雄狐绥绥。鲁道有荡。齐子由归。既曰归
止。曷又怀止。

1   High and large is the south hill,
     And a male fox is on it, solitary and suspicious.
     The way to Loo is easy and plain,
     And the daughter of Ts'e went by it to her husband's.
     Since she went to her husband's,
     Why do you further think of her?

moning him to the audience;' 令之 ,—'with some orders to be executed.' I translate the 之 in the 1st person; but the whole ode might be given in the 3d.

St. 3. This st. is metaphorical. A feeble fence served to mark the distinction between forbidden and other ground, and the most reckless paid regard to it; in the court of Ts'e, however, the evident distinction of morning and night was disregarded, and times and seasons confounded. 柳 is the drooping willow, the wood of which has little strength. 樊＝蕃, 'a fence' or 'to fence:'—'Break a willow tree and fence your garden.' 瞿瞿 is 'the appearance of looking at with awe.' 辰＝时, 'time,' used here as a verb, 'to time,' 'to fix the time of.' 莫,—read as, and＝暮, 'late.'

The rhymes are—in st. 1, 明 *, 裳, cat. 10; 倒, 召, cat. 2: in 2, 晞, 衣, cat. 1, t. 1: 颠, 令 *, cat. 12, t. 1: in 3, 圃, 瞿, 夜 *, 莫 *, cat. 5, t. 1.

Ode 6. Allusive. ON THE DISGRACEFUL CON-NECTION BETWEEN WAN KEANG, THE MAR-CHIONESS OF LOO, AND HER BROTHER:—AGAINST SEANG OF TS'E AND HWAN OF LOO. There is

a substantial agreement among the critics as to the intention of this piece, though they differ in the interpretation of several of the lines. In B.C. 708, Kwei, the marquis of Loo, known as duke Hwan, (轨, 桓公), married a daughter of the House of Ts'e, known as Wan Keang (文 姜). There was an improper affection between her and her brother; and on his suc-cession to Ts'e, the couple visited him. The consequences were—incest between the brother and sister, the murder of the husband, and a disgraceful connection, long continued, between the guilty pair. The marquis of Ts'e is known in history as duke Seang (襄 公). If we translate the verbs in the last lines in the pre-sent tense, the time of the piece must be referred to the visit to Ts'e,—before the death of the marquis of Loo. The first two stt. are com-monly taken as directed against duke Seang, and the last two as against duke Hwan. It is not worth the space to point out other construc-tions of the words, which slightly modify this view.

St. 1. 'The south hill' is the *New* hill (牛 山) of Mencius, VI. Pt. i. VIII. 崔 崔 describe its appearance as high and large. The allusion in it is understood to be to the greatness of the State of Ts'e. L.2,—see on v.IX. 1. 雄, pro-perly the male of birds, is here used of a quad-

二章
葛屦五两。冠緌双止。鲁道有荡。齐子庸止。既曰庸
止。曷又从止。

三章
艺麻如之何。衡从其亩。取妻如之何。必告父母。既
曰告止。曷又鞠止。

2　The five kinds of dolichos shoes are [made] in pairs,
And the string-ends of a cap are made to match;
The way to Loo is easy and plain,
And the daughter of Ts'e travelled it.
Since she travelled it,
Why do you still follow her?

3　How do we proceed in planting hemp?
The acres must be dressed lengthwise and crosswise.
How do we proceed in taking a wife?
Announcement must first be made to our parents.
Since such announcement was made,
Why do you still indulge her desires?

ruped,—the fox. Duke Sëang is understood to be thus contemptuously alluded to. L.3. 荡 is explained by 平 易 'level and easy.' L. 4. The daughter of Ts'e is Wăn Këang, who had gone to Loo by this way (由 = 从) to her husband's (归,—as in i.VI.) The 止 in lines 5, 6, and below, is the final particle. So, the 曰 is only a particle. The subject of 怀 is most naturally understood to be duke Seang.

St.2. 两 (3d tone), is explained of two, or a pair of shoes. 五 两, 'five pairs,' must be taken as in the translation, the 'five' referring, probably, to the five different colours of which shoes were made of the dolichos fibre. What the writer would say, is simply that shoes were made in pairs,—alluding to the union of man and wife. L.2. 緌 denotes the ends of the strings, by which the cap was tied under the chin, which were then left hanging down of equal lengths (双). The line thus conveys the same idea, and contains the same allusion, as the former one. L.4. 庸 = 用, 'to use,'—

here applied to travelling the road to Loo. L.6. 从, like 怀 above, is to be understood of duke Sëang, following his sister, unable to leave her to her husband.

St.3. L.1. 艺 = 树, 'to plant, or sow.' L.2. For hemp the ground had to be carefully prepared, and was ploughed both cross-wise (衡 = 横), or from east to west, and length-wise, or from north to south. L.3. 取 = 娶, 'to marry.' L.4. 告, is now in the 4th tone. The 'parents' are those of the bridegroom. As the parents of the marquis of Loo were dead, he had announced to their spirits in the ancestral temple his intention to marry a princess of Ts'e. He thus obtained their sanction to the union. The marriage was concluded with every formality. It was for him to maintain it as strictly; but instead of this, he weakly allowed his wife to visit her brother. The 鞠 of 1.6 is understood of duke Hwan, 'allowing his wife to carry out her licentious desires (使 之 得 穷 其 欲).'

四章

析薪如之何。匪斧不克。取妻如之何。匪媒不得。既

曰得止。曷又极止。

4　How do we proceed in splitting firewood?
　　Without an axe it cannot be done.
　　How do we proceed in taking a wife?
　　Without a go-between it cannot be done.
　　Since this was done,
　　Why do you still allow her to go to this extreme?

VII.　*Foo t'een.*

甫田

一章

无田甫田。维莠骄骄。无思远人。劳心忉忉。

二章

无田甫田。维莠桀桀。无思远人。劳心怛怛。

1　Do not try to cultivate fields too large;—
　　The weeds will only grow luxuriantly.
　　Do not think of winning people far away;—
　　Your toiling heart will be grieved,

2　Do not try to cultivate fields too large;—
　　The weeds will only grow proudly,
　　Do not think of winning people far away;—
　　Your toiling heart will be distressed.

St. 4. Here another formality in contracting a marriage is mentioned, and illustrated by an indispensable condition in the splitting of firewood. This also had been complied with by the marquis of Loo; and as he had begun his marriage, so he should have continued it. 极, —as 鞠 in the former stanza.

The rhymes are—in st. 1, 崔, 绥, 归, 归, 怀, cat. 15, t. 1: in 2, 两, 双, 荡, cat. 10; 庸, 庸, 从, cat. 9: in 3, 何, 何, (and in 4), cat. 17; 亩 *. 母 *, cat. 1, t. 2; 告 *, 鞠 *, cat. 3, t. 3: in 4, 克, 得, 得, 极, cat. 1, t. 3.

Ode 7. Metaphorical. THE FOLLY OF PURSUING OBJECTS BEYOND ONE'S STRENGTH. So, Choo. The Preface refers the piece to duke Seäng, possessed by a vaulting ambition which over-leapt itself. It may be applied to the insane course which he pursued to acquire the foremost place among the States, but there is nothing in the language to indicate that it was in the first place directed against him.

Ll. 1, 2, in stt. 1, 2. 无 = 母, though we might also translate it as a simple negative— 'There is no such thing,' &c. 田 (read *teen*, in 3d tone) is a verb,—'to cultivate,' *i. q.* 亩 in 亩 尔 田, Shoo, V.xviii. 21. Ying-tah, indeed, quotes that passage here as 田 尔 田. 甫 = 大, 'large.' Maou explains it by 'large beyond measure,' so that the labour put forth on it is inadequate to secure any return. 莠,—see Men. VII. Pt.ii.XXXVII. 12. 骄骄

三章

婉兮娈兮。总角卯兮。未几见兮。突而弁兮。

3   How young and tender
    Is the child with his two tufts of hair!
    When you see him after not a long time,
    Lo! he is wearing the cap!

VIII. *Loo ling.*

卢令

一章

卢令令。其人美且仁。

二章

卢重环。其人美且鬈。

三章

卢重鋂其人美且偲。

1   *Lin-lin* go the hounds;—
    Their master is admirable and kind.
2   There go the hounds with there double rings;—
    Their master is admirable and good.
3   There go the hounds with there triple rings;—
    Their master is admirable and able.

expresses the 'app. of luxuriant growth.' So, 榛榛. Leu Tsoo-k'ëen says that both combinations give us to see the darnel growing luxuriantly, to the injury of the good grain.

Ll· 3, 4. 远人, 'distant men,' are people removed from us so far as to be beyond our influence. 忉忉 and 怛, 怛 (*tah*) express 'the app. of being grieved and distressed.'

St. 3, 婉 and 娈—'young and tender-like.' 总=聚, 'to gather.' 角,—'a horn.' Yen-Ts'an says, 'The hair of a child was gathered into two tufts, so as to have the form of the character 卯.' 突=忽, conveying the ideas of suddenness and growth. 而=然 弁 is here simply = 冠, 'a cap,' worn by the youth grown up. In this st. we have an instance of natural and legitimate development, surely taking place;—in contrast with the fruitless strain and effort indicated in the other stanzas.

The rhymes are—in st. 1, 田, 人 (and in 2), cat. 12, t. 1; 骄, 忉, cat. 2: in 2, 桀, 怛 (prop. cat. 14), cat. 15, t. 3: in 3, 娈, 卯, 见 ＊, 弁, cat. 14.

Ode 8. Narrative. THE ADMIRATION IN TS'E OF HOUNDS AND HUNTERS. This piece is akin to ode 2. We are only to find in it the foolish estimation in which hunting was held in Ts'e. The Preface makes it out, indeed, to have been directed against duke Sëang's wild addiction to hunting, and to set forth the sympathy which the people had with their good rulers of a more ancient time in their hunting expeditions (See Men I. Pt. ii. II. 6), as a lesson to him. This, however, is much too far-fetched.

L. 1, in all the stt. 卢 (more fully with 犬 at the side) is the name for a hunting dog (田 犬). 令 令 is intended to give the sound of the rings which the hounds carried at their necks. The Shwoh-wǎn gives 狣, 狣, with 犬 at the side,—meaning 'strong.' 重环, 'a double ring,' denotes a large ring carrying a smaller one attached; and 重鋂, a larger ring with two smaller ones attached. L. 2. The 人 is best taken of the owner of the hounds, and not of the hunters generally. 美 且 仁,— see on vii. III. 1. Here, as there, the application of 仁 is an exaggeration. We may accept Maou's explanation of 鬈 by 好 貌, 'good-like,' and of 偲 by 才, 'able,' 'talented.' Choo explains these terms by 'whiskered,' 'bearded.'

IX.　*Pe kow.*

敝笱

一章
敝笱在梁。其鱼鲂鳏。齐子归止。其从如云。

二章
敝笱在梁。其鱼鲂鱮。齐子归止。其从如雨。

三章
敝笱在梁。其鱼唯唯。齐子归止。其从如水。

1　Worn out is the basket at the dam,
　　And the fishes are the bream and the *kwan.*
　　The daughter of Ts'e has returned,
　　With a cloud of attendants.

2　Worn out is the basket at the dam,
　　And the fishes are the bream and the tench.
　　The daughter of Ts'e has returned,
　　With a shower of attendants.

3　Worn out is the basket at the dam,
　　And the fishes go in and out freely.
　　The daughter of Ts'e has returned,
　　With a stream of attendants.

The rhymes are—in st. 1, 令 *, 仁, cat. 12, t. 1: in 2, 环, 鬈, cat. 14: in 3, 鲔, 偲, cat. 1, t. 1.

Ode 9. Metaphorical. THE BOLD LICENTIOUS FREEDOM OF WAN KEANG IN RETURNING TO TS'E. The Preface says, further, that the piece was directed against duke Hwan of Loo, unable in his weakness to impose any restraint on his wife;—see on ode 6. Choo, on the contrary, makes it to be directed against their son, duke Chwang;—and with reason. All critics understand the 归, in the 3d lines, of Wăn Kĕang's repeated returns to Ts'e after her husband's death, to carry on her intrigue with her brother, duke Sĕang. If any marquis of Loo, therefore, was in the writer's mind, it must have been the son, unable to control the conduct of his mother.

敝,—see on vii. I.　笱 and 梁,—see on iii. X. 3.　鲂,—see on i. X. 3.　鱮 is the tench,

described as 'like the bream, but with a large head, and weak scales.' The 鳏 has not been identified. The Shwoh-wăn simply calls it 'a fish.' Maou calls it 'a large fish;' and a story is given by K'ung Ts'ung (孔 从 子, 抗 志 篇) of a *kwan* being taken in Wei, large enough to fill a cart. K'ang-shing says the word means 'spawn.' Neither of these accounts is admissible in the connection. 唯 唯 in st. 3 denotes the freedom with which the fishes went in and out of the broken basket (唯 唯 者, 惟 所 出 入, 而 无 忌 之 貌). The concluding lines set forth the multitude of the marchioness's followers,—'like clouds,' 'like rain,' 'like water.'

The rhymes are—in st. 1, 鳏, 云, cat. 13; in 2, 鲔 雨, cat. 5, t. 2: in 3, 唯 水, cat. 15, t. 2.

X. *Tsae k'eu.*

载驱

一章

载驱薄薄。簟茀朱鞹。鲁道有荡。齐子发夕。

四骊济济。垂辔沵沵。鲁道有荡。齐子岂弟。

四章

汶水汤汤。行人彭彭。鲁道有荡。齐子翱翔。

1 She urges on her chariot rapidly,
   With its screen of bamboos woven in squares, and its vermilion-
       coloured leather.
   The way from Loo is easy and plain,
   And the daughter of Ts'e started on it in the evening.

2 Her four black horses are beautiful,
   And soft look the reins as they hang.
   The way from Loo is easy and plain,
   And the daughter of Ts'e is delighted and complacent.

3 The waters of the Wăn flow broadly on;
   The travellers are numerous.
   The way from Loo is easy and plain,
   And the daughter of Ts'e moves on with unconcern.

Ode 10. Narrative. THE OPEN SHAMELESS-NESS OF WAN KEANG IN HER MEETINGS WITH HER BROTHER. There is an agreement among the critics that this is the subject of the piece. Maou differs, however, from Choo in referring the first two lines of the stanzas to duke Sëang, driving to the place of assignation; but even Yen Ts'an agrees in this point with Choo. The ode has thus a better unity, and Sëang had no need to cross the Wăn.

St. 1, 载 is the initial particle,—as often. 薄 薄 expresses the sound of the carriage driven rapidly, and so seeming to touch the ground *slightly*. 簟—as in iii. X. 3. Here the screen is made of 簟, 'slender bamboos,' which were made or woven in squares. 鞹 is the name for hides dressed and curried,=leather. This was employed in the construction of the carriage, but for what part of it, it is difficult to say. In this case it was painted vermilion. As that colour was used in one of the car-

riages of the princes of States, Maou contends that the 1st and 2d lines should be referred to duke Sëang; but there is no evidence that their wives might not ride in chariots of the same colour. 发,—nearly as in IV. 2. I follow Maou in taking 夕 as the time when Wăn Këang commenced her journey (自 夕 发 至 日). Choo makes it the place where she had passed the night,—as Lacharme translates, '*ex diversorio capescit iter.*'

St. 2. 骊 tells the black colour of the horses; Maou only says their rich and well-groomed appearance. 济 济＝美貌, 'the app. of beauty.' 沵沵, acc. to Choo,＝柔貌, 'soft-like;' this gives a better meaning than Maou's 众, 'numerous:'—Maou reads simply 尔 尔. 岂弟＝乐易, 'pleased and easy,' setting forth the complacency with which Wăn Këang went on her way of vice.

四章

汶水滔滔。行人儦儦。鲁道有荡。齐子游敖。

4　　The waters of the Wăn sweep on;
　　　The travellers are in crowds.
　　　The way from Loo is easy and plain,
　　　And the daughter of Ts'e proceeds at her ease.

XI. *E tseay.*

猗嗟

一章

猗嗟昌兮。顾而长兮。抑若扬兮。美目扬兮。巧趋跄兮。射则臧兮。

1　　Alas for him, so handsome and accomplished!
　　　How grandly tall!
　　　With what elegance in his high forehead!
　　　With what motion of his beautiful eyes!
　　　With what skill in the swift movements of his feet!
　　　With what mastery of archery!

Stt. 3, 4. 汶,—see on Ana. VI. vii. The Wăn divided Ts'e and Loo, and it was necessary that Wăn Këang should cross it. 汤汤 denotes the 'full appearance of the waters;' and 滔滔, 'the app. of their flow.' 彭彭 and 儦儦 both denote the multitude of the travellers on the way, whom the lady might have been afraid to face. But instead of this, she went on with unconcern, as described in the synonymous phrases with which the stt. conclude.

The rhymes are—in st. 1, 薄, 鞹 *, cat. 5, t. 3: in 2, 济, 沵 *, 弟, cat. 15, t. 2: 汤, 彭 *, 荡, 翔, cat. 10.

Ode 11. Narrative. LAMENT OVER DUKE CHWANG, NOTWITHSTANDING HIS BEAUTY OF PERSON, ELEGANCE OF MANNERS, AND SKILL IN ARCHERY. The Preface and subsequent critics are, probably, correct in their account of this piece as referring to duke Chwang of Loo, notwithstanding his various accomplishments, yet allowing his mother to carry on her disgraceful connection with her brother, and himself joining the marquis of Ts'e in hunting, oblivious of his mother's shame and his father's murder. Some say the piece should have a place in 'Lessons from Loo;' but to this it is replied that here is the wisdom of Confucius, who would not directly publish the shame of his native State, and yet took care, by giving this and the other pieces about Wăn Sëang a place in the odes of Ts'e, that that shame should not be concealed. All these odes, however, were, no doubt, written in Ts'e. The point of this one is found in the exclamation with which all the stanzas commence.

St. 1. 猗 嗟, 'oh alas!'—an exclamation of lamentation. The prefixing of this to the praises which follow shows the writer's opinion of the deficiencies of Chwang's character, notwithstanding his various accomplishments. 昌 —as in II. 3. It covers all the lines that follow. L. 2. 顾 而 describes 'the app. of Chwang's tallness.' 而 = 然. The combination is adverbial.

L. 3 若, like 而, = 然, and 抑若, describes the beauty or elegance of the high forehead Maou defines 抑 by 美色, 'admirable beauty, where 色 is probably a misprint for 儿 or 貌 and accepting this account of 抑, we must take 扬 as in iv. III. 2, et al. To account for this meaning of 抑, Wang Taou says that the character may originally have been 懿, homophonous with it, and having the signification o

二章
猗嗟名兮。美目清兮。仪既成兮。终日射侯。不出正
兮。展我甥兮。

三章
猗嗟娈兮。清扬婉兮。舞则选兮。射则贯兮。四矢反
兮。以御乱兮。

2   Alas for him, so famous!
     His beautiful eyes how clear!
     His manners how complete!
     Shooting all day at the target,
     And never lodging outside the bird-square!
     Indeed our [ruler's] nephew!

3   Alas for him, so beautiful!
     His bright eyes and high forehead how lovely!
     His dancing so choice!
     Sure to send his arrows right through!
     The four all going to the same place!
     One able to withstand rebellion!

美. L. 4. Choo defines 扬 here as 目之动, 'the movement of the eyes;' and this we may accept, as the term would hardly be repeated with the same meaning as in the preceding line.

L. 5. 跄 describes 'the app. of his artful and quick walk (巧趋);'—Choo says, 'as if he were on wings,' i. e., equable and graceful. L. 6. 'When he shoots, then he is skilful.'

St. 2. L. 1. 名, 'famous,' or rather 'worthy of fame,' is evidently like 昌, in st. 1, covering the rest of the stanza. This is decisive against Maou's definition of it as 目上为名, 'above the eyes is called 名.' L. 3. I take 成 with Yen Ts'an, as= 备, 'complete.' Ll. 4, 5. Ying-tah observes that, at trials of archery, the parties engaged thrice discharged their arrows, each time four, and then stopped. The 'whole day' mentioned here is an exaggeration; what we are to think of is Chwang's skill, and the length of time for which he could exhibit it. 正 (1st tone) denotes the square in the centre of the target, in the centre of which again was the figure of a bird called ching. L. 6. 展= 诚, 'truly.' The 我 proves that the writer was a native of Ts'e; and by his words he refutes a calumny which was current, that Chwang was the son of duke Sëang.

St. 3. L. 2,—see on vii. XX. 1. L. 3, 选, 'choice,'= 异于众, 'different from—better than—all others.' L. 5. 反=复, 'again;' i. e., arrow after arrow went to the same place. (皆得其故处). L. 6. We have an instance of duke Chwang's prowess with his arrows in the Tso-chuen, under the 10th year of his rule.

The rhymes are—in st. 1, 昌, 长, 扬, 扬, 跄, 臧, cat. 10: in 2, 名, 清, 成, 正, 甥, cat. 11: in 3, 娈, 婉, 选, 贯, 反, 乱, cat. 14.

CONCLUDING NOTE ON THE BOOK. The odes of which duke Sëang is, more or less directly, the subject, are the only pieces in this Book, the time of which can be determined. It is strange that from none cf the others do we get any definite ideas of the history of the State before him, and still more strange that there is no celebration of the famous duke Hwan, subsequent to him,—the hero of Ts'e. His exploits, it has been said, would be sung of in a boasting style, and the sage therefore purposely excluded them from his collection; but much more might we have expected him to exclude the odes about duke Sëang! Only the 1st ode presents us with a pleasing picture. The 2d and 8th show us the vaingloriousness of the officers of the State, and their excessive estimation of skill in hunting. The 6th seems to give an indication of lewd manners; and the 5th, of how ill the court was regulated.

BOOK IX. THE ODES OF WEI.

I. *Koh keu.*

魏一之九　　葛屨

一章

糾糾葛屨。可以履霜。摻摻女手。可以縫裳。要之襋

之。好人服之。

1　Shoes thinly woven of the dolichos fibre
　　May be used to walk on the hoarfrost.
　　The delicate fingers of a bride
　　May be used in making clothes.
　　[His bride] puts the waistband to his lower garment and the
　　　　collar to his upper,
　　And he, a wealthy man, wears them.

THE TITLE OF THE BOOK.—魏 一之九, 'The odes of Wei; Book IX. of Part I.' In B.C. 660, duke Hëen of Tsin extinguished the State of Wei, and incorporated it with his own dominions. At the division of the kingdom, after the subjugation of the Shang dynasty, Wei had been assigned to some chief of the Kœ stock; but no details of its history have been preserved. In consequence of this, many critics are of opinion that the odes of Wei are really odes of Tsin, and that they are here prefixed to those of T'ang, just as those of P'ei and Yung are prefixed to the odes of Wei, all really belonging to that Wei (丿). We shall find expressions in some of the odes which bear this view out; but, as Choo observes, the question cannot be positively settled. The territory of Wei was small, and the manners of the people were thrifty and industrious. It was within the present Këae-chow (解 州) of Shan-se, but did not extend over all the territory now forming that department.

Ode 1. Narrative. THE EXTREME PARSI-MONIOUSNESS EVEN OF WEALTHY MEN IN WEI. The piece explains itself in a way which no other ode has yet done, the last two lines stating plainly the reason of its condemnation of its subject. This has been accounted for on the

ground that in the Chinese code of morals, sanctioned afterwards by Confucius, an excessive economy even was commended; and the writer therefore felt it necessary to point out that he branded it as interfering with generosity of soul.

St. 1. Ll. 1, 2. 糾 糾 are explained by Maou as = 繚 繚, which was in use in his time;—the combination denotes the thin texture of the woven fibres (稀 疏 之 貌; Ying-tah). Dolichos shoes were for summer wear; yet necessity might require and justify the use of them in winter. These two lines are taken as allusive, introducing the next two; but I prefer to regard them as narrative, giving an instance of allowable economy. Ll. 3, 4. 摻摻 = 纖 纖, 'small,' 'delicate.' 女 is 'a bride,'—a wife during the three months that elapsed before her presentation in the ancestral temple of her husband's family, which ceremony was the full and solemn recognition of her in the new relation. Until it took place, it was not the rule for her to engage in all the domestic work of the family; but still circumstances might justify her in doing so. 裳 = 衣裳, 'clothes,' generally. Ll. 5, 6. 要, (or with 衣 at the

二章

好人提提。宛然左辟。佩其象揥。维是褊心。是以为

刺。

2　Wealthy, he moves about quite at ease,
　　And politely he stands aside to the left.
　　From his girdle hangs his ivory comb-pin.
　　It is the narrowness of his disposition,
　　Which makes him a subject for satire.

II.　*Hwun tseu-joo.*

汾沮洳

一章

彼汾沮洳。言采其莫。彼其之子。美无度。美无度。

殊异乎公路。

二章

彼汾一方。言采其桑。彼其之子。美如英。美如英。

1　There in the oozy grounds of the Hwun
　　They gather the sorrel.
　　That officer
　　Is elegant beyond measure.
　　He is elegant beyond measure
　　But, perhaps, he is not what the superintendent of the ruler's
　　　carriages ought to be.

2　There along the side of the Hwun,
　　They gather the mulberry leaves.
　　That officer

side) 之 襋 之 have a verbal force. 好 人
一 大 人 or 贵 人, 'a great or noble man,'
i. e., one occupying a high position in society.
Whatever poverty might justify, it was not for
one like him to be wearing dolichos shoes in
winter, or to put his bride to such tasks.

St. 2, 提 提 is descriptive of 'the gentle-
manly ease' of the husband. The right was
the place of honour anciently in China; the
husband therefore is represented as moving to
the left, to give the precedence to others. 揥,
—see iv.III. 2. The man's manners and dress in
public were such as became his position. The
facts in st.1, however, showed a stinginess of
disposition in his family which made him a
proper subject for reprehension.

The rhymes are—in st. 1, 霜, 裳, cat. 10;
襋, 服 *, cat. 1, t. 3: in 2, 提 *, 辟, 揥 *,
刺 *, cat. 16, t. 3.

Ode 2. Allusive. AGAINST THE PARSIMONI-
OUSNESS OF THE OFFICERS OF WEI. The argument of this piece is akin to that of the last;
only the 'good' or wealthy man there appears
here as a high officer of the State. It belongs to
the allusive class, and we are not to suppose
that the officer or officers spoken of actually did
the things mentioned in the second lines, but
only that they did things which parties per-
forming such tasks might have done. If we
make 彼 其 之 子 the subject of 采, as
K'ang-shing does, then the ode will be narrative.
Ll. 1, 2, in all the stt. The Hwun rises in the
pres. dis. of Tsing-loh (静 乐), E Chow (忻

殊异乎公行。

三章

彼汾一曲。言采其藚。彼其之子。美如玉。美如玉。

殊异乎公族。

Is elegant as a flower.
He is elegant as a flower;
But, perhaps, he is not what the marshaller of the carriages
    ought to be.

3   There along the bend of the Hwun,
    They gather the ox-lips.
    That officer
    Is elegant as a gem.
    He is elegant as a gem;
    But, perhaps, he is not what the superintendent of the ruler's
    relations should be.

III.   *Yuen yew t'aou.*

园有桃

一章

园有桃。其实之殽。心之忧矣。我歌且谣。不知我

者。谓我士也骄。彼人是哉。子曰何其。心之忧矣。

1   Of the peach trees in the garden
    The fruit may be used as food.
    My heart is grieved,
    And I play and sing.
    Those who do not know me
    Say I am a scholar venting his pride.

州), and flows into the Ho, in the dis. of Yung-ho (荣 河), dep. P'oo-chow (蒲 州). The capital of Wei was near its junction with the Ho. 沮 洳 = 'low and oozy.' 一方 = 一边, 'one side;' but the —— is not to be pressed, as appears from the 一 曲, designating the bend of the Hwun where it joins the Ho. The 莫 (moo) is, perhaps, the *rumex acetosa*. Medhurst, after Luh Ke, says—'A kind of sorrel, the stalk of which is as large as a goose-quill, of a red colour, and giving out at every joint a leaf like the willow; it is provided with hairy prickles, sour, and when young, can be boiled into soup.' The Urh-ya calls the 藚 the 牛 唇, which I have adopted in the translation. Medhurst says,—'water plantago;' and Williams,—'a marshy, grassy, and (?) climbing plant, with leaves like purslane, called also cow's lips.'

Ll.3,4. 彼其之子,—as in vi.VI. 其 is the particle; 彼 and 之, a double demonstrative. 无 度 is laudatory. Maou takes

其谁知之。其谁知之。盖亦勿思。

二章

园有棘。其实之食。心之忧矣。聊以行国。不知我

者。谓我士也罔极。彼人是哉。子曰何其。 心之忧

'Those men are right;
What do you mean by your words?'
My heart is grieved;
Who knows [the cause of] it?
Who knows [the cause of] it?
[They know it not], because they will not think.

2　Of the jujube trees in the garden
The fruit may be used as food.
My heart is grieved,
And I think I must travel about through the State.
Those who do not know me
Say I am an officer going to the verge of license.
'Those men are right;

英 in the sense of 'a man of ten thousand;' but the 如, and 如 玉 of st.3, require the meaning I have given.

L.6. 公路＝掌公之路车者，—as in the translation. 公行 is another name for the same officer, as regulating the order of the carriages (以其主兵车之行列). 公族＝掌公之宗族者, 'the superintendent of the branches of the ducal family.' There were, as we learn from the Tso-chuen, such officers in the state of Tsin; and hence it is contended that this piece is really an ode of Tsin. But there may have been officers so called in Wei, at an earlier time. The appointment of them in Tsin took place 54 years after its extinction of the ancient Wei. The 公族 were more honourable than the 公行. It seems very unnatural to refer the 3d and 6th lines to different subjects,—as Ho K'eae (何 楷) does.

The rhymes are—in st. 1, 泚, 莫, 度, 度, 路. cat.5, t.1: in 2, 方, 桑, 英 ＊, 英 ＊,

行 ＊, cat. 10: in 3, 曲, 蓫, 玉, 玉, 族, cat. 3, t. 3.

Ode 3. Allusive. AN OFFICER TELLS HIS GRIEF BECAUSE OF THE MISGOVERNMENT OF THE STATE, AND HOW HE WAS MISUNDERSTOOD. The idea of the misgovernment of the State is not evident, but it is found in the allusion in the first two lines. 'The peach,' says Ch'ing E, 'is but a poor fruit; but while there are peach-trees in the garden, their fruit can be used as food. This suggests the idea of the people of the State as few, and yet, if they were only rightly used and dealt with, good government would ensue.' This may seem far-fetched, yet it is the most likely interpretation of the words. The ode may be compared with the first of the 6th Book; but there the speaker is mourning over ruin accomplished, and makes his moan to Heaven, while here the speaker is grieved by the prospect of ruin approaching, and indicates the authors of it.

Ll.1—4, in both stt. 殽, 'viands,' is here ＝ 食 in st. 2, 'to eat,' or 'to use as food.' The 之 in l.2 is a difficulty; we must call it a mere particle, and translate as I have done. The 'Complete Digest' gives— 其实可为殽·

矣。其谁知之。其谁知之。盖亦勿思。

What do you mean by your words?'
My heart is grieved.
Who knows [the cause of] it?
Who knows [the cause of] it?
[They do not know it], because they will not think.

IV. Chih hoo.

陟岵

一章

陟彼岵兮。瞻望父兮。父曰嗟予子行役。夙夜无已。

上慎旃哉。犹来无止。

1 I ascend that tree-clad hill,
And look towards [the residence of] my father.
My father is saying, 'Alas! my son, abroad on the public service,
Morning and night never rests.
May he be careful,
That he may come [back], and not remain there!'

In l.3 also, 之 may be taken as a particle. 歌 is distinguished from 谣, as 'singing with the accompaniment of an instrument, while the latter term denotes singing simply.' Standing alone, 歌 does not necessarily imply playing, as well as singing. 聊,—as in vii.XIX. 1,2; et al. 行国 indicates that the speaker thought of travelling about to dissipate his grief (出游于国中以泻忧).

L1.5—8. The speaker's dissatisfaction is perceived, but not understood. People say he is conceited and 罔极, 'without a well-balanced judgment,' taking 极 = 中, according to Maou); or 'without any bounds to his condemnation of the government' (so, Choc). Ll.7,8 give their words directly. 彼人,—'those men,'—meaning the conductors of the govt. 是,—'to be right.' 其 is a final particle, used in interrogations, to be distinguished from that in Ll. 3 last ode.

L.12. 盖 takes up the question in the preceding lines, as if it were said directly,—'They do not know me, for '————. 勿 is used as an indicative negative,=非 or 不. 亦 is a mere particle. Wang Yin-che makes a rule that 亦 preceded by 盖 has never any substantive force.

The rhymes are—in st. 1, 桃, 殽, 谣, 骄, cat. 2; 哉, 其, 之, 之, 思, (and in 2), cat. 1, t. 1: in 2, 棘, 食, 国, 极, ib., t. 3.

Ode 4. Narrative. A YOUNG SOLDIER ON SERVICE SOLACES HIMSELF WITH THE THOUGHT OF HOME. The marquis D'Hervey-Saint-Denys, having translated into French Lacharme's very inaccurate Latin translation of this ode, proceeds to found on it some ingenious reflections on the unwarlike character of the Chinese. He finds in it 'regrets for the loss of the domestic hearth; the longing of a young soldier who ascends a mountain to try to discover in the distance the house of his father; a mother whom Sparta would have driven from its walls; a brother who counsels the absent one, not to make his race illustrious, but before every thing to come back.' 'We feel ourselves,' he adds, 'in I know not what atmosphere of quietude and rural life.' The sentiment of the piece, however, should not make such an impression upon us. According

二章
陟彼屺兮。瞻望母兮。母曰嗟予季行役。夙夜无寐。

上慎旃哉。犹来无弃。

三章
陟彼冈兮。瞻望兄兮。兄曰嗟予弟行役。夙夜必偕。

上慎旃哉。犹来无死。

2   I ascend that bare hill,
And look towards [the residence of] my mother.
My mother is saying, 'Alas! my child, abroad on the public service,
Morning and night has no sleep.
May he be careful,
That he may come [back], and not leave his body there!'

3   I ascend that ridge,
And look towards [the residence of] my elder brother.
My brother is saying, 'Alas! my younger brother, abroad on the public service,
Morning and night must consort with his comrades.
May he be careful,
That he may come back, and not die!'

to the Preface, the service in which the young soldier was engaged was service exacted from Wei by a more powerful State, in which there was no room for patriotism, no opportunity for getting glory. The sentiment is one of lamentation over the poor and weak Wei whose men were torn from it to fight the battles of its oppressors.

L.1, in all the stt. 岵 and 屺 are defined in the Urh-ya, as I have translated them. Maou strangely reversed the definitions, and Choo followed him. I cannot but agree with Ying-tah in thinking that in Maou's account of the characters we have errors of transcription.

L.2. 瞻 is properly 'to look up to,' and 望, 'to look out to,' or 'to look towards.'

L.3. 行役, 'has gone away on service,' or 'is doing public service.' 季＝少子, 'younger son,'＝child. This term is appropriately put into the mother's mouth. 无已＝不得止息 'gets no rest.' The mother says, naturally again, 无寐, 'gets no sleep.' 必偕＝

必与同役者偕,—as in the translation. This language is natural from the elder bother.

Ll.4,5. 上 ＝ 尚, with the optative force of that term. 旃 ＝ 之. It gives force to the verb. 犹,—'still,' 'and so, notwithstanding.' It carries on the wish, and converts it into a hope. The 'Complete Digest' says, 犹来，不敢必之词. 无止,—as in the translation, or according to a meaning of 止, to which Choo refers, 'not be taken prisoner.' 弃＝弃其尸, 'cast away his corpse.'

Yen Ts'an observes that we are not to suppose that the soldier ascended three different heights;—the writer merely, as is usual in these odes, varied his terms for rhyme's sake.

The rhymes are—in st.1, 岵, 父, cat.5, t.2; 子, 已, 止, cat.1, t.2: in 2, 屺, 母,, ib.; 季, 寐, 弃, cat.15, t.3: in 3, 冈, 兄,, cat. 10: 弟, 偕, 死, cat.15, t.2.

V. *Shih mow che këen.*

十亩之间

一章
十亩之间兮。桑者闲闲兮。行与子还兮。

二章
十亩之外兮。桑者泄泄兮。行与子逝兮。

1   Among their ten acres
The mulberry-planters stand idly about.
'Come,' [says one to another], 'I will return with you.'

2   Beyond those ten acres,
The mulberry-planters move idly about.
'Come,' [says one to another], 'I will go away with you.'

VI. *Fah t'an.*

伐檀

一章
坎坎伐檀兮。寘之河之干兮。河水清且涟猗。不稼不

1   *K'an-k'an* go his blows on the sandal trees,
And he places what he hews on the river's bank,
Whose waters flow clear and rippling.

Ode 5. Narrative. THE STRAITS OF THE PEASANTRY OF WEI. The interpretation of this short piece is not a little difficult. Acc. to the Preface, it was directed against the times when the State of Wei was so much reduced by the loss of territory, that there was not room for the people to live in it. Acc. to Choo, on the other hand, a worthy officer, disgusted with the irregularities of the court, proposes to his companion to withdraw from the public service to a quiet life among the mulberry trees in the country. The old view seems to me the preferable.

L. 1, in both stt. Why *ten* acres are here specified, or what ten acres are meant, cannot be determined. According to the ancient regulations, often spoken of by Mencius, each farmer, the head of a family, received 100 acres. Here, it is said, so much was Wei reduced, that such a man could only receive a tenth part of his proper allotment. But those hundred acres were for the cultivation of grain; the mention of the mulberry trees in the 2d line shows that the farm is not intended here. Rather must we think of the 'homesteads with their five acres (Men. I. Pt. i. VIII. 24), about which mulberry trees were planted. Those 5 acres were divided into two portions, half in the fields, and half in

the villages. The eight families which constituted a *tsing* (井) had thus 20 acres of mulberry ground in each place, which here appear, it is supposed, reduced to 10. This is more likely. 亩 was anciently written 畮. Six cubits (尺) formed a pace (步), and 100 paces was the length of an acre.

L.2. 桑者,—'mulberriers.' We are to understand, probably, the gatherers of the mulberry leaves. 闲闲 or 间间,—as in the translation. Choo makes it—'placidly or contentedly going about.' 泄泄 may be regarded as synonymous with 闲闲. Maou makes it mean—'the app. of a multitude,' the people being too numerous for the space.

L. 3 is to be taken as the language of the mulberry planters to one another. They have no work to do, and think they may as well go home empty-handed, or go and amuse themselves in the neighbouring lot. 行, acc. to Choo,=将, the sign of the future. 逝=往,

檣。胡取禾三百廛兮。不狩不猎。胡瞻尔庭有县貆

兮。彼君子兮。不素餐兮。

二章
坎坎伐辐兮。寘之河之侧兮。河水清且直猗。不稼不

檣。胡取禾三百亿兮。不狩不猎。胡瞻尔庭有县特

兮。彼君子兮。不素食兮。

You sow not nor reap;—
How do you get the produce of those three hundred farms?
You do not follow the chase;—
How do we see the badgers hanging up in your court-yards?
O that superior man!
He would not eat the bread of idleness!

2   *K'an-k'an* go his blows on the wood for his spokes,
And he places it by the side of the river,
Whose waters flow clear and even.
You sow not nor reap;—
How do you get your three millions of sheaves?
You do not follow the chase;—
How do we see those three-year-olds hanging in your court-
    yards.
O that superior man!
He would not eat the bread of idleness!

'to go to another place.' The use of 还 and 逝 respectively respondst o the 间 and 外 of ll. 1, the ground of the speakers, and the ground beyond it.

The rhymes are—in st. 1, 间, 闲, 还, cat. 14: in 2, 外, 泄, 逝, cat. 15, t. 3.

Ode 6. Allusive. AGAINST THE IDLE AND GREEDY MINISTERS OF THE STATE. CONTRAST BETWEEN THEM AND A STALWART WOODMAN. Choo does not, in his work on the She, admit the allusive element, and puts the lines from the 4th downwards into the mouth of the woodcutter, solacing himself under his toil, and with the results to which it might lead. The interpretation which I have given, more in accordance with the Preface, seems preferable; Choo himself held it, when commenting on Mencius, VII. Pt. i. XXXII.

Ll. 1—3, in all the stt. 坎 坎 is intended to convey the sound of the woodman's blows;—like 丁 丁 in i. VII. 檀,—see on vii. II. 3. The wood was prized for making carriages, and was specially good for the spokes and other parts of the wheels. 于=厓, 'a river's bank.' 漘,—as in vi. VII. 3. 涟 is the 'rippling' appearance of the water; 直, its being 'even and unagitated;' 沦, the 'rippling circles' caused by a slight wind. Choo thinks the third line always describes the condition of the river,

三章

坎坎伐轮兮。寘之河之漘兮。河水清且沦猗。不稼不

穑。胡取禾三百囷兮。不狩不猎。胡瞻尔庭有县鹑

兮。彼君子兮。不素飧兮。

3   *K'an-k'an* go his blows on the wood for his wheels,
And he places it by the lip of the river,
Whose waters flow clear in rippling circles.
You sow not nor reap;—
How do you get the paddy for your three hundred round binns?
You do not follow the chase ;—
How do we see the quails hanging in your court-yards?
O that superior man!
He would not eat the bread of idleness !

VII.   *Shih shoo.*

硕鼠

一章

硕鼠硕鼠。无食我黍。三岁贯女。莫我肯顾。逝将去

1   Large rats! Large rats!
Do not eat our millet.
Three years have we had to do with you,
And you have not been willing to show any regard for us.

unfit to carry away the wood which the worker's toil produced. 猗 is used as 兮.

Ll. 4—7. 稼 is properly 'the spike' of grain, and 穑, the grain fit to be reaped. 稼穑 intimates the business of husbandry; but from the constant use and order of the terms, they have come to get the respective meanings in the translation. So in l. 6. 狩 and 猎 together denote hunting. 廛 denotes the ground assigned for the dwelling of a farmer, and the land, or 100 acres, attached to it, so that we can render it here by 'farms.' 取禾三百廛＝取三百廛所出之禾. The 3 millions of st. 2. are understood to refer to the sheaves or bundles in which the cut paddy was gathered (禾秉之数); and the binns (囷 denotes their round form) of st 4, the repositories in which the grain was stored. 貊 is a species of 貊 ;—see on Ana. IX. xxviii. Here, as there, it might mean badgers' skins, but for the 特 and 鹑 below. Maou gives the former of those terms as meaning any animal of the chase, three years old. These four lines set forth the great revenues of the officers intended in the ode, acquired and enjoyed without any proper services performed for them.

Ll. 8, 9, return to the woodman, as truly a superior man, earning his support. 素＝空, 'emptily,' or 'idly.' 飧＝食, 'to eat.'

The rhymes are—in st. 1, 檀, 干, 涟, 廛, 貊, 飧, cat. 14: in 2, 辐 *, 侧, 直, 亿, 特, 食, cat. 1, t. 3: in 3, 轮, 漘, 沦, 囷 *, 鹑, 飧, cat. 13.

女。适彼乐土。乐土乐土。爰得我所。

二章

硕鼠硕鼠。无食我麦。三岁贯女。莫我肯德。逝将去

女。适彼乐国。乐国乐国。爰得我直。

三章

硕鼠硕鼠。无食我苗。三岁贯女。莫我肯劳。逝将去

女。适彼乐郊。乐郊乐郊。谁之永号。

We will leave you,
And go to that happy land.
Happy land! Happy land!
There shall we find our place.

2 Large rats! Large rats!
Do not eat our wheat.
Three years have we had to do with you,
And you have not been willing to show any kindness to us.
We will leave you,
And go to that happy State.
Happy State! Happy State!
There shall we find ourselves right.

3 Large rats! Large rats!
Do not eat our springing grain!
Three years have we had to do with you,
And you have not been willing to think of our toil.
We will leave you,
And go to those happy borders,
Happy borders! Happy borders!
Who will there make us always to groan?

Ode 7. Metaphorical. AGAINST THE OPPRES-
SION AND EXTORTION OF THE GOVERNMENT OF
WEI. The piece is purely metaphorical, the
writer, as representative of the people, clearly
having the oppressive officers of the govt. before
him, under the figure of *large rats*. The Preface
is wrong in supposing it to be intended directly
against the ruler of Wei. It would serve as an
admonition to him, but it would be too licentious
if it designated him as the *large rat*.

Ll. 1, 2, in all the stt. 无 = 毋, imperative.
The term 'millet' is varied by the others, merely
for the sake of the rhythm.

Ll. 3, 4. There must have been a reason for
specifiying 'three years;' so long, probably, had
the ministers complained of been in office. Choo
defines 贯 by 习, 'to practise,' 'to be accus-
tomed to;' and Maou by 事, 'to serve.' The
translation gives the exact idea. 顾 = 念, 'to

think of,' 'to regard;' 德,—used as a verb, 'to show kindness to;' 劳 我 = 以 我 为 勤劳, 'to consider our toil.'

Ll. 5, 6. 逝,—a particle, as in iii. IV. 去, —'to go away from,' 'to leave.' 'That happy land' was, probably, some neighbouring State, where there was kindly government.

Ll. 7, 8. 爰 —'there,' as iii. VI. 3, et al. 我 所, —'our place,' i. e., our right place. 我 直, 'our right,' i. e., be dealt with righteously. 谁 之 永 号,—号 = 呼, 'to cry out;'—'whose will be our constant crying out?' As Choo expands it— 当 复 为 谁 而 永 号 乎.

The rhymes are—in st. 1, 鼠, 黍, 女, 顾, 女, 土, 土, 所, cat. 5, t. 2: in 2, 鼠, 女, 女, (and in 3), ib.; 麦, 德, 国, 国, 直, cat. 1, t. 3: in 3, 苗, 劳, 郊, 郊, 号, cat. 2.

CONCLUDING NOTE ON THE BOOK. Yen Ts'an calls attention to the fact that there are no licentious songs among the odes of Wei. The characteristics of excessive parsimony in the higher classes, and oppressive extortion practised by them on the people, leave no room for surprise at the early extinction of the State as an independent fief. The best pieces are IV. and VI.

174

BOOK X. THE ODES OF T'ANG.

I. *Sih-tsuh.*

唐一之十

蟋蟀

一章

蟋蟀在堂。岁聿其莫。今我不乐。日月其除。无已大
康。职思其居。好乐无荒。良士瞿瞿。

1 The cricket is in the hall,
   And the year is drawing to a close.
   If we do not enjoy ourselves now,
   The days and months will be leaving us.
   But let us not go to great excess;
   Let us first think of the duties of our position;
   Let us not be wild in our love of enjoyment.
   The good man is anxiously thoughtful.

TITLE OF THE BOOK.—唐一之十, 'The *odes of* T'ang; Book X. of Part I.' The odes of T'ang were the odes of Tsin,—the greatest, perhaps, of the fiefs of Chow, until the rise and growth of Ts'in. King Ching, in B. C. 1106, invested his younger brother, called Shuh-yu (叔虞), with the territory where Yaou was supposed to have ruled anciently as the marquis of T'ang;—in the pres. dep. of T'ae-yuen, Shan-se, the fief retaining that ancient name. In the south of the territory was the river Tsin (晉水), and Shih-foo (燮父), the son of Shuh-yu, gave its name to the marquisate. Choo He says that 'the soil was thin and the people poor; that they were diligent, thrifty and plain in their ways, thinking deeply and forecasting;—characteristics which showed the influence among them of the character and administration of Yaou.' It is difficult to say why the name of the State, which had gone into disuse, was given to the collection of its poems. We should set it down, probably, to a fondness for ancient legends and traditions. The State of Tsin developed greatly, having the Ho as its boundary on the west, and extending nearly to it on the south and east.

Ode 1. Narrative. THE CHEERFULNESS AND DISCRETION OF THE PEOPLE OF TSIN, AND THEIR TEMPERED ENJOYMENT AT FITTING SEASONS. The Preface refers the piece to the time of the marquis He (僖侯; B.C. 839-822), who was too parsimonious, and did not temper his economy by the rules of propriety. This ode therefore, it says, was made, through compassion for him, and to suggest to him to allow himself proper indulgences. But there is nothing in the language to make us think of the ruler of the State; we have only to see in it a pleasant picture of the manners of the people.

Ll. 1—4, in all the stt. The 蟋蟀, no doubt, is the cricket. It has many names. In xv. I. 5, it is said in the 9th month to be at the door, and in the 10th under the bed. By the door we must understand that of the bedchamber, so that the 在戶 there and 在堂 here are equivalent, and we conclude that the time intended is the 9th month, when the year had entered on its last quarter. 聿 is used as a particle, synonymous with 于, 曰, 奧, and 越. Choo defines it by 遂. 莫=晚, 'late.'

二章

蟋蟀在堂。岁聿其逝。今我不乐。日月其迈。无已大

康。职思其外。好乐无荒。良士蹶蹶。

三章

蟋蟀在堂。役车其休。今我不乐。日月其慆。无已大

康。职思其忧。好乐无荒。良士休休。

2　The cricket is in the hall,
　　And the year is passing away.
　　If we do not enjoy ourselves now,
　　The days and months will have gone.
　　But let us not go to great excess;
　　Let us first send our thoughts beyond the present;
　　Let us not be wild in our love of enjoyment.
　　The good man is ever diligent.

3　The cricket is in the hall,
　　And our carts stand unemployed.
　　If we do not enjoy ourselves now,
　　The days and months will have gone by,
　　But let us not go to an excess;
　　Let us first think of the griefs that may arise;
　　Let us not be wild in our love of enjoyment.
　　The good man is quiet and serene.

其 in the 4th line is by Wang Yin-che brought under the category of 将,='will.' In the 2d line we may take it as descriptive, or emphatic, equivalent to our use of the subject proper and of the 3d personal pronoun in the same sentence. 除 =去, 'to go,' 'pass away;' so also, both 逝 and 迈. 慆=过, 'to pass by,' 役车, 'service carriages,'=our 'carts,' or perhaps, only 'barrows.'

Ll. 5—8. The first four lines are to be taken as the language of a party of the people, as there rises among them the idea of their having a jovial time. At this point we may suppose that one among them, of a more serious and thoughtful character, interjects the remarks that follow, in order to temper their mirth. 已 is defined by Maou as meaning 其, 'greatly.' 康 = 乐, 'pleasure.' 大康 = 过于

乐. 职=主, 'to make the first business.' 其居, 'where we dwell,' 'where we occupy;'—as in the transl. 其外, 'what is beyond,' i. e., what yet may remain for us to do. 荒,—'to go wildly to excess;'—comp. Men. I.Pt.i.IV. 良士,—士, is here not more than our 'man.' 瞿瞿 denotes 'the app. of looking round and out;' 蹶蹶, that of 'sedulous movement;' and 休休, that of 'calm composure.'

The rhymes are—in st.1, 堂. 康, 荒 (and in 2, 3), cat.10; 莫, 除, 居, 瞿, cat. 3, t.1: in 2, 逝, 迈, 外, 蹶, cat. 15, t. 3: in 3, 休, 慆 忧, 休, cat.3, t.1.

II. *Shan yëw ch'oo.*

山有枢

一章

山有枢。隰有榆。子有衣裳。弗曳弗娄。子有车马。

弗驰弗驱。宛其死矣。他人是愉。

二章

山有栲。隰有杻。子有廷内。弗洒弗埽。子有钟鼓。

弗鼓弗考。宛其死矣。他人是保。

1   On the mountains are the thorny elms,
     In the low, wet grounds are the white elms.
     You have suits of robes,
     But you will not wear them ;
     You have carriages and horses,
     But you will not drive them.
     You will drop off in death,
     And another person will enjoy them.

2   On the mountains is the *k'aou*,
     In the low wet grounds is the *nëw*.
     You have courtyards and inner rooms,
     But you will not have them sprinkled or swept ;
     You have drums and bells,
     But you will not have them beat or struck,
     You will drop off in death,
     And another person will possess them.

Ode 2. Allusive. THE FOLLY OF NOT EN-
JOYING THE GOOD THINGS WHICH WE HAVE, AND
LETTING DEATH PUT THEM INTO THE HANDS OF
OTHERS. The Preface says that this piece was
directed against the marquis Ch'aou (B. C. 744-
738), who could not govern the State well, nor
use the resources which he had, so as to secure
himself against the enemies who were plotting
his ruin. I must believe, with Choo, that such
an interpretation is 'very wrong.' He considers it himself to be a response to the previous
ode, bringing in the idea of death, to remove all
hesitation in accepting the counsel to enjoyment
there given. The two pieces would seem to
have some connection.

Ll.1,2, in all the stt. 荎 is another name
for the 枢, which is described as 'the thorny

elm (刺 榆).' I have seen the tree, with its
trunk all covered with spinous protuberances,
making it very difficult to climb. 榆 is the
general name for elms. The one intended in
the text is understood to be 'the white elm
(白 粉).' The 栲 is said to be like the varnish tree ; the 杻 affords good material for bows.
It goes also by the name of 'the myriad years
(万岁),' or 'the everlasting.' 山 and 隰,
—see iii.XIII. 4. These two lines are allusive,
but they suggest no idea apropriate to the
subject which they introduce. As Choo says,

别 无 意 义,只 是 兴 起 下 面
子 有 车 马,子 有 衣 裳 耳.

三章

山有漆。隰有栗。子有酒食。何不日鼓瑟。且以喜
乐。且以永日。宛其死矣。他人入室。

3　On the mountains are the varnish trees,
　　In the low wet grounds are the chestnuts.
　　You have spirits and viands;—
　　Why not daily play your lute,
　　Both to give a zest to your joy,
　　And to prolong the day?
　　You will drop off in death,
　　And another person will enter your chamber.

III.　Yang che shuy.

扬之水

一章

扬之水。白石凿凿。素衣朱襮。从子于沃。既见君子。

1　Amidst the fretted waters,
　　The white rocks stand up grandly.
　　Bringing a robe of white silk, with a vermilion collar,
　　We will follow you to Yuh.

Ll.3—6. 子 — 'you,' any one to whom we may suppose the speaker to be addressing himself. 曳 and 娄 are synonyms, signifying 'to drag or trail along.' The two terms together give us the idea of the man's moving along in full dress. 驰 驱,—see iv. X. 1. 廷 = 庭; 内 is probably the hall and apartments, inside from the courtyard. 考 = 击, to 'strike.' This term is more appropriate to the bells, though in the 3d st. 鼓 is used for to play on the lute. In l.4 of st. 3, 日, on Choo's view of the piece, is taken to mean 'the days of the year that remain;' but that is not necessary. Moreover, to explain 以 永 日, he says that 'when men have many anxieties, the days seem short,' whereas the contrary is the case.

Ll.7,8. 宛, with Choo, is 坐 见 貌, 'the app. of sitting and seeing,' i.e., anything happening without warning or excitement. 愉 —

乐, 'to enjoy;' 保 = 居 有, 'to dwell in the possession of.'

The rhymes are—in st. 1, 枢, 榆 *, 娄 *, 驱 *, 愉 *, cat. 4, t. 1 : in 2, 栲 *, 杻, 埽 *, 考 *, 保 *, cat. 3, t. 2 : in 3, 漆, 栗, 瑟, 日, 室, cat.12, t.3.

Ode 3. Allusive. REBELLION PLOTTED A-GAINST TSIN BY THE CHIEF OF K'EUH-YUH AND HIS PARTIZANS. At the beginning of his rule, the marquis Ch'aou invested his uncle, called Ching-sze (成师) and Hwan-shuh (桓叔), with the great city of K'ёuh-yuh, thus weaken-ing greatly his own power; and by this pro-ceeding there resulted long disorder in the State of Tsin. A party was soon formed to displace the marquis, and raise Hwan-shuh to his place. The piece is supposed in the Preface, and by Choo, to describe the movement for this object, the people declaring in it their devotion to the chief of K'ёuh-yuh, who is intended by the 君

云何不乐。

二章

扬之水。白石皓皓。素以朱绣。从子于鹄。即见君子。

云何其忧。

三章

扬之水。白石粼粼。我闻有命。不敢以告人。

> When we have seen the princely lord,
> Shall we not rejoice?

2   Amidst the fretted waters,
    The white rocks stand glistening.
    Bringing a robe of white silk, with a vermilion collar, and
        embroidered,
    We will follow you to Kaou.
    When we have seen the princely lord,
    What sorrow will remain to us?

3   Amidst the fretted waters,
    The white rocks clearly show.
    We have heard your orders,
    And will not dare to inform any one of them.

子 of the first two stanzas. But, as a matter of fact, the conspiracy against Ch'aou was the affair of a faction, and not shared in by the mass of the people. I prefer, therefore, to adopt the view of Yen Ts'an, that the piece describes the plottings of conspirators in the capital of Tsin. The 'we,' the speakers, are only the adherents of the conspiracy, and the 子 in l. 4 is an emissary of Hwan-shuh, who is the 君子 of l. 5. The object of the piece, therefore, was to warn the marquis Ch'aou of the machinations against him. The K'ang-he editors rather incline in favour of this interpretation.

Ll. 1, 2, in all the stt. 扬之水,—see on vi. IV., and vii. XVIII. 凿 凿,—'the rugged, lofty app. of the rocks;' 皓 皓,—'their shining appearance;' 粼 粼 is obscure. The Shwoh-wăn explains it as 'the water about the banks and rocks;' Maou, as='clear;' Choo, as 'the stones visible amid the clear water.' What meaning we are to get from these allusive lines, it is as difficult to determine as in the previous odes which began with 扬之水.

Ll.3—6 in stt.1,2. The robe described in l.3 was one worn by the princes of States in sacrificing. It was an inner robe, made of white silk, with a collar which is here called poh. On this were embroidered the axes of authority, and it was fitted also with a hem or edging of vermilion-coloured silk. Hwan-shuh had no right to such a robe; and the people of the capital, in saying to his emissary (子) that they would go with one to Yuh, promise, in effect, to make him the marquis of Tsin. 鹄 was the name of a town or city in the territory of K'ëuh-yuh. 云 in l.6 is the particle. In stanza 3, 'we have heard your orders,' means the orders from Hwan-shuh communicated to his partizans in Tsin.—Lacharme has erred egregiously in translating the 3d and 4th lines of stt.1,2, and the 3d line of st.3.—'Homines simplici cultu induti, in vestibus quibus collare rubrum assuitur, &c., se dedunt viro cuidam in regione Kou dicta.'...'Ego quæ audivi Imperatoris mandata,' &c.

The rhymes are—in st. 1, 凿 *, 襮 *, 沃 *, 乐 *, cat. 2: in 2, 皓 *, 绣, 鹄, 忧, cat. 3, t. 2: in 3, 粼, 命 *, 人, cat.12, t. 1.

IV. *Tsëaou lëaou.*

椒聊

一章

椒聊之实。蕃衍盈升。彼其之子。硕大无朋。椒聊

且。远条且。

二章

椒聊之实。蕃衍盈匊。彼其之子。硕大且笃。椒聊

且。远条且。

1   The clusters of the pepper plant,
    Large and luxuriant, would fill a pint.
    That hero there
    Is large and peerless.
    O the pepper plant!
    How its shoots extend!

2   The clusters of the pepper plant,
    Large and luxuriant, would fill both your hands.
    That hero there
    Is large and generous.
    O the pepper plant!
    How its shoots extend;

V. *Chow-mow.*

绸缪

一章

绸缪束薪。三星在天。今夕何夕。见此良人。子兮子

1   Round and round the firewood is bound;
    And the Three Stars appear in the sky.
    This evening is what evening,
    That I see this good man?

Ode 4. Allusive and metaphorical. SUPPOSED TO CELEBRATE THE POWER AND PROSPERITY OF HWAN-SHUH, AND TO PREDICT THE GROWTH OF HIS FAMILY. The Preface gives this interpretation of the piece, and Choo allows that he does not know to what to refer it.

Ll. 1, 2, in both the stt. 椒 is the pepper plant; 聊 is to be taken as a mere particle. 蕃 = 茂, 'luxuriant;' 衍 = 广, 'wide,' 'large.' 升 is a pint measure, and 匊 is the two hands full. Both words express the great productiveness of the plant; and as Yen-she observes, it is folly to go about trying to determine the size of the old pint. Evidently there is a metaphorical element in the allusion in these lines, and the two last.

Ll 3, 4. 彼其之子 has often been met with. 硕 and 大 intensify each other. 朋 = 比, our 'peer.' 笃 = 厚, 'generous.'

Ll. 5, 6. 且,—as in iv. III. 2, *et al.* It here gives the sentiment a tinge of regret.

兮。如此良人何。

二章

绸缪束刍。三星在隅。今夕何夕。见此邂逅。子兮子

兮。如此邂逅何。

三章

绸缪束楚。三星在户。今夕何夕。见此粲者。子兮子

兮。如此粲者何。

O me! O me!
That I should get a good man like this!

2   Round and round the grass is bound;
And the Three Stars are seen from the corner.
This evening is what evening,
That we have this unexpected meeting?
Happy pair! Happy pair!
That we should have this unexpected meeting!

3   Round and round the thorns are bound;
And the Three Stars are seen from the door.
This evening is what evening,
That I see this beauty?
O me! O me!
That I should see a beauty like this!

The rhymes are—in st.1, 升 朋, cat. 6; 聊 *, 条 * (and in 2), cat. 3, t.1: in 2, 蒭, 笃, *ib.*, t.3.

Ode 5. Allusive. HUSBAND AND WIFE EXPRESS THEIR DELIGHT AT THEIR UNEXPECTED UNION. The Preface says that the piece was directed against the disorder of Tsin, through which the people were unable to contract marriages at the proper season assigned for them. Hence Maou would make it out that we have here the joy of husband and wife, as married at the fitting time, in contrast with the existing disappointment and misery. Choo, on the contrary, says we have here simply the joy of a newly married pair. So far I must agree with Choo; the joy indicated is not that of a past age, but of the time then being. The pair, however, would seem to rejoice in the realization of a happiness from which they had seemed hitherto debarred.

L. 1 in all the stt. 绸缪 denotes 'the app. of the bundles bound or tied together.' 刍

means 'grass,' generally fodder; but here we must think of it as gathered for the purpose of fuel. The point of the allusion in this line is hard to tell. The idea of *union*, in the bringing things together, may, possibly, be it.

L. 2. By the 'Three Stars,' we are to understand a constellation so denominated. Maou understood by it the constellation of Ts'an (参 宿) in Orion; and K'ang-shing, whom Choo follows, that of Sin (心 宿) in Scorpio. The *Ts'an* would be visible at dusk in the horizon in the 10th month, a proper time according to Maou for contracting marriage;—hence his view of the ode. The *Sin* would be visible in the 5th month, when, acc. to Ch'ing, the proper season was past. The mention of the constellation as opposite the corner (*i. e.*, the south-east corner of the house), and the door, ought not to be pressed to a special significance. It is only the usual variation for the sake of rhythm.

Ll.3—6. In st.1 the lady is supposed to be soliloquizing, and calls her husband 良人,

VI. *Te too.*

杕杜

一章

有杕之杜。其叶湑湑。独行踽踽。岂无他人。不如我

同父。嗟行之人。胡不比焉。人无兄弟。胡不佽焉。

二章

有杕之杜。其叶菁菁。独行睘睘。岂无他人。不如我

同姓。嗟行之人。胡不比焉。人无兄弟。胡不佽焉。

1   There is a solitary russet pear tree,
     [But] its leaves are luxuriant.
     Alone I walk unbefriended;—
     Is it because there are no other people?
     But none are like the sons of one's father.
     O ye travellers,
     Why do ye not sympathize with me?
     Without brothers as I am,
     Why do ye not help me?

2   There is a solitary russet pear tree,
     [But] its leaves are abundant.
     Alone I walk uncared for;—
     Is it that there are not other people?
     But none are like those of one's own surname.

'the good man.' Mencius, IV.Pt.ii.XXXIII., is decisive in favour of this view; and the opinion of Maou, that it is a designation of the wife, must be rejected. In st.2, both husband and wife are supposed to be the speakers, congratulating each other. 邂逅 gives the idea of 'a meeting,' and one which is unexpected, 'not previously arranged.' Maou erroneously understands it of 'mutual delight.' In st. 3, the husband soliloquizes. 粲 = 美, 'beautiful.' Maou, from an expression in the 国语, that 'three ladies make a ts'an,'—a bevy of beauties, understands the term of the wife and two concubines of a great officer! The 如...何 in all the stanzas expresses the delight of the parties.

The rhymes in st. 1 are— 薪, 天, 人, 人, cat. 12, t. 1; in 2, 刍 *, 隅 *, 逅, 逅, cat. 4, t. 1: in 3, 楚, 户, 者 *, 者 *, cat. 5, t. 2.

Ode 6. Allusive. LAMENT OF AN INDIVIDUAL DEPRIVED OF HIS BROTHERS AND RELATIVES, OR FORSAKEN BY THEM. A historical interpretation of the piece is given, as we should have expected, in the Preface, which refers it to the marquis Ch'aou, opposed by his uncle of K'ëuh-yuh, and plotted against by other members of his House. This, however, is only conjecture. The words may have a manifold application.

Ll. 1, 2. in both stt. 杜,—see on ii. V. 杕 = 特. 'the app. of standing alone.' 有 is, I think, the descriptive, to be construed with 杕. 湑湑 and 菁菁 are synonymous, and describe the abundant frondage of the tree. The allusion is understood to be by way of contrast. —The tree, though solitary, was covered by its leaves; the speaker was solitary and desolate of friends.

O ye travellers,
Why do ye not sympathize with me?
Without brothers as I am,
Why do ye not help me?

VII.　*Kaou k'ew.*

羔裘
一章
羔裘豹袪。自我人居居。岂无他人。维子之故。
二章
羔裘豹襃。自我人究究。岂无他人。维子之好。

1　Lamb's fur and leopard's cuffs,
　　You use us with unkindness.
　　Might we not find another chief?
　　But [we stay] because of your forefathers.

2　Lamb's fur and leopard's cuffs,
　　You use us with cruel unkindness.
　　Might we not find another chief?
　　But [we stay] from our regard to you.

Ll. 3—5. 踽 踽,—see Men. VII. Pt. ii. XXXVII. 9. Ll. 4, 5 express the speaker's pain in being forsaken by his brothers and relatives. 同父 = 'brothers by the same father,' 同姓 = blood relations, 'descended from the same ancestor.'

Ll. 6=8. 嗟 行 之 人 = 嗟 叹 行 路 之 人, 'O ye wayfaring men!' 比 and 佽 are both explained by 'to help;' but the former is referred to the sympathy of the mind, the latter to its demonstration in the act. The rhymes are—in st. 1, 杜, 湑, 踽, 父, cat. 5, t. 2: in 2, 菁, 睘 (prop. cat. 14), 姓, cat. 11: in both stt., 比, 佽, cat. 15, t. 3.

Ode 7. Narrative. THE PEOPLE OF SOME GREAT OFFICER COMPLAIN OF HIS HARD TREAT- MENT OF THEM, WHILE THEY DECLARE THEIR LOYALTY. Choo does not attempt to interpret these verses, but dissents from the view of the Preface which I have followed.

L. 1, in both stt.—See on vii. VI. The great officer, to whose territory the speakers belonged, is here indicated by his dress. 袪 and 襃 are synonyms, signifying the cuff of the jacket. L. 2. Maou explains 自 by 用, 'to use.' He also says that 居 居 and 究 究 are synonyms, denoting 'the app. of evil intentions, and of want of sympathy.'

Ll. 3, 4 tell how the speakers might seek the lands of some other great officer, who would treat them better, but that they felt an attach- ment to the family of their chief, and even to himself. 故 = 子 故 旧 之 人,—as in the translation.

The rhymes are in st. 1—袪, 居, 故, cat. 5, t. 1: in 2, 襃, 究, 好 *, cat. 3, t. 2.

VIII. *Paou yu.*

鸨羽
一章
肃肃鸨羽。集于苞栩。王事靡盬。不能艺稷黍。父母
何怙。悠悠苍天。曷其有所。
二章
肃肃鸨翼。集于苞棘。王事靡盬。不能艺黍稷。父母
何食。悠悠苍天。曷其有极。

1 *Suh-suh* go the feathers of the wild geese,
    As they settle on the bushy oaks.
    The king's affairs must not be slackly discharged,
    And [so] we cannot plant our sacrificial millet and millet;—
    What will our parents have to rely on?
    O thou distant and azure Heaven!
    When shall we be in our places again?

2 *Suh-suh* go the wings of the wild geese,
    As they settle on the bushy jujube trees.
    The king's affairs must not be slackly discharged,
    And [so] we cannot plant our millet and sacrificial millet;—
    How shall our parents be supplied with food?
    O thou distant and azure Heaven!
    When shall [our service] have an end?

Ode 8. Allusive or metaphorical. THE MEN OF TSIN, CALLED OUT TO WARFARE BY THE KING'S ORDER, MOURN OVER THE CONSEQUENT SUFFERING OF THEIR PARENTS, AND LONG FOR THEIR RETURN TO THEIR ORDINARY AGRICULTURAL PURSUITS. The piece is referred, we may presume correctly, to some time after duke Ch'aou, when, for more than 50 years, a struggle went on between the ambitious chiefs of K'euh-yuh, and the marquises proper of Tsin. The people were in the main loyal to Tsin, and one king and another sent expeditions to support them. There were of course great trouble and confusion in the State, and the work of agriculture was much interfered with. Këang Ping-chang compares the ode with the 4th of last Book. The strength of the home feeling in the ancient Chinese appears in both pieces. 'Here,' says Këang, 'the interest turns more on

the destitution of the parents, because the filial son of Wei could rely on his elder brother at home, to provide for the wants of the family.'

Ll. 1, 2, in all the stt. The *paou* is described as similar to a wild-goose, but larger, without any hind toe. The last particular may be doubted. I think the bird intended may be the Grey Lag. 行, in st. 4, is descriptive of the *rows* or orderly manner which distinguishes the flight of wild geese. *Suh-suh* is intended to give the sound of the birds in flying. 集,—as i. II.

1. 苞＝丛生, 'growing thickly together,' 'bushy.' 栩 is a species of oak; 棘,—as in iii. VII. The *paou* is said not to be fond of lighting on trees, the attempt to perch occasioning it trouble and pain. That is not the proper

三章
肅肅鴇行。集于苞桑。王事靡盬。不能蓺稻粱。父母

何嘗。悠悠蒼天。曷其有常。

3　　*Suh-suh* go the rows of the wild geese,
　　　As they rest on the bushy mulberry trees.
　　　The king's business must not be slackly discharged,
　　　And [so] we cannot plant our rice and maize ;—
　　　How shall our parents get food?
　　　O thou distant and azure Heaven!
　　　When shall we get [back] to our ordinary lot?

IX.　　*Woo e.*

无衣

一章
豈曰无衣。七兮。不如子之衣。安且吉兮。

二章
豈曰无衣。六兮。不如子之衣。安且燠兮。

1　　How can it be said that he is without robes?
　　　He has those of the seven orders;
　　　But it is better that he get those robes from you.
　　　That will secure tranquillity and good fortune.

2　　How can it be said that he is without robes?
　　　He has those of the six orders;
　　　But it is better that he get those robes from you.
　　　That will secure tranquillity and permanence.

position for it; and Choo thinks that the soldiers introduce it in this position as metaphorical of the hardship of their lot.

Ll. 3—5. The 'king's business' was the operations of his commissioners aginst K'ëuh-yuh, in which the men of Tsin were, of course, required to take part. 盬 is defined as 'not strong or durable;' and also by 略, 'perfunctory,' 'slackly performed.' 靡 = 无, and must here be construed as in the translation. 黍 and 稷,—see on vi.I. 稻 is paddy; and 粱 = 粟類, 'a kind of maize.' 嘗 = 食, 'to eat.'

Ll.6,7. L.6,—see on vi.I. 曷, 'when,'—as in vi.II. 2. 其 must be translated 'in the 1st person; or we might keep its demonstrative force,—'when shall there be this, the getting the [proper] place [for us]?' &c.

The rhymes are—in st.1, 羽, 栩, 盬, 黍, 怙, 所, cat. 5, t. 2: in 2, 翼, 棘, 稷, 食, 极, cat. 1, t. 3: in 3, 行 *, 桑, 粱, 嘗, 常, cat.10.

Ode 9. Narrative. A REQUEST TO THE KING'S ENVOY FOR THE ACKNOWLEDGMENT OF DUKE WOO AS MARQUIS OF TSIN. In B. C. 678, the struggle between the branches of the House of

X. *Yëw te che too.*

有杕之杜

一章

有杕之杜。生于道左。彼君子兮。噬肯适我。中心好

之。曷饮食之。

二章

有杕之杜。生于道周。彼君子兮。噬肯来游。中心好

之。曷饮食之。

1　There is a solitary russet pear tree,
　　Growing on the left of the way.
　　That princely man there!
　　He might be willing to come to me.
　　In the centre of my heart I love him,
　　[But] how shall I supply him with drink and food?

2　There is a solitary russet pear tree,
　　Growing where the way makes a compass.
　　That princely man there!
　　He might be willing to come and ramble [with me].
　　In the centre of my heart I love him;
　　[But] how shall I supply him with drink and food?

Tsin was brought to a termination, and Ching, earl of K'ëuh-yuh, called after his death duke Ching (成 公), made himself master of the whole State, 67 years after the investiture of his grandfather, Hwan-shuh. It was an act of spoliation, but the usurper bribed the reigning king, He (僖 王), and got himself acknowledged as marquis of Tsin. In this piece we must suppose that an application is made in his behalf, by one of his officers, to an envoy from the court, for the royal confirmation. The daring of the application is equalled by the arrogance of its terms. Choo supposes the application was made directly by Woo himself, so that by the 子 of l.2 the emperor is meant. This is not likely. The remark of the Preface, that the piece is expressive of admiration for duke Woo, is not worth discussion.

Ll.1,2, in both stt. The different ranks in ancient China were marked by the number of carriages, robes, &c., conferred by the king. The prince of a great State had *seven* of the symbols of rank or, as we may call them here, orders, on his robes: on the upper robe three; on the lower robe four. Those robes had previously belonged to the marquisate of Tsin, which Woo had now seized; and he might have pro-

ceeded to assume them at once, but he preferred to get the sanction of the king to his doing so, because that would tranquillize the minds of men, and strengthen his own position. The prince of a State, when serving at court as a minister of the crown, was held to be of lower rank by one degree; hence the seven orders of st.1 appear in st.2 as only 6. 曰,—as in the translation; it is not a particle merely. 子 = 'you;'—spoken to the king's envoy.

L.3. 燠 = 暖, 'warm;' but Choo makes it = 久, 'long-lasting;'—in consequence, that is, of the thickness of the robes, and their good quality. Others give the character the meaning of 安, 'tranquil,' 'secure.'

Both Maou and Choo note that each stanza consists of three lines; but the rhythm shows that each should be arranged in 4 lines, 七 兮 and 六 兮 forming lines themselves.

The rhymes then are—in st.1 衣, 衣 (and in 2), cat.1, t.1; 七, 吉, cat.12, t.3: in 2, 六, 燠. cat.3,t.3.

XI.　*Koh sang.*

葛生

一章
葛生蒙楚。蔹蔓于野。予美亡此。谁与独处。

二章
葛生蒙棘。蔹蔓于域。予美亡此。谁与独息。

三章
角枕粲兮。锦衾烂兮。予美亡此。谁与独旦。

1　The dolichos grows, covering the thorn trees;
　　The convolvulus spreads all over the waste.
　　The man of my admiration is no more here;—
　　With whom can I dwell?—I abide alone.

2　The dolichos grows, covering the jujube trees;
　　The convolvulus spreads all over the tombs.
　　The man of my admiration is no more here;
　　With whom can I dwell?—I rest alone.

3　How beautiful was the pillow of horn!
　　How splendid was the embroidered coverlet!
　　The man of my admiration is no more here;—
　　With whom can I dwell?—Alone [I wait for] the morning.

Ode 10. Metaphorical. SOME ONE REGRETS THE POVERTY OF HIS CIRCUMSTANCES, WHICH PREVENTED HIM FROM GATHERING AROUND HIM COMPANIONS WHOM HE ADMIRED. The Preface finds in this piece a censure of duke Woo, who did not seek to gather worthy officers around him. Choo repudiates, correctly, such an interpretation, and the K'ang-he editors make no attempt to support it.

Ll. 1, 2, in both stt. L. 1,—see on the 6th ode. The 'left' of the road means the east. 周 is explained by 曲, 'a bend.' 'The way went round the spot (周绕之),' says Ying-tah. Such a solitary tree would afford little or no shelter, and so the speaker sees in it a resemblance to his own condition.

Ll. 3—6. 噬 is an initial particle. We have previously had 逝, with the same pronunciation, used in the same way; and Han Ying here read 逝. 饮 and 食 are now both in the 3d tone, with the meaning which I have given.

The rhymes are—in st. 1, 左, 我, cat. 17: in 2, 周, 游, cat. 3, t. 1. The last two lines do not rhyme, unless we make those in the one stanza rhyme with those in the other.

Ode 11. Allusive and narrative. A WIFE MOURNS THE DEATH OF HER HUSBAND, REFUSING TO BE COMFORTED, AND WILL CHERISH HIS MEMORY TILL HER OWN DEATH. The Preface says that the piece was directed against duke Heen (献公 ; B. C. 675—650), who occasioned the death of many by his frequent wars. This charge could, indeed, be made against him; but there is nothing in the piece to make us refer it to his time.

Ll. 1, 2, in stt. 1, 2. With the names 葛, 楚, and 棘 we are by this time familiar 蔹 is a convolvulus; probably the *ipomœa pentadactylis*,—a creeper found abundantly in Hongkong, and called by the common people, from the way in which its leaves grow, 五爪龙, 'the five-clawed dragon.' 域 is in the sense of 茔域, 'a place of graves.' These two lines are taken by Maou and Choo as allusive; the speaker being led by the sight of the weak plants supported by the trees, ground, and tombs, to think of her own

四章

夏之日。冬之夜。百岁之后。归于其居。

五章

冬之夜。夏之日。百岁之后。归于其室。

4　Through the [long] days of summer,
　Through the [long] nights of winter [shall I be alone],
　Till the lapse of a hundred years,
　When I shall go home to his abode.

5　Through the [long] nights of winter,
　Through the [long] days of summer [shall I be alone],
　Till the lapse of a hundred years,
　When I shall go home to his chamber.

XII.　*Ts'ae ling.*

采苓

一章

采苓采苓。首阳之巅。人之为言。苟亦无信。舍旃舍

旃。苟亦无然。人之为言。胡得焉。

1　Would you gather the liquorice, would you gather the liquorice,
　On the top of Show-yang?
　When men tell their stories,
　Do not readily believe them;
　Put them aside, put them aside.
　Do not readily assent to them;

desolate, unsupported condition. But we may also take them as narrative, and descriptive of the battle ground, where her husband had met his death.

Ll. 3, 4, 予美＝我所美之人,—as in the translation, a designation of the husband. Yen Ts'an makes 亡此＝死于此, 'died here;' but I prefer the version I have adopted. 谁与独处＝谁与乎独处而已,—as is the translation. Some critics call attention to the rhyme between 与 and 处 in the line; but it is not carried out in st. 2.

St. 3. The pillow of horn and embroidered coverlet had been ornaments of the bridal chamber; and as the widow thinks of them, her grief becomes more intense. 独旦＝独处至旦, 'I dwell alone till the morning.' Some would construe ll. 1, 2 in the pres. tense, and

infer that the speaker had not been long married. Maou takes the pathos out of the stanza by explaining it of some ancient sacrificial usages.

Stt. 4, 5. The lady shows the grand virtue of a Chinese widow, in that she will never marry again. And her grief would not be assuaged. The days would all seem long summer days, and the nights all long winter nights; so that a hundred long years would seem to drag their course. The 'dwelling' and the 'chamber' are to be understood of the grave.

The rhymes are—in st. 1, 楚, 野*, 处, cat. 5, t. 2: in 2, 棘, 域, 息, cat. 1, t. 3: in 3, 粲, 烂, 旦, cat. 14: in 4, 夜*, 居, cat. 5, t. 1: in 5, 日, 室, cat 12, t. 3.

Ode 12. Metaphorical. AGAINST GIVING EAR TO SLANDERERS. This piece, like the last, is supposed to have duke Hëen for its object; but such a reference is open to the same remark as there.

二章
采苦采苦。首阳之下。人之为言。苟亦无与。舍旃舍

旃。苟亦无然。人之为言。胡得焉。

三章
采葑采葑。首阳之东。人之为言。苟亦无从。舍旃舍

旃。苟亦无然。人之为言。胡得焉。

And, when men tell their stories,
How will they find course?

2　Would you gather the sowthistle, would you gather the sow-
　　　　thistle,
At the foot of Show-yang?
When men tell their stories,
Do not readily approve them;—
Put them aside, put them aside.
Do not readily assent to them;
And, when men tell their stories,
How will they find course?

3　Would you gather the mustard plant, would you gather the
　　　　mustard plant,
On the east of Show-yang?
When men tell their stories,
Do not readily listen to them;—
Put them aside, put them aside.
Do not readily assent to them;
And, when men tell their stories,
How will they find course?

Ll. 1, 2, in all the stt. These lines are metaphorical of baseless rumours, carrying their refutation on the face of them. The plants mentioned were not to be found about Show-yang. That any one might know, and a person, asked to look for them in it, would never think of doing so. In the same way baseless slanders might, by a little exercise of sense and discrimination, be disregarded. The lines are in the imperative mood, but I have translated them interrogatively, the better to indicate their relation to those that follow. 苓,—see on iii. XIII.

4; 苦,—i. q. the 荼 of iii. X. 2; 葑,—see on iii. X. 1. Show-yang,—see on Ana. XVI. xii.

Ll. 3—5. 之 may be construed as the sign of the genitive. 为言,—'make words,'— tell their stories. Some take 为 = 伪, 'hypocritical,' 'false;' but it is not necessary to do so. Maou takes 苟 in the sense of 诚, 'really' or 'if really.' It is better to take it in the sense of 且, as I have done, and treat 亦 as a particle; unless, indeed, we take the two terms as a compound particle, as Wang Yin-che says that 蓋 亦 always is, and not attempt to translate them at all. 与 = 许, 'to grant,' 'to approve of;' 从, 'to follow,' is here, both by Maou and Choo, explained by 听, 'to hearken to.' 痏,—as in ix. IV.

Ll. 6—8. 然 — 'to account correct.' Choo makes 人 the nominative to 得,—'How will those men attain to spread their slanders.?' I think we should take the whole of the 7th line as the subject. The meaning comes to the same.

The rhymes are—in st. 1, 苓*, 巅, 信, cat. 12, t. 1: in 2, 苦, 下 *, 与 , cat. 5, t. 2: in 3, 莳, 东, 从, cat. 9: and in all the stanzas, 痏, 言 , 然 , 焉, cat. 14.

CONCLUDING NOTE ON THE BOOK. As the omission in Book VIII. of all odes about duke Hwan was matter of surprise, so in this Book we must think it strange that there is silence about duke Wăn, the hero of Tsin. In the odes, as we have them, there is a good deal that is pleasing, and has more than a local interest. The 1st, as a picture of cheerful, genial ways; the 8th, as an exhibition of filial regard and anxiety; and the 11th, as a plaintive expression of the feelings of a lonely widow, bear to be read and read again. The 2d, in the view which it gives us of death, and the 5th, in the joy which it describes of a union unexpectedly attained, have a human attraction. And in none of the others is there any of the lewdness which defiles so many of the odes of Wei and Ch'ing.

190

BOOK XI. THE ODES OF TS'IN.

I. *Keu lin.*

秦一之十一

车邻

一章
有车邻邻。有马白颠。未见君子。寺人之令。

二章
阪有漆。隰有栗。既见君子。并坐鼓瑟。今者不乐。

逝者其耋。

1 He has many carriages, giving forth their *lin-lin*;
　He has horses with their white foreheads.
　Before we can see our prince,
　We must get the services of the eunuch.

2 On the hill-sides are varnish trees;
　In the low wet grounds are chestnuts.
　When we have seen our prince,
　We sit together with him, and they play on their lutes.
　If now we do not take our joy,
　The time will pass till we are octogenarians.

TITLE OF THE BOOK.—秦一之十一,. 'The odes of Ts'in; Book XI. of Part I.' The State of Ts'in took its name from its earliest principal city,—in the pres. dis. of Ts'ing-shwuy (清 水), Ts'in-chow (秦 州), Kan-suh. Its chiefs claimed to be descended from Yih, or Pih-yih (伯 益), Shun's forester, and the assistant of the great Yu in his labours on the deluge, from whom he got the clan-name of Ying (嬴). Among his descendants, we are told, there was a Chung-keuh (仲 滴), who resided among the wild tribes of the west for the protection of the western borders of the kingdom of Shang. The sixth in descent from him, called Ta-loh (大 骆), had a son, Fei-tsze (非 子), who had charge of the herds of horses belonging to king Hëaou (B.C. 908—894), and in consequence of his good services

was invested with the small territory of Ts'in, as an attached State. His great-grandson, called Ts'in-chung, or Chung of Ts'in (秦 仲), was made a great officer of the court by king Seuen, in B.C. 826; and his grandson, again, known as duke Sëang (襄 公), in consequence of his loyal services, in 769, when the capital of Chow was moved to the east, was raised to the dignity of an earl, and took his place among the great feudal princes of the kingdom, receiving a large portion of territory, which included the ancient capital of the House of Chow.—In course of time, Ts'in, as is well known, superseded the dynasty of Chow, having gradually moved its capital more and more to the east, after the example, in earlier times, of Chow itself. The people of Ts'in were, no doubt, composed of the wild tribes of the west, though the ruling chiefs among them may have come originally from the more civilized China on the east. The descent from Pih-yih belongs to legend, not to history.

三章

阪有桑。隰有杨。既见君子。并坐鼓簧。今者不乐。

逝者其亡。

3   On the hill-sides **are mulberry trees**;
      In the low wet grounds are willows.
      When we have seen our prince,
      We sit together with him, and they play on their organs.
      If now we do not take our joy,
      The time will pass till we are no more.

II.   *Sze t'ëeh.*

驷驖

一章

驷驖孔阜。大辔在手。公之媚子。从公于狩。

1   His four iron-black horses are in very fine condition;
      The six reins are in the hand [of the charioteer].
      The ruler's favourites
      Follow him to the chase.

Ode 1. Narrative and allusive. CELEBRATING THE GROWING OPULENCE AND STYLE OF SOME LORD OF TS'IN, AND THE PLEASURES AND FREEDOM OF HIS COURT. The Preface says that the lord of Ts'in here intended was Ts'in-chung, mentioned in the note above. Choo, however, remarks that there is nothing in the piece to make us refer it to Ts'in-chung. This is true; but we must believe it was made at an early period, when the State was emerging from its obscurity and weakness.

St.1. 邻 邻 is defined as 'the noise of many chariots.' The character here was probably formed originally by 车, with the phonetic on the right. 颠, here, = 额, 'forehead.' The horses would have a white spot in their foreheads. By 君 子 we are to understand 'the ruler of Ts'in.' 寺 人 = 阉 官 'a eunuch-officer.' There were eunuchs about the court of Chow, though not in any great number. From the Tso-chuen we know that in the Ch'un-ts'ëw period, they were in the great feudal courts. The mention of one here, whose services were necessary to announce the wish of a high officer (such we must suppose the speaker to have been) to have an interview with the ruler, is intended to show that the court of Ts'in was now assuming all the insignia of the other States of the kingdom.

Stt. 2, 3, ll. 1, 2. Perhaps the allusion here is to indicate that as the hill-sides and low grounds had their appropriate trees, so music was appropriate to the court. 阪,—see vii. XV. 1. Here 'banks,' however had better give place to 'hill-sides.' The Shwoh-wǎn defines the term by 山 胁.

Ll. 3, 4. Hwang Tso observes on 并 坐, that it is to be understood of the ruler and his guests, sitting together in the same apartment, but not of their doing so, 'shoulder to shoulder,' without distinction of rank. We are not to suppose that the ruler and his guests played themselves on the instruments mentioned; the music was from the proper officers, an accompaniment of the feasting which was going on. 簧,—see on vi. III. 1.

Ll. 5, 6. 今 者 makes the meaning of 逝 者 plain enough. In x. I. 2, 逝 is used of the passing away of the year. We might translate 逝 者 by 'hereafter;'—comp. 往 者 in Men. VII. Pt. ii. XXX. 2. I take 其 as in x.I., = 将. Eighty years old is called 耋.

The rhymes are—in st. 1, 邻, 颠, 令 *, cat. 12, t. 1: in 2, 漆, 栗, 瑟 耋 , *ib.*, t. 3: in 3, 桑, 杨, 簧, 亡 , cat. 10.

二章
奉时辰牡。辰牡孔硕。公曰左之。舍拔则获。

三章
游于北园。四马既闲。辖车鸾镳。载猃歇骄。

2   The male animals of the season are made to present themselves,
    The males in season, of very large size.
    The ruler says, 'To the left of them;'
    Then he lets go his arrows and hits.

3   He rambles in the northern park;
    His four horses display their training.
    Light carriages, with bells at the horses' bits,
    Convey the long and short-mouthed dogs.

Ode 2. Narrative. CELEBRATING THE GROW-
ING OPULENCE OF THE LORDS OF Ts'IN, AS
SEEN IN THEIR HUNTING. The Preface refers
this piece to duke Sëang, also mentioned in the
introductory note, on his being raised to the
dignity of earl by king P'ing, and assuming the
style becoming his rank; but such a reference
is entirely outside the piece itself.

St.1. 铁 is descriptive of the colour of the
horses. Luh Tëen says that the term has reference not only to their iron colour, but also to
their iron strength (坚 壮 如 铁). Maou
explains 阜 by 'large (大);' Choo adds 肥,
'fat.' L.2. We must understand that the reins
were in the hand of the charioteer; but I do not
see, with Maou, that the line is intended to indicate his skill, but simply his holding the reins in
his hand. With a team of 4 horses, there were of
course 8 reins, but the two inner reins of the
outsiders were somehow attached to the carriage; so that the driver held only 6 in his hand.
L.3. 公,—as in iii.XIII. 3, et al. We need not
translate it by 'duke.' 媚 is in the sense of
爱, 'to love.' Yen Ts'an and Choo both understand the line as in the translation; Maou's
view of it is much too far-fetched,—'the duke's
officers, who love him above them, and the people below them.' L.4. 狩, 'the winter hunt,'
is here probably='the chase,' generally.

St. 2 describes the action of the chase. As a
nominative to 奉 we must understand 虞 人,
'the forester,' and his attendants, who have
surrounded the animals in season, so as to
afford plenty of sport. 时 = 是 'these;'
辰 = 时, 'season;' 牡 = 兽 之 牡 者,
'the males of the animals.' The 'these' represents the scene graphically, as if passing before
the speaker's eye. L.3. 左 之, 'left it,'= to

the left with the carriage. L.4. 拔 = 矢
末, 'the end of an arrow,' not 'the barb,' as
Williams says; so that 舍 拔 = 放 矢,
'he discharges his arrows.'

St. 3 supposes the hunting finished. The
action is now transferred to some park, north
of the capital of Ts'in. 园 is here evidently
synonymous with 囿, 'a park,' though it is now
confined mainly to the signification of 'garden.'
Ying-tah says that the difference between them
was in their being enclosed, the 囿 by a wall,
and the 园 by a hedge or fence. L2. 闲 = 习
or 调 习, 'to put through their practice.'
The horses now went gently along, not driven
about as in the chase, and displayed the skill
with which they had been trained. 辖 = 轻,
'light.' These were used to prevent the animals of the chase from escaping out of the
circle in which they were enclosed, and for the
purpose here mentioned. On each side of the
bits (镳) of the horses in them were suspended bells, called here 鸾, being supposed to
emit a sound like that of the fabulous bird so
called. L.4. Both Maou and Choo say that 猃
was the name for 'long-muzzled dogs,' and
歇 骄, that for 'dogs with short muzzles.'
These last characters, if we are to accept this
explanation of them, should be formed with
犬, instead of 欠 and 马, as indeed they
are in the Shwoh-wän.

The rhymes are—in st.1, 阜, 手 狩, cat.
3, t. 2: in 2, 硕, 获, cat. 5, t. 3: in 3, 园, 闲,
cat. 14; 镳, 骄, cat. 2, t.1.

III.　*Sëaou jung.*

小戎

一章

小戎伐收。五楘梁辀。游环胁驱。阴靷鋈续。文茵畅

毂。驾我骐𬳿。言念君子。温其如玉。在其板屋。乱

1　[There is] his short war carriage;—
　　With the ridge-like end of its pole, elegantly bound in five
　　　　places;
　　With its slip rings and side straps;
　　And the traces attached by gilt rings to the masked transverse;
　　With its beautiful mat of tiger's skin, and its long naves;
　　With its piebalds, and horses with white left feet.
　　When I think of my husband [thus],
　　Looking bland and soft as a piece of jade;
　　Living there in his plank house;
　　It sends confusion into all the corners of my heart.

Ode 3. Narrative. THE LADY OF AN OFFICER ABSENT ON AN EXPEDITION AGAINST THE TRIBES OF THE WEST GIVES A GLOWING DESCRIPTION OF HIS CHARIOT, AND PRAISES HIMSELF, EXPRESSING, BUT WITHOUT MURMURING, HER OWN REGRET AT HIS ABSENCE. The Preface says the piece is in praise of duke Sëang; which is altogether foreign to its spirit, though it may, or may not, have belonged to his time. He received a charge from king P'ing to subdue the tribes referred to in it, and the struggle between them and Ts'in long continued. Both the Preface and Choo suppose two speakers in each stanza, referring the 1st six lines to the followers of the officer, and the last four to his wife. This destroys the unity of the verses. They are, evidently, all the language of the wife, and we thus have in her a fine specimen of a Ts'in matron, public-spirited and tender-hearted;— see Këang Ping-chang, *in loc.*

St.1. L.1. 戎 here denotes the ordinary war-chariot, called 'small (小),' to distinguish it from a larger one, which we shall by and by meet with. 收 is used in the sense of 轸, 'the boards forming the back and front of the carriage.' They are called 'shallow (伐 = 浅),' or short as we must translate, because the war chariot was much shorter than the carriage or waggon used for ordinary purposes. The width of both was the same,—6 ft. 6 in; but the latter was 8 ft. long, and the former only 4 ft. 4 in. L.2. 辀 was the end of the pole, where the yoke for the two inside horses was attached. It rose in a curve, like the ridge of a house (梁).

and was bound in 5 places with leather, which gave it an elegant appearance. 楘 ='ornamental bands of leather.' L. 3. 'The slip (游 =moving) rings' were attached somehow to the backs of the inside horses, and the off reins of the outsides were drawn through them, so that the driver could keep those horses in control, if they tried to start off from the others. 'The side straps,' it is said, were fixed to the ends of the yoke and the front of the carriage, running along the 'sides' of the insiders, and so preventing the other horses from pressing in upon them. The force of the 驱 I cannot discover.—The student must bear in mind, that in those times the team of a chariot consisted of 4 horses, which were driven abreast or nearly so, and not yoked two behind, and two in front. L.4. 靷 means a trace (所以引). What is here spoken of are the traces attached in front to the necks or breasts of the outsiders, and behind to the front of the chariot. The places where they were so attached to the carriage were somehow masked or concealed (阴); the attachment (续) was made by means of gilt rings. L.5. 文茵 is the mat of tiger's skin' which was spread in the carriage. 畅 = 长, 'long,' For the sake of greater strength the naves of the wheels in a warchariot were made of extraordinary size. L.6. 'Yoked in it are our piebalds,' &c. The terms descriptive of the horses are defined as in the translation.

我心曲。

二章

四牡孔阜。六辔在手。骐骝是中。騧骊是骖。龙盾之

合。鋈以觼軜。言念君子。温其在邑。方何为期。胡

然我念之。

三章

伐駟孔群。厹矛鋈錞。蒙伐有苑。虎韔镂膺。交韔二

2   His four horses are in very fine condition,
    And the six reins are in the hand [of the charioteer].
    Piebald, and bay with black mane, are the insides;
    Yellow with black mouth, and black, are the outsides;
    Side by side are placed the dragon-figured shields;
    Gilt are the buckles for the inner reins.
    I think of my husband [thus],
    Looking so mild in the cities there.
    What time can be fixed for his return?
    Oh! how I think of him!

3   His mail-covered team moves in great harmony;
    There are the trident spears with their gilt ends;
    And the beautiful feather-figured shield;

Ll. 7—10. 言 is the particle. 君 子,— 'husband,' as in i. X., *et al.* The 其 in l. 8, and in the next st., increases the descriptive force of 温. The tribes of the west lived in plank houses or log huts. The lady sees her husband in one, which he had taken, we may suppose, from the enemy. 心 曲,—'bends of the heart.'

St. 2. 四 牡—the horses were entire. 孔 阜,—as in II. 1. L. 3. 骝 is 'a red horse, with a black mane.' 中 denotes the 'middle' horses, the insiders, called 服 马. L. 4. The outsiders were called ts'an. Maou defines 騧 as in the transl. L. 4. The shields are called 'dragon,' from having the figure of a dragon drawn upon them. They were set up in the front of the carriage, and helped to protect those in it from the missiles and arrows of the enemy.

L. 6. By 軜 is meant the two inner reins of the outsiders, which were attached by buckles (觼 = 环 之 有 舌 者) to the front of the carriage, leaving only 'six reins' for the driver to manage.— 以 must be disregarded, as a mere particle, and the line='the reins with their gilt buckles.'

Ll. 7, 10. 邑 may be taken of the cities or towns on the western border of Ts'in, or those of the western tribes. 方 = 将, 'there will be.' 胡 然,—as in iv. III. 2.

St. 3. L. 1. 伐 has here the sense of 'mailed,' the mail for the horses being made of 'thin' plates of metal, scale-like. 群 = 和, 'harmonious,' referring to the unison of their movements. L. 2. The k'ew maou is defined as 'a three cornered spear (三 隅 矛);' but it is figured as a trident. The end of its shaft (錞) was gilt. L. 3. 伐 is here used in the sense of 'shield,' specifically one of middle size. The Shwoh-wăn gives the character as 旱 with 戈 on the right. 蒙 denotes the feathers, which were fixed (Maou), or painted (Ch'ing), on the shield. 有 苑 describes the effect as elegant (文 貌). L. 4. 韔 was the 'bow-case (弓

弓。竹闭绲滕。言念君子。载寝载兴。厌厌良人。秩

秩德音。

With the tiger-skin bow-case, and the carved metal ornaments
    on its front.
The two bows are placed in the case,
Bound with string to their bamboo frames.
I think of my husband,
When I lie down and rise up.
Tranquil and serene is the good man,
With his virtuous fame spread far and near.

IV. *Këen këa.*

蒹葭
一章
蒹葭苍苍。白露为霜。所谓伊人。在水一方。溯洄从

1   The reeds and rushes are deeply green,
    And the white dew is turned into hoarfrost.
    The man of whom I think
    Is somewhere about the water.
    I go up the stream in quest of him,

室)，' 镂膺，—lit., 'engraven breasts.' Maou
and Choo take the phrase of the carved metal
ornaments on the horses' breast-bands; but I
agree with Yen Ts'an that it is very unlikely the
speaker should start off from the bow-case to
the breast-bands of the horses, and then in the
next line return to the bow-case again. We must
take the phrase as descriptive of the ornaments
on the front of the case.

L.5. 交韔 二弓＝交二弓于
韔 中. 'there were placed together two bows
in the case.' L.6. The 闭 (composed elsewhere of 韦 and 必) was an instrument of
bamboo, strapped to the bow when unstrung, to
keep it from warping. It appears here, as so
strapped to it with string (绲), and placed
along with it in the case.

Ll.6—7. 载—as in iii.XIV. 3. 厌厌
describes 'the tranquil serenity of the husband's
virtue.' 秩 秩 ＝ 'orderly.' Choo Kung-
ts'een says, 'The manifestation of his virtuous
fame proceeded from the inside to the outside,

from near to far. This is what is meant by its
being *an orderly fame.*'

   The rhymes are—in st.1, 收, 辀, cat.3, t.1;
驱, 续, 毂, 异, 玉, 曲, *ib.*, t.3 (驱
prop. belongs to cat. 4): in 2, 阜, 手, *ib.* t.2;
中, 骖 (this is very doubtful); 合, 钠 (prop.
cat. 15), 邑, cat.7, t.3: in 3, 群, 镎, 苑
(prop. cat.14), cat.13, t.1; 膺, 弓*, 滕, 兴
and 音 (prop.cat.7), cat. 6, t. 1.

Ode 4. Narrative. SOME ONE TELLS HOW HE
SOUGHT ANOTHER WHOM IT SEEMED EASY TO
FIND, AND YET COULD NOT FIND HIM. This
piece reads very much like a riddle, and so it
has proved to the critics. The Preface says it
was directed against duke Sëang, who went on
his course to strengthen his State by warlike
enterprises, without using the proprieties of
Chow, and so would be unable to consolidate it.
In developing this interpretation, on which the
first two lines are allusive, Ch'ing K'ang-shing
makes 'the man' in the 3d line to be a man or
men versed in the proprieties; Gow-yang and

之。道阻且长。溯游从之。宛在水中央。

二章
蒹葭凄凄。白露未晞。所谓伊人。在水之湄。溯洄从

之。道阻且跻。溯游从之。宛在水中坻。

三章
蒹葭采采。白露未已。所谓伊人。在水之涘。溯洄从

But the way is difficult and long.
I go down the stream in quest of him,
And lo! he is right in the midst of the water.

2　The reeds and rushes are luxuriant,
And the white dew is not yet dry.
The man of whom I think
Is on the margin of the water.
I go up the stream in quest of him,
But the way is difficult and steep.
I go down the stream in quest of him,
And lo! he is on the islet in the midst of the water.

3　The reeds and rushes are abundant,
And the white dew has not yet ceased.
The man of whom I think
Is on the bank of the river.

others think duke Sëang himself is meant; and Lëu Tsoo-k'ëen takes 'the man' as 'the proprieties of Chow.' All this is what Choo well calls 'chiselling,' and gives no solution of the riddle. He himself takes the whole as narrative, and does not attempt any solution;—nor do I venture to propose one.

Ll. 1, 2, in all the stt. The *këen* is described as like the *hwan* (萑), which Medhurst calls a tough sedge or rush, but smaller, though it rises to the height of several feet. For the *këa*, see on ii. XIV. 苍 苍 describes their appearance of a deep green. Maou and Choo say that 凄 凄 is synonymous with this;—comp. 萋 萋 in i. II. 1. 采 采 must have a similar meaning; Choo tries to keep to the meaning in it of 采, 'to gather.' The 2d line indicates the time as towards the close of autumn, when frost was beginning to make itself felt;

and the time of the day as in the morning, when the dew still lay in hoarfrost, or a semblance of it. 干,—'to be dry.'

Ll. 3. 伊人＝彼人, 'that man.' Maou makes 伊＝维, as in ii. XIII. 3, but the term has here a demonstrative force. Wang Yin-che explains it by 是. 一 方, 'one quarter,'— somewhere. 湄 is the margin, 'the place where the water and grass meet.' 涘,—as in vi. VII. 2. To go up against the stream is called 溯 (or with 水 at the side) 洄 ; to go down with the stream is called 溯 游;'—so, the Urh-ya. 从 之,—'follow him,' *i.e.*, go in quest of him. 阻 ＝ 险, 'dangerous,' 'precipitous and difficult.' 跻 ＝升, 'ascending,' 'steep.'

之。道阻且右。溯游从之。宛在水中沚。

I go up the stream in quest of him,
But the way is difficult and turns to the right.
I go down the stream in quest of him,
And lo! he is on the island in the midst of the water.

V.   *Chung-nan.*

终南
一章
终南何有。有条有梅。君子至止。锦衣狐裘。颜如渥

丹。其君也哉。
二章
终南何有。有纪有堂。君子至止。黻衣绣裳。佩玉将

1   What are there on Chung-nan?
    There are white firs and plum trees.
    Our prince has arrived at it,
    Wearing an embroidered robe over his fox-fur,
    And with his countenance rouged as with vermilion.
    May he prove a ruler indeed!

2   What are there on Chung-nan?
    There are nooks and open glades.

右,—'to the right.' The meaning is, as Chóo says, that 'he did not meet with the man, and turned away to the right of him.' 坻 and 沚 both mean 'islet;' but 坻 is the smaller of the two. 宛,—as in x.II.

The rhymes are—in st. 1, 苍, 霜, 方, 长, 央, cat. 10; it is not worth while to put down ll. 5 and 7 as rhyming: in 2, 凄, 晞, 湄, 跻, 坻, cat. 15, t. 1: in 3, 采, 已, 涘, 右*, 沚, cat. 1, t. 1.

Ode 5. Allusive. CELEBRATING THE GROW-ING DIGNITY OF SOME RULER OF TS'IN, AND ADMONISHING, WHILE PRAISING, HIM. The piece is akin to the first and second. The Preface refers it to duke Sëang, who was the first of the chiefs of Ts'in to be recognized as a prince of the kingdom, and we need not question the reference.

Ll. 1, 2, in both stt.   Chung-nan was the most famous mountain in the old demesne of Chow, lying south of the old capital of Haou,—in the

pres. dep. of Se-gan, in Shen-se. It came to belong to Ts'in, when king P'ing had granted to duke Sëang the old possessions of Chow. The *t'eaou* is another name for 'the mountain *ts'ëw* (山 楸),' 'a kind of fir,' distinguished by the whiteness of its bark, and leaves, and affording good materials for making chariots, coffins, &c. Choo defines 纪 by 山 之 廉 角, 'corners of a hill,' and 堂 by 山 之 宽 平 处, 'open, level, places.' It is hard to tell in what the allusion in these two lines lies.

Ll. 3. 5.   I construe 止 as the particle, and suppose that the lines are descriptive of the prince of Ts'in's arrival in the neighbourhood of the mountain, from a visit to the court of Chow, or in some progress through his territories.   On l. 4, st. 1, Ying-tah says that the prince of a State wore a white fox-fur at the royal court, and on his return to his own dominions when he announced in his ancestral temple what gifts he had received from the son of Heaven; after which he no more wore it. The same would probably be true of the dress mentioned in the corresponding line of st. 2.   On the

将。寿考不忘。

Our prince has arrived at it,
With the symbol of distinction embroidered on his lower gar-
    ment,
And the gems at his girdle emitting their tinkling.
May long life and an endless name be his?

VI. *Hwang nëaou.*

黄鸟

一章

交交黄鸟。止于棘。谁从穆公。子车奄息。维此奄

息。百夫之特。临其穴。惴惴其栗。彼苍者天。歼我

1   They flit about, the yellow birds,
   And rest upon the jujube trees.
   Who followed duke Muh [to the grave]?
   Tsze-keu Yen-seih.
   And this Yen-seih
   Was a man above a hundred.
   When he came to the grave,
   He looked terrified and trembled.
   Thou azure Heaven there!

symbol of distinction, see the Shoo on II.iv. 4. Ying-tah, after Ch'ing, observes that as the symbol was represented on the lower garment, we are not to find two article of array in this line. The 黻 衣 and the 绣裳 are merely variations of expression for the same thing. We have indeed, two articles in st.1, and we know that the embroidered robe was worn over the fur. 渥 丹,—comp. on iii.XIII. 3. 将 将 gives the sound of the gems.

L.6. expresses a wish, in which a warning or admonition is also supposed to be conveyed. The 其, as optative, may be pleaded in favour of the admonition in st.1, and Këang finds the same in 2, by taking 不 忘 as = 自 始 至 终，时 以 王 命 为 念, 'from first to last, ever mindful of the king's orders.' I prefer to take the 忘 passively. Elsewhere in

Ptt. II. and III., we find 寿 考 combined, in the sense of 'to live long.'

The rhymes are—in st.1, 梅, 裘 ", 哉, cat. 1.t.1: in 2, 堂, 裳, 将, 忘, cat.10: 有 ", 止 may also be taken as rhymes in both stt., cat. 1, t. 2.

Ode 6. Allusive. LAMENT FOR THREE WOR-THIES OF TS'IN WHO WERE BURIED IN THE SAME GRAVE WITH DUKE MUH. There is no difficulty or difference about the historical interpretation of this piece; and it brings us down to the year B.C. 620. Then died duke Muh, after playing an important part in the northwest of China for 39 years. The Tso-chuen, under the 6th year of duke Wăn, makes mention of his requiring the three officers here celebrated to be buried with him, and the composition of the piece in consequence. The 'Historical Records' say that the barbarous practice began with duke Ching,

良人。如可赎兮。人百其身。

二章

交交黄鸟。止于桑。谁从穆公。子车仲行。维此仲

行。百夫之防。临其穴。惴惴其栗。彼苍者天。歼我

良人。如可赎兮。人百其身。

三章

交交黄鸟。止于楚。谁从穆公。子车鍼虎。维此鍼

　　　Thou art destroying our good men.
　　　Could he have been redeemed,
　　　We should have given a hundred lives for him.

2　They flit about, the yellow birds,
　　　And rest upon the mulberry trees.
　　　Who followed duke Muh [to the grave]?
　　　Tsze-keu Chung-hang.
　　　And this Chung-hang
　　　Was a match for a hundred.
　　　When he came to the grave,
　　　He looked terrified and trembled,
　　　Thou azure Heaven there!
　　　Thou art destroying our good men.
　　　Could he have been redeemed,
　　　We should have given a hundred lives for him.

3　They flit about, the yellow birds,
　　　And rest upon the thorn trees.
　　　Who followed duke Muh [to the grave]?

Muh's predecessor, with whom 66 persons were buried alive, and that 170 in all were buried with duke Muh. The death of the last distinguished man of the House of Ts'in, the emperor I., was subsequently celebrated by the entombment with him of all the inmates of his harem. Yen Ts'an says that though that House had come to the possession of the demesne of Chow, it brought with it the manners of the barbarous tribes among which it had so long dwelt.—Have we not in this practice a sufficient proof that the chiefs of Ts'in were themselves sprung from those tribes?

In all the stt. Ll. 1, 2. I take 交交 in the sense adopted by Choo, 'the app. of flying about, coming and going.' Maou makes it='small-like.' The allusion is variously explained, some say there is in it the idea of the people's loving the three victims as they liked the birds; others, that the birds among the trees were in their proper place,—very different from the worthies in the grave of duke Muh. 从＝从死, 'to follow in death.' 殉 is the more common term in this sense. L. 4. 子车 was the clan-name of the victims, brothers, whose names follow in

虎。百夫之御。临其穴。惴惴其栗。彼苍者天。歼我

良人。如可赎兮。人百其身。

Tsze-keu K'ëen-hoo.
And this Tsze-keu K'ëen-hoo
Could withstand a hundred men.
When he came to the grave,
He looked terrified and trembled.
Thou azure Heaven there!
Thou art destroying our good men.
Could he have been redeemed,
We should have given a hundred lives for him.

VII. *Shin fung.*

晨风
一章

鴥彼晨风。郁彼北林。未见君子。忧心钦钦。如何如

1 Swift flies the falcon
To the thick-wooded forest in the north.
While I do not see my husband,
My heart cannot forget its grief.
How is it, how is it,
That he forgets me so very much?

the several stanzas. L. 6. 特 gives the idea of 'standing out eminent;' 防, that of 'a dyke or bulwark;' 御, that of 'a combatant.' Ll. 7, 8. 穴 is explained by 圹, 'the pit of a tomb.' 惴惴 ='terrified-like.' I follow Choo in understanding these lines of the victims themselves. Ch'ing is followed by Yen Ts'an in taking them of the spectators. The other view is more natural. L. 9. This line is equivalent to 悠悠苍天 in x. VIII. *et al.* The appeal is, literally, to 'that which is azure, the sky,' but we must understand really to the Power dwelling in the heavens. 歼＝尽, 'to make an end of.' L. 12. Choo makes this='men would all have wished to make their lives a hundred to give in exchange for him.' But the construction is, perhaps,—'*The price would have been* a hundred.'

The rhymes are—in st. 4, 棘, 息, 息, 特, cat. 1, t. 3: iu 2, 桑, 行*, 行*, 防, cat. 10:

in 3, 楚, 虎, 虎, 御, cat. 5, t. 2. Also 穴 栗, and 天, 人, 身, in all the stt.

Ode 7. Allusive. A WIFE TELLS HER GRIEF BECAUSE OF THE ABSENCE OF HER HUSBAND, AND HIS FORGETFULNESS OF HER. Such is the account of the piece given by Choo, drawn from the language of the different verses. The Preface says it was directed against duke K'ang (B. C. 619—608), the son and successor of Muh, who slighted the men of worth whom his father had collected around him, leaving the State without those who were its ornament and strength. But there is really nothing in the piece to suggest this interpretation;—it is, indeed, far-fetched.

Ll.1,2, in all the stt. 鴥 expresses ' the app. of the rapid flight of a bird.' 晨风 is a name for the 鹯, which Williams calls 'a falcon, goshawk, or kite.' It is described as 'fulvous, with a short swallow-like neck, and a hooked beak, flying against the wind with great

何。忘我实多。

二章

山有苞栎。隰有六驳。未见君子。忧心靡乐。如何如

何。忘我实多。

三章

山有苞棣。隰有树檖。未见君子。忧心如醉。如何如

何。忘我实多。

2   On the mountain are the bushy oaks;
     In the low wet grounds are six elms.
     While I do not see my husband,
     My sad heart has no joy.
     How is it, how is it,
     That he forgets me so very much?

3   On the mountain are the bushy sparrow-plums;
     In the low wet grounds are the high, wild pear trees.
     While I do not see my husband,
     My heart is as if intoxicated with grief.
     How is it, how is it,
     That he forgets me so very much?

VIII.   *Woo e.*

无衣

一章

岂曰无衣。与子同袍。王于兴师。修我戈矛。与子同

1   How shall it be said that you have no clothes?
     I will share my long robes with you.
     The king is raising his forces;
     I will prepare my lance and spear,
     And will be your comrade.

rapidity.' 郁 describes 'the thick and extensive growth of the forest.' In st.2 there is great difficulty with 六驳, and there is, probably, a corruption of the text. Acc. to Maou, 驳 is the name of an animal, 'like a white horse, with a black tail, and strong teeth like a saw, which eats tigers and leopards!' But an animal of any kind is entirely out of place here. We must take the term as the name of a tree, and Lnh Ke says the *poh* is a kind of elm. Why *six* trees are mentioned we cannot tell, unless it were that a meadow with that number of elms in it was in the writer's view or in his mind's eye, when he wrote the verse. In the Japanese plates the tree would seem to be the *celtis muku*. The 棣 is the 唐棣 of ii.XIII. The *suy* yields a fruit like a pear, but smaller and sour. It is called 'the hill, or wild pear tree,' 'the deer pear tree,' 'rat pear tree,' &c. 树 must have a meaning, to correspond to the 苞 of the prec. line, and 六 in st 2. I translate it by 'high.' The allusion in all the stt. seems to be simply in the contrast between the falcon and the trees, all in

仇。

二章
岂曰无衣。与子同泽。王于兴师。修我矛戟。与子偕

作。

三章
岂曰无衣。与子同裳。王于兴师。修我甲兵。与子偕

行。

2   How shall it be said that you have no clothes?
     I will share my under clothes with you.
     The king is raising his forces;
     I will prepare my spear and lance,
     And will take the field with you.

3   How shall it be said that you have no clothes?
     I will share my lower garments with you.
     The king is raising his forces;
     I will prepare my buffcoat and sharp weapons,
     And will march along with you.

the places and circumstances proper to them, and
the different condition of the speaker.

Ll. 3–6. 君子,—in the sense of 'husband,'
as often. 钦钦 represents the speaker to us as
'unable to forget' her grief. 未见, 'not yet
seen,' suggests the thought that the husband had
been long absent. 靡乐,—'with no joy.' All
was grief.

The rhymes are—in st. 1, 风 (all through
the She, 风 rhymes thus), 林, 钦, cat. 7, t.
1: in 2, 栋, 驳, 乐, cat. 2; in 3, 棣, 檖, 醉,
cat. 15, t.3: also in all the stt., 何, 多, cat. 17.

Ode 8.   Narrative.   THE PEOPLE OF TS'IN
DECLARE THEIR READINESS, AND STIMULATE ONE
ANOTHER, TO FIGHT IN THE KING'S CAUSE.   I can
get no other meaning but the above out of this
perplexing piece.   The Preface says it is condemnatory of the frequent hostilities in which
the people were involved by a ruler who had no
fellow feeling with them; but I can see no trace
in it of such a sentiment.   Some refer it to duke
K'ang; others to Sëang; others to Chwang.   With
some it expresses condemnation; with others
praise.   Evidently it was made at a time when
the people were being called out in the king's
service; and the loyalty which they had felt,
when they were subjects of Chow, still asserted
its presence, and made them forward to take
the field.

Ll.1,2 in all the stt.   Here we have one of the
people stimulating another who had been excus-
ing himself, perhaps, from taking the field on
the ground that he had but a scanty wardrobe.
The friend will share his own with him.   袍 is
the term for a long robe or gown.   The critics
all speak of it here as quilted.   Choo, after
Ch'ing, defines 泽 as in the translation.   The
Shwoh-wăn gives the character with 衣 at the
side,—no doubt correctly.

Ll.3–5.   于 must be taked as the particle.
I translate both 戈 and 戟 by lance.   The
former is said to have been of all spear-like
weapons the most convenient for use.   It was 6
ft. 6 in. long, and you could pound, cut, smite,
and hook with it.   The kih here is said to have
been that used in the chariot, 16 feet long,
used both for thrusting and hooking.   甲 is
the corselet, made in those days of leather.
兵 means sharp weapons generally.   I take
仇, with Maou, in the sense of 匹, 'mate,'
'comrade,'—like 逑 in i.I.   作, 'to rise to
action,'=to take the field.

The rhymes are—in all the stt. 衣, 师, cat.
15, t.1: in 1, 袍, 矛, 仇, cat.3, t.1: in 2,
泽, 戟, 作, cat.5. t.3; in 3, 裳, 兵*, 行*,
cat. 10.

IX. *Wei yang.*

渭阳

一章
我送舅氏。曰至渭阳。何以赠之。路车乘黄。

二章
我送舅氏。悠悠我思。何以赠之。琼瑰玉佩。

1   I escorted my mother's nephew,
     To the north of the Wei
     What did I present to him?
     Four bay horses for his carriage of state.

2   I escorted my mother's nephew;
     Long, long did I think of him.
     What did I present to him?
     A precious jasper, and gems for his girdle-pendant.

X. *K'euen yu.*

权舆

一章
于我乎夏屋渠渠。今也每食无余。于嗟乎不承权舆。

二章
于我乎每食四簋。今也每食不饱。于嗟乎不承权舆。

1   He assigned us a house large and spacious;
     But now at every meal there is nothing left.
     Alas that he could not continue as he began!

2   He assigned us at every meal four dishes of grain;
     But now at every meal we do not get our fill.
     Alas that he could not continue as he began!

Ode 9. Narrative. THE FEELINGS WITH WHICH DUKE K'ANG ESCORTED HIS COUSIN, DUKE WAN, TO TSIN, AND HIS PARTING GIFTS. Duke Hëen of Tsin had a daughter who became the wife of Muh of Ts'in, and was the mother of his son who became duke K'ang. The eldest son and heir of Hëen was driven to suicide by the machinations of an unworthy favourite of his father, and his two sons fled to other States. One of them, Ch'ung-urh, afterwards the famous duke Wăn of Tsin, took refuge finally in Ts'in, and by the help of duke Muh was restored to his native State, and became master of it, after he had been a fugitive for 19 years. K'ang was then the heir-apparent of Ts'in, and escorted his cousin into the State of Tsin when he undertook his expedition to recover it. These verses are supposed to have been written by him at a subsequent time, when he recalled with interest the event.

Ll. 1, 2, in both stt. 舅 denotes a mother's brothers, and 舅氏 will therefore be one bearing their surname, and little removed from them; here it='cousin.' Lacharme translates it *avunculus*, which is here incorrect. 渭,—see iii.X. 3. The north of a river is called 阳. The capital of Ts'in at this time was Yung (雍), in pres. dis. of Hing-p'ing, dep. Se-gan. The one prince accompanied the other to the territory of the pres. dis. of Heen-yang (咸阳). 悠悠我思,—see iii.V. 2, Maou says that he thought of his mother, now long dead. But whether she were dead or not at this time does not appear;—the line simply expresses the anxious regard which he felt for his cousin, embarked on a hazardous enterprize.

Ll. 3, 4. We are not to understand that the carriage was given by the prince of Ts'in. Such a carriage the princes of States received from the king. If Ch'ung-urh succeeded, he would have such a carriage as the marquis of Tsin; and now his cousin, anticipating his success, gave him the horses for it. 琼 as in v.X. *et al.*

Williams says the 琼瑰 was 'a kind of jasper.' We cannot tell whether this jasper was to be worn at the girdle-pendant, or whether it was given in addition to the usual stones worn there.

The rhymes are—perhaps, in both stanzas 氏, 之 (not given by Twan): in 1, 阳, 黄, cat. 10: in 2, 思, 佩, cat. 1, t. 1.

Ode 10. Narrative. SOME PARTIES COMPLAIN OF THE DIMINISHED RESPECT AND ATTENTION PAID TO THEM. The Preface says the complainers were men of worth, old servants of duke Muh, in his attentions to whom K'ang, his successor, gradually fell off. It may have been so, but we cannot positively affirm it. In the common editions, the stanzas are printed in 5 lines, 于我乎 and 于嗟乎 being each regarded as one. Koo-she observes that these expressions can hardly be treated as separate lines.

In both stt., l. 1. 于我乎 is an exclamation,—'for us,' 'in the treatment of us.' 夏 =大, 'large.' 渠渠 expresses 'the appearance of being deep and wide.' The 簋 were vessels of earthenware or wood, round outside, and square inside, in which grain was set forth at sacrifices and feasts. A prince, in entertaining a great officer, had two of these dishes on the mat, or, as we should say, on the table, and the dishes of meat and other viands corresponded. Here there are 4 such dishes, intimating the abundance of the entertainment which was provided.

L. 2. The student will observe the appropriateness of 无 in st. 1, and of 不 in 2.

L. 3. 承=继, 'to continue.' 权舆=始, 'a beginning.' How the two characters have this signification is attempted to be made out in this way. 权 is the weight or stone attached to a steel yard, and with a stick and stone the first rude attempts at weighing were made; 舆 is the bottom of a carriage, and the first attempts at conveying things were made on a board. However this be, the two characters are now recognized as meaning 'the beginnings of things.'

CONCLUDING NOTE ON THE BOOK. From the first three odes, the fifth, and the seventh, we get the idea of Ts'in as a youthful State, exulting in its growing strength, and giving promise of a vigorous manhood. The people rejoice in their rulers; wives are proud of the martial display of their husbands, while yet they manifest woman's tenderness and affection. The sixth ode shows what barbarous customs still disfigured the social condition; but there is in the whole an auspice of what the House of Ts'in became,—the destroyer of the effeminate dynasty of Chow, and the establisher of one of its own, based too much on force to be lasting. Many of the critics think that Confucius gave a place in his collection of odes to those of Ts'in, as being prescient of its future history!

The rhymes are—in st. 1, 渠, 余, 舆, cat. 5, t. 1: in 2, 簋*, 饱*, cat. 3, t. 2. The 舆 in st. 2 rhymes with 1.

BOOK XII. THE ODES OF CH'IN.

I. *Yuen-kew.*

陈一之十二

宛丘

一章

子之汤兮。宛丘之上兮。洵有情兮。而无望兮。

二章

坎其击鼓。宛丘之下。无冬无夏。值其鹭羽。

1 How gay and dissipated you are,
There on the top of Yuen-k'ëw!
You are full of kindly affection indeed,
But you have nothing to make you looked up to!

2 How your blows on the drum resound,
At the foot of Yuen-k'ëw!
Be it winter, be it summer,
You are holding your egret's feather!

TITLE OF THE BOOK.—陈, 一之十二, '*The odes of* Ch'in; Book XII. of Part I.' Ch'in was one of the smaller feudal States of Chow, and its name remains in the dep. of Ch'in-chow (陈州), Ho-nan. It was a marquisate, and its lords traced their lineage up to the verge of historic times, and boasted of being descended from the famous emperor Shun, so that they had the surname of Kwei (妫). At the rise of the Chow dynasty, one of Shun's descendants, called Ngoh-foo (阏父), was potter-in-chief to king Woo, who was so pleased with him that he gave his own eldest daughter (大姬) to be wife to his son Mwan (满), whom he invested with the principality of Ch'in. He is known as duke Hoo (胡公), and established his capital near the mound called Yuen-k'ew, in the present district of Hwae-ning (淮宁), dep. Ch'in-chow. His marchioness is said to have been fond of witches and wizards, of singing and dancing, and so to have affected badly the manners and customs of the people of the State;—a character of her, a daughter of king Woo, which perplexes many of the critics.

Ode 1. Narrative. THE DISSIPATION AND PLEASURE-SEEKING OF THE OFFICERS OF CH'IN. The Preface says the piece was directed against duke Yew (幽公; B.C. 850–834), and Maou interprets the 子 in st. 1 of him. Choo, however, says that there is no evidence of Yew's dissipation but in the bad title given to him after his death, and that 'he does not dare to believe' that the ode speaks of him. To make the 子 refer to him supposes a degree of familiarity with his ruler on the part of the writer, which is hardly admissible. Yet we

三章

坎其击缶。宛丘之道。无冬无夏。值其鹭翿。

3 How you beat your earthen vessel,
    On the way to Yuen-k'ëw!
    Be it winter, be it summer,
    You are holding your egret-fan!

II. *Tung mûn che fun.*

东门之枌

一章

东门之枌。宛丘之栩。子仲之子。婆娑其下。

二章

谷旦于差。南方之原。不绩其麻。市也婆娑。

1 [There are] the white elms at the east gate.
    And the oaks on Yuen-k'ew;
    The daughter of Tsze-chung
    Dances about under them.

2 A good morning having been chosen
    For the plain in the South,
    She leaves twisting her hemp,
    And dances to it through the market-place.

may infer from st. 1, l. 4 that the subject of the piece was an officer, a man of note in the State, and a representative, I assume, of his class.

St. 1. I have mentioned that Maou refers the 子 to duke Yëw. Ch'ing, however, supposes it is addressed to some 'great officer;'—which is more likely. 汤 is taken as = 荡, 'dissipated,' 'unsettled.' Maou, after the Urh-ya, understands 宛丘 as 'a mound, high on the 4 sides, and depressed in the centre;' while Kwoh Puh gives just the opposite account of the name, as 'a mound rising high in the centre.' Evidently, however, we need not try to translate the words. Whatever was its shape, Yuen-k'ew was the name of a mound, inside, some say, the chief city of Ch'in, certainly in its immediate neighbourhood, and a favourite resort of pleasure-seekers. 有情 is here about = our word 'jolly.'

Stt. 2,3. 坎, followed by the descriptive 其, is intended to give the sound of the blows on the instruments. 缶 is a vessel of earthen-ware. We find it used of a vessel for holding wine, and a vessel for drawing water. It is used also, as here, for a primitive instrument of music. 无冬无夏 = 无问 (or 论), 冬夏, —with the meaning I have given. 值 = 植, or 持, 'to hold in the hand.' We generally translate 鹭 by 'heron;' but according to Kwoh, who says that both from the crest and from the back arose a plume of long feathers, we must understand the bird here to be the Great White Egret (*Ardea Egretta*). Those feathers, either single or formed into fans, were carried by dancers, and waved in harmony with the movements of the body.

The rhymes are—in st. 1, 汤, 上, 望, 'cat. 10: in 2, 鼓, 下*, 夏*, 羽, cat. 5, t. 2: in 3, 缶, 道*, 翿*, cat. 3. t. 2.

Ode 2. Narrative. WANTON ASSOCIATIONS OF THE YOUNG PEOPLE OF CH'IN. The Preface says the piece was intended to express detestation of the lewd disorder of the State. Këang

三章

谷旦于逝。越以鬷迈。视尔如荍。贻我握椒。

3　The morning being good for the excursion,
　　They all proceed together.
　　'I look on you as the flower of the thorny mallows;
　　You give me a stalk of the pepper plant.'

III.　*Hăng mûn.*

衡门

一章

衡门之下。可以栖迟。泌之洋洋。可以乐饥。

1　Beneath my door made of cross pieces of wood,
　　I can rest at my leisure;
　　By the wimpling stream from my fountain,
　　I can joy amid my hunger.

Ping-chang explains it of some celebration by witches and wizards, of which I can discover no trace in the language.

St. 1. Going out at the east gate, it would appear, parties proceeded, to the mound of Yuen-k'ëw, as the great resort of pleasure-seekers. 枌,—*i. q.* 榆, x. II. 1; 栩,—see x. VIII. 1. The Tsze-chung was one of the clans of Ch'in, and we must understand that a daughter of it is here introduced. This is much more likely than the view of Ch'ing, who takes 之子 as =‘that man (男子).' Indeed, we must take 子 as feminine, if the same person be the subject of the 3d line in st. 2. 婆娑 is explained as = 舞貌, ‘the app. of dancing.' The action in this stanza is subsequent to that in the two others.

Stt. 2, 3. 谷 = 善, ‘good;’ here = bright. 差 is explained by 择, ‘to choose.' The dict. refers to this passage, under the pronunciation of 差 as *ch'ae*, which it cannot have here. 于 is the expletive particle. L. 2, st. 2. Maou takes 原 as a surname or clan-name, and understands by the line—‘a lady of the Yuen clan living in the south.' Gow-yang was the first to discard this unnatural construction. ‘The plain in the south' was, probably, at the foot of Yuen-k'ëw, and to reach it, the parties went through the city, and out at the east gate. In st. 3, 越以 must be taken as a compound particle; like 于以 in ii. II., *et al.* 逝 = 往, ‘to go,’ = to make the excursion. 鬷 = 众, ‘all,’ or, as Ch'ing says, 总, ‘all together.' 迈 = 行, to go.' Ll. 3, 4 in st. 3 give the words of some gentleman of the party addressed to a lady. There is a difficulty about them, because l. 3 is directly addressed to the lady, whereas l. 4 is narrative, unless 贻 be taken in the imperative which no critic has ventured to do. I have called 荍, ‘the thorny mallows,' after Medhurst. This is, indeed, a literal translation of another name for the same plant,—荆葵. The figure of it is evidently that of one of the *malvaceœ*.

The rhymes are—in st. 1, 栩, 下 *, cat. 5, t. 2: in 2, 差, 麻, 娑, cat. 16; Twan also makes 原 rhyme here, by poetic license, but unnecessarily: in 8, 逝, 迈, cat. 15, t. 3; 荍*, 椒*, cat. 3, t. 1.

Ode 3. Narrative. THE CONTENTMENT AND HAPPINESS OF A POOR RECLUSE. These simple verses, sufficiently explain themselves. The Preface, however, finds in them advice, thus metaphorically suggested to duke He (僖公; B. C. 830—795), whom some one wished to tell that, though Ch'in was a small State, he might find it every way sufficient for him. We need not take that view, and go beyond what is written.

St. 1. 衡门 is an apology for a door,—one or more pieces of wood placed across the opening in a hut or hermitage. The meaning of 下 is not to be pressed. 栖迟,—lit., ‘roost

二章
岂其食鱼。必河之鲂。岂其取妻。必齐之姜。

三章
岂其食鱼。必河之鲤。岂其取妻。必宋之子。

2   Why, in eating fish,
    Must we have bream from the Ho?
    Why, in taking a wife,
    Must we have a Këang of Ts'e?

3   Why, in eating fish,
    Must we have carp from the Ho?
    Why, in taking a wife,
    Must we have a Tsze of Sung?

IV. *Tung mûn che ch'e.*

东门之池

一章
东门之池。可以沤麻。彼美淑姬。可与晤歌。

二章
东门之池。可以沤纻。彼美淑姬。可与晤语。

1   The moat at the east gate
    Is fit to steep hemp in.
    That beautiful, virtuous, lady
    Can respond to you in songs.

2   The moat at the east gate
    Is fit to steep the bœhmeria in.
    That beautiful, virtuous, lady
    Can respond to you in discourse.

and be at leisure.' 泌＝毖 in iii. XIV. 1, 'the app. of water bubbling up from a spring.' The term here, however, refers us more to the spring itself. 洋 洋 gives the idea of a gentle flow of the water, which then spreads itself out (安 流 广 长 貌). The last line is expanded by Choo—亦 可 以 玩 乐 而 忘 饥 也, 'I can still enjoy myself, and forget my hunger.'

Stt. 2, 3. The marquises of Ts'e had the surname of Këang, and the dukes of Sung that of Tsze. Not bream or carp only could be eaten; one might be satisfied with fish of smaller note.

And so, one could be happy with a wife, though she were not a noble Këang or Tsze.

The rhymes are—in st. 1, 迟, 饥, cat. 15, t. 1: in 2, 鲂, 姜, cat. 10: in 3, 鲤, 子, cat. 1, t. 2.

Ode 4. Allusive. THE PRAISE OF SOME VIRTUOUS AND INTELLIGENT LADY. Choo thinks that in this piece we have a reference to a meeting between a gentleman and lady somewhere near the moat at the eastern gate; but the K'ang-he editors remark correctly that there is nothing in the language indicating any undue familiarity. The Preface says it was directed

三章

东门之池。可以沤菅。彼美淑姬。可与晤言。

3　The moat at the east gate
　　Is fit to steep the rope-rush in.
　　That beautiful, virtuous lady
　　Can respond to you in conversation.

V.　*Tung mûn che yang.*

东门之杨

一章

东门之杨。其叶牂牂。昏以为期。明星煌煌。

二章

东门之杨。其叶肺肺。昏以为期。明星晣晣。

1　On the willows at the east gate,
　　The leaves are very luxuriant.
　　The evening was the time agreed on,
　　And the morning star is shining bright.

2　On the willows at the east gate,
　　The leaves are dense.
　　The evening was the time agreed on,
　　And the morning star is shining bright.

against the times, and the writer is thinking of the weak character of the ruler, and wishing that he had a worthy partner, like the lady who is described, to lead him aright. This view has been variously expanded; but I content myself with the argument of the piece which I have given.

Ll. 1, 2, in all the stt. From its association with the east gate, the 池 here is understood of the 城 池, or moat surrounding the wall. 沤＝渍, 'to soak,' 'to steep.' The stalks of the hemp had, of course, to be steeped, preparatory to getting the threads or filaments from them. 纻 is described as 'a species of hemp,' a perennial, and not raised every year from seed. In the Japanese plates, it is, evidently, the bœhmeria, or nettle from which the grass-cloth is made. The 菅 resembles the 茅. Strings, and cordage generally, could be made from the fibres of the long leaf. It produces a white flower.

Ll.3,4. 姬,—Ke was the surname of the House of Chow,—of all who could trace their lineage, indeed, up to Hwang-te, just as Këang was the surname of the House of Ts'e, and of all descended from the still more ancient Shin-nung. These were the most famous surnames in China; and hence to say that she was 'a Ke,' or 'a Këang,' was the highest compliment that could be paid to a lady. So Ying-tah explains the 姬 here. Choo explains 晤 by 解 'to explain,'＝intelligently. I prefer the explanation of Ch'ing,— 对, ＝ 'responsively.'

The rhymes are—in st. 1, 池 *, 麻, 歌, cat. 17: in 2, 纻, 语, cat. 5, t.2: in 3, 菅, 言, cat. 14.

Ode 5. Allusive. THE FAILURE OF AN ASSIGNATION. The old and new schools differ here as they do in the interpretation of vii.XIV. Here, as there, I prefer the view of Choo. Why should we suppose that there had been any contract of marriage between the parties? or embarrass ourselves with speculations as to the time of the year for the regular celebration of marriages?

VI. *Moo mûn.*

墓门

一章

墓门有棘。斧以斯之。夫也不良。歌以知之。知而不

已。谁昔然矣。

二章

墓门有梅。有鸮萃止。夫也不良。国人讯之。讯予不

顾。颠倒思予。

1　At the gate to the tombs there are jujube trees;—
　　They should be cut away with an axe.
　　That man is not good,
　　And the people of the State know it.
　　They know it, but he does not give over;—
　　Long time has it been thus with him.

2　At the gate to the tombs there are plum trees,
　　And there are owls collecting on them.
　　That man is not good,
　　And I sing [this song] to admonish him.
　　I admonish him, but he will not regard me;—
　　When he is overthrown, he will think of me.

Both stanzas. 羊 羊 and 肺 肺 are synonymous expressions, denoting the dense and luxuriant appearance of the foliage. 明星,—as in vii.VIII. 1. 煌 煌 and 晰 晰 are also synonymous.

The rhymes are—in st. 1, 杨, 羊, 煌, cat. 10: in 2, 肺, 晰, cat. 15, t. 3.

Ode 6. Allusive. On SOME EVIL PERSON WHO WAS GOING ON OBSTINATELY TO HIS RUIN. The Preface gives an historical interpretation of this piece which Choo at one time accepted. It was directed, we are told, against T'o of Ch'in. This T'o was a brother of duke Hwan (B. C. 743—706), upon whose death, he killed his eldest son, and got possession of the State,—to come to an untimely end himself the year after. Yet the critics do not refer the third line directly to him, but to his tutor and guardian, who was unfaithful to his duty, and ruined the prince, who was naturally well inclined. The two first or allusive lines in the stanzas are explained so as to support this view, but it is too complicated. Choo did right in changing his opinion.

Ll.1,2, in both stt. Maou understands by 墓门 'the gate at the path leading to the tombs;' and this interpretation need not be questioned, though Wang Taou tries to make out that one of the gates of the capital of Ch'in was thus named,—'Tomb-gate.' 斯＝析, 'to split wood,' 'to lop.' 鸮, also called 鸱, appears to be the barn owl,—'a bird of evil voice.' 萃＝集, 'to collect.' 止 is the particle. The thorns about the gate of the tombs, and the owls collected on the plum trees, were both things of evil omen; and thence are here employed to introduce the subject of the ode.

Ll 3—6. 夫 is here the demonstrative,＝'this,'—the individual in the speaker's mind. The 'Complete Digest' says that 不已＝不改, 'does not alter.' That is the meaning, but we cannot define 已 by 改. 谁 must be taken here as merely an introductory particle. The Urh-ya says that 谁昔 is no more than 昔. The wickedness of the person referred to was ingrained, had matured for long, and was now not

VII. *Fang yëw ts'ëoh ch'aou.*

防有鹊巢

一章

防有鹊巢。邛有旨苕。谁侜予美。心焉忉忉。

二章

中唐有甓。邛有旨鷊。谁侜予美。心焉惕惕。

1　On the embankment are magpies' nests;
On the height grows the beautiful pea.
Who has been imposing on the object of my admiration?
—My heart is full of sorrow.

2　The middle path of the temple is covered with its tiles;
On the height is the beautiful medallion plant.
Who has been imposing on the object of my admiration?
—My heart is full, of trouble.

sensible to shame. Ch'ing refers 歌 to the present ode (作 此 诗);—most naturally I think. 讯 = 告, 'to inform,'—to admonish. 颠倒 = 至 于 颠 倒 之 时, 'when he is overthrown.'

The rhymes are—in st. 1, 斯, 知, cat. 16, t. 1; 已, 矣, cat. 1, t. 2: in 2, 萃, 讯 (this rhyme, however, is attained by reading 译 for 讯; the text is, no doubt, corrupted), cat. 15, t. 3; 顾, 予, cat. 5, t. 2.

Ode 7. Allusive. A LADY LAMENTS THE ALIENATION OF HER LOVER BY MEANS OF EVIL TONGUES. The Preface says we have here 'sorrow on account of slanderous villains,' and goes on to refer the piece to the time of duke Seuen (宣 公; B C. 691—647), who believed slanderers, filling the good men about his court with grief and apprehension. Much more likely is the view of Choo, that the piece speaks of the separation between lovers effected by evil tongues. He does not give his opinion as to the speaker, whether we are to suppose the words to be those of the gentleman or of the lady. In this I have ventured to supplement his interpretation.

Ll. 1, 2 in both stt. 防 and 邛 are taken by some as the names of places in Ch'in. There might be places so styled, the speaker having in view what were known as 'the embankment' and 'the height;' but the spirit of the ode does not require as to enter on this question. 邛 (the radical is 邑, not 阝, as in Williams)= 邱, 'a mound.' Maou here simply explains 苕 by 草, 'a grass or plant.'—It is different from the same character in II. viii. IX., and is figured as a pea. 旨 = 美, 'beautiful.' 唐 was the designation of the path in a temple from the gate up to the hall or raised platform; and 甓, of the tiles with which it was paved;—tiles of a peculiar and elegant make. I do not know where Williams got his account of the term as—'a sort of tiles which is to be partly covered with other tiles, and in which lines are made.' Maou explains 鷊 as 'the ribbon plant.' The character is properly the name of the medallion pheasant (*tragopan satyrus*), and the plant may have got its name from its resemblance to the neck of that bird. It should be written in the text with 艹 at the top.—I cannot tell wherein lies the point of the allusion in these lines to those that follow.

Ll. 3, 4. 侜,—'to cover,'= to impose upon. 予美,—see on x. XI.; here = 'my lover.' 忉忉 and 惕惕 are synonymous, denoting 'the app. of sorrow or trouble.'

The rhymes are—in st. 1, 巢, 苕, 忉, cat. 2; in 2, 甓, 鷊, 惕 cat. 16, t. 3.

VIII.   *Yueh ch'uh.*

月出
一章
月出皎兮。佼人僚兮。舒窈纠兮。劳心悄兮。
二章
月出皓兮。佼人懰兮。舒懮受兮。劳心慅兮。
三章
月出照兮。佼人燎兮。舒夭绍兮。劳心惨兮。

1   The moon comes forth in her brightness;
    How lovely is that beautiful lady!
    O to have my deep longings for her releved!
    How anxious is my toiled heart!

2   The moon comes forth in her splendour;
    How attractive is that beautiful lady!
    O to have my anxieties about her relieved!
    How agitated is my toiled heart!

3   The moon comes forth and shines;
    How brilliant is that beautiful lady!
    O to have the chains of my mind relaxed!
    How miserable is my toiled heart!

Ode 8. Allusive. A GENTLEMAN TELLS ALL THE EXCITEMENT OF HIS DESIRE FOR THE POSSES- SION OF A BEAUTIFUL LADY. There is no differ- ence of opinion as to the character of the piece, only the Preface moralizes overs it, according to its wont, and says that it was directed against the love of pleasure.

L. 1, in all the stt. 皎 and 皓 both describe the bright, 'white,' light of the moon; and 照, its 'enlightening.' The speaker is supposed to be led on from his view of the moon to speak of the object of his affections.

L. 2. 佼 = 美, 'beautiful;'—comp. 姣 in Men. VI. Pt. i. VII. 7. 僚 and 懰 are both ex- plained by 好 貌, 'good, elegant-like.' 燎 = 明, 'bright,' 'brilliant.' In this line we have the description of the lady.

L. 3 is more difficult than the others. Maou interprets it as a continuation of the description of the lady, explaining 舒 by 迟, 'leisurely,' and understanding it of her movements. 窈 纠, he says, denotes 'the elegance of those

movements.' He does not touch the other lines, but Yen Ts'an and other critics of the Maou school interpret them in the same way. Choo on the other hand interprets the line of the gentleman,—as in the translation. 舒 has the meaning of 解, 'to relieve,' 'to untie;' and the other two characters describe his feelings towards the lady, pent up, and chain-bound. 窈 is descriptive of their depth, and 纠 of their intensity, as if they were knotted together in his breast; 懮 受, of the grief with which they possessed him; and 夭 绍, of the sorrow- ful desire in which they held him fast.

L.4. describes the gentleman's feelings unable to compass the object of his desire, rising from the condition of sorrowful anxiety to that of misery.

The rhymes are—in st. I, 皎, 僚, 纠 (prop. cat. 3), 悄, cat. 2: in 2, 皓, 懰, 受, 慅 *, cat. 3, t. 2: in 3, 照, 燎, 绍, 惨 (this character ought to be 懆. In the Han. dyn. 参 and 桑 were constantly confounded), cat. 2.

IX. *Choo-lin.*

株林

一章

胡为乎株林。从夏南。匪适株林。从夏南。

驾我乘马。说于株野。乘我乘驹。朝食于株。

1　What does he in Choo-lin?
　　He is going after Hëa Nan.
　　He is not going to Choo-lin;
　　He is going after Hëa Nan.

2　'Yoke for me my team of horses;
　　I will rest in the country about Choo.
　　I will drive my team of colts,
　　And breakfast at Choo.'

X. *Tsih p'o.*

泽陂

一章

彼泽之陂。有蒲与荷。有美一人。伤如之何。寤寐无

为。涕泗滂沱。

1　By the shores of that marsh,
　　There are rushes and lotus plants.
　　There is the beautiful lady;—
　　I am tortured for her, but what avails it?
　　Waking or sleeping, I do nothing;
　　From my eyes and nose the water streams.

Ode 9. Narrative. THE INTRIGUE OF DUKE LING WITH THE LADY OF CHOO-LIN. Choo observes that this is the only one of the odes of Ch'in, of which the historical interpretation is certain. The intrigue of duke Ling (B. C. 612 —598) with the lady Hëa makes the filthiest narrative, perhaps, of all detailed in the Tso-chuen. She was one of the vilest of women; and the duke was killed by her son Hëa Nan, who was himself put to a horrible and undeserved death, the year after, by one of the viscounts of Ts'oo.

St. 1. We have here the people of Ch'in intimating, with bated breath, the intrigue carried on by their ruler. Choo-lin was the city of the Hëa family,—in the pres. dis. of Se-hwa (西华), dep. Ch'in-chow. 乎 may be taken as 于, 'in,' 'at.' The question is put as to what the duke meant by being constantly at Choo-lin, and the answer is given that he was cultivating the acquaintance of Hëa Nan, the writer not daring to say openly, that the object of attraction was Nan's mother. The son's name was Ching-shoo (征舒), and his designation, Tsze-nan.

St. 2. I think we should take these lines as spoken by the duke. The critics all refer them to the people, and interpret them as narrative; but the 我 becomes in that case very awkward. 说 = 舍, to rest;' here meaning to pass the night, in opp. to 朝食, in l. 4. Maou interprets 驹, of the 'horses of a great officer,' probably finding in l. 3 a reference to two officers of Ch'in, each of whom had an intrigue

二章
彼泽之陂。有蒲与蕳。有美一人。硕大且卷。寤寐无

为。中心悁悁。

三章
彼泽之陂。有蒲菡萏。有美一人。硕大且俨。寤寐无

为。辗转伏枕。

2　By the shores of that marsh
　　There are rushes and the valerian.
　　There is the beautiful lady,
　　Tall and large, and elegant.
　　Waking or sleeping, I do nothing;
　　My inmost heart is full of grief.

3　By the shores of that marsh,
　　There are rushes and lotus flowers.
　　There is that beatiful lady,
　　Tall and large, and majestic.
　　Waking or sleeping, I do nothing;
　　On my side, on my back, with my face on the pillow, I lie.

at the same time with the lady; but it is simpler to suppose that the character is synonymous with 马. The stanza indicates the frequency with which the duke sought the company of his mistress.

The rhymes are—in st. 1, 林, 南 *, cat. 7, t. 1: in 2, 马 *, 野 *, cat. 5, t. 2; 驹 *, 株 *, cat. 4, t. 1.

Ode 10. Allusive. A GENTLEMAN'S ADMIRATION OF AND LONGING FOR A CERTAIN LADY. Choo observes that the piece is of the same nature and to the same effect as the 9th. It is of no use seeking for a historical interpretation of it, as the Preface does, in the lewd ways of duke Ling and his ministers.

Ll. 1, 2, in all the stt. 陂 is here explained by 障, 'a dyke,' 'an embankment;' but it is better to take it as the natural shores, 蒲,—not as in vi. IV. 3. but='rushes.' Mats were made of them. 荷 is the nelumbium or lotus plant. Its flower, unopened, is callen as in the 3d st. 蕳,—as in vii. XXI. From the pool and its beautiful flowers, the writer is led to think of the object of his affection.

Ll. 3—6. Choo expands ll. 3, 4 of st 1 thus: 有美一人而不可见,则虽忧伤而如之何哉, 'there is that

beautiful lady, but I cannot see her, so that, though I am wounded in consequence with grief, it is of no avail.' L. 4 in stt. 2, 3 describes the person of the lady. 卷=好貌, 'beautiful-like.' Choo explains it of the fine appearance of the hair; and the critics refer us to 鬈 in viii. VIII, but that term is there used of a gentleman. 寤寐,—as in i. I. 2; so also 辗转. 涕 is used of tears; 泗, of water from the nose. 滂沱 indicates the abundance of the tears. 悁悁, like 悒悒,—'the app. of grief or disquiet.' 伏枕,—'I lie prostrate on the pillow.'

The rhymes are—in st. 1, 陂 荷 何, 为 *, 沱, cat. 17: in 2, 蕳, 卷, 悁, cat. 14: in 3, 萏, 俨, 枕, cat. 8: 陂 in stt. 2, 3, is supposed to rhyme with the same character in st. 1.

CONCLUDING NOTE ON THE BOOK. The odes of Ch'in are of the same character as those of Wei and Ch'ing, and the manners of the State must have been frivolous and lewd. Only in the 3d, 4th, and 6th pieces have we an approach to correct sentiment and feeling. The 9th is the latest of all the odes in the Classic, as if the sage had intended to represent duke Ling as the *ne plus ultra* of degeneracy and infamy.

BOOK XIII. THE ODES OF KWEI.

I. *Kaou k'ëw.*

桧一之十三

羔裘

一章
羔裘逍遥。狐裘以朝。岂不尔思。劳心忉忉。
二章
羔裘翱翔。狐裘在堂。岂不尔思。我心忧伤。

1 In your lamb's fur you saunter about;
In your fox's fur you hold your court.
How should I not think anxiously about you?
My toiled heart is full of grief.

2 In your lamb's fur you wander aimlessly about;
In your fox's fur you appear in your hall.
How should I not think anxiously about you?
My heart is wounded with sorrow.

TITLE OF THE BOOK.—桧，一之十三, 'The odes of Kwei; Book XIII. of Part I.' Kwei was originally a small State, in the pres. Ch'ing Chow (郑州), dep. K'ae-fung, Ho-nan, or acc. to others, in the dis. of Meih (密), same dep. Its lords were Yuns (妘), and claimed to be descended from Chuh-yung (祝融), a minister of the ancient emperor Chuen-hëuh. Before the period of the Ch'un-ts'ëw, it had been extinguished by one of the earls of Ch'ing, the one, probably, who is known as duke Woo (武公; B. C. 770—743), and had become a portion of that State. Some of the critics contend that the odes of Kwei are really odes of Ch'ing, just as those of P'ei and Yung belonged to Wei. It may have been so; but their place, away from Bk. VII., instead of immediately preceeding it as Bkk. III. and IV. do Bk. V., may be accepted as an argument to the contrary.

Ode 1. Narrative. SOME OFFICER OF KWEI LAMENTS OVER THE FRIVOLOUS CHARACTER OF HIS RULER, FOND OF DISPLAYING HIS ROBES, INSTEAD OF ATTENDING TO THE DUTIES OF GOVERNMENT. The Preface says further that the officer, rightly offended by the ruler's ways, left his service; but this does not appear in the piece.

Ll. 1, 2, in all the stt. A jacket of lamb's fur was proper to the prince of a State in giving audience to his ministers; but should have been changed when that ceremony was over. One of fox's fur was proper to him, when he appeared at the court of the king; but it was irregular for him to wear it in his own court. 逍遥, —as in vii. V. 2. 翱翔—as in viii. X. 3, *et al.* 堂 is here the hall or State-chamber, to which the ruler retired, after giving audience to his officers, and where he transacted business with them. 有曜＝有光, 'to have effulgence,' *i. e.,* 'to glisten.'

三章
羔裘如膏。日出有曜。岂不尔思。中心是悼。

3   Your lamb's fur, as if covered with ointment,
    Glistens when the sun comes forth.
    How should I not think anxiously about you?
    To the core of my heart I am grieved.

II.   *Soo kwan.*

素冠
一章
庶见素冠兮。棘人栾栾兮。劳心怛怛兮。
二章
庶见素衣兮。我心伤悲兮。聊与子同归兮。

1   If I could but see the white cap,
    And the earnest mourner worn to leanness!—
    My toiled heart is worn with grief!

2   If I could but see the white [lower] dress!—
    My heart is wounded with sadness!
    I should be inclined to go and live with the wearer!

Ll. 3, 4. 思 has here the meaning, as frequently, of 'to think of with interest and longing.' 忉 忉,—as in xii. VII. 1. 悼, 'to be pained in mind,' 'afflicted.'

The rhymes are in st. 1, 遥, 朝, 忉, cat. 2: in 2, 翔, 堂, 伤, cat. 10: in 3, 膏, 曜, 悼, cat. 2.

Ode 2. Narrative. SOME ONE DEPLORES THE DECAY OF FILIAL FEELING, AS SEEN IN THE NEGLECT OF THE MOURNING HABIT. Both Maou and Choo quote, in illustration of the sentiment of the piece, various conversations of Confucius on the three years' mourning for parents;—see Ana; XVII. xxi.

St. 1. 庶,—as in viii. I. 3. It is here defined from the Urh-ya by 幸 'fortunately,' 'luckily; but it has also an optative or conditional force. By the 'white cap' we are to understand the cap worn by mourners for their parents at the end of two years from the death (大祥之后), and which was properly

called 缟冠. Maou supposes it was another, called 练冠, which was assumed in the 13th month;—but this is not so likely. 棘 =急; 'earnest,' 'forward.' 棘人 is a man earnest to observe all the prescribed forms of mourning. 栾栾=瘠貌, 'thin and worn-like,' *i.e.*, by grief and abstinence. 怛 怛 =忧 劳 之 貌, 'the app. of sorrow and toil.'

St. 2. 素衣 was the proper accompaniment of the 素冠. The skirt or lower robe was then also of plain white silk. Ying-tah observes that 衣, as the general name for any article of dress, is here used for 裳, for the sake of the rhyme. 伤 悲,—as in ii. III. 3. 聊,—as in iii. XIV. 1, *et al.* 子 must here be translated in the 3d person, meaning 'such a mourner.' The 同归 expresses the speaker's love and admiration of him.

三章
庶见素韠兮。我心蕴结兮。聊与子如一兮。

3　If I could but see the white knee-covers!—
Sorrow is knotted in my heart!
I should almost feel as of one soul with the wearer!

III.　*Sih yëw ch'ang-ts'oo.*

隰有苌楚
一章
隰有苌楚。猗傩其枝。天之沃沃。乐子之无知。
二章
隰有苌楚。猗傩其华。天之沃沃。乐子之无家。
三章
隰有苌楚。猗傩其实。天之沃沃。乐子之无室。

1　In the low wet grounds is the carambola tree;
Soft and pliant are its branches,
With the glossiness of tender beauty.
I should rejoice to be like you, [O tree], without consciousness.

2　In the low, damp grounds is the carambola tree;
Soft and delicate are its flowers,
With the glossiness of its tender beauty.
I should rejoice to be like you, [O tree], without a family.

3　In the low, damp grounds is the carambola tree;
Soft and delicate is its fruit,
With the glossiness of its tender beauty.
I should rejoice to be like you, [O tree], without a household.

St. 3. The 'white 韠,' was a sort of leather apron covering the knee,—also the accompaniment of the white cap and skirt. 我心蕴结,—lit., 'my heart is a collection of knots.' 如一, 'as one,'= 其志同, 'of the same mind.'
The rhymes are—in st. 1, 冠, 栾, 慱, cat. 14: in 2, 衣, 悲, 归, cat. 15, t. 1: in 3, 韠, 结, —, cat. 12, t. 3.

Ode 3. Narrative. Sᴏᴍᴇ ᴏɴᴇ, ɢʀᴏᴀɴɪɴɢ ᴜɴ-ᴅᴇʀ ᴛʜᴇ ᴏᴘᴘʀᴇssɪᴏɴ ᴏꜰ ᴛʜᴇ ɢᴏᴠᴇʀɴᴍᴇɴᴛ, ᴡɪsʜᴇs ʜᴇ ᴡᴇʀᴇ ᴀɴ ᴜɴᴄᴏɴsᴄɪᴏᴜs ᴛʀᴇᴇ. The Preface says the piece was composed to indicate the writer's disgust at the licentiousness of his ruler. On this view, the 子 in the 4th line must be referred to the ruler, and the piece becomes allusive. In carrying out this interpretation, however, Maou and his followers are put to such straits, that the K'ang-he editors content themselves with giving Choo's view, and do not refer to the older one at all.

IV. *Fei fung.*

匪风

一章
匪风发兮。匪车偈兮。顾瞻周道。中心怛兮。

二章
匪风飘兮。匪车嘌兮。顾瞻周道。中心吊兮。

三章
谁能亨鱼。溉之釜鬵。谁将西归。怀之好音。

1   Not for the violence of the wind;
    Not for the rushing motion of a chariot;—
    But when I look to the road to Chow,
    Am I pained to the core of my heart.

2   Not for the whirlwind;
    Not for the irregular motion of a chariot;—
    But when I look to the road to Chow,
    Am I sad to the core of my heart.

3   Who can cook fish?
    I will wash his boilers for him.
    Who will loyally go to the west?
    I will cheer him with good words.

All the stt. The *ch'ang-ts'oo* is also called 羊桃, 'the goat's peach.' I agree with Williams in identifying it with the *averrhoa carambola*, though Medhurst calls it 'a sort of cherry.' 猗傩 is explained as meaning 'soft and pliant-looking,' 'soft and delicate.' Luh Ke says that 'the leaves of the plant are long and narrow, its flowers of a purplish red, and its branches so weak, that, when they are more than a foot long, they go creeping along on the grass.' 夭,—as 夭夭 in i.VI. 沃沃,—'glossy-like.' The point of the ode is in the 4th line. So grew the plant in beauty and exuberance;—it was better under such a government to be a plant than a man. 无家 and 无室 are synonymous,—'without a family' to care for.

The rhymes are—in st. 1, 枝, 知, cat. 16, t. 1: in 2, 华 *, 家 *, cat. 5, t. 1: in 3, 实, 室, cat. 12, t. 3.

Ode 4. Narrative and allusive. SOME ONE TELLS HIS SORROW FOR THE DECAY OF THE POWER OF CHOW. The difference between Choo's view of this piece and that of the Preface will appear in the interpretation of the phrase 周道.

Stt. 1, 2. 风发, 'a wind rushing forth,'—a violent wind; 风飘,—'a wind whirling about.' 偈 denotes 'the app. of a chariot driven along furiously;' 嘌, 'the app. of one driven irregularly.' 周道,—'the way to Chow,' acc. to Choo; acc. to Maou, 'the way of Chow.' On this latter view, the sorrow which the ode expresses is because of the misgovernment of Kwei, contrary to the good rules of the Chow dynasty. 顾瞻, however, agree better with Choo's view, and the 3d line of st. 3 is decisive in its favour. Maou defines both 怛 and 吊 by 伤, 'to be pained,' 'wounded.'

St. 3. It is certainly a homely subject which the writer employs to introduce the expression of his sympathy with the friends of Chow. 烹, 'to boil or stew;'—to cook. The 釜, was a deep pan or boiler without feet;—see ii. IV. 2; the 鬵 was a utensil of the same kind, larger at the mouth than at the bottom. 溉之, 'clease him,' *i.e.*, cleanse for him. The capital of the western Chow lay west from Kwei; hence the expression 西归. 怀 = 安 'to cheer or comfort.' 音 = 语, 'words.' The writer means, probably, this ode which he had made.

The rhymes are—in st. 1, 发, 偈, 怛 (prop. cat. 14), cat. 15, t. 3: in 2, 飘, 嘌, 吊, cat. 2: in 3, 鬵, 音, cat. 7, t. 1.

CONCLUDING NOTE ON THE BOOK. In these few odes of Kwei we have the picture of a small State, misgoverned and hastening to ruin. Dissoluteness, decay of filial affection, and oppression are sapping its foundations; yet there are men in it, who are painfully conscious of these evils, and see that the decay of Kwei is but a part of the general decay that is at work in the whole kingdom. Of the four odes the third has the greatest merit.

Këang Ping-chang says, 'Kwei became a part of Ch'ing, at the time of king P'ing's removal to the east. When duke Woo extinguished the independent existence of the State, these four odes were carried with king P'ing to the east, and afterwards the Grand Recorder found them in the archives of the kingdom. Thus it was that Confucius was able, in his labours on the poems, to give them a place in the Classic. Ah! Kih (虢) and Kwei were both extinguished by Ch'ing; but while no odes of Kih remain, we have these four odes of Kwei.—Such was the good fortune of this State!'

BOOK XIV. THE ODES OF TS'AOU.

I. *Fow-yëw.*

曹一之十四

蜉蝣

一章

蜉蝣之羽。衣裳楚楚。心之忧矣。于我归处。

二章

蜉蝣之翼。采采衣服。心之忧矣。于我归息。

1　The wings of the ephemera
　　Are robes, bright and splendid.
　　My heart is grieved;—
　　Would they but come and abide with me!

2　The wings of the ephemera
　　Are robes, variously adorned.
　　My heart is grieved;—
　　Would they but come and rest with me!

TITLE OF THE BOOK.— 曹，一之十四, 'The odes of Ts'aou;' Book XIV. of Pt. I.' Ts'aou was a small State, corresponding to the pres. dep. of Ts'aou-chow, Shan-tung, having as its capital T'aou-k'ew,—in the pres. dis. of Ting-t'aou (定陶). Its lords were earls, the first of them, Chin-toh (振铎), having been a younger brother of king Woo. It continued for 646 years, when it was extinguished by the larger Sung.

Ode 1. Metaphorical. AGAINST SOME PARTIES IN THE STATE, OCCUPIED WITH FRIVOLOUS PLEASURES, AND OBLIVIOUS OF IMPORTANT MATTERS. The Preface says the piece was directed against duke Ch'aou (昭公 ; B. C. 660—652), who indulged in a vainglorious extravagance, and gave his confidence to mean and unworthy creatures. Maou tries to interpret it on this view, and makes it allusive, the second line being descriptive of the *dandyism* of Ch'aou and his officers. There is nothing in the words, however, nor in any existing records, to lead us to refer it to duke Ch'aou; and Choo, therefore, gives the argument of it which I have proposed. On this view the piece is metaphorical, and the first two lines belong to the beetle, which is the emblem of the parties intended.

Ll. 1, 2, in all the stt. Williams says that the *fow-yëw* is 'a dung-fly,' and Medhurst calls it 'a sort of *aleochora*, or tumble dung.' The name originally was 浮 游, 'floating wanderer,' and the 水 gave place to 虫, only to make it clear that the character was the name of an insect. No doubt one of the coleoptera is intended,—'narrow and long, the wing-cases yellow and black, produced from dung and the ground, coming out in the morning, and dying in the evening.' Though its wing-cases are so splendid, it is only an ephemera. 羽 and 翼 are

三章

蜉蝣掘阅。麻衣如雪。心之忧矣，于我归说。

3　The ephemera bursts from its hole,
　　With a robe of hemp like snow.
　　My heart is grieved;—
　　Would they but come and lodge with me!

II.　*How-jin.*

候人

一章

彼候人兮。何戈与祋。彼其之子。三百赤芾。

1　Those officers of escort
　　Have their carriers of lances and halberds.
　　But these creatures,
　　With their three hundred red covers for the knees!—

synonymous, being varied for the sake of the rhyme. Choo says he does not understand 掘 阅. 阅 may be taken as= 穴, 'a hole,' and 掘, as= 堀, which, indeed, the Shwoh-wän gives, of the same meaning. The phrase will then indicate the insect making its first appearance out of the ground. 楚 楚 ='fresh and bright-looking.' 采采,—'variegated.' Both these phrases are descriptive of the wing-cases of the creature. L. 2 in st. 3 is descriptive of the wings, under the cases, like snow-white linen.

Ll. 3, 4.　The 4th line is all but unintelligible. It must be taken as optative. If the speaker could only get the parties he is complaining of to go with him, and take his counsels, he would guide them to a better way. But the 于我 is a great difficulty. 于我乎 in xi. X. does not help us here. The critics have various ways of developing the meaning, but none satisfactory. Këang Ping-chang says 君 于 我 谋 归 处 之 道, 'if the ruler would consult with me *(chez moi)* about the way of coming to a permanent security,'—. Le Kwang-te (李光地)says,— 我 心 于 何 忧 乎, 于 我 之 所 归 宿 者 尔, 'About what is my heart grieved? About where I shall turn to for rest.' It is of no use quoting more attempts to throw light on the darkness.

The rhymes are—in st. 1, 羽, 楚, 处, cat. 5, t. 2: in 2, 翼, 服 *, 息 , cat. 1, t. 3: in 3, 阅, 雪, 说 , cat. 15, t. 3.

Ode 2. Allusive and metaphorical. LAMENT OVER THE FAVOUR SHOWN TO WORTHLESS OFFICERS AT THE COURT OF TS'AOU, AND THE DISCOUNTENANCE OF GOOD MEN. The Preface refers this piece to the time of duke Kung (共公 ; B. C. 651—617), and he was chargeable, no doubt, with the error which is here condemned, for we are told in the Tso-chuen, that when duke Wän of Tsin entered Ts'aou in B. C. 631, his condemnation of its ruler was based on the ground of his having about him 300 worthless and useless officers. It has been argued, however, that when duke Wän specified the number of 'three hundred,' he was speaking from this ode, previously in existence. But we may contend, on the other hand, that it had only become current in the previous years of Kung.

St. 1.　候人 was an officer for the reception and convoy of guests or visitors. There were six of them of the 1st degree (上 士), and twelve of a lower (下 士), attached to the court of Chow,—with their attendants. The number at the court of Ts'aou would be smaller. 何 (2d tone)= 揭, 'to carry.' 祋 = 父, as in v. VIII. 1. The second line is to be understood of the attendants of the officers. These all had their use, and from them the writer goes on to point out the useless favourites. L. 3,—as in vi. IV, but is here to be undertood as the expression of contempt. 芾 = 韠 , in xiii. II. 3.

二章
维鹈在梁。不濡其翼。彼其之子。不称其服。

三章
维鹈在梁。不濡其咮。彼其之子。不遂其媾。

四章
荟兮蔚兮。南山朝隮。婉兮娈兮。季女斯饥。

2　The pelican is on the dam,
　　And will not wet his wings!
　　These creatures
　　Are not equal to their dress!

3　The pelican is on the dam,
　　And will not wet his beak!
　　These creatures
　　Do not respond to the favour they enjoy.

4　Extensive and luxuriant is the vegetation,
　　And up the south hill in the morning rise the vapours.
　　Tender is she and lovely,
　　But the young lady is suffering from hunger.

III. *She-këw.*

鸤鸠

一章
鸤鸠在桑。其子七兮。淑人君子。其仪一兮。其仪一

1　The turtle dove is in the mulberry tree,
　　And her young ones are seven.
　　The virtuous man, the princely one,
　　Is uniformly correct in his deportment.

Ying-tah observes that when the two terms are to be distinguished, the former is the name of the article in sacrificial dress, and the latter, as worn on other occasions. Great officers and those of higher rank were entitled to this appendage to their dress. The '300' is not to be pressed. It indicates the multitude of the 'creatures' spoken of.

Stt. 2, 3. The 鹈 is the pelican, called also 鹈鹕, and by other names. It is here represented as sitting on a dam, contriving somehow to get its food, without effort or labour of its own;—resembling the useless officers who had

their salaries and positions, without doing anything for them. 称 (3d tone),—'to weigh;' hence meaning 'to balance,' 'to be equal to.' 媾 is here defined by 厚 and 宠, 'the favour' which the 'creatures' enjoyed. 遂,—'to be according to,' synonymous with 称.

St. 4 is metaphorical:—the first two lines, of the number and forwardness of the 'creatures;' the last two, of the men of worth, kept in obscurity and poverty, or of the poor, weak people, suffering from the misgovernment of the State. These interpretations are forced out of

兮。心如结兮。

二章

鸤鸠在桑。其子在梅。淑人君子。其带伊<u>丝</u>。其带伊

<u>丝</u>。其弁伊骐。

三章

鸤鸠在桑。其子在棘。淑人君子。其仪不忒。其仪不

忒。正是四国。

> He is uniformly correct in his deportment,
> His heart is as if it were tied to what is correct.
>
> 2　The turtle dove is in the mulberry tree,
> 　　And her young ones are in the plum tree.
> 　　The virtuous man, the princely one,
> 　　Has his girdle of silk.
> 　　His girdle is of silk,
> 　　And his cap is of spotted deer-skin.
>
> 3　The turtle dove is in the mulberry tree,
> 　　And her young ones are in the jujube tree.
> 　　The virtuous man, the princely one,
> 　　Has nothing wrong in his deportment.
> 　　He has nothing wrong in his deportment,
> 　　And thus he rectifies the four quarters of the State.

the words; but we must be content with them. 荟蔚 are taken to denote 'the app. of vegetation, luxuriant and abundant.' 阶＝升, 'to ascend,' is taken of vapours or clouds. 婉娈,—as in viii. VII. 3. 季女,—see ii. IV. 3; but it is not necessary to understand here that the lady is married. 斯＝ 'this,' giving emphasis to the antecedents.

The rhymes are—in st. 1, 役, 茷, cat. 15, t. 3: in 2, 翼, 服 *, cat. 1, t. 3: in 3, 昧 *, 媤, cat. 4, t. 2: in 4, 阶, 饥, cat. 15, t. 1.

Ode 3. Allusive. THE PRAISE OF SOME ONE, SOME LORD, PROBABLY, OF TS‘AOU, UNIFORMLY OF VIRTUOUS CONDUCT AND OF EXTENSIVE INFLUENCE. Acc. to the Preface, the praise in this piece is of some early ruler of Ts‘aou, who is celebrated by way of contrast with the very different characters of the writer's time. But we can gather nothing of this from the language of the piece;—nor from history.

Ll. 1, 2, in all the stt. The she-këw is, no doubt, the turtle dove, the same as the këw in ii. I. There is a difficulty, indeed, in the statement that the young ones of the bird amount to 'seven,' as the turtle dove, like all other birds of the same species, has only two young at a time. It is highly characteristic of the critics, that the only one I have met with who touches on this point is Maou K‘e-ling. He observes that we have the 七 simply because it rhymes with 一, and are not to understand the text as if it gave definitely the number of the turtle's young! As if this misstatement in the text were not enough, almost all the critics, follow the old Maou in saying that the dove has a uniform method in feeding her young, giving them their food in the evening in the reverse order of that in which she had supplied them in the morning! And this equality and justice form the ground of the allusion in the piece, they say, the dove being thus the counterpart of the uniformly virtuous man. Something of the same kind is brought out from the 2d and other stanzas, the mother dove *always* appearing in a mulberry tree, while her young continually change their place. All this seems to be mere fancy.

四章

鸤鸠在桑。其子在榛。淑人君子。正是国人。正是国

人。胡不万年。

4   The turtle dove is in the mulberry tree,
    And her young ones are in the hazel tree.
    The virtuous man, the princely one,
    Rectifies the people of the State.
    He rectifies the people of his State:—
    May he continue for ten thousand years!

IV.   *Hëa ts'euen.*

下泉

一章

冽彼下泉。浸彼苞粮。忾我寤叹。念彼周京。

二章

冽彼下泉。浸彼苞萧。忾我寤叹。念彼京周。

1   Cold come the waters down from that spring,
    And overflow the bushy wolf's-tail grass
    Ah me! I awake and sigh,
    Thinking of that capital of Chow.

2   Cold come the waters down from that spring,
    And overflow the bushy southernwood.
    Ah me! I awake and sigh,
    Thinking of that capital of Chow.

Ll. 3—6.   君子 would here seem to be not only one in authority (在 位), but one in the highest authority, whose influence extends to the whole State (正 是 四国). The meaning of 仪, 'deportment,' is well illustrated by referring to Ana. VIII. iv. 3. ── gives the ideas of uniformity, and equality or correctness. 如 结 ,—'as if tied;' *i.e.*, the mind is tied to what is correct, as things are tied together so that they cannot separate. It is a great descent from this, when we come in st. 2 to read of the girdle and cap. 伊,—as in ii. XIII. 3. 骐 弁, *i.q.* 綦 弁, in the Shoo, V. xxii. 21. 忒 = 差忒, 'error.' 四国 = 曹四境, 'all within the four borders of Ts'aou. 胡 不 万年 is a wish for the long life of one so worthy (愿 其 寿 考 之 词).

The rhymes are—in st. 1, 七, 一, 一, 结, cat. 12, t. 3: in 2, 梅*, 丝, 丝, 骐, cat. 1, t. 1: in 3, 棘, 忒, 忒, 国, cat. 1, t. 3: in 4, 榛, 人, 人, 年, cat. 12, t. 1.

Ode 4. Metaphorical-allusive. THE MISERY AND MISGOVERNMENT OF TS'AOU MAKES THE WRITER THINK OF CHOW, AND OF ITS FORMER VIGOUR AND PROSPERITY.

Ll. 1, 2 in stt. 1—3.   冽 (formed from 冫) is descriptive of the coolness of the waters. 下 泉 ,—'descending spring,' *i.e.*, a spring whose waters flow away downwards. Both Maou and Choo seem to take 苞 as—'bushy grass,' difft. from the other productions mentioned; but it is better to follow the analogy of x. VIII., and other places, where we have met with the term as an adjective. 粮 is explained by some as 'blasted ears of grain;' but it is better

三章
冽彼下泉。浸彼苞蓍。忾我寤叹。念彼京师。
四章
芃芃黍苗。阴雨膏之。四国有王。郇伯劳之。

3 Cold come the waters down from that spring,
  And overflow the bushy divining plants.
  Ah me! I awake and sigh,
  Thinking of that capital-city.

4 Beautifully grew the fields of young millet,
  Enriched by fertilizing rains.
  The States had their sovereign,
  And there was the chief of Seun to reward their princes.

taken as a kind of weed or darnel. I have translated it by one of the names which it receives. 萧,—see on vi. VIII. 2. 蓍 is a plant said by the Chinese to be of the same order as 萧,—one of the *artemisiœ*. Its stalks were used for the purpose of divination. In the Japanese plates it is the *achillea*. The cold water overflowing these plants only injured them;—an image of the influence of the government of Ts'aou on the people.

Ll. 3, 4. 忾 is onomatopoetic of a sigh. 周京 appears in st. 2 as 京周 for the rhyme; the same may be said of 京师 in st. 3, though those characters are often associated in the sense of 'a capital-city.'

St. 4. The writer here speaks of the former and prosperous period of the House of Chow, and we must translate in the past tense. 芃芃 ='beautiful-like.' 苗 is not to be taken of other grain, besides the millet (黍苗=黍之苗). The millet is metaphorical of the States of the kingdom. 阴雨,—compare 以阴以雨, iii. X. 1. The phrase denotes abundant and fertilizing rains, rains impregnated with the masculine, generating influences of nature. 膏, 'to anoint.'= to moisten and enrich. 四国=四方之国, 'the States in the four quarters of the kingdom.'

Seun was a small State,—in the pres. district of Lin-tsin (临晋), dep. P'oo-chow (蒲州), Shan-se. It was first conferred on a son of king Wăn, one of whose descendants was the chief mentioned in the text,—so called, as presiding with viceregal authority over a district embracing many States. We do not know when he lived.

The rhymes are—in st. 1, 泉, 叹, cat. 14; 粮, 京 *, cat. 10: in 2, 泉, 叹; 萧 *, 周, cat. 3, t. 1: in 3, 泉, 叹; 蓍, 师, cat. 15, t. 1: in 4, 苗, 膏, 劳, cat. 2.

CONCLUDING NOTE UPON THE BOOK. To none of the odes of Ts'aou does there belong any great merit. The second, taken in connection with the statement in the Tso-chuen referred to in the notes on it, shows one of the principal reasons of the decay and ruin of the State,—the multiplication of useless and unprincipled officers. The last ode is strikingly analogous to the last in the preceding Book. In both, the writers turn from the misery before their eyes, and can only think hopelessly of an earlier time of vigour and prosperity.

BOOK XV. THE ODES OF PIN.

I. *Ts'ih yueh.*

豳一之十五

七月

一章

七月流火。九月授衣。一之日觱发。二之日栗烈。无
衣无褐。何以卒岁。三之日于耜。四之日举趾。同我
妇子。馌彼南亩。田畯至喜。

1　In the seventh month, the Fire Star passes the meridian;
In the 9th month, clothes are given out.
In the days of [our] first month, the wind blows cold;
In the days of [our] second, the air is cold;—
Without the clothes and garments of hair,
How could we get to the end of the year?
In the days of [our] third month, they take their ploughs in hand;
In the days of [our] fourth, they take their way to the fields.
Along with my wife and children,
I carry food to them in those south-lying acres.
The surveyor of the fields comes, and is glad.

THE TITLE OF THE BOOK.—豳，一之十五，'The odes of Pin; Book XV. of Part I.' Of Pin I have spoken sufficiently in the note on the title of Book I. There the chiefs of the House of Chow dwelt for nearly five centuries, from B. C. 1796—1325. The first piece in this Book is accepted as a description by the famous duke of Chow of the ways of the first settlers in Pin, under Kung-lëw, and hence the name of Pin is given to all the odes in the Book. No other of them, however, is descriptive of so high an antiquity. They were made by the duke of Chow about matters in his own day, or they were made by others about him, and, it would be difficult to say for what reason, were arranged together under this common name of Pin. The character 豳 is now 邠, the form having been changed in the period K'ae-yuen (开元; A. C. 713-741) of the T'ang dynasty. From a narrative in the Tso-chuen, under B. C. 543, it appears that at that time the odes of Pin followed those of Ts'e. That its place now is at the end of the 'Lessons from the States' is attributed to the arrangement of Confucius, 'showing,' says Yen Ts'an, 'the deep plan of the sage.' What that deep plan was I have not been able to ascertain.

Ode 1. Narrative. LIFE IN PIN IN THE OLDEN TIME ; THE PROVIDENT ARRANGEMENTS THERE TO SECURE THE CONSTANT SUPPLY OF FOOD AND RAIMENT,—WHATEVER WAS NECESSARY FOR THE SUPPORT AND COMFORT OF THE PEOPLE. I do not wish to deny here this universally accepted account of the ode; but it is not without its difficulties. Pin is not once mentioned in it, nor Kung-lëw. The note of time with which the first three stanzas commence is not a little perplexing:—'In the seventh month, the Fire star, or the Heart of Scorpio (see on the Shoo, I. 5), passes on,' i.e., passes to the westward of the meridian at night-fall. Mr. Chalmers has observed that this could not have been the case if the year of Chow commenced, as it is said to have done, with our December ; but the critics meet this difficulty by saying that in this ode, and indeed throughout the She, the specification of the months is according to the calendar of the Hëa dyn., and not that of Chow. They add, moreover, that it was proper in this piece, occupied with the affairs of Pin during the Hëa dynasty, to speak of its months. This is granted ; but it only leads us to a greater difficulty. Scorpio did pass to the westward in August, or the 7th month of the Hëa dynasty, in the time of the duke of Chow,—say about B. C. 1114 ; but it did not do so in the time of Kung-lëw, or B. C. 1,796. Lew Kin (刘瑾) observes on this:—'In the Canon of Yaou it is said, "The day is at its longest, and the star is Ho. You may thus exactly determine midsummer." In the time of Yaou, the sun was, at midsummer, in Cancer-Leo, and the Ho star culminated at dusk. More than 1,240 years after came the regency of the duke of Chow during the minority of king Ching ; and the stars of the Zodiac must have gone back during that time, through the retrocession of the equinoxes, 16 or 17 degrees. It would not be till the sixth month, and after, therefore, that the sun would be in the same place, and the Ho star pass away to the westward at nightfall. But in this poem which relates the customs of Pin in the times of Hëa and Shang, it is said that the star passed in the 7th month, the duke of Chow mentioning the phænomenon, as he himself saw it.' We are thus brought to one of two conclusions :—that the piece does not describe life in Pin about 700 years before the days of Chow's time ; or that he supposed the place of the sun in the heavens in the time of Kung-lëw to have been the same as it was in his own days. I think we must adopt the latter conclusion, nor need we be stumbled by the lack of astronomical science in the great statesman. I adhere to the ordinary view of the ode, mainly because of the 2d line in the stanzas already referred to, that clothes were given out in the 9th month, in anticipation of the approaching winter. This must evidently be the 9th month of Hëa, and not of Chow. Were the author telling of what was done in his time, soon after the commencement of the Chow dyn., we cannot conceive of

his thus expressing himself. Why then should we not translate the piece in the past tense, as being a record of the past ? I was for some time inclined to do so. The 9th and 10th lines of st. 1 determined me otherwise. The speaker there must be an old farmer or yeoman of Pin, and the whole ode must be conceived of as coming from him.

St. 1. 流 'flows down,' is explained by 下, 'descends,' i.e., goes on towards the horizon. The giver out of the clothes was the head of each family, distributing their common store according to the necessities of the household (授者家长，以与家人也). The expressions, 一之日，二之日, &c., 'the days of the first, of the second, &c., are taken on all hands as meaning the days of the 1st month, of the second month, &c., according to the calendar of Chow. I accept the conclusion, without attempting to explain the nomenclature, and have indicated it by the addition of 'our' in the translation. The use of the two styles in the same piece, and even in the same stanza, is certainly perplexing. 觱发 are explained together, as ＝风寒, 'winds cold,' and 栗烈 as ＝气寒, 'the air cold.' 觱 was the name of a horn blown by the Këangs to frighten the horses of the Chinese, and is here used as giving the sound of the wind as it began to blow in December. 烈 should, probably, be 洌, as in the last ode of the prec. Book. 褐＝毛布, 'cloth of hair,' of which the clothes of the inferior members of the household were made. But a supply of clothes was necessary for all, in order to get through the rigour of the second month of Chow, and so conclude the year of Hëa. L. 7 brings us to the 3rd month of Chow, and the 1st of Hëa, when the approach of spring required preparations to be made for the agricultural labours of the year. 耜, the part of the plough which enters the ground, is here used for the plough, and agricultural implements in general; I take 于 as a particle, as in i. II., et al. Choo explains it here by 往 'to go to;' but even then we should have to supply another verb to indicate that 'they went to prepare their ploughs.' 举趾, 'lifted up their toes,'—the meaning is as in the translation. In l. 9, the narrator appears in his own person, an aged yeoman, who has remained in the house, with his wife (or 妇 may mean the married women on the farm generally) and young children, while the able-bodied members of the household have all gone to work in the fields. 馌＝饷田, 'to carry food to those in the fields.' 畯田 was an officer who superintended the farms over a district of considerable extent. It is a pleasant picture of agricultural life which these last five lines give us.

二章

七月流火。九月授衣。春日载阳。有鸣仓庚。女执懿

筐。遵彼微行。爰求柔桑。春日迟迟。采蘩祁祁。女

心伤悲。殆及公子同归。

三章

七月流火。八月萑苇。蚕月条桑。取彼斧斨。以伐远

2　In the seventh month, the Fire Star passes the meridian;
In the ninth month, clothes are given out.
With the spring days the warmth begins,
And the oriole utters its song.
The young women take their deep baskets,
And go along the small paths,
Looking for the tender [leaves of the] mulberry trees.
As the spring days lengthen out,
They gather in crowds the white southernwood.
That young lady's heart is wounded with sadness,
For she will [soon] be going with one of our princes as his wife.

3　In the seventh month the Fire Star passes the meridian;
In the eighth month are the sedges and reeds.
In the silkworm month they strip the mulberry branches of
their leaves,

St. 2. *Care of the silkworm.* L. 3. 载 = 始, 'to begin.' 阳 = 温和, 'genial.' L. 4. The *ts'ang-kăng* is, probably, the same as the 'yellow bird' of i. II.;—a kind of oriole. It begins its song contemporaneously with the hatching of the eggs of the silkworm. L. 5. I translate 女 by 'young women,' in consequence of its recurrence in l. 10. L. 6. 'The small paths' are those about the homesteads, around which the mulberry trees were planted;—see Men. I. Pt. i. VII. 24. L. 7. 爰,—as in iii. VI. 3, *et al.* L. 8. Maou explains 迟 迟 by 舒 缓, 'slow and easy.' The meaning is what I have given. L. 9. 蘩,—as in ii. II. Choo says that the leaves of this were used to feed the young worms which were later in being hatched. More correctly, Seu Kwang-k'e (徐 光 启) says that the eggs are washed with a decoction from the leaves to assist their hatching. 祁 祁 = 众 多, 'all;' meaning that all the ladies, of noble families as well as of others, engaged in this

work. The last two lines are variously explained. I have adopted the view of Choo which is certainly the most poetical, and I believe is correct also. He says, 'At that time the princes of the State still married ladies of it; and those of noble families, who might be engaged to be married to them, took their share of the labour of feeding the silkworms. Hence at this time, those of them who were so engaged, thinking of the time when they would be going home with their husbands and leave their parents, felt sad!' Maou explains l. 10 of sorrow from the fatigue of the labour, and l. 11 of returning home along with the princes who came to see the labour, as the surveyor of the fields had done in st. 1. Others take 公 子 of the daughters of the ruling House. 殆 = 将 然 之 词, 'a word indicating what will be.'
St. 3. *Further labour with the silkworms, and the weaving of silk.* L. 2. Choo observes that 萑 苇 = 兼 葭 in xi. IV. These things are mentioned here, it is said, simply as a note of time. The leaves were made into baskets for collecting the mulberry leaves, and also into the frames on which the silkworms were placed.

扬。猗彼女桑。七月鸣鵙，八月载绩。载玄载黄。我

朱孔阳。为公子裳。

四章

四月秀葽。五月鸣蜩。八月其获。十月陨萚。一之日

于貉。取彼狐狸。为公子裘。二之日其同。载缵武

And take their axes and hatchets,
To lop off those that are distant and high;
Only stripping the young trees of their leaves.
In the seventh month, the shrike is heard;
In the eighth month, they begin their spinning;—
They make dark fabrics and yellow.
Our red manufacture is very brilliant,
It is for the lower robes of our young princes.

4　In the fourth month, the Small grass is in seed.
In the fifth, the cicada gives out its note.
In the eighth, they reap.
In the tenth, the leaves fall.
In the days of [our] first month, they go after badgers,
And take foxes and wild cats,
To make furs for our young princes.
In the days of [our] second month, they have a general hunt,

L. 3. No month is specified, as the eggs might be hatched, now in one month, now in another, according to the heat of the season. 条桑,— 'branch the mulberry trees,' i. e., bring down the branches to the ground, and then strip them of their leaves.
L. 4. The foo and the ts‘ëang were both axes, differing in the shape of the hole which received the handle;—in the former it was oval, in the latter, square. L. 6. 猗 should be 掎, which the Shwoh-wăn defines as 'to draw on one side.' It means here, says Choo, 'to take the leaves and preserve the branches.' 女桑 = 小桑, 'small mulberry trees.' The Japanese plates, however, give here the female mulberry tree. L. 7. The keih is the shrike or butcher bird, commonly called 伯劳. As the oriole gave notice of the time to take the silkworms in hand, so

the note of the shrike was the signal to set about spinning. L. 8. 绩 is the term appropriate to the twisting of hemp. L. 9 describes the dyeing operations on both the woven silk and the cloth. 玄 denotes a black colour with a flush of red in it. L. 10. 阳 = 明, 'bright.'

St. 5. Hunting;—to supplement the provision of clothes. L. 1. Both Maou and Choo simply say of 葽 that it is 'the name of a grass.' Others describe it as like hemp, with flowers of a yellowish red, and a sharp-pointed leaf. Among other names given to it is that of 细草, 'the small grass.' In the Japanese plates, it is the polygala Japonica. 秀 is said to be used of 'a plant that seeds without having put forth flowers.' L. 2. 蜩 is the cicada or broad locust. L. 3. The reaping here must be of the earlier crops.

功。言私其豵。献豜于公。

五章

五月斯螽动股。六月莎鸡振羽。七月在野。八月在

宇。九月在户。十月蟋蟀。入我床下。穹窒熏鼠。塞

向墐户。嗟我妇子。曰为改岁。入此室处。

And proceed to keep up the exercises of war.
The boars of one year are for themselves;
Those of three years are for our prince.

5 　In the fifth month, the locust moves its legs;
　In the sixth month, the spinner sounds its wings.
　In the seventh month, in the fields;
　In the eighth month, under the eaves;
　In the ninth month, about the doors;
　In the tenth month, the cricket
　Enters under our beds.
　Chinks are filled up, and rats are smoked out;
　The windows that face [the north] are stopped up;
　And the doors are plastered.
　'Ah! our wives and children,
　'Changing the year requires this;
　Enter here and dwell.'

L. 4. 陨 — 落, 'to fall.' 萚,—as in vii. XII.
L. 5. 于,—as in st. 1, l. 7. 貉 —as in Ana.
IX. xxvi. It appears to be the same with the
hwan of ix. VI. 1. L. 6. We often take 狐狸
together, as signifying a fox. The characters
denote different animals, however. The 狸 is
a sort of wild-cat. Yen Ts'an supposes that the
badgers' skins were for the hunters themselves,
and only the others for the princes. L. 8. 其
同 indicates a great hunting, when the chiefs
all went forth, and which was intended as a
preparation for the business of war. L. 9.
载 is the particle. 缵,—'to continue,' or 'to
keep up.'

L. 10. 豵,—as in ii. XIV. 2. L. 11. 豜
denotes a boar three years old, *i. e.*, full-grown.

Down to this point the ode tells of the arrangements in Pin to provide a sufficiency of raiment
against the cold.

St. 5. *Further provision made by the people
against the cold of winter.* Choo supposes that
sze-chung, so-ke, and *suh-suh* are only different
names for the same insect,—the cricket. But I
do not see why they should be thus identified.
Sze-chung is the same as *chung-sze* in i. V. The
so-ke appears to be, likewise, a kind of locust,
called 纺绩娘, 'the spinner,' from the
sound which it makes with its wings. Ll. 3—5
may be assigned to the cricket. 宇,—'the sides
of a roof,' 'the eaves.' L. 8. Maou explains
穹 by 穷, 'entirely,' 'thoroughly.' I prefer
Choo's account of the term, as meaning 'chinks.'
窒 = 塞, 'to shut, or stuff, up.' L. 9. 向 is
to be understood of windows, or openings in the

六章
六月食郁及薁。七月亨葵及菽。八月剥枣。十月获

稻。为此春酒。以介眉寿。七月食瓜。八月断壶。九

月叔苴。采荼薪樗。食我农夫。

七章
九月筑场圃。十月纳禾稼。黍稷重穋。禾麻菽麦。嗟

6 In the sixth month they eat the sparrow-plums and grapes;
In the seventh, they cook the *k'wei* and pulse;
In the eighth, they knock down the dates;
In the tenth, they reap the rice,
And make the spirits for the spring,
For the benefit of the bushy eyebrows.
In the seventh month, they eat the melons;
In the eighth, they cut down the bottle-gourds;
In the ninth, they gather the hemp-seed;
They gather the sowthistle and make firewood of the Fetid tree;
To feed our husbandmen.

7 In the ninth month, they prepare the vegetable gardens for
their stacks,
And in the tenth they convey the sheaves to them;

wall, looking towards the north. 堇 = 涂, 'to plaster.' The doors of the houses of the people were made of wicker-work. In l. 10, the 曰 is not the verb 'to say,' but the particle' 为 is that now in the 3d tone,—'because of.' The measures just detailed were all taken, because of the extreme cold which was at hand. Stress is not to be laid on the use of the terms 改岁 , as if there were an indication in the employment of them after the 10th month, that the people did not use among themselves the calendar of Hëa.

St. 6. *Various articles of food; the richer for the old, and the others for the husbandmen.* L. 1. The 郁 is a kind of plum. The tree grows to the height of 5 or 6 cubits, and produces a large red fruit. One of its names is 雀李, which I have adopted. The 薁 is called also 蘡薁; and must be a sort of vine. Williams calls it 'a wild grape, or a plant like it.' 'The fruit,' it is said, 'is like a grape, small and round, with a sour taste, and purplish.' L. 2. Choo simply says that 葵 is the name of a vegetable. One

name of it is *chung kwei*, which Medhurst says is alsine, or pimpernel; but the name *k'wei*, with various adjunets, is given to a multitude of plants. L. 3. 剥 = 击, 'to strike,' 'knock down.' Ll. 4—6. The spirits distilled from the rice cut down in the 10th month would be ready for use in the spring. But in those days the use of spirits was restricted to the aged, who need their exhilaration. L. 6 is literally, 'to help the longevity of the eyebrows;' Maou explains 眉寿 by 豪眉, 'bristly eyebrows.' L. 7. 瓜 is the general name for gourds melons, &c. L. 8. 壶,—*i.q.* 瓠. L. 9. 叔 = 拾, 'to gather.' 苴 = 麻子, 'hemp-seed.' L. 10. 荼,—as in iii. X. 2. The 樗 is like the varnish tree 'with Fetid leaves. It is good for nothing but to be used as fuel. It is commonly called 'the fetid tree (臭树).' Another name is 'imps' eyes (鬼目).'

St. 7. *Harvesting; and repairs of houses, to be ready for the work of the spring.* L. 1. 筑场圃 = 筑场于圃, 'They form the areas

我农夫。我稼既同。上入执宫功。昼尔于茅。宵尔索

绹。亟其乘屋。其始播百谷。

八章

二之日凿冰冲冲。三之日纳于凌阴。四之日其蚤。献

羔祭韭。九月肃霜。十月涤场。朋酒斯飨。曰杀羔

The millets, both the early sown and the late,
With other grain, the hemp, the pulse, and the wheat.
'O my husbandmen,
Our harvest is all collected.
Let us go to the town, and be at work on our houses.
In the day time collect the grass,
And at night twist it into ropes;
Then get up quickly on our roofs:—
We shall have to recommence our sowing.'

8 In the days of [our] second month, they hew out the ice with
harmonious blows;
And in those of [our] third month, they convey it to the ice-
houses,
[Which they open] in those of the fourth, early in the morning,
Having offered in sacrifice a lamb with scallions.
In the ninth month, it is cold, with frost;

for stacks in the kitchen gardens.' Williams translates the words incorrectly, 'to form a kitchen garden.' Ground was valuable. In the early part of the year, this space was cultivated for the growth of vegetables. When the harvest of the fields was ready, they beat the same space into a hard area, to place in it the produce of the fields. L. 2. Choo says that 禾 denotes the grain and the stalk together; and 稼 the same as being in the fields. L. 3. 重 denotes what is first sown, and ripens last; 穋, the opposite of this. L. 4. 禾 is a general name for rice and all the grains mentioned. L. 6. 同 = 聚, 'to be collected. L. 7. 宫 denotes the houses of the people in their towns or villages where they lived in the end of autumn and in winter, when their labours in the field were completed. These were to them, compared with their huts in the fields, as the capital

to the other towns in a State; hence the use of 上, 'to go up to.' Some, however, take 宫 of the palace and other public buildings of the State; but this is very unnatural. L. 8. 于, —as in st. 1. 茅,—as in ii. XII. L. 9. 索= 绞, 'to twist.' 绹=索, 'ropes.' L. 10. 乘 = 升, 'to get upon.'

St. 8. *Preparation of ice against the summer heat; the harvest feast.* L. 1. The ice was dug out of deep recesses in the hills. 冲 冲 = 和, 'harmoniously,' or 'with harmonious blows.' L. 2. 凌阴 = 冰室, 'an ice-house,' Ll.3,4, This sacrifice was in connection with the opening of the ice houses, and henceforward ice could be taken from them as it was required. It was offered to 'the Ruler of the cold (司寒).'

羊。跻彼公堂。称彼兕觥。万寿无疆。

In the tenth month, they sweep clean their stack-sites.
The two bottles of spirits are enjoyed,
And they say, 'Let us kill our lambs and sheep,
And go to the hall of our prince,
There raise the cup of rhinoceros horn,
And wish him long life,—that he may live for ever.'

II.   Ch'e-hëaou.

鸱鸮
一章
鸱鸮鸱鸮。既取我子。无毁我室。恩斯勤斯。鬻子之

闵斯。

1   O owl, O owl,
You have taken my young ones;—
Do not [also] destroy my nest.
With love and with toil
I nourished them.—I am to be pitied.

The collecting and depositing of ice, and the solemn opening of the ice-house, as here described, was appropriate, I suppose, only to great Families; but there would be something analogous to it in the customs of the people also.

The remaining lines belong to the customs of the people, and show the sympathy there was between them and their rulers. L. 6. This cleansing of the farm-yards was after the harvest had all been brought into them. L. 7. 朋, —'two bottles of spirits' were so denominated. L. 8. The lambs and sheep would be an offering, I suppose, to the ruler. L. 9. 跻＝升, 'to ascend to.' L. 10. 称＝举, 'to raise up.' The last lines give the words in which they would drink their ruler's health.

[While I have accepted the ordinary view of this ode, as descriptive of the ways of Pin in the olden time, and explained it accordingly, I must state my own disbelief that the tribe in Pin had attained to anything like the civilization here described, in the time of Kung-lew, or for centuries after.]

The rhymes are—in st. 1, 火*, 衣, cat. 15, t. 2 (but 衣 is more commonly t. 1); 发, 烈, 褐, 岁, cat. 15, t. 3; 耜, 趾, 子, 亩*, 喜, cat. 1, t. 2: in 2. 火*, 衣, 阳, 庚*, 筐, 行*,

桑, cat. 10; 迟, 祁, 悲, 归, cat 15, t. 1: in 3, 火*, 苇, cat. 15, t. 2; 桑, 斯, 扬, 桑, 黄, 阳, 裳, cat. 10; 鹐, 绩, cat. 16, t. 3: in 4, 萋, 蜩, cat. 2, but 蜩, prop. belongs to cat. 3, acc. to the analogy of 周; 获, 蒦, 貉, cat. 5, t. 3; 狸, 裘*, cat. 1, t. 1; 同, 功, 豵, 公, cat. 9: in 5, 股, 羽, 野, 宇, 户, 卜*, 鼠, 户, 处, cat. 5, t. 2: in 6, 薁, 菽, cat. 3, t. 3; 枣*, 稻*, 酒, 寿, cat. 3, t. 2; 瓜, 壶, 苴, 樗, 夫, cat. 5, t. 1: in 7, 圃, 稼*, cat. 5, t. 2; 穋 (prop. cat. 3), 麦 *, cat. 1, t. 3; 同, 功, cat. 9; 茅*, 绹*, cat. 3, t. 1; 屋, 谷, cat. 3, t. 3: in 8, 冲, 阴 (prop. cat. 7), cat. 9; 蚤 *, 韭 *, cat. 3, t. 2; 霜, 场, 飨, 羊, 堂, 觥 *, 疆, cat. 10.

Ode 2. Metaphorical. THE DUKE OF CHOW, IN THE CHARACTER OF A BIRD, WHOSE YOUNG ONES HAVE BEEN DESTROYED BY AN OWL, VINDICATES THE DECISIVE COURSE HE HAD TAKEN WITH REBELLION. We have an account of the composition of this piece in the Shoo, V. vi. 15.

二章

迫天之未阴雨。彻彼桑土。绸缪牖户。今女下民。或

敢侮予。

三章

予手拮据。予所捋荼。予所蓄租。予口卒瘏。曰予未

有室家。

2   Before the sky was dark with rain,
    I gathered the roots of the mulberry tree,
    And bound round and round my window and door.
    Now ye people below,
    Dare any of you despise my house?

3   With my claws I tore and held.
    Through the rushes which I gathered,
    And all the materials I collected,
    My mouth was all sore;—
    I said to myself, 'I have not yet got my house complete.'

Two of his brothers, who had been associated with the son of the dethroned king of Shang in the charge of the territory which had been left to him by king Woo, joined him in rebellion, having first spread a rumour impeaching the fidelity of the duke to his nephew, the young king Ching. He took the field against them, put to death Woo-kăng and one of his own brothers, dealing also with the other according to the measure of his guilt. It is supposed that some suspicions of him still remained in the mind of the king, and he therefore made this ode to show how he had loved his brothers, notwithstanding he had punished them, and that his conduct was in consequence of his solicitude for the consolidation of the dynasty of his family.

St. 1. *Ch'e-heaou*,—see on xii. VI. 2. It is generally supposed that by the owl Woo-kăng was intended. I should refer it rather to rebellion generally. The 子, 'young ones' is referred to the duke's brothers. 'My house,' the bird's nest, denotes the infant dynasty of Chow, the fortunes of his family, and involving the welfare of king Ching himself. The last two lines are difficult and perplexing, though Choo's view of them, which I have followed, is preferable to any other. The 斯, as pointed out by Wang Yin-che, is merely a final particle. 恩斯, 勤斯, both qualify 鬻子,—as in the translation. Of the 之 I can make nothing, and can only regard it as a meaningless particle,

introduced for the sake of euphony. 閔斯 tells how the duke was to be pitied in the circumstances. This exegesis is harsh; but, as I said, it is the best which any critic has devised.

St. 2 indicates how the duke of Chow had laid the foundations of their dynasty. 迨 = 及, 'while.' Followed by 未, the two characters = our 'before.' 阴雨,—as in xiv. IV. 4. 彻 = 取, 'to take away,' 'to gather.' 土 is here = 根, 'roots.' Han Ying gives here 杜 for 土; and hence the meaning assigned to the term. 绸缪,—as in x. V. L. 4 is interrogative, and 或 which gives to it that force may further be translated by 'any.' See Confucius' eulogium of this stanza in Mencius, II. Pt. i. IV. 3.

St. 3 is to the same effect as the preceding. Choo, after the Shwoh-wăn and Han Ying, says that 拮据 denotes 'the app. of hands and mouth working together.' But in that case they would not appear as a predicate of 手 alone. They describe the intense action of the bird's legs and claws in gathering the materials of its nest. 捋 = 取, 'to take.' 荼 is here the same as that in vii. XIX. 2. 蓄,—'to accumulate.' 租, —'to collect.' 卒 = 尽, 'all,' 'entirely.'

四章

予羽谯谯。予尾翛翛。予室翘翘。风雨所漂摇。予维

音哓哓。

4   My wings are all-injured ;
     My tail is all-broken ;
     My house is in a perilous condition ;
     It is tossed about in the wind and rain:—
     I can but cry out with this note of alarm.

III.   *Tung shan.*

东山

一章

我徂东山。慆慆不归。我来自东。零雨其濛。我东曰

归。我心西悲。制彼裳衣。勿士行枚。蜎蜎者蠋。烝

1   We went to the hills of the east,
     And long were we there without returning,
     When we came from the east,
     Down came the rain drizzlingly.
     When we were in the east, and it was said we should return,
     Our hearts were in the west and sad;
     But there were they preparing our clothes for us,

瘏,—as in i. III. 4. 曰 may be taken as I have done. The 5th line gives the reason of all the laborious toil in the preceding ones.

St. 4 gives the reason of the vehement feeling in the ode. 谯谯 describes the appearance of the wings, frayed and injured. Maou and Choo explain it by 杀, 'to clip,' 'to pare.' 翛 翛 = 敝, 'broken,' 'worn' (Medhurst has strangely erred in his account of this character). 翘 翘 = 危, 'perilous.' 漂摇 = 动, 'to move,' 'to shake.' 哓哓 is intended to indicate a note or cry of alarm.

The rhymes are—in st. 1, 子 (prop. cat. 1), 室, cat. 12, t. 3; 斯, 斯, cat. 16, t. 1: in 2, 雨, 土, 户, 予, cat. 5, t 2: in 3, 据, 茶, 租, 瘏, 家 ₊, cat. 5, t. 1: in 4, 谯 (prop. cat. 3), 翛, 翘, 摇, 哓, cat. 2.

Ode 3. Narrative. THE DUKE OF CHOW TELLS OF THE TOILS OF HIS SOLDIERS IN THE EXPEDITION TO THE EAST AND ON THEIR RETURN, OF THEIR APPREHENSIONS, AND THEIR JOY AT THE LAST. The piece nowhere says that it was made by the duke of Chow; but I agree with Choo and the critics generally, who assign to him the composition of it as a sort of compliment to his men.

Ll. 1—4, in all the stt. The expedition here referred to was that mentioned in the notes on the last ode,—undertaken by the duke of Chow against the son of the last king of Shang, and his own rebellious brothers. The seat of the rebellion was mainly in the north-eastern parts of the present Ho-nan, lying of course east from the capital of Chow: hence the expedition is spoken of as 'towards the hills of the east.' 徂,—as in v. IV. 4. 滔滔,—'for a long time.' 零 = 落, 'to fall.' The Shwoh-wăn defines 濛 by 微雨, 'small rain;' 其濛 = 'drizzlingly.'

在桑野。敦彼独宿。亦在车下。

二章

我徂东山。慆慆不归。我来自东。零雨其濛。果臝之

实。亦施于宇。伊威在室。蠨蛸在户。町畽鹿场。熠

燿宵行。亦可畏也。伊可怀也。

As to serve no more in the ranks with the gags.
Creeping about were the caterpillars,
All over the mulberry grounds;
And quietly and solitarily did we pass the night,
Under our carriages.

2   We went to the hills of the east,
And long were we there without returning.
When we came back from the east,
Down came the rain drizzlingly.
The fruit of the heavenly gourd
Would be hanging about our eaves;
The sowbug would be in our chambers;
The spiders' webs would be in our doors;
Our paddocks would be deer-fields;

St. 1. Ll. 5—12. I take the 曰 in l.5 of what was said about the soldiers—of the orders for their return to the west. Ll.7—12 are descriptive of the preparations being made by the wives and families of the soldiers to receive them on their return, and of their thoughts about them during their march. For this I am indebted to Këang Ping-chang (此 制 裳 衣 是 室 家 初 闻 捷 音，喜 而 预 待), and it is much preferable to the usual construction which assigns them to the soldiers themselves. All critics take 裳 衣 of the unmilitary, ordinary dress; why should the soldiers set about making this for themselves, when they were commencing their march? Choo says he does not understand l.8; but he adopts the view of it given by Ch'ing, that 士 = 事，'to do service;' 行 = 行阵，'ranks;' and 枚 = 'gags.' 勿 is appropriate as the thought of their no more doing such service, in the minds of their families. 蜎 蜎 = 动貌，'the app. of creeping.' 蠋 is the name of a cater-

pillar like the silkworm, 'as large as a finger,' found on the mulberry trees. 烝 is to be taken as simply an initial particle; as is 亦 in l. 12. 敦 (tuy) is descriptive of the soldiers as 'lodging alone,' and 独, of their 'solitariness,' away from their families. The sight of the caterpillars on the mulberry trees made their wives think of them thus under their carriages.

St. 2, 5—12. These lines describe the thoughts of the men on their journey home,—the foolish fancies which crowded into their minds. Medhurst calls the kwo-lo the papaya; but this is a creeper, not a tree. Another name for it is 括 楼   It is also called 天瓜,—as in the translation. The leaves come out, two and two, opposite to each other. A flour, beautifully white, is made from the root, and much used in medicine. The plant grows wild, and here the men see it encroaching on their houses. In the Japanese plates it is the musk-melon. 施,—as in i. II. 亦 is the initial particle. 伊 威 (or with 虫 at the side of the characters) is the large sow-bug, or oniscus.

三章
我徂东山。慆慆不归。我来自东。零雨其濛。鹳鸣于

垤。妇叹于室。洒扫穹窒。我征聿至。有敦瓜苦。烝

在栗薪。自我不见。于今三年。

四章
我徂东山。慆慆不归。我来自东。零雨其濛。仓庚于

The fitful light of the glow-worms would be all about.
These thoughts made us apprehensive,
And they occupied our breasts.

3　We went to the hills of the east,
And long were we there without returning.
On our way back from the east,
Down came the rain drizzlingly.
The cranes were crying on the ant-hills;
Our wives were sighing in their rooms;
They had sprinkled and swept, and stuffed up all the crevices.
Suddenly we arrived from the expedition,
And there were the bitter gourds hanging
From the branches of the chestnut trees.
Since we had seen such a sight,
Three years were now elapsed.

4　We went to the hills of the east,
And long were we there without returning.

The *seaou-shaou* is a small spider. Maou wrongly explains *t'ing-t'un* by 鹿迹, 'deers' foot-prints.' The phrase means the vacant ground about the peasants' hamlets. The men fancy that through their absence the deer must have encroached upon it. Maou takes 熠燿 as the name of the fire-fly (萤火); but the error was pointed out by Ying-tah. These two characters denote 'the appearance of a bright but fitful light.' The name of the insect is 宵行, 'a glow-worm.' The 11th line is to be construed interrogatively, so that it is really affirmative. 伊＝惟, 'only,' or 'but.'

St. 3 describes the experiences and feelings of the men immediately on their return, so different from the apprehensions they had felt. Ll. 5

—12. 鹳 is the white crane. 垤 is an anthill. When it is about to rain, the ants show themselves. The crane has in the meantime taken its place on their hill or mound, screaming with joy in anticipation of its feast. This 5th line serves to introduce the 6th and 7th. 穹窒, —see on I. 5. 聿＝忽, 'suddenly.'—'we, who had been on the expedition, suddenly arrive.' 瓜苦＝苦瓜;—the characters are reversed for the sake of the rhyme. 敦,—as in st. 1, 'the app. of the gourds, hanging one by one, on the trees.' 烝,—also as in st. 1. 薪, —as in iii. VII. 2.

St. 4, ll. 5—12. These lines should be translated in the pres. tense. The men are now at home, and in their own joy at reunion with their

飞。熠燿其羽。之子于归。皇驳其马。亲结其缡。九
十其仪。其新孔嘉。其旧如之何。

On our way back from the east,
Down came the rain drizzlingly.
The oriole is flying about,
Now here, now there, are its wings.
Those young ladies are going to be married,
With their bay and red horses, flecked with white.
Their mothers have tied their sashes ;
Complete are their equipments.
The new matches are admirable ;—
How can the reunions of the old be expressed?

IV. *P'o foo.*

破斧
一章
既破我斧。又缺我斨。周公东征。四国是皇。哀我人

1   We broke our axes,
     And we splintered our hatchets ;
     But the object of the duke of Chow, in marching to the east,
     Was to put the four States to rights.

families, sympathize with all of a joyful nature around them. 仓庚 ,—as in I. 2. 于 is the particle. 熠燿 ,—as in st. 2. L. 7 may be construed in the plural. 皇 ='yellow, with white spots;' 驳 ='red, with white spots.' 亲 here =母, 'mother.' Williams' account of 缡 is—'an ornamental girdle put on a bride by her mother.' 仪 denotes here the equipments, all the things sent with the brides.   They are said to be 九十 , 'nine or ten,' to indicate how numerous they were.   Great as was the joy of the new couples, it was not equal to that of the husbands and wives, now reunited after so long a separation.

The rhymes are—in all the stt., 东 , 濛 , cat. 9: in st. 1, 归 , 归 , 悲 , 衣 , 枚 , cat. 15, t. 1; 蜩 , 宿 , cat. 3, t. 3; 野 *, 下 *, cat. 5, t. 2 : in 2, 宇 , 户 , *ib.*; 实 , 室 , cat. 12, t. 3; 场 , 行 *, cat. 10; 畏 , 怀 , cat. 15, t. 1: in 3, 垤 , 室 , 窒 , 至 *, cat. 12, t. 3; 薪 , 年 , cat. 12, t. 1: in 4, 飞 , 归 , cat. 15, t. 1 羽 , 马 *, cat. 5, t. 2; 缡 *, 仪 *, 嘉 , 何 , cat. 17.

Ode 4. Narrative. RESPONSIVE TO THE LAST ODE.—HIS SOLDIERS PRAISE THE DUKE OF CHOW FOR HIS MAGNANIMITY AND SYMPATHY WITH THE PEOPLE.   With both the old and the new school the praise of the duke of Chow is the subject of

斯。亦孔之将。

二章

既破我斧。又缺我锜。周公东征。四国是吪。哀我人

斯。亦孔之嘉。

三章

既破我斧。又缺我銶。周公东征。四国是遒。哀我人

斯。亦孔之休。

His compassion for us people
Is very great.

2   We broke our axes,
And splintered our chisels;
But the object of the duke of Chow, in marching to the east,
Was to reform the four States.
His compassion for us people
Is very admirable.

3   We broke our axes;
And splintered our clubs.
But the object of the duke of Chow, in marching to the east,
Was to save the alliance of the four States.
His compassion for us people
Is very excellent.

this piece. The Preface, however, refers its composition to some great officer; Choo, much better, to the soldiers of the duke.

Ll. 1, 2, in all the stt. 破 and 缺 are evidently synonymous. The latter term properly denotes 'a cracked or broken vessel.' I take it here as meaning 'to splinter.' 斧 and 斨,—see on I.

3. Both Choo and Maou take 锜 here as 'a sort of chisel.' Han Ying made it some wooden instrument. The last thought that 銶 was 'a kind of chisel,' whereas the other two critics say it was a club (木属). Yen Ts'an is struck with the specification of such implements instead of the ordinary weapons of war; and infers from it that the duke of Chow had accomplished the object of his expedition without any fighting.

Ll. 3–6. 四 国 does not here, as sometimes. denote all the States of the four quarters, but what had been the royal domain of Shang.

and which had been assigned in four portions to Woo-kăng, and three of the duke of Chow's brothers. It was there where the rebellion had been. See the Shoo, V. xiv. 21, and xviii. 2. 皇 is taken as=匡 'to rectify;'—such, moreover was the reading in the Ts'e recension of the poems. 吪 = 化, 'to reform,' or rather 'to transform.' 遒 is 'to collect and make firm,' 'to consolidate.' L. 5. The duke's compassion for the people was seen in the object he had in view in his operations against the rebellious States, and the way in which he reduced them to order with little effusion of blood. In l. 6, 亦 is the initial particle, and 之 is a mere expletive. 将,—'great.' 休=美, 'excellent.'

The rhymes are—in st 2, 斨, 皇, 将, cat. 10: in 2, 锜 *, 吪 , 嘉, cat. 17: in 3, 銶, 遒, 休, cat. 3. t. 1.

V.　*Fah ko.*

伐柯
一章
伐柯如何。匪斧不克，取妻如何。匪媒不得。
二章
伐柯伐柯。其则不远。我觏之子。笾豆有践。

1　In hewing [the wood for] an axe-handle, how do you proceed?
　　Without [another] axe it cannot be done.
　　In taking a wife, how do you proceed?
　　Without a go-between it cannot be done.

2　In hewing an axe-handle, in hewing an axe-handle,
　　The pattern is not far off.
　　I see the lady,
　　And forthwith the vessels are arranged in rows.

Ode 5. Metaphorical. IN PRAISE OF THE DUKE OF CHOW. So say the old critics and the new, and I say with them, hardly knowing why, but having nothing better to say. On the different interpretations of the piece, see at the end of the notes.

St. 1. Comp. viii. VI. 4. 柯 = 斧柄, 'the handle of an axe.' It is interesting to find the go-between existing as an institution in those early times. Such an agent was thought to be necessary, and helpful to the modesty of both the families interested in the proposed marriage. Originally, the go-between was an arranger of marriages only; now he or she is often a purveyor of them.

St. 2. 则 = 法, 'pattern.' 'The pattern is not far off;' *i. e.*, the handle in the hand is the model of that which is to be made. I cannot do other than understand 之子 of the lady, with whom the marriage has been arranged. The last two lines of this stanza must surely be connected with the last two of the preceding. Choo, with his correct, critical discrimination, thus understands the characters. Maou and his school refer them to the duke of Chow. The *peen* were vessels of bamboo, and the *tow* vessels of wood, of the same size, lackered within, and with stands rather more than a foot high. They were used at feasts and sacrifices, to contain fruits, dried meat, vegetables, sauces, &c. 践 denotes 'the app. of rows,'—the way in which those vessels were arranged. The meaning seems to be that when the go-between had done his work, all subsequent arrangements were easy, and the marriage-feast might forthwith be celebrated.

THE INTERPRETATION. The Preface says that the piece is in praise of the duke of Chow, and was made by some great officer to condemn the court for not acknowledging the worth of the great statesman. 'There is a way,' says one of the great Ch'ings, 'to hew an axe-handle, and a way to get a wife; and so, if the duke of Chow was to be brought back to court, there was a way to do it.' Is not this mere trifling with the text? Then the second stanza is interpreted.—'The axe in the hand is the pattern of that which is to be made. If you would bring the duke home, you have only to arrange a feast, and receive him with the distinction which is his due.' This is trifling, and moreover, as I have observed in the notes, 之子 cannot be referred to the duke of Chow. Choo He, seeing that the old interpretation was untenable, assigned the piece to the people of the east, whose feelings towards the duke it expresses. St. 1, acc. to him, intimates how they had longed to see the hero, and their difficulty to get a sight of him; st. 2, how delighted they were, when they could now see him with ease. But neither can I get for myself this meaning out of the lines.

A most important principle is derived by Confucius from the first two lines of st. 2 in the 'Doctrine of the Mean,' xiii. 2,—that the rule for man's way of life is in himself. There is, probably, no reference at all to the duke of Chow in the ode. May not its meaning be that *while there is a necessary and proper way for every thing, men need not go far to find out what it is?*

The rhymes are—in st. 1, 何, 何, cat. 17; 克, 得, cat. 1, t. 3: in 2, 远, 践, cat. 15.

VI. *Këw yih.*

九罭
一章
九罭之鱼。鳟鲂。我觏之子。衮衣绣裳。
二章
鸿飞遵渚。公归无所。于女信处。
三章
鸿飞遵陆。公归不复。于女信宿。

1　In the net with its nine bags
　　Are rud and bream.
　　We see this prince
　　With his grand-ducal robe and embroidered skirt.

2　The wild geese fly [only] about the islets.
　　The duke is returning;—is it not to his proper place?
　　He was stopping with you [and me] but for a couple of nights.

3　The wild geese fly about the land.
　　The duke is returning, and will not come back here?
　　He was lodging with you [and me] but for a couple of nights.

Ode 6. Allusive and narrative. THE PEOPLE OF THE EAST EXPRESS THEIR ADMIRATION OF THE DUKE OF CHOW, AND SORROW AT HIS RETURNING TO THE WEST. On better grounds than in the case of the last ode, Choo He assigns this to the people of the east, sorry that the duke of Chow was now being recalled to court. The Preface on the other hand gives the same argument of this ode as of the other, and assigns it to some officer of Chow, who wished to expose the error of the court in not acknowledging the merits of the great man. The K'ang-he editors seem to think that other differences of view are unimportant, while there is an agreement in finding in the piece the praise of the duke of Chow.

St. 1. The Shwoh-wăn explains *yih* as meaning 'a fish-net;' but the Urh-ya gives that definition for *këw yih* together. The net in question was, no doubt, composed somehow of nine bags or compartments. Medhurst says that 鳟 is the roach; Williams says, 'a fish like the roach.' It has 'red eyes,' and must be the rud or red-eye (*leucismus erythrophthalmus*). Both this and the bream are good fish; and the writer therefore passes on from them to speak of the duke of Chow. The other stanzas make it plain that he is the 之子 of l. 3. 衮衣 is explained in the dict. as 天子服, 'the dress of the Son of Heaven.' But a 'high duke,' one of the three *kung* of the Chow dyn. (Shoo, V. xx. 5), had also the right to wear it, with a small difference in the blazonry of the upper robe. The emblematic figures of rank (Shoo,

II. iv. 4) were all depicted on the robes of both, but whereas on the royal robe there were two dragons, 'one ascending and one descending,' on that of a grand-duke there was only the descending dragon. The same four figures were embroidered on the skirts of both. It was only the 'high,' or grand duke, whose dress approximated so nearly to that of the king.

St. 2. 鸿,—as in iii. XVIII. 3. 渚,—as in ii. XI. 2. The 2d line is understood interrogatively.—公归岂无所乎. The connection between the first line and this seems to be:—'The geese come here among the islands, but it is only for a time. We know they will soon leave us. We should have known, that the duke was only temporarily among us.' 信,—'to rest two nights in the same place is called *sin*.' The 于女, 'among you,' is a difficulty in the way of Choo's view, that the piece should be assigned to the people of the east. He meets it by saying that the people of the east in speaking to each other would naturally say 'you;' so that 'among you' is really equivalent to 'among us.'

St. 3. 陆 is often used of the land in distinction from the water. Here the speaker has reference, probably, to the departure of the geese for the dry, northern regions; yet it might have occurred to him that they would be back among the islands in the next season. 宿 is here=the 处 in st. 2.

四章

是以有袞衣兮。无以我公归兮。无使我心悲兮。

4   Thus have we had the grand-ducal robe among us.
Do not take our duke back [to the west];
Do not cause us such sorrow of heart.

VII. *Lang poh.*

狼跋   论语

一章

狼跋其胡。载疐其尾。公孙硕肤。赤舄几几。

二章

狼疐其尾。载跋其胡。公孙硕肤。德音不瑕。

1   The wolf springs forward on his dewlap,
Or trips back on his tail.
The duke was humble, and greatly admirable,
Self-composed in his red slippers.

2   The wolf springs forward on his dewlap,
Or trips back on his tail.
The duke was humble, and greatly admirable;
There is no flaw in his virtuous fame.

St. 4 is all narrative, and must be taken as an address to the people of the west, complaining of the recall of the duke to the court. 无 = 毋, imperative.

The rhymes are—in st. 1, 鲂, 裳, cat. 10: in 2, 渚, 所, 处, cat. 5, t. 2: in 3, 陆, 复, 宿, cat. 3, t. 3: in 4, 衣, 归, 悲, cat. 15, t. 1.

Ode 7. Allusive. THE PRAISE OF THE DUKE OF CHOW, THE MORE DISTINGUISHED THROUGH HIS TRIALS. Choo again assigns this piece to the people of the east, while the Preface and Maou's school assign it, like the two odes that precede, to some officer of Chow. In other points they agree.

Both stanzas. The wolf in the text is supposed to be an old wolf, in which the dewlap (胡) and tail have grown to a very large size. He is further supposed to be taken in a pit, and to be making frantic efforts to escape,—all in vain, for his own dewlap and tail are in his way. The duke of Chow, under suspicion of disloyalty, and because of his dealing with his brothers, might have been expected to fret and rage; but his mind was too good

and great to admit such passions into it. 跋 = 蹳, 'to jump,' 'to spring forward.' 疐,— 'to be hindered,'— 踣, 'to trip or stumble.' 载 = 则. It is here equivalent to our 'or.' 孙 = 逊 or 让, 'complaisant,' 'yielding;' with reference to the meekness with which the duke bore his trials. 肤 = 美, 'admirable.' The 'red slippers' were worn both by the king and the princes of States. 几几 denotes 'the app. of quiet composure.' Wang Gan-shih observes, '几 is used by men to lean and rest themselves on; hence 几几 means *quiet*.' 德音,—as in vii. IX. 2, *et al.* 瑕 = 疵病, 'a blemish,' 'a flaw.'—It is astonishing with what lengthened eloquence the critics dilate here on the marvellous virtues of the duke of Chow

The rhymes are—in st. 1, 胡, 肤, cat. 5, t. 1; 尾, 几, cat. 15, t. 2: in 2, 胡, 肤, 瑕*, cat. 5, t. 1.

CONCLUDING NOTE UPON THE BOOK. The last three of the pieces are of a trifling character;

but the 1st and 3d, as they are longer than the other odes in this 1st part of the She, so they are of a superior character. The 1st, could we give entire credit to it, would be a valuable record of the manners of an early time, with touches of real poetry interspersed; and the 3d has also much poetical merit. Various speculations, into which we need not enter, have been indulged as to the place given to the odes of Pin at the very end of these Lessons from the States.

With regard to the order of the odes themselves, there is also a difference of opinion; and I transfer here what Këang Ping-chang has said upon it, especially as it illustrates what the critics have to say about the 'deep plans' of Confucius in the arrangement of the Books and of the odes:—' Heu K'ëen, in his scheme of the order of the pieces in the odes of Pin (爾風 次序图), places the *Fah ko*, the *Lang poh*, the *Ch'e-heaou* and the *Këw yih* immediately after the *Ts'ih yueh*, and makes the *Tung shan* and the *P'o foo* the last odes; but I venture to think that he thus misses the idea of the Master in arranging the odes as he did. The *Ts'ih yueh*, the *Ch'e-heaou*, and the *Tung shan*, were all made by the duke of Chow himself. They are placed first; and all the particulars of the rumours against the duke, his residence in the east, his return to the capital, and his expedition to the east, become quite plain. The *P'o foo*, and the three odes that follow, were all made by others in the duke's praise. The *P'o foo* fol-

lows the *Tung shan*, because they are on kindred themes. The other three pieces were all made by the people of the east, and we are not to think that the Master had no meaning in placing the *Lang poh* last. The duke's assumption of the regency looked too great a stretch of power; his vesting such authority as he did in his two brothers seemed like a want of wisdom; his residing in the east seemed to betoken a fear of misfortune; the *Ch'e-heaou* seemed to express resentment; his expedition to the east seemed to show impetuous anger; and his putting Kwang-shuh to death seemed to indicate cruelty :—all these things might be said to be blemishes in his character. The master, therefore, puts forth that line,—

" There is no flaw in his virtuous fame,"

as comprising the substance of the odes of Pin, and to show that the duke of Chow was what he thus was through the union in him of heavenly principle, and human feelings, without the least admixture of selfishness. His purity in his own day was like the brightness of the sun or moon, and it was not to be permitted that any traitorous and perverse people in subsequent times should be able to fill their mouths with his example. Thus though the author of the *Lang poh* had no thought of mirroring in it the duke's whole career, yet the Master, in his arrangement of the odes, comprehended the whole life of the great sage.'